Praise for
PETER LINEY

Also by Peter Liney

The Detainee

Into the Fire

IN
CONSTANT
FEAR

PETER LINEY

Jo Fletcher
BOOKS

First published in Great Britain in 2015
This edition published in Great Britain in 2016 by

Jo Fletcher Books
an imprint of Quercus Editions Ltd
Carmelite House
50 Victoria Embankment
London EC4Y 0DZ

An Hachette UK company

A CIP catalogue record for this book is available
from the British Library

MMP ISBN 978 1 78206 043 7
EBOOK ISBN 978 1 78429 997 2

10 9 8 7 6 5 4 3 2 1

Typeset by CC Book Production

Printed and bound in Great Britain by Clays Ltd, St Ives plc

To my readers

On the brightest of days, you'll find the darkest of shadows

CHAPTER ONE

I didn't know what it was. Really, I had no idea. It wasn't a howl and it wasn't a scream, it was something in between, but whatever was making it – and I guess it was some kinda animal – it sure was in a bad way. For a moment I just stood there, every fibre of my body locked, my breath hanging out in mid-air, hugging my precious little bundle that bit closer to me.

I'd heard it first a few days earlier – around about the same time, in the early hours – just the one animal, and much further away, over towards the mountain, but now there were two or more, and a whole lot closer, maybe only on the far side of the woods.

God, but that was one helluva disturbing sound. Worse than torture, that made you think that, like it or not, you were *part* of it – it couldn't just be dismissed as particular to another species. It was a universal pain, and I'd bet there wasn't one living creature in the valley that wasn't holding its breath or feeling sick to the stomach the same way I was.

It did go through my head to go over there, or at least get that bit closer – maybe someone had set traps or something? A herd of deer had wandered in, steel jaws snapping shut all around, and now they howled and screamed as they tried to wrench their limbs free, ready to tear their bodies apart in their blind urge for freedom? But I didn't dare risk it, not with who I had with me.

A pizza moon with an extra large bite out of it continued its slow descent towards the mountaintops, ghostlike and abandoned, the occasional dark cloud passing before it, creating monochrome and murk. I waited 'til the howling had died down, 'til whatever it was fell exhausted – maybe even dead? – then resumed my slow pacing of the farmyard, knowing I'd soon be in a whole lotta trouble if I didn't.

It was over a year since we'd escaped from the City: a year of relentlessly being pursued, always having to move on, looking over our shoulders even in our sleep – and you wanna know something? – the best year of my life.

I guess that's one of the things about life: we might think we do, but the truth is, we got no idea what's waiting for us – no matter how much we might plan or how far we think we can see ahead. That's just a projection, a *possibility*, us trying to make order out of chaos. We got no idea what might be waiting for us around the next bend – in fact, I hate to tell ya this, but we might not even make it round that next bend. Take me, for example: if you'd told me a couple of years back when I was imprisoned on that stinking, merciless Island how my life would change, where I'd be now, I probably would've laughed in your face. In fact, I was such a bad-tempered sonofabitch, I might've laid you out cold for trying to make fun of me. But here I am, at an age where a lot of folk might think it's time to start taking things easy, and guess what? . . . I'm a *father*.

It's true! From this wrinkled old body has sprung the most unbelievably tender of new life.

I have a son. His name is Thomas, and I love him every bit as much as I love his mother, but in a different way, which was why I was walking him around the yard at three in the morning, 'cuz although

2

he wanted to inform everyone he was exactly seven months old that very day, I had a fair idea no one else was interested.

I owed it all to Lena, of course. She'd given me back my life – in fact, she'd returned it to me a thousand times better than it ever was before. All those years of being one of society's unwanted, no longer the 'Big Guy' but just a ragged, bitter old hulk scratching out the most pathetic of existences on that Island . . . I'd given up. Then she came along: this remarkable blind young woman hiding in the old subway tunnels, and with her came hope, a reason not just to go on but to fight against the vicious scum who ran that place – if you can call terrorising the old and abusing the young 'running' a place – 'til finally, with the aid of our own little techno genius, Jimmy, and one or two other equally unlikely allies, we managed to destroy that hell that held us and escape to a better life.

The only problem with that was, it *wasn't* better, it was a whole lot worse. When we finally left the Island and got ashore, the night of the big exodus, the City was burning from one end to the other. The streets were a battlefield: rioting, looting, people killing each other for no good reason. What was more, the fires spread and with the whole city ringed by flame, there was no way out. We had to find somewhere to hide, somewhere safe not only from fires and mobs but also from Infinity; those in control, who made the Wastelords look like nothing scarier than kids who pulled the wings off butterflies. And at their head – a whole new development of the human species, and one who, though female, I'd freely admit, frightened me more than anyone else had in my life.

If you'll forgive the presumption of a guy who took sixty-four years to become a father, a little tip for those of you planning on having a kid: it's a real convenience if one of you's an insomniac. I've always had periods when I couldn't sleep – a couple of months on, a couple of months off, just one of those things, I guess. It can drive you crazy – I mean, literally, you get some pretty dark characters come calling for you in the middle of the night. But now I had someone to keep me company: this little bundle I was always carrying around with me. Mind you, his choice of conversation wasn't exactly wide-ranging, being pretty well limited to what went in and what came out. To be fair, when he wasn't hollering, he made a damn fine listener; just lying there, staring up at me with those drunken blue eyes as if he was in shock that someone like me could be his father.

Can I say that again? I've always hated those people who go on and on about kids and parenthood like it's the greatest thing ever, but you know, I *am* the boy's father, and dumb old big guy or not, I did help make him . . . not that you need to be that intelligent to produce children, as you may have noticed.

We never actually discussed it, but gradually Lena and me fell into this routine where she mostly took care of him in the day and I did what I could at night: answering that shrill call, assessing his needs and passing him over if all else failed so that greedy little mouth of his could start snuffling out mother's milk on draught. The only problem with that was, it didn't take him long to work out that I was always there, at his beck and call right throughout the night, and he really played on it.

Like that night: I knew there was nothing wrong with him – he'd been changed, fed, winded, whatever and just wanted a bit of company. Still, it had given me the excuse to take him outside, to pretend I didn't wanna disturb the others, when actually, I was feeling that bit disturbed myself.

We'd been squatting on the farm for five months or so by then, and apart from the occasional unwanted visitor, the many crazies roaming around, we'd slowly begun to relax, to pray that maybe Infinity had given up on finding us. To be honest, it was more of a smallholding than a farm. There were any number of them abandoned out there:

family concerns whose proud owners would rather walk away than sell up to the creeping conglomerates.

The irony of those smallholdings was that they'd had people busily working on them, while the giant spreads where the big boys'd got their own way and everything was flattened up to the horizon, were computer-operated, 'ghost farms', watched over by satellites and with everything done by machine: planting, watering, harvesting – so all the company had to do was to come out and pick up the packed crates.

'course, everything got messed up when some of the commercial and communication satellites were brought down with the punishment ones. They tried bringing workers out here, reverting to good old-fashioned people-power, but the fires, the remoteness, no way to enforce protection – or discipline – thanks to the absence of punishment satellites, meant there weren't too many prepared to give it a go.

Our place had belonged to a family, that was clear 'cuz of the stuff left behind – not just bats and balls and bikes, things like that, but pencil marks on the kitchen wall showing how the kids were growing – and for some reason it made me feel that bit more warmly disposed towards it.

Mind you, the first time we laid eyes on the place, it looked pretty sorry for itself: two small fields, once laid to wheat, all dried up and flattened like a pair of straw tablemats, vegetables rotting in the ground or run to seed, worm-riddled fruit fermenting under the trees. We salvaged every last ounce we could, and were grateful for it, but it was clear that if we were gonna stay there, we had to plant more.

Without any kind of vehicle or livestock, we had no choice but to restore the old plough Jimmy'd found in the lean-to at the back of the barn and drag it across the fields by hand. We took it in turns, working in teams of four, me trying to insist on doing more than my share and keeping going 'til my old legs felt like a couple of condemned tower blocks.

What really did surprise me was how much the kids took to it out there – it was as if they were growing along with everything else. Gordie was starting to look like a proper young man, and actually, with the sun on him, plenty of exercise, his hair that bit longer, not a bad-looking one at that. Gigi didn't change that much, just grew a bit taller, a bit more substantial – she let her old clothes out rather than come up with anything new, maybe so she could keep her 'style', that odd, multi-layered look; she even kept the same seagull feathers in her hair. But Hanna – well, she was the one who really blossomed. She'd completely lost that slightly startled look she used to have about her, as if every oncoming moment of her life was a potential threat, and with all that tall measured grace and tumbling dark hair, I tell ya, was becoming quite a beauty. She gained in confidence, no longer keeping her ballet just for when she was alone but dancing all over, especially out in the fields – she didn't care if you stood and watched her or not.

As for the more senior members of the gang, well, our new situation had done Jimmy and Delilah a power of good: they were more content, more in harmony, than I ever could've imagined back when I first met them on the Island. Not only were they finally free, they weren't tripping over each other any more either. The little guy spent most of his time out in the barn (or should I say, 'his workshop'), playing around with an impressive stockpile of assorted technology, powered by the old solar panel tree he cleaned up and restored; while Lile sat out on the porch, quietly smiling to herself and counting and then recounting all her belated blessings.

As for Lena and me, well, I guess I don't have to tell you how well things'd worked out for us. I'd thought we were happy before, but now, with Thomas, I knew I'd got more – way more – than anyone had a right to. It's true we had our problems when we first left the City. That day we escaped and stood there looking down from the hills and she told me she'd gone blind again – I can't tell you how bad I felt. I wanted to turn around then and there and go right back, find Doctor Evan Simon and get him to operate on her again, but with Infinity chasing after us – well, it wasn't exactly an option. Over and over I told her that as soon as it was safe we'd go back and get them fixed, until eventually she started getting that bit impatient with me, going all silent or changing the subject, and I realised it was best to shut up, though that didn't mean I wasn't still thinking about it.

When we first settled on the farm I came up with all sorts of ideas to make her life easier: some worked out, others didn't. I found these rolls of wire in the barn and used them to map out the surrounding area. I hammered in posts and hung lines with identifying markers on each one, so the wire leading to the woods had twigs attached; the one to the barn had steel washers, and to the road, small rocks – and so on. I mean, she would've mapped everything out in her head soon enough – she's always had this unnatural gift for it – but I wanted to give her a head start. 'course, she didn't need them for long, but I left them there just in case.

But great as it was not just to have our own place but to be out in the country, smelling fresh air for the first time in more years than I could recall, it was having Thomas that really transformed us from being a couple to a family, and that's a helluva leap, believe me.

Almost as if I couldn't go another second without seeing him, without having proof of his existence, I paused in my slow, jigging circuit of the farmyard and looked down into the folds of the little guy's favourite blanket – the blue and white checked one that, even at his age, he was reluctant to be parted from. I was greeted by that same dazed expression that hinted at a terrible mistake: surely his father should've been the next guy in line, or the one after that? The banker or the businessman, the one with all the money and comfort in the world, not this wheezy old big guy squatting on someone else's abandoned property?

It's kinda odd to build your life around something that barely fits into the palm of your hand – well, my hand anyway. Though I guess that's why you do it: 'cuz he or she is so vulnerable they need your constant protection. Sometimes it'd frighten the hell outta me that in this insane and brutal world we'd voluntarily created our own weakness, an Achilles heel which could so easily destroy us, then again, we wouldn't've had it any other way.

I was about to return into the house and try to settle him back down when that terrible howling started up again, and much closer this time, almost sounding like it was on *this* side of the woods – like whatever it was had been silently stealing over in my direction.

What the hell? It wasn't like anything I'd ever heard before. Not so much threatening in itself, but more like I could feel their pain, how terrified they were.

I stood there for a moment, debating whether to take Thomas inside and grab a torch, when I heard the door of the farmhouse close behind me.

'Clancy?' Lena whispered into the darkness.

'Yeah,' I answered, and in a moment she'd honed in on my voice and was at my side, her expression almost as pained as the howling. 'What *is* that?'

'I dunno,' I replied.

'Sounds like something's being tortured,' she said, instinctively taking Thomas from me, I guess also feeling that urge to protect.

'Hey. What do we know?' I replied, trying not to sound that concerned. 'City folk. Could be anything. An owl maybe.'

'We've been out in the country for a year now and I've never heard anything like that,' she pointed out, 'and I don't think you have either.'

I sighed to myself, all those dark thoughts churning away inside me again, that in some way this might be connected with Infinity.

'You sure it's an animal?' Lena asked.

'I'm not sure of anything.'

We stood there listening for a few moments as the noise thankfully started to subside again. 'Come to bed,' she said, as if she'd made a decision, and turned towards the house, Thomas firmly clutched in her arms.

'Gimme a moment.'

'Clancy.'

'Okay, I'm coming.'

Still more concerned than I was letting on, I slowly followed after her. The fly-screen clicked shut just as I reached it and I was about to swing it back open, to follow Lena inside, when – Jeez, I don't how to describe it – the weirdest thing happened: *something* passed me by. Something was there – and then it wasn't. There was a disturbance, like a ripple throughout the night, and then it was gone.

I turned back to the step, looking all around me, the hairs on the back of my neck twanging away like they had electricity passing through them.

What the hell *was* that? There was nothing in the sky, I couldn't see anything moving across the land, but something had been there, all right. Even the howling had stopped abruptly, as if whatever it was had been sufficiently unnerved to forget their distress.

I stayed there for several minutes, squinting hard into the darkness, checking all around, those hairs on the back of my neck springing up again every time I recalled how I'd felt, but nothing else happened.

Finally I followed Lena in, locking and bolting the door, then taking one last look outta the window. There was still nothing to see, but I had this strong sense that a shadow had somehow stretched its way over the mountains, across the valley and the road and now was travelling up the slope towards us.

CHAPTER TWO

Those first couple of days out of the City, skimming along country roads in the limo we took from Doctor Simon, were really something. At first I described everything to Lena – the mountains, the forest, a beautiful view – trying to make sure she didn't miss a thing, but again she got all impatient with me, telling me to pipe down and complaining that I was spoiling the moment. I guess the thing was, she could feel the freedom every bit as much as anyone else, and as far as she was concerned, that was all that mattered.

It took me a while to see it her way, to appreciate I'd been creating a bit of tension; when I finally did, the mood in the limo noticeably lifted: four adults and three kids blasting off to Planet Delirium. We sang endlessly, laughed long and hard for no particular reason, and for ever hung outta the windows calling out to every animal, tree and rock we passed. Okay, so there was still the occasional fire that meant a lengthy detour, and any number of times we crested the top of a hill to be met by nothing but a blackened wasteland, but we knew it would grow back again – and so would we.

Jimmy had reprogrammed the limo, taken out most of the security features – locator, return-to-owner, voice recognition – so we could go wherever we wanted (and more importantly, I suspect, so *he* could add to his growing collection of scavenged technology). The only problem was, once we got off the main road and left the power strip, the limo switched to auxiliary – good old-fashioned gas – and we had to be real careful about every mile we covered.

I can't tell you how many close shaves we had during those first couple of months, the number of times we almost got caught. Infinity Dragonflies were coming and going day and night, swinging from one side of the sky to the other, stopping dead and hovering over one particular spot; that thunderous thrumming pulsating across the forest floor, their spotlights arrowing down like they were borne on silver stilts. Some days there were so many we had to stay put, camouflaging the limo with branches and hiding amongst the trees. They even brought in armoured pursuit vehicles, each one carrying half a dozen or so Specials, roaring around all over the place, smashing up everything in their way. A couple of times they were upon us almost before we knew and all we could do was make a run for it, desperate to draw them away from the hidden limo, going deeper and darker into the forest, like parent birds distracting predators from the nest, slipping back only after we were sure they'd gone.

It got to the point where we were utterly exhausted, starved of sleep and food, and though no one was saying it, there was this growing sense that it could only be a matter of time. But Jimmy – God bless that little guy – worked out that we had to be close to the limit of a Dragonfly's range; if we travelled on another twenty or thirty miles, maybe up into the mountains, we'd be out of their reach.

That night we all piled into the limo and slowly worked our way out of the forest and onto the deserted country road. 'course I couldn't use the headlights and it wasn't long before I was reminded that my old eyesight ain't what it used to be by going off the road, not once, but twice, putting more dents into the Doc's precious vehicle, a lotta swearing and cussing going into getting us out of the ditch and back onto the road.

I got us as far as I could, to the foothills that led up to the mountains, but was forced to stop the moment I saw the dawn starting to clamber up over the horizon. We returned the limo to the forest, again disguising it with branches, everyone splitting up to explore the immediate area.

It was the kids who found the cave – hidden away behind this big slab of upended rock, like it was the front door or something. Gordie, competitive as ever, claimed it was him, but Gigi got so annoyed that in the end he had to acknowledge it might've been more her. They called us over, jumping up and down and getting all excited, like they'd found an abandoned castle or something. Mind you, it *was* quite a find, especially how roomy it was. A little damp, which proved a bit of a problem, but we still ended up living there for the best part of six months. And, of course, it was where Thomas was born.

Thank God, Delilah took over that afternoon, what with me rushing around like a wild-eyed headless chicken. I didn't have a clue what to do and couldn't have been more panicked if Lena'd had half a dozen bullets inside her. Lile sent the kids off for a walk before ordering Jimmy to get lost too – telling him outright it wasn't seemly for him to be that close to a woman in her condition. All I can remember is her screaming at Lena to push, ignore the pain it rewards you with and '*Push! Push! Push!*' for all she was worth.

If you've never seen it, when that baby starts to come out, and no matter how natural you tell yourself childbirth is, it is one *helluva* shock – as if you can't believe that's where it's been hiding all that time. I cut the cord myself, with the hunting knife I'd spent for ever sharpening and sterilising (the same one I once used to scar my side that time, to make out I'd had a kidney transplant so I'd be taken into the fortress of the Infinity building to have it removed).

Afterwards, Lena just lay there, cuddling little Thomas and looking so proud of herself. She kept gently feeling him all over, working out what he looked like, and if she was frustrated at not being able to see him, if she was feeling the weight of her disability, she sure didn't mention it.

For a while everything seemed to work out just fine. 'course, it was a helluvan adjustment having another person around, especially such a demanding one, and maybe it was my age – I was beginning to feel every one of those sixty-four years – but he really tired me out. Yet gradually, I guess as all new parents do, we got used to him. Then one day the little guy developed a cough, his tiny lungs started to clog and we knew we had to move on, that the cave was too damp for such a new life.

Jimmy suggested we go over the mountains, that not only would we be safer from Infinity, but the lie of the land would mean there'd be far less hydrazine residue left over from the punishment satellites. The only problem with that was there wasn't a direct route: if we'd taken the limo, we would've had to have headed down to the pass and gone around that way, but it would've meant the best part of a day and just about all of our gas.

In the end, it was Hanna who came up with the answer: why not just hide the limo in the cave and make our way over the mountain on foot?

That poor vehicle took a real battering on its way up the slope and into the cave. The slab just outside the entrance meant I had to keep going back and forth, back and forth, 'til eventually I managed to manoeuvre it into place. And as for the mountain, once we started to climb – it might not've been that steep or high, but it was still one helluva challenge for someone like Lile and that old sawing single lung of hers. Not that I reckoned any of us felt we had a choice: not where the baby's health was involved.

There were times when I wondered if Thomas was the real reason why Lena didn't wanna talk about her blindness any more. Perhaps some animal instinct had kicked in and shifted all her priorities from her to him. She was always *aware* of the little guy, no matter what the situation, where he was and what he was doing – as if my knife hadn't cut that cord at all, and never could do.

It took a while of waiting for what I hoped was the right moment, but in the end I told her what Doc Simon had said: about her being the only woman he was aware of who was able to bear a child, that those four years of living underground in the tunnels had meant she'd avoided the effects of the hydrazine poisoning that'd been spilling out of punishment satellites – or 'til Jimmy went and brought them all down.

I thought she'd be really shocked, that she wouldn't know how to deal with it, but she just dismissed it as another of the Doc's games – which I guess made a kinda sense. As far as she was concerned, Thomas was *our* little miracle and that was an end to it. It would've worried the hell out of her to have to entertain the idea of him being *other people's* miracle too; that we might have some kinda moral responsibility to share the little guy.

Anyway, in terms of our survival, of Infinity's pursuit, I don't reckon it made a whole heap of difference. They had more than enough reasons for hunting us down: like Gigi double-crossing Nora Jagger, and both of us briefly thinking that we'd put an end to her miserable life.

I tell ya, I've come across some pretty vile examples of humanity in my time. Some of the scum Mr Meltoni used to send me to deal with – well, let's be honest, some of the scum he had working *for* him – were so randomly vicious and violent, so beyond redemption, you felt like you wanted to burn out what they had in their heads, set them to default, and hope you ended up with something better. But Nora Jagger? . . . Jesus, she's something else. She's got no arms and legs, just these specially-made prosthetics – or to be more accurate, *weapons* – she attaches to herself. They're stronger, more powerful than you could ever imagine, and utterly lethal at her bidding.

I'd seen enough of her to know she'd never give up searching for us, no matter what the reason; that she probably spent hours each and every day dreaming up new ways to torture and kill us and wouldn't stop 'til she'd used each and every one. If that was the reason why those animals were screaming into the night, 'cuz they could sense her on her way, for sure, I didn't blame them – in fact, if that did turn out to be the case, I'd start screaming too.

The following morning, Jimmy, Gigi and me headed up over the hill towards the next valley. It said a lot that I often left Gordie behind now, trusting him to look after Lena and the baby in case any crazies came a-calling. And if he stayed, generally that meant that Hanna did too, and Gigi would immediately make a point of volunteering to go along, so who stayed and who went pretty well resolved itself.

Our smallholding was kinda on the edge of things. You only had to get over the hill and there were half a dozen other groups and families who'd done the same as us: taken over abandoned spreads, done any necessary repairs, dismantled any automatic machinery that could be used by hand. Several of them had even got livestock: not much, maybe a dozen or so cows and a bull, a horse to help out with the ploughing (though, apparently it had a mule-like habit of occasionally refusing), a couple of goats – some had been rounded up but most just wandered in of their own accord, like they'd given independence a shot but hadn't much cared for it.

We would've preferred to have lived over there, too – strength in numbers, after all – but by the time we'd arrived there was nowhere left. Mind you, they did tell us about *our* place – how it'd been left empty, that no one had moved in 'cuz it was out on its own and considered too vulnerable.

I don't know how many people were living in that valley, maybe thirty or so, and all sorts, young and old. No kids, I noticed, and no babies – I mean, it could've been just coincidence, but I wouldn't have wanted to bet on it.

We were going to see this guy, Nick, in his fifties, short but heavy, of Greek extraction. He didn't exactly care for the title, but most of those over there saw him as the village elder, mainly 'cuz him and his grown-up family were the first there. Jimmy'd done this trade with him – his wheat seed for a signal-booster – and it was time to make the exchange. There's not a lotta communication gets over that side of the mountains, not since Jimmy prompted the punishment satellites to have their little shoot-out in the sky. There were one or two places where you *might* get a signal, but you'd better be prepared to climb way up, and even then, it's weak or intermittent at best. I didn't know whether Jimmy's booster would make any difference, but I guessed Nick thought it was worth playing around with.

For our part, we were really hoping that if we could plant some wheat, get a good harvest, we could start grinding flour, for bread, pies, cakes, whatever. Nick'd cautioned us that it was getting a little late for summer wheat, but as long as the weather was kind, it should be okay.

I wasn't gonna say anything about what had happened the previous night, but Gigi brought it up, complaining it'd disturbed her sleep.

'We didn't hear nothing,' Jimmy commented, which didn't exactly surprise me, not with him and Lile.

'Kinda scary,' Gigi admitted.

Jimmy turned to me, wondering if I'd heard anything.

'Something,' I admitted. 'Screech Owl p'haps?' Though I had no real idea what that was or even what it sounded like.

'Maybe around your side of the house,' he said, as if to head off any suggestion that his hearing wasn't what it used to be, and to my relief, promptly lost interest in the subject.

I don't know what it was about that little community in the valley but normally there's this real nice atmosphere over there, a sense that everyone's a damn sight happier than they've been in a long time, and that they appreciate every moment of it. But as we approached, I began to get this feeling, like all wasn't entirely well.

'What's bothering them?' Jimmy asked, as if confirming my concerns.

I shook my head. Normally you'd get a couple of cheery waves and a 'how-are-ya?', but it looked like they had something pretty heavy on their minds.

'Maybe it's me?' Gigi suggested, knowing there was still a certain amount of distrust of Island kids.

'Nah. 'course not,' I replied, just for a moment wondering if it might have more to do with whatever I'd heard in the early hours.

I saw Nick from some way off, crouched down on his porch step, that oversize stomach filling the gap between his chest and knees. There was a large frown hacked across his heavy brow, his long curly black and silver hair even more dishevelled than usual.

He stood up as we approached, starting to take a few steps in our direction, as if he couldn't wait to tell us something.

'Everything okay?' I asked.

'Not really,' he replied. 'Someone's been around again.'

'Crazies?'

'Some real sick bastards.'

'What d'ya mean?'

'You know Sandy—?' At my blank look he added, 'George's little mutt?'

'Yeah—'

George was Nick's youngest, only just in his twenties but already a real gentleman; fresh-faced and blue-eyed, there with help even before you knew you needed it. Sandy was this little Jack Russell cross who'd befriended the family on their way outta the City and had barely left George's side since. He wasn't just cute as hell; he'd become an invaluable part of the team, being as he killed just about every rat within a mile radius which might've had ideas about setting up home.

'I don't know what they did to him,' Nick said, pausing for a moment like he really didn't want to say the words, then he sighed and led us to a small store at the back of the house. Just before he opened the door, he put his hand up to Gigi, forbidding her entrance. 'Not you.'

Gigi gave a rather disgusted snort, but she stayed where she was, leaving Nick, Jimmy and me to head into the store.

At first I didn't even recognise it as a dog – I didn't recognise it as anything very much. I mean, Sandy hadn't been that big, but he had been a stocky little guy. All that remained now was a burnt-out carcase about the size of a large turkey lying on the ground.

Jimmy groaned. 'What the hell did they do that for?'

'Just hope he was dead before they did,' I commented.

Nick stared at us for a moment, as if there was still more to tell. 'Look closer,' he said.

We advanced a couple of paces, studying the small, blackened skeleton. Out of the corner of my eye I spotted Gigi peering round the doorway and warned her off with a look, though actually, I didn't know why – it might be natural to wanna protect kids from that sorta stuff, but it was way too late for her. She'd been beaten, bruised and abused by human nature a million times over.

She gave this groan of protest and pretended to back out, but almost immediately returned.

'*Jesus!*' Jimmy suddenly cried, obviously having worked out what Nick was talking about, but I was still in the dark.

'What?' I asked, forgetting all about Gigi.

'He's been burned from the *inside*.'

I scrutinised the remains of the corpse, immediately appreciating what Jimmy was saying, that the fire had been lit from within.

'Must've given him something – made him swallow it,' Nick said, his big brown eyes misting up. 'Gas maybe – then struck a match and put it down his throat.'

'Not cool,' Jimmy whined. 'Not cool one little bit.'

'When did you find him?' I asked.

'This morning. Someone picked him up on the hill, over in the direction of your place.'

'Shit,' I muttered.

'What?'

'Last night – we heard some noises in the woods, maybe something in pain. We didn't know what it was.'

Nick met my gaze and I immediately felt guilty I hadn't investigated. 'But—'

'What?'

'There were several of them, or that's what it sounded like.'

'Only got one dog,' he replied. 'Or we *had*.'

'And it wasn't just last night either,' I went on. 'I've heard it before.'

'I never heard nothing,' Jimmy chipped in, like that was important.

For several moments there was silence, the three of us transfixed by that small charred frame of blackened bone. We hadn't solved the mystery at all; if anything, we'd made it worse.

'Anyone else gotta dog?' Gigi asked from the doorway, but we ignored her.

Jimmy crouched down over the remains of the animal. 'No smell of gas,' he said with a frown. 'No smell of anything combustible.'

Eventually Nick led us back outside, the three of us filing past a plainly unimpressed Gigi. 'It's just a dog,' she muttered, like she'd seen a whole lot worse and we should put it into perspective.

'*This* time,' Nick told her.

He invited us into his home. His other two sons, Edward and Daniel, were in the kitchen, both silent and subdued, as if more concerned by what had been done to the family than the dog. George came out to greet us but only stayed for a few minutes. His smile was as sad as an orphan's at Christmas, his eyes red and raw, and I had to fight off the urge to put my arm around his shoulders in case it triggered more tears. As for Nick's wife, Miriam – well, she was in bed, like she always was. No one had ever said exactly what was wrong with her, but there was a kind of unspoken understanding that the only way she'd be leaving that place was in a coffin. Nick shouted to her all the time, telling her who was there, what they were talking about, but I'd never ever heard her reply.

He made us coffee – well, more like some kinda instant coffee substitute, which tasted pretty well as it sounded. He was chatting away about all manner of stuff, avoiding returning to the subject of the dog, telling us how to plant and take care of the wheat, then later, took us back out to his store and gave us a hundred-pound bag of seed-grain. 'It's good stuff,' he added, 'fast-growing, high yield.'

I thanked him with a warm handshake, aware he was providing us with a real chance to make a life for ourselves out there.

'Keep an eye out,' he warned, as we set off. 'Crazies are everywhere.'

'Probably miles away by now,' I said, trying to sound reassuring.

'Beats me where they're coming from,' he complained.

I hesitated for a moment, letting the others go on ahead; I wanted to speak to him on my own, but wasn't sure how to bring up the subject.

Nick scratched his gut for a moment, watching Jimmy and Gigi walking away, and I realised he too was waiting for us to be alone.

'I don't think it was Sandy you heard,' he eventually muttered.

'No,' I agreed.

For a moment he just stood there, gazing around the valley as if expecting to see an invading force come streaming down the surrounding slopes at any moment. 'Something's going on.'

I stared into his face, not sure what to say; his unease was ramping up mine.

'Big Guy!' Jimmy called back.

'Coming,' I replied.

I thought that was all Nick was gonna say, but maybe he'd just been trying to think of a way of phrasing it.

'Whatever it is,' he sighed, 'I don't think we've seen it before.'

This time Gigi called to me as well and I turned to go, telling Nick to take care before setting off, but I hadn't gone more than twenty or thirty paces before I glanced back, his words still echoing inside my head. He hadn't moved an inch, just stayed where he was, staring after us. I waved, and after a moment's hesitation he did the same, but there was an unease about him, a sense that he felt it was madness for anyone to be heading off on their own.

On the way back over the hill, Jimmy had to stop for a few moments to get his breath back. Not that he was carrying anything – but I guess he wasn't getting any younger.

'You okay, Big Guy?' he asked.

'Yeah.'

'Kinda quiet?'

'We're gonna have to be more vigilant,' I announced. 'Keep a closer eye on things.'

'It was just a dog,' Gigi sneered.

I stared at her for a moment. She had a point: it *was* just a dog, but it was still a senseless act of violence. On its own, it mightn't amount to much, but with what else was going on, I didn't care for it one little bit.

Without making any further comment, I heaved my sack back up onto my shoulder and resumed our walk, the others soon following on behind.

At the very top of the hill you could see down into both valleys. It really was quite a view: all the many smallholdings looked like some kinda marquetry on fancy furniture. To one side the hills rolled on into the Interior, to the other, to our valley and then the mountains beyond. Nothing could've looked more idyllic, more peaceful – and yet, try as I might, I couldn't shake this growing sense that it was happening again. I didn't know from what direction, nor by what means, but somehow I knew our little world was about to be shattered once more.

CHAPTER THREE

That afternoon we went out sowing the two fields we'd spent so much time ploughing, still bearing the bruises and blisters of all that hard work, Gordie with a bandage on his leg where he hadn't got outta the way of the blade quickly enough, Lena with a bruise on her forehead from when we ran into a buried rock and she'd collided with the plough handle.

We collected everything we could use for seed containers: flour bags, buckets, some of the old tin cans piled up behind the lean-to at the back of the barn, and I cut a long gash in the sack the wheat came in so I could poke my head through and hang it over my shoulders. We knew we couldn't waste a single precious seed, that we had to really take our time up and down those haphazard furrows and make sure that each and every one had their chance at life. Even with this new souped-up, fast-growing variety it would probably be a month or more before we could harvest. But with the little bit of food we still had stored, some foraging and the occasional trade, we should be okay.

Hanna and Gordie had somehow managed it so they were seeding adjacent rows, so they could physically bump into each other now and then, or exchange words or giggles. He had that look about him that every man gets, irrespective of age, when he's trying to impress a woman: strutting his stuff, rolling his sleeves up as far as they'd go to display newly filled-out muscles, and I noticed he'd redrawn the dragon on his bicep again. He did that every now and then, in honour of little Arturo, that time they both had tattoo transfers on their arms – his a dragon, and Arturo's, Mickey Mouse – in remembrance of the day that the little guy got killed and brought a premature end to the magic duo of 'Dragon Boy and the Mickey Mouse Kid'.

Gordie rarely said anything about it, but I knew he still missed his little buddy. On the other hand, I guessed Hanna was some kinda agreeable compensation.

I didn't know exactly what was going on with those two, and to tell you the truth, I didn't wanna, either. A year or so back, when I first realised they had a crush on each other, it was kinda cute, but with them now grown into young adults, it was all a bit intimidating. I know it was human nature and all, and maybe it'd become physical already – although I didn't think so – but I really wasn't sure how to handle it. If they so much as put an arm around each other, I looked the other way. Lena said I was being 'old-fashioned', that it was none of my business, and I guess, strictly speaking, they weren't our kids, so she was right – but that didn't stop me from doing their blushing for them now and then.

The other problem, of course, was that none of this was going down very well with Gigi. At one stage she'd undoubtedly been under the impression that it'd be *her* teaming up with Gordie. 'course she did everything she could to pretend total indifference, that she didn't give a damn, but the occasional snap of resentment or lash of jealousy betrayed her over and over. Not to mention made for one helluva uncomfortable atmosphere.

Hanna and Gordie used to try to include her in whatever they did, inviting her on their outings, but I reckon she thought that was just rubbing her nose in it and after a while they didn't bother. It'd been plain right from the start the two girls had issues; when Gigi got really irked, when she got that 'Island blade' look about her, she called Hanna 'the princess'— which could've been a term of endearment, but out of her mouth sounded more like something she couldn't wait to spit out. It was an aggravation we could've well done without, though more than that, it worried me that one day it might erupt somehow and affect us all.

Gigi'd never actually come out with it, but at times she must've thought she would've been better off staying back in the City. Though bearing in mind what was waiting for her there, who was after her with murder in her heart, I wouldn't have recommended it.

Neither Lena or me ever talked to the others about the night we got into Infinity; that Gigi had obviously been playing some kinda double game with Nora Jagger, no more than I'd ever asked her for an explanation. In the end she came good and that was all that mattered – maybe she'd planned it that way, maybe she hadn't. I thought she might talk to me about it one day, but with a year and more passed, I was beginning to think that she just wanted to forget the whole thing.

As well as her heavy bucket of seed, Lena also had Thomas with her, his blanket tied into this kinda homemade papoose. I'd told her not to worry, that we could manage without her, but I knew how important it was for her to prove she could do most things as well as us, and after all, she could follow a furrow as easily as a length of string.

Thankfully it was overcast, so she didn't have to worry about the little guy getting all hot and bothered, though later in the day he did do that thing where he starts crying and simply refuses to stop, and she was forced to take him inside, which I reckon was what he was after all along, that he'd just got bored with looking at the same view all the time.

The rest of us finished seeding round about seven and trudged wearily back to the house, Jimmy and Delilah too tired even to speak, Hanna and Gordie still fooling around, Gigi making a solemn point of ignoring them.

With the light starting to fade, my thoughts had gone back to what'd happened the previous night – not just here, but also over in the next valley – and I had an idea.

'Kids – can you give me a hand?'

Jimmy glanced back but was too weary to show any further interest, whilst the kids followed along in the direction of the barn without a word.

It wasn't exactly inspired, nor that original, but I'd been pondering on what Nick'd said and it'd occurred to me that with crazies around and weird things going on, any kind of early warning system would be useful – and we had the beginnings of one already in place: Lena's wires, that'd helped her find her way around when we first arrived. We could retrieve all those cans piled at the back of the barn and attach them to the lines, along with old bottles, anything that would make a noise when they knocked together.

Gordie was a long way from impressed – he'd wanted infrared beams at the minimum, maybe some kind of disguised animal traps – but it was better than nothing, and when I demonstrated how it would work, how much noise it could make, he did kinda nod with grudging approval.

We stayed out 'til the light was just about gone, threading all manner of stuff to clang and clink together. In total, with all the different lines star-bursting away from the farmhouse, we must've set up half a mile or so. Admittedly, it couldn't have been much more basic, but at least it felt like we'd done something, that we weren't entirely at the mercy of anyone who came a-calling.

Delilah came out on the porch and hollered for us to come in and eat. The last thing I did before I closed and locked the front door, even though I didn't understand the impulse, was to take a long, hard look at the sky. It was if my instincts were telling me that if any invaders were on their way, that was the direction they were going to come from.

I'd anticipated the atmosphere in the house would be a little anxious, but with the assistance of a bottle of the homemade hooch we'd found stashed in the barn when we'd first arrived, Lena, Jimmy, Lile and me talked things out 'til we felt much more relaxed. Over dinner I told them what we'd been up to, tying stuff on the wires, what purpose I hoped it'd serve – but apart from a half-hearted nod of approval from Jimmy, there was little else in the way of reaction.

'Let's hope they've moved on,' Lile croaked.

'What kind of person does that to a dog?' Lena asked, pouring herself more hooch.

'Kids—' Jimmy started to say, old attitudes dying hard, but though he stopped himself, Hanna jumped on him.

'We wouldn't do that!' she protested.

'*Other* kids,' Jimmy explained.

'Last night – we should've gone over,' Lena said to me, 'checked it out.'

'That wasn't just the one dog in the woods,' I said, not for the first time.

'Woke me up,' Gordie complained, like that'd been the real tragedy of the night. 'If it happens again, I'll make sure it's dead.'

We discussed it a while longer, 'til eventually a long, thoughtful pause became the cue to retire. We were country people now, early to bed and early to rise, needing to make the most of every daylight hour.

One of the great things about living in a proper home – and after some of the hellholes we'd bedded down in, there were *lots* – was that we had a measure of privacy: a bedroom for Lena and me, another for

Jimmy and Delilah, and, unavoidably, the last one for the two girls (and wouldn't I've liked to have heard those 'goodnight' conversations!) while Gordie slept on the sofa.

That night Lena and me made love, something that, since the birth of Thomas, hadn't happened that often, and it crossed my mind that we were reverting to old behaviour, that 'cuz we were feeling threatened, we wanted to reaffirm our love for each other, as if to fortify ourselves against whatever might be on its way.

When the little guy was first born he slept with us, but I got so nervous of rolling over in the middle of the night and crushing him, I couldn't close my eyes for a second. When we moved into the farm, we fixed him up a bed in the bottom drawer of the wardrobe – it might sound odd, but it worked a treat. Wrapped in his favourite blanket, the little guy looked as comfy as a baby bird in its nest.

The one thing I didn't normally have trouble with was *falling* asleep, it was staying that way that was the problem. After a few hours, Thomas had only to snuffle and snort to wake me – and later that night, that's exactly what he did. I lay there for a while, feeling an impending bout of attention-seeking coming on, knowing if I was going to nip it in the bud I had to get up straight away.

I just about made it: on my way outta the bedroom he was already taking in as much air as his little lungs could hold and by the time I'd reached the front door, he was choosing the opening note of his I Want Overture.

I paused out on the step, looking all around, mindful of what'd happened the previous night, and seeing nothing, took Thomas on his usual circuit of the yard, the little guy going back to sleep almost immediately. The night was exactly as before – one moment bathed in moonlight, the next plunged into darkness. The only difference was the occasional clank or scraping noise from the items we'd tied to Lena's wires, which I'll tell ya, did nothing to settle my nerves.

I wasn't that surprised when the howling started again: those same tortured cries cutting across the night like slithers of flying glass. Once more it was in the woods, but this time much further away, down the slope towards the road. It also sounded like just the one animal this time, though the pain, the agony, was exactly as before, as if something was being tortured.

I never heard anything like that in my life. All that time out on the Island, the terrible things that went on, the 'clean-ups' in the City when hundreds – including dear little Arturo – got slaughtered? They were all nightmares, but I never heard pain expressed like that before.

I pulled back Thomas's blanket to see if he was registering anything, if there was a change of expression, but thankfully there wasn't. Maybe down the line, when he was older, he'd have the worst nightmare and we'd all wonder why, what'd possibly brought it on – unquestionably, it would be this. It sounded like whatever-it-was was being skinned alive, slain and driven crazy all in the same moment. I still didn't have the faintest idea what kinda animal it was. In fact, in that moment, I wasn't even sure it was an animal.

I ran back into the house, putting Thomas back to bed, grateful that once he did nod off, he could sleep through just about anything. As I crept back out through the parlour, Gordie started mumbling sleepy complaints about the recurring wailing, but never seemed to really wake and was asleep again before I even got outta the door.

I hurried over to the far side of the yard, the howls getting slightly louder, more distressed. I broke into a trot but had to stop the moment I got into the woods to allow my eyes time to adjust to the almost complete darkness. In the day it was a nice place to be; at night it damn near frightened the life outta you.

Slowly I edged my way forward, but the closer I got to that noise, the more confused I became. Something was definitely going on – some kinda disturbance, a struggle maybe – as well as the repeated howling, I could hear heavy, thumping collisions. For the briefest of moments the moon's light filtered down through the branches and I caught a glimpse of something big and dark rolling across the forest floor. *What the hell was that?* But the light was extinguished before I could get a proper view.

I crept a little closer, trying to be as quiet as I could, though with all the noise going on, the grunting and howling, I wasn't sure if there was a need. It took me several seconds to realise that whatever it was, whatever creature was involved, had got to its feet and was now running my way.

I couldn't move, as much frozen by confusion as fear. Did it know I was there? Was this an attack? It continued to scream and howl towards me, but it sounded so crazed, so completely deranged, as if it didn't have the slightest idea where it was or what it was doing.

I did think about running, but whatever it was, it was moving a damn sight quicker than I could, and I realised I had no choice but to stand my ground. It was approaching at such speed, with such pounding heavy footsteps, I got it into my head that it might be a bull. I crouched behind a tree, fearing the worst as it got ever closer, that I was about to be crushed to death, but it thundered past with barely a foot or two to spare, those panicked screams of terror like some shrill squealing alarm.

It was so dark in that moment, I still couldn't say exactly what it was. I had this idea it had four legs rather than two, and it was certainly big and heavy, but more than that, I couldn't even guess. I half-expected to hear something chasing after it; that it'd escaped its torturers and they were in hot pursuit, but there was nothing, just that endlessly repeated howl slowly fading into the night, occasionally coming to an abrupt stop, as if it'd fallen, or maybe even collided with a tree, then just when you started to hope it was over, it would start up again.

Finally it was gone, absorbed into the deadness of night, and the breath I'd unknowingly been holding onto exploded out of me. *What the hell was that?* Why had it been so distressed? Was it running from *something* – or running from *itself*?

Whatever the answer, I didn't want to spend another minute in those woods in the middle of the night. I headed back towards the farmhouse, keeping a real watchful eye out, and yeah, I don't mind admitting it, spinning round now and then to make sure I wasn't being followed.

I can't tell you how grateful I was to finally see a dull light straining through the trees. At the very moment that I emerged into the open, the moon came out from behind the clouds and lit up the whole night, as if to reassure me I was now safe . . . yeah, thanks a lot for that.

I hurried back to the house, my footsteps the only sound on what now seemed to be an eerily silent night. Nothing else stirred: no distant owl hooted, no echoing unspecified grunt or call from somewhere down the valley. It was almost as if everything was as shocked as I was; as if they were perched in their trees and peering out of their burrows, the pounding of their hearts only now subsiding.

I'd just about made it to the farmyard when damned if I didn't get that feeling again, that same sense that something or someone was whispering into the darkest of the night. I doubled back a few yards and slipped into the shadow of the barn, having no idea what I was waiting for, but waiting all the same.

I don't how long I was there, ten minutes or more maybe, over and over telling myself it was nothing, 'til finally I actually believed it. I had a warm bed and a wonderful woman waiting for me, and after what'd happened over in the woods, I wanted to be back in her arms. Whatever I'd heard or felt the previous night – and I wondered if the most likely explanation was some kind of meteorological phenomenon – it could wait 'til morning.

I started to make my way over towards the porch, feeling like at last I might be able to give sleep a really good go, then suddenly stopped, this time even more frightened than before. What in God's name was *that*?

Something big and black had just slid across the land, triggering the objects on the wires, setting the cans rattling, the bottles chinking – like the rumbling approach of an earthquake. Again I looked up into the night sky, but nothing passed across the face of the moon or the stars, not as far as I could see. So what the hell was it?

CHAPTER FOUR

The following morning dawned so bright and uncompromised it was hard to believe the events of the previous night. I told the others what had happened but found myself backing away a little from the final part of the story. Bad enough they had to deal with me coming face to face with whatever had been howling in the night, let alone some mysterious dark force stealing across the land like a hunting shark; which was probably why they concentrated on what had happened in the woods and treated the rest a bit like it might be the product of the over-stimulated imagination of an insomniac.

'Gotta be an animal,' Delilah said, 'ain't it?'

'I guess,' I replied.

'Are there wolves around here?' Hanna asked.

I shrugged; Nick *had* mentioned he'd once caught a glimpse of a small pack, but what had swept past me had been on its own and much bigger than a wolf.

'Should've brought the lasers,' Jimmy grumbled. 'I told ya. Not cool.'

I sighed; God knew how many times he'd brought that up – and maybe it irritated me so much 'cuz I knew he was probably right. Once we'd decided we were coming over the mountains and getting well away from our previous life I'd kinda insisted we got rid of the lasers, convinced that we'd have no need of that sort of thing any more.

Lena and Hanna had been in complete agreement, Gigi – a little surprisingly – had sat on the fence, but Jimmy, Gordie and Lile had been dead against it. In fact, they'd gone on about my stupidity so much that, in a spirit of compromise, when I hid the limo in the cave, I stashed the lasers in the trunk, just in case. Now, of course, that wasn't looking like such a great decision.

'Someone could go back for them?' Lile suggested, though Gordie's mind was heading off elsewhere.

'Why don't we set traps?'

Hanna stared at him as if he'd betrayed her in some way. '*No!*' she cried.

'Why not?'

'It's cruel!'

'Cruel to what?' he asked, pointing out that we had no idea what we were dealing with.

'I think it's a good idea,' Gigi ventured, always ready to seize the chance to stir things up a little.

'Wouldn't hurt,' Delilah commented. 'Least we might find out what it is.'

Jimmy nodded. 'I can make something up – we might even get a little fresh meat out of it.'

Hanna made this face, like she wanted to argue some more but knew there was something in what they were saying. Since we'd arrived on the farm we'd been mainly living off the stored fruit and vegetables and what we'd been able to dig up, most of it well past its eat-by date, 'specially as we'd traded a lot of the better stuff with those in the next valley. But there was very little left, and gradually we'd become more and more reliant on trading Jimmy's know-how or

34

my muscle for food. For sure a little fresh meat of our own wouldn't go amiss. Mind you, I had to wonder, once we saw what we'd caught, would we actually want to eat it?

In the end we agreed Jimmy would make up some traps and Lena, Gordie and me would go and set them in the woods. Hanna still wasn't happy about it – bad enough hunting animals, let alone trapping them, when that often resulted in a long and painful death – and when Gordie asked her to come along, she refused. Which, of course, meant Gigi immediately said she'd come.

Jimmy was as good as his word, and later that morning emerged from the barn with not just one but two types of trap: a simple snare to catch smaller animals – which Hanna got so upset about I said we didn't need – and several examples of what looked like good old-fashioned bear traps.

As ever, the little guy made a real production of explaining them to us, insisting we showed him that we understood how they worked and that we could set them correctly, and when I tried to make light of it, warned me that was how people lost limbs. Finally, when each of us had satisfied him that we really did understand, he left us to it, scuttling back to his workshop as if there was something there much more suited to his talents.

The four of us made our way over to the woods, the daylight still embarrassing me, the way everything looked so peaceful and unthreatening. But the moment we crossed the treeline, you could feel the mood change: it was cooler, darker, the trees so dense in places anyone or anything could've been hiding in there.

We didn't set the traps straight away, just took a general look around for anything that didn't feel right. Lena was stopping every now and then, sniffing the air, this slightly concerned look growing on her face.

'What's the matter?' I asked.

She shook her head, like she was getting a bit of an idea but wasn't yet ready to share it.

We went deeper into the woods, still not seeing anything unusual, taking the gentle slope down towards the road, then suddenly Lena picked up speed and I realised she was leading us somewhere.

'What is it?' I asked, and again she didn't reply, but I knew she was onto something, calling on those specially honed senses of hers, negotiating her way by sound and smell.

At first I wasn't sure what it was. I could see something up ahead, strewn out across the forest floor, and even though my instincts told me it was bad, it took me a while to work out exactly how. As we got nearer I could see there were four of them, blackened and burned, each one so twisted and contorted by death I couldn't even make out what sorta animals they were.

'What is it?' Lena asked, stopping along with the rest of us, though the smell was so strong, she must've had a pretty good idea.

'Four burned animals,' I told her, moving forward to take a better look, the kids following but looking distinctly queasy.

At first I thought they were all the same animal – all those sets of razor-sharp teeth, they had to be wolves, maybe the same ones Nick had seen – but then I realised that the one partly hidden under the others was something else, possibly a deer.

'All burned?' Lena asked.

It was the way she said it that made me stop and think, consider what I'd seen – what I should've seen straight away.

'Jeez,' I groaned, bending over the charcoaled bodies, studying them, but sure enough, with the possible exception of the deer, which I couldn't see clearly unless I extracted it from the pile of carcases, they were all burned the way George's dog had been. 'It's the same thing: burned from the inside out.'

'Same as Sandy?' Gordie asked.

'Yeah,' Gigi sneered, like it was surely obvious to anyone with a brain.

By the look of the ground around us and a couple of nearby trees there'd been a bit of a fire, but thankfully it'd burned itself out and all that remained now was this grotesque sculpture of skeletons in the middle of a blackened canvas.

'Anything else?' Lena asked, starting to sniff again.

'Whaddya mean?'

She looked a little confused. 'Nothing?'

I took a more careful look around, even up in the trees, and it was there that I made yet another gruesome discovery. 'Jesus!'

'What?'

'There's a bird – a really big one – just hanging from a branch by one of its claws. It's been burned, too.'

I don't know why, but for some reason that was even more disturbing than the wolves and the deer, maybe 'cuz of the way it was just hanging there, like some ghostly sacrifice, or maybe 'cuz it immediately struck me that if this was the work of crazies, how the hell had they managed to get up there and do that?

In the end we moved on, wondering what other surprises lay in store for us, though as it turned out, the answer was none. There was one place where a tree had been badly damaged, but as there were deer around, maybe that'd been caused by a stag? Mind you, if that was the case, he must've had a real sore head afterwards, 'cuz it looked like he'd gone crazy, butting that trunk over and over, leaving a canvas of blood smears, and I couldn't help but wonder what sort of state he'd ended up in.

We didn't bother to set the traps. It looked like we'd solved the mystery of what'd been howling in the middle of the night, and odd as it might sound, if there were others, we weren't of a mind to eat them when they were in such distress.

I did my best to play the whole thing down, but I gotta say, it disturbed me far more than I let on. Animals dying by being burned from the inside out, both wild and domestic? How could that be, for chrissake? That night, lying in bed with Lena softly breathing beside me, I found sleep even more elusive than usual. I wanted Thomas to wake so I had an excuse to get up, and when he didn't, I got up anyway and went to sit out on the porch in Delilah's favourite chair.

I reckon it was that bird as much as anything that unnerved me: suspended up there all black and naked. Jimmy said it sounded like some kind of raptor, maybe even an eagle, but it'd felt like more like a crucified angel maybe? As if someone had murdered an ambassador sent here from Heaven.

I stayed out on that porch for a good hour or more, the atmosphere in the valley now feeling so different, as if everything we'd built, everything we'd discovered, was now under threat. Hanna came out to see me, all tousled-haired and heavy-lidded, asking if I'd heard anything and not looking that reassured when I said I hadn't. For a while she sat with me, but eventually tiredness got the better of her and she went back inside.

No more than five minutes later, Jimmy replaced her – Jeez, things had to be really bad if the little guy couldn't keep his head down.

'Everything okay?' he asked, slumping up against a wooden post, taking in the surrounding countryside. For the third night running, clouds were darting in and out of the path of the moon, like sheep playing soccer with a luminous ball.

'Yeah,' I said, trying to sound confident. 'God knows what caused it – maybe they ate or drank something they shouldn't – but it looks like they were the problem.'

For a while he didn't reply, just stood there with his back to me, then he turned. 'D'you really think so?'

'Why not?'

He took in a deep breath, then slid it out, like it would help ease the passage of his words. 'She's gonna come over those mountains one day.'

There was no need to ask who he meant. 'Maybe not.'

'You don't believe that any more than I do.'

I stared at the little guy, for some reason it finally occurring to me that he'd resurrected his thinning ponytail; that like many old people, he'd tried a new look – shaving his head in his case – but now had reverted to the one he'd had most of his life. Whatever his taste in hairstyles, he was one helluva smart cookie, and if *he* didn't know what was going on, sure as hell I didn't.

'It's not often you can say that the death of one person would improve the world a thousand times over,' he commented, 'but in this case – that is one mean, evil, uncool daughter-of-a-bitch.'

'You got that right.'

He took one last look out into the night before hurrying back to Lile and their bed, almost as if he was concerned they might not have much more time together.

I only stayed a few more minutes myself, just long enough to go over my checklist of worries: there'd been no more howling in the night, no dark spectres consuming everything in its path, no rattling of cans or chinking of bottles. In the morning I'd be able to give everyone the encouraging news, maybe even predict that our troubles were over . . .

I just wished I believed it.

It was a surprise, yet not an altogether unexpected one (if that makes any sense?) when the following day Gigi told me she was going back to the City. We were out walking the ploughed fields, making sure that every one of those seeds we'd sown had been covered by soil and had its chance of growing. It hadn't occurred to me, but she'd obviously been waiting for a moment when we were alone to tell me.

'Why?' I asked.

As always, her first line of communication was a shrug, but I waited for something a bit more informative. 'Might as well,' she told me.

'Is this 'cuz of Gordie and Hanna?' I asked, the seriousness of the subject provoking me to say what I'd normally avoid like a plague.

God, did she lose her cool. '*No!*' she shouted, jutting her bottom teeth out like a piranha. 'Jesus—! What's that got to do with anything?'

'I dunno.'

'I was never interested in *him*!' she snarled.

I nodded, crouching down to cover a couple of exposed seeds, turning away from what seemed like a telling degree of anger.

'The princess is welcome to him,' she sneered. For a while she went quiet, maybe fearing she'd given herself away, doing her best to restore her air of indifference before going on, 'I wanna see some friends, that's all,' she said at last. 'Make sure they're all right.'

I really didn't know what to say – that whole area was so hazy with her. She'd mentioned friends before, but in such a way that I'd never been sure they even existed. There were so many mysteries surrounding Gigi – the main one as far as I was concerned being, of course, what'd gone on with her and Nora Jagger.

'But you're coming back?' I asked.

Again she shrugged. 'Depends.'

I paused for a moment, all sorts of thoughts going through my head, and shit to admit, the one that was disturbing me the most was: did I trust her on her own in the City? I guess after all that time of living and working together that sounds a little strange, but Gigi was always a complicated person; there was a side to her I'd never been able to isolate, let alone understand. Despite recent events, none of us wanted to have to flee the farm. There were plenty of people in the City who would've given anything to know the whereabouts of Lena and Thomas, who'd be offering all manner of inducements – certainly possessions and a lifestyle that an Island kid couldn't even dream of. On the other hand, she'd sampled some of that with Nora Jagger, but had still ended up 'killing' her – or she would have if I'd set my laser correctly. And bearing that in mind, going back there and risking confronting that woman again seemed like just about the stupidest thing she could do.

'She'll still be looking for you,' I said. 'You know that, don't you?'

'I can take care of myself,' Gigi told me fiercely.

For a while the two of us walked in silence, still scouring the ground for seeds, Gigi covering a few more over. She wasn't asking my permission – she didn't need to. We might be a kinda family, but it was up to her what she did. After all, she was an adult . . . well, more or less.

'I'll come with you,' I said eventually.

'*Why?*' she asked, taken aback.

'I want to.'

She gave this half grunt, half chuckle. 'You don't trust me.'

'Sure I do.'

'No, you don't.'

'I do!' I said, trying to sound convincing. 'I just wanna see what's been happening. The way things are going. Maybe look someone up.'

'Who?' she challenged.

I declined to say and she obviously took that as proof of my lack of trust; that she should never have mentioned her plan to one of the two people who'd seen her with Nora Jagger that night. But later, over lunch, when the subject came up again, the others' reactions were equally concerned.

'Gigi!' Gordie protested. 'You gotta be kidding!'

41

'What's it got to do with you?' she challenged, and he had the good sense not to reply. 'Huh!' she still grunted, as if he'd said something anyway.

'You wanna go *back*?' Delilah cried in disbelief.

'Yeah.'

Delilah exchanged looks with Jimmy, as if barely believing what she was hearing. 'Think on, girl,' she muttered. 'Think on.'

I turned to Lena, hoping for some kinda guidance from the only other person who knew the whole story, and despite feeding Thomas, she sensed me looking at her.

'Why risk what we've got?' she asked.

'Don't worry, I'll be real careful,' Gigi promised, knowing what Lena was saying. 'The last thing I'd do is endanger you or Thomas.'

'But *why*?' Lile repeated, as if suspecting the first symptom of madness. 'Why d'ya wanna go?'

There was a frustrated and uncomprehending pause that was eventually interrupted in a way I didn't think any of us would've anticipated.

'Maybe we should all go?' Hanna half-suggested.

Gigi glared at her. The others, as one, were shaking their heads. But this was approval from the most unlikely of quarters, and all the more surprising for it. It was a bit like when we were out on the Island and finally accepted that we couldn't hide in the tunnels any more, that we had to go out and face the Wastelords.

'I'm not going anywhere,' Lena announced.

I took a deep breath. It was high time I told Lena what I had in mind. 'I was thinking of going along too.'

'*What?*'

'Big Guy!' Jimmy protested. 'Not cool. Not one little bit.'

'Just to take a look,' I said, ignoring Gigi's grunting, obviously still convinced I was lying.

'Clancy!' Lena wailed, a little like she'd suddenly realised she was drowning.

'I'll keep a real low profile, I promise.'

'You're too big to keep a low profile,' she replied, in all seriousness.

The discussion got increasingly heated, what with Gigi saying she wished she'd just snuck away and Lena getting angry with me, reminding me – as if I needed reminding! – that I was a father now. It even went on later, when we went to bed; which was unusual for us.

'We need to know what's going on,' I told her again.

'I don't see why?'

''cuz it's beginning to affect us.'

'In what way?'

'I don't know! That's what we need to find out.'

She turned over, punching her pillow a few times in frustration. 'What about Gigi?' she asked, her voice dropping to a whisper.

'What about her?' I replied, though I knew what she meant.

'Do you trust her?'

'Yeah,' I said, not entirely convincingly.

'You sure?'

'After all this time – yeah, why not?'

'You're prepared to risk everything?'

I paused for a moment, feeling like I was getting boxed in and wanting to fight my way out. 'I'm used to working with people I'm not sure of. I can handle it,' I told her. 'I'm just gonna take a quick look . . . put our minds at rest.'

'Jesus, Clancy!' she groaned, and without another word, turned off the light.

For a while we both lay there in the half-light of a peeping-tom moon, then I heard, as clearly as if it'd dropped from the highest leaf of a tree to the forest floor, a tear fall onto her pillow and I immediately pulled her to me.

'I'm scared,' she told me.

'You think I'm not?' I replied. 'All the more reason to find out what's going on.'

'But we've got so much more to lose now!'

She was right, of course, and I was all too aware of it. It wasn't just the house and farm, or living in this picturesque valley, or this new and unsuspected lifestyle, but that little guy quietly dreaming away over in the bottom drawer of the wardrobe.

'It'll be all right,' I told her – the four most useless words in the English language.

She sighed like she knew there was nothing else she could say; the two of us gradually stepping onto the top of that slow slide down to sleep. I think my eyes had just about closed when she suddenly jolted me back.

'*What was that?*'

'What?'

For a moment she didn't speak, her concentration positively crackling beside me. 'I felt something.'

'What?' I repeated.

'I don't know. It felt like something passed over us.'

'I didn't notice anything,' I replied.

'Really?'

'Nope.'

Again she paused, all her heightened sensors quivering away, searching in places I knew I couldn't go, 'til finally she began to relax. 'It was something,' she said, making herself comfortable again before returning to her search for sleep.

For a while I just lay there, listening to her breathing slowly getting heavier. I hadn't noticed anything, but I was pretty sure she was right and I had a fair idea what it'd been: that thing had swept across our land again, taking in the farm and the house, threatening everything and everyone before it.

The following morning – and I wouldn't have minded putting money on it – a fight broke out about who else was going to the City. Gordie was of a mind to come along; in fact, he was of the opinion the venture wouldn't stand a chance without him. He'd grown a lot over the last year, not just upwards and outwards but in confidence too. I'd trained him a little, taught him a few tricks of the old trade. They call prostitution the world's oldest profession, but I bet you they were only there to service soldiers – we been beating the hell outta each other a lot longer than we been paying someone to love a little heaven into us.

I'd been through some fairly basic stuff with him, how to cause the most damage with the minimum amount of effort, tricks we've probably been using since the beginning of time. No matter how much I might've disapproved of violence now, I didn't seem able to get away from it. But it was because he *had* become that much more formidable, so much better at handling himself, that I wanted him to stay at the house. With all the strange things that'd been going on, I knew I'd feel a whole lot better knowing he was there looking out for everybody.

Hanna debated it for a while – she did actually want to come with us even if Gordie wasn't there – but Gigi made it perfectly plain she wasn't welcome. Jimmy and Delilah kept insisting that no one should be going anywhere, their fear of what they might lose on their faces for everyone to see, so that, in the end, things stayed as they were: with just Gigi and me going alone.

Saying goodbye to Lena and Thomas in the midst of all that uncertainty was something I could've well done without. It was the first time the three of us had been parted and we had this kind of awkward three-way group hug, with little Thomas getting squashed in the middle, protesting in the only way he knew how.

Gigi acted as if she would definitely be coming back, that there was no need to say a proper goodbye, but I reckoned that was as much down to her hating emotional outpourings as anything else. Over and over I told Lena I'd be back as soon as I could, certainly no more than a few days, though really, I couldn't be sure. All I knew was I wanted to get in and back out again as quickly as I could.

As we made our way down the track and past the two small wheat fields, still calling back or giving the occasional wave, we gotta real nice surprise. Damned if in some places there weren't a few tiny green shoots already poking their way out, like stubble on the face of the Incredible Hulk. I shouted back to the others, told them to come and take a look, but we continued on our way rather than risk getting delayed and having to say our goodbyes all over again. But something about seeing that new life clawing its way outta the ground flushed out a whole new area of unsuspected optimism. It was a sign, a promise for a brighter future, and I was more than ready to put my faith in it.

Once we reached the road, we had to turn in the direction of the pass, walk for thirty minutes or so, then leave the road and make our way across country and up the mountain.

If it'd been a straightforward journey without the occasional stretch of dense forest or boggy soil I might've tried to persuade Gigi to make use of the present Jimmy made for Lena and me – for sure it would've saved us several hours – but I couldn't imagine her ever getting on that thing, no matter how much easier it might've been.

I think he did it partly for the challenge – for the pleasure of designing and making something, using that side of his brain, but also, as so often with the little guy, purely outta the goodness of his heart. I'd known he was up to something 'cuz when I went over to the barn one day I found my entrance blocked and I was pushed away. All he would say was he was working on something but wasn't ready to tell me what – mind you, if he'd given me a thousand guesses, I never would've come up with it.

Finally the day arrived when he proudly called Lena and me outside and we walked out to find him standing at the bottom of the steps, this huge smile on his face, waiting for me to get over the surprise so I could explain to Lena what he'd made for us.

Maybe I gave him the idea the day he saw me fooling around with one of the kids' bikes the previous occupants had left behind, circling the farmyard like a circus clown, Delilah laughing at the way my knees kept hitting the handlebars, the many times I almost wobbled my way off. What you'd describe it as exactly, I dunno; I guess you'd call it a 'tandem', though I don't think the world'd ever seen one quite like his. He'd used both of the kids' bike frames as a kinda base, but then had to weld in a part of an old iron bedstead to extend it. The original wheels weren't up to a tandem and two adults, so it had two at the back, one in the middle, and one at the front for steering. Apart from that, it had all kinds of bits and pieces holding it together – some from the barn, even some from the kitchen – and he obviously must've felt the end product wasn't as aesthetically pleasing as it could be, 'cuz to top it all off, he'd found some paint – the colour we'd done Hanna and Gigi's bedroom – and coated the whole thing in this particularly vivid shade of green.

To be honest, though I thanked him, my first reaction wasn't that different to Gigi's – that you wouldn't get me on that thing if you paid me – but when I saw how proud he was of it, when I appreciated just how enthusiastic Lena was, I swallowed my pride and clambered aboard, the two of us, slightly nervously, heading off on our maiden trip.

It didn't take me long to appreciate that, as usual, I'd underestimated the little guy. It was ingenious. With me at the front peddling and steering and Lena at the back peddling and taking in the day – I can't tell you how much pleasure it brought us. We went all over with it, clashing the centuries: old-fashioned techno in an unspoilt world.

But like I said, Gigi thought it was distinctly uncool – worse, in fact, just plain embarrassing – though that might have had something to do with the fact that Hanna'd managed to persuade Gordie to go out on it a few times, and they'd come back all happy and smiling and saying how great it was.

We slept that night on the other side of the mountain, neither of us wanting to make the descent in the dark. It might not be that high, but it still got pretty cold up there. We hung one of our blankets on a bush to give us a little shelter; the other we used to keep warm. Neither of us said much. I've never been much of a talker and Gigi was never gonna be anything but a dyed-in-the-wool ex-Island kid who found it impossible to empathise with any adult. Sometimes when I overheard her chattering away to Gordie I could barely recognise her: so animated, so emotional, so relaxed and full of life. But as soon as an adult appeared, the drawbridge went up, fires were lit and the tar was brought to the boil. She didn't trust us and I didn't believe she ever would, which was one helluvan irony, bearing in mind the concerns I had about her.

The following morning, to our immense relief, we found the limo still in the cave just as we'd left it. It looked a bit sorry for itself, covered in various slimy substances, some looking on the point of taking root, but whatever you might say about modern vehicles, they're one helluvan improvement on what used to be, 'cuz believe it or not that thing fired up first time.

As for the lasers I'd hidden in a secret well in the trunk, they were fine, though their power-packs had got badly corroded. No way were they gonna fire, though I hoped that at least they'd act as a kind of deterrent, something we could wave around to impress people.

I slowly backed out the limo, manoeuvred around the slab and went slithering and slipping down the slope, Gigi screaming at me at one point 'cuz she thought we were gonna topple over. When I got to the forest floor and started to make my way through the trees we got lost a coupla times, my memory fooled by how fast some of the undergrowth had grown since we were last there. I also managed to dent the final untouched panel on the limo, that poor, mistreated, mechanical beast now looking like it had paid a consultation trip to the breaker's yard. Yet at length we burst out of the undergrowth, leapt across a small ditch and landed on the dirt track.

I knew I had to take it real easy: it was more than a hundred miles to the first bit of power strip and we were unlikely to come across any gas. And maybe it was our slow progress, one too many degrees of boredom, that finally prompted Gigi to speak to me properly – though I gotta say, it wasn't the subject I'd expected.

'It was this guy on the garbage boat,' she suddenly said, as if I'd just asked her a question.

You didn't have to be a genius to work out what she was talking about, nor where the conversation was heading. I never said a word, nor even glanced her way, just in case it frightened her off.

'He started making these jokes about all the spies on the Island – kids and wrinklies – I guess seeing how I'd react. Slowly it became more serious – more of an 'offer'. Not 'spying', just . . . keeping an eye on things.'

Those 'guys' on the garbage boats, men and women, had a bit of a reputation. They'd been our only possible contact with the Mainland but something about them often hadn't seemed quite right. They'd trade you stuff, get it to order, but it'd arrive looking like it'd been sourced straight from a warehouse. Clothing or food, stuff you hadn't seen in years, providing you had something they wanted in exchange. At the time I assumed they were just taking the opportunity to make a little on the side, a dabble in the black market; since then I'd come to realise that some of them were probably working for Infinity.

'Didn't take it seriously at first – more fool them; I wasn't telling them anything everyone didn't already know – but the more it went on, the more they gave me, the more I got sucked in,' Gigi continued, her voice flat and emotionless. 'Then one day, when I told them to leave me alone, that I wouldn't do it any more, they threatened to tell all the other kids . . . I knew I was in deep shit.'

She spoke nonstop for about twenty minutes – which was about ten times longer than I'd ever heard her speak before, all about how they picked her up the night we escaped from the Island and briefed her about what was going on, the places she needed to hang out where she might be recruited by enemies of Infinity, where to report if she got any information. A few days later she was befriended by 'the resistance', taken to a kinda halfway house and kept there 'til they were sure they could trust her, then finally brought up to speed about their activities: how they were fighting back against Infinity, stepping up techno-terrorism to try to cut off the many tendrils of Big Sister.

It's funny how that expression came into use: 'Big Sister'. Makes you realise how devious big business can be. For so long we used to talk about Big Brother, the government, spying on us, abusing our rights, ignoring our privacy, but then things began to change and it wasn't so much *government* spying any more as private enterprise. At first it was just to assist in their marketing, to direct the appropriate goods and services our way, but then it became something else. They used our secrets for all manner of reasons, and those they had no use for, they sold on to others. But the worst thing was they were watching us all the time, checking our techno-footprints, seeing what we were up to, making sure we did nothing to harm their commercial interests – 'editing' us out of normal life if we did, making us 'non-people'.

Sound familiar? You don't have to go too far from there to get to where Infinity are now: 'cleaning up' their society, keeping it the way they want, the way it's easiest for them to manage and exploit.

It was them who came up with the expression 'Big Sister', the conglomerates – or probably some high-end ad agency they hired. They knew people'd find a nickname for their behaviour and decided to invent one and plant it into the nation's consciousness before someone arrived at something more sinister. I mean, 'Big Sister'? That's someone who's always looking out for you, who might make the odd unpopular decision but at heart she's always on your side, always there to protect your interests . . . Sneaky, huh?

At first Gigi didn't take 'the resistance' too seriously – they were just this bunch of weirdoes and losers, right? She didn't *know* them, and didn't give a damn about informing on them . . . but the more they hung out, the more she started to respect them, to suspect there might be something in what they had to say. The only problem was, just like before, she'd already got in too deep and there was no way back – if she'd tried, she'd probably've had both sides after her.

Then, to make matters worse, this one time she went to the Infinity building, she came to the attention of Nora Jagger. She started to receive star treatment, little favours, luxuries she'd never known before in her life.

In the end, she'd just resigned herself to being a victim of circumstance, that she might as well carry on and enjoy her lifestyle as best she could. It was only when she infiltrated our world that her loyalties started jostling again, things finally coming to a head the night we broke into Infinity. If she'd killed Nora Jagger, if I'd set my laser properly, that would've been an end to it, but as she didn't, just like me, she'd made probably the worst enemy she possibly could, and frankly, the very last place either of us should be heading was back to that City.

When she finally finished, when she'd said all she wanted to say, she lapsed back into silence with no ceremony whatsoever. If you'd nodded off on the back seat and just woken up, you wouldn't've known anything had taken place.

She hadn't *had* to tell me and I think she knew that, but I guess she'd wanted to get the story out, and being Gigi she'd made it all very matter-of-fact, like a long, articulated shrug. Or maybe she felt she owed it to me 'cuz we were on our way back to the City, 'cuz she knew how much I needed to trust her.

Not that I made a big thing of it. It was what it was and both of us knew that; no matter how long we lingered over it, it would never entirely sit right for either of us. I mean, the thing about human nature is that despite what some people tell ya, very few of us are one hundred per cent good or bad, and Gigi's a perfect example: when she's in the light, you're not sure what's going on in the shadow; and when she's in the dark, you wonder where that glow's coming from. I mean, I *had* to trust her, that was all there was to it . . . but I had to keep an eye on her, too.

It took us more than three hours to reach the highway, and when we did, we were in for a bit of a shock. The power strip wasn't working. Well, I say it wasn't working, when I checked, it *was* working – it just wouldn't connect to *us*. I didn't know why; maybe there was something wrong with the limo's reader, or perhaps Doctor Simon had withdrawn the credit? Though I'd always thought he'd try to maintain any link with us he could, no matter how tenuous – well, not 'us', exactly, more Lena – and now, of course, little Thomas.

With Jimmy having taken out most of its technology, the limo wasn't talking to me or telling me what was going on, but the read-out indicated we had less than a gallon of gas in the tank and would fail to reach the City by eighty-eight point three miles, though it had no answer to my question about where we might find more.

That didn't leave us with too many options: either we went as far as we could and then walked the rest, or tried hitching – which I didn't have a great deal of faith in, being as there were so few vehicles around. The only other possible alternative was to call on a few private dwellings and see if they had any gas.

We tried a couple of likely-looking smallholdings – being as I reckoned they'd be more likely to keep a store – but they'd been abandoned and stripped of anything of value.

'You gotta go where no one else's been,' Gigi told me. 'Outta sight of the road.'

She was right, of course: all this stuff left in full view of everyone, like the occasional discarded vehicle – someone was bound to have checked it out. The next track that headed off the road and out into nowhere, I ventured down, taking it slowly, lurching left and right, trying to ignore a slight grinding noise coming from the back suspension.

It must've been the best part of three-quarters of a mile before we got to the farmhouse, but it was the same story all over again: the place'd been abandoned, ransacked, and Mother Nature was already starting to get to work, having her way with the upstart interlopers.

We gave it a quick once-over but there was nothing so I returned to the road, drove another couple of miles, then tried again, this time finding the homestead even further down the track.

The *good* thing was that this one wasn't deserted; the *bad* thing was that the residents weren't all that friendly. Even before we'd come to a halt they'd started shooting, sending bullets ricocheting off the limo's reinforced body. I reversed back as rapidly as I could, spun around when I had enough room, and got outta there a helluva lot quicker than I went in.

'You okay?' I asked Gigi.

She nodded, glancing over at the fuel read-out, obviously as worried as I was.

By the time that we got back to the road, the limo was flashing up that we had precisely twelve point four miles of gas. Either we could go that far down the highway and hope for the best, or try another track or two. A little further on, I made the decision for us, this time diving off on the other side of the road, almost immediately entering a thick pine forest.

'Fingers crossed,' Gigi commented dolefully.

'Yeah,' I replied, feeling a whole canyon away from a point of hopeful.

We came to this sun-starved clearing with a faded wooden two-storey house and a coupla barns. Through the open double-doors of the nearest one I could see a large circular saw – in fact, going by the wood stacked everywhere, timber had obviously been – and maybe still was – the occupants' business. There didn't look to be anyone around. I went and knocked on the front door, then returned to the limo and started blowing the horn, but still no one appeared.

I gave a frustrated sigh and turned to Gigi, but she was staring into the nearby forest.

'What's up?'

'Thought I saw someone.'

Both of us stood there for several moments, scrutinising the dense darkness of the pine trees, not able to see more than a few feet inside the treeline. I was concerned we were about to be shot at again and ready to jump back into the limo.

'Can't see nothing,' I told her. 'Maybe a deer?'

Gigi shrugged and followed along behind me as I cautiously went to enter the nearest barn. Everything inside – miscellaneous tools, numerous parts, general junk, a workbench – looked like it had just been left, like the owner had walked out five minutes ago.

We immediately started to hunt around for gas; me going one way, Gigi the other, soon building up confidence and becoming more invasive, shifting stuff around in our search. Suddenly Gigi stopped, giving this little grunt and staring at the ground.

'What's the matter?' I asked, making my way over.

There was a large pool of dried blood soaked into the dirt, deep and dark, like it was several inches deep.

'Something got itself slaughtered,' she said.

'Yeah,' I replied, not wanting to pay it too much attention; just at that moment we had other, far more pressing, things to worry about. I noticed this large tarp covering something bulky stacked up against the wall and went over to yank it off – to our delight, we were confronted by several large drums. I gave the nearest one a kick – whatever was in there, it was full.

I screwed the top off and took a sniff. Yep, it was gas all right.

'I'll get the limo,' I said, our mood immediately lifting.

I turned for the doorway, but stopped. There were two guys standing there, haunted-looking, pale to the point of sickness, one holding a rifle, the other an axe. For a moment we all stared at each other as if words were unnecessary, that we all knew what the situation was.

Finally the guy with the rifle broke into this sick, nigh-on toothless grin – the very image of a mass murderer you saw on the screen when you were a kid but no one would talk to you about.

'We got ourselves a girl,' he kinda sang, with just the hint of celebration.

His companion merely grunted; Gigi, with all her strange clothes and feathers in her hair plainly not to his taste.

'Fine by me,' the first guy smirked.

'We don't want any trouble,' I told them. 'Just gas. We're happy to trade.'

'Oh, you'll trade,' the guy with the rifle sneered.

'She your daughter?' his companion asked.

'No.'

'So what you doing in here with her?'

'Ya dirty old bastard,' the first guy taunted.

He wasn't pointing the rifle directly at me, but it wouldn't take a split moment to swing it in my direction. And for sure I didn't like the look of the polished blade on his companion's axe, nor the thought that it might have some connection with the bloodstain on the ground.

'Come here,' the first guy ordered Gigi.

'Go fuck yourself,' she replied, as gutsy as ever.

'Whoa! I'm gonna enjoy this even more than I thought,' he purred, moving towards her.

'Leave her alone,' I told him.

He turned towards me, a look of irritation on his face, as if I was of about as much consequence as a single fly at a barbecue. 'Shut up, old man,' he said.

'Leave her.'

'Why? . . . 'cuz you can't manage it any more you don't want me to either? Tell you what, you can watch,' he said, taunting me by sliding the zipper on his pants up and down.

I took a step towards him but he swung the rifle up and pointed it directly at my chest. 'Ya know something, I really can't see the point of you.'

'Just leave her alone,' I persisted.

He almost burst into laughter, as if he couldn't believe I'd have the nerve, then braced the muzzle of his rifle hard up against me, so all it would take would be the lightest of touches. His smile grew with the slow tightening of his trigger finger, the expression he could see on my face, the fact that I was about to be blown all over the wall behind me.

I knew exactly how far that trigger needed to travel, that one more barely perceptible movement would end my life, but ya know something . . .? It never happened.

Suddenly he got this look about him as if somewhere deep inside he'd just been dealt the most resounding blow. His body somehow contorted and twisted and he fell to his knees, his eyes gaping wider and wider, becoming coloured and clouded, and then – *Jesus, what the hell?* – steam started coming out of them! His eyes were *evaporating*, the liquid inside boiling, and sure enough, they began to dry and crack, to smoke and finally burst into flame.

He gave the worst possible scream you could imagine, and you know what? . . . As his mouth gaped wide open, I could see down his throat – there were flames in there, too.

For some reason his companion blamed me, as if he thought I'd used some kinda invisible weapon on him. He came at me with his axe, swinging that big, shiny blade back and forth, intent on chopping me into pieces – but then he suddenly froze too, giving out with a cry of agony as the same thing happened to him: his eyeballs swelling and steaming, his entire body starting to smoulder and burn.

I thought about trying to douse their flames, throwing water over them as they screamed and rolled on the ground – as much 'cuz I couldn't bear what I was seeing and hearing as any other reason – but it was too late, already they were starting to shrivel up like bacon in a pan.

At that moment, and thank God I did, I saw we had to get out of there, that the fire was spreading from the two guys and over towards the gasoline store. I tipped over the nearest drum and Gigi and me rolled it outta the door as fast as we could.

The limo was parked some distance from the barn and we didn't quite make it before there was this almighty *kerrumph!* and a rushing wave of hot air scorched the back of my neck as flames, metal and timber flew all around, and Gigi and me threw ourselves down behind our vehicle.

We had to wait there for the fire to die down, 'til I thought it was safe, then we rolled the drum back around to the other side of the limo, where the filler cap was. Jeez, those flames must've been quite something: there were blisters all along the paintwork of the limo like the body of some scaly reptile.

I managed to pour some gas in, but the drum was so unwieldy, and without a funnel, a helluva lot of it was ending up on the ground and starting to run in the direction of the barn. I had to continue pouring, all the while keeping an eye on that building trail of gas, 'til eventually I knew we had to get out of there, and pretty damn quick.

Wouldn't you know it? For the first time ever, that engine didn't start straight away. Gigi screamed, her hand going to the door-button, but I pressed start once more and thankfully, this time the engine hummed into life and I stamped on the gas and swept outta that place with the flames chasing after us.

There was another explosion as the drum went up, another huge burst of intense flame, but d'you know what? That fire was nothing, not compared to what we'd seen start it.

What the hell – I always thought 'spontaneous human combustion' was an urban myth, one of those things you hear about as a kid, but as you get older you realise couldn't happen. To actually *see* it, people bursting into flames like that—? Jesus! *How*, for chrissake?

CHAPTER FIVE

I couldn't help myself – maybe I saw it as some kind of sentimental symmetry – when we got to the same lookout where over a year ago we'd said goodbye to the City, I stopped to say hello. Standing there with Gigi, wordlessly gazing down at that dark, intimidating sprawl, my thoughts drawn to the last time I'd stood there, when Lena had told me she'd gone blind again. How panicked I was, but how calm *she* was, almost as if she'd been expecting it.

We hadn't heard a whole lot about what'd been going on in the City since we'd gone over the mountains, and most of what we *had* heard was second- or third-hand. Jimmy spent some time trying to get a signal on his screen (and knowing him, he probably would've managed it eventually) but everyone else was so firmly against it, particularly Lile, who warned him that if he upset her peaceful world she would make his hell, that in the end he reluctantly gave up. Though now, going on some of the things we'd witnessed, what we'd seen back at that barn, maybe we should've kept ourselves better informed.

Spontaneous human combustion! . . . Come on. There had to be a reason for it – and I wouldn't've minded betting we'd find it in the City.

The thought of returning to that place, all the bad memories it held, made me feel quite sick. As long as I live, I'll never forget those nights they came for us: the mass beating and screaming of the Specials as they cleaned yet another area of undesirables; the Dragonflies thundering overhead, the panic and fear as they drove everyone to that evening's hunting ground to be slaughtered – the old, the poor, the homeless and the sick, all those they regarded as society's waste . . . and of course, I had to deal with the hardest memory of all to shift: the death of little Arturo, the Mickey Mouse Kid.

You probably wouldn't be surprised to know that we'd thought about naming the baby after him. The kids, especially Gordie, were all for it. But, I dunno, Lena and me just felt that everyone should have their *own* name, be an individual, a memory in their own right. Arturo was a really special little guy and we didn't think he should be confused with *anyone* else, no matter how precious they might be.

'Drop me near the Square,' Gigi suddenly announced, gesturing over in that general direction.

I turned to her, momentarily confused. 'What?'

'Somewhere around that way.'

'I ain't dropping you off anywhere,' I told her.

'Why not?'

'We gotta stick together.'

She groaned, plainly having a gripe, and it was all too obvious what.

'We don't have a clue what's been going on,' I continued, doing my best to head her off. 'We gotta look out for each other – I need your help as much as you need mine.'

'Yeah, yeah,' she sneered, not hearing a word, only that I didn't trust her.

I turned and made my way back to the limo, a long and heavily exaggerated sigh issuing out from behind me, but at least she'd followed.

'So where we going?' she asked as the doors slid shut beside us.

I pulled away, rejoining the highway, for a few moments saying nothing.

'First there's someone I gotta see,' I told her.

Driving back down those hills and into the suburbs was one helluva barbed education. Unbelievably, there was still the occasional fire around, though why and what could be burning after all that time, I couldn't imagine. Surely all that hydrazine-derivative stuff that'd powered the punishment satellites was long gone?

There were a lot more vehicles around, people trying to go about their daily business, doing their best to keep things moving along, though it was soon obvious that notions of 'normality' had taken a helluva disturbing turn.

The first one I saw, I'll tell ya, my stomach took the express elevator to the basement and hit the bottom with a real jolt. The posters weren't so much a surprise – Nora Jagger looking out all stern and steely, dressed in quasi-military uniform – nor the many screens showing videos of her performing various duties. What put the damn fear of God into me were the holograms.

They were everywhere: pedestrian squares, road junctions, cleared blocks where fires had once raged – these huge laser statues of Nora Jagger, probably thirty or forty feet high.

She looked so damn real, so damn menacing, and what I knew of that woman, some of the things I'd witnessed her do – well, to see her towering over us as if she was about to swallow us in one gulp, was something I could've done without.

'The Bitch is everywhere,' Gigi spat, never one to mince her words.

Whoever'd been in charge when we were last there was obviously gone, and I wouldn't want to guess at their fate. In fact, looking back on it, the process of her accession had obviously been well underway even then. We never saw anyone else, just assumed, but whatever Nora Jagger had been then, now she was obviously the very embodiment of Infinity: the public face. And Gigi was right, the Bitch really was all over: open spaces, blank walls, any place where her image could be projected or hung, there she was, glaring down at us, daring us to do anything wrong.

The City was still surprisingly scarred; the after-effects of the fires, blackened and collapsed buildings, were everywhere. In some places it looked like it could've happened yesterday – nothing had been touched – but in the wealthier suburbs it was clear someone'd been put to work cleaning up. A little further on we got to see who: a large work-gang had been assembled, a motley group of the unwashed and unwanted, busy toiling away while armed Specials lounged about watching over them like guards surveying a chain-gang.

'Jesus,' I muttered, partly 'cuz of what was going on, partly 'cuz I couldn't believe we'd been stupid enough to return. I'd never felt such an overwhelming sense of submission, of a city under siege from within.

I turned to Gigi. No way was she gonna admit it, but she was looking distinctly frightened.

'You okay?' I asked.

''course, I am,' she said, as if I'd just insulted her in some way.

I nodded, doing her the favour of taking her at face value, swinging down Union, ignoring all the beggars at the lights.

'Where ya going?' she asked.

'Won't take long.'

'I wanna go to the house!' she protested, but nothing was gonna divert me from what I had in mind.

I hadn't told anyone, especially not Lena, but I had an ulterior motive for returning to the City. I knew there'd be no chance of seeing Doctor Simon at his home surgery, not with all its many layers of security, but I was hoping there might be a way at St Joseph's, presuming he still did his two days a week there. All I needed was somewhere discreet where the two of us could have a cosy little chat.

Actually, it wasn't that difficult. I wasn't gonna risk going to his office or surgery, but I knew somewhere where I could pretty well guarantee he'd show up at some point. Gigi and me managed to bluff our way into the underground car park by pretending she was my daughter and in excruciating pain, her putting on quite a show, me acting like an over-protective and possibly unstable parent. The guy did give the limo a bit of a look, but in a city where there was so much damage and destruction, it didn't seem to concern him that much, and yet another blood-curdling scream from Gigi finally prompted him to wave us through.

It wasn't hard to pick out the Doc's new auto; there was this big, elegant Bentley, looking all custom-made and optioned to the hilt. You could've lived in that thing for a coupla years and still not known your way around. I found a place almost opposite it, easing his battered old limo into the shadows in the corner, knowing he'd get a horrible shock when he saw it.

'You sure that's his?' Gigi asked, looking at the Bentley.

'Oh yeah,' I said, noticing the pools of water around it, that someone had cleaned and polished it 'til it looked like it was made of mirrors.

We didn't have to wait that long. A little after five, the familiar figure of Doctor Simon appeared from the elevator and walked briskly towards the Bentley, his clothes and his restored immaculate appearance belying that little trick Jimmy'd played on him the last time we saw him, removing his implant and changing his records so he was locked out of his privileged existence for a while.

I waited 'til he was almost at the Bentley, then jumped out and made my way over so I arrived as he was opening the door. The look on his face, the collapse of his jaw, was a real picture. I never said a word, just pushed him inside and immediately followed.

'Long time no see,' I said, closing the door behind me.

For a moment he was apparently too stunned to do anything, then his hand went to his inside pocket, presumably for some kinda security device. I immediately grabbed his forearm.

'Just keep them where I can see them,' I told him.

'What do you want?' he asked.

'A history lesson – what the hell's been going on?'

He paused for a moment, still staring at me, then his expression started slowly changing and I could've sworn there was part of him that was almost relieved to see me. 'Lots of things,' he eventually replied.

'Like what?'

'Clancy,' he said, ignoring my question, 'why the hell did you come back?'

'Various reasons.'

'You must've seen on your way in—?'

I nodded. 'D'you still take care of her?'

'I've got no choice,' he replied. 'She's insane.'

'This is gonna come as a helluva shock to ya,' I told him, 'but you never needed to be a doctor to know that.'

'That was before … Now,' he said, 'she's introduced all these emergency powers. She's in total control of every second of our lives. Everyone's *terrified*.'

'I'm not surprised,' I muttered, remembering the beating she gave me, how she'd damn near killed me with those special limbs of hers, the gruesome way she punished all those who disappointed her.

'And she's not the only one,' the Doc informed me. 'Not any more.'

'Whaddya mean?'

'She's got this elite Bodyguard – they've all got prosthetics.' He stared at me as if a little fascinated by the expression slowly appearing on my face.

'You're *kidding* . . . ?'

'They had to choose between arms or legs; they weren't allowed to have both – just to be sure she'd always be the strongest.'

'They had their limbs removed too? How many—?'

'I don't know how many there are . . . Enough.'

I was damn near speechless: things were even worse than I'd imagined. The way I saw it, they'd only need about twenty or thirty of those damn mutants to take out the whole City. 'Is she still searching for us?' I asked.

'Yeah, but she's had other things on her mind. She'll get to you,' he said, like it was nothing if not inevitable.

'Does she know where we are?'

'I don't know – maybe. I did hear you'd gone over the mountains.'

'Shit!' I groaned.

'Why did you come back?' he repeated, as if there was plainly no logical answer to that question.

'There's a lotta weird stuff going on,' I told him. 'I wanna know why.'

'Like what?'

'Well, for one, people spontaneously combusting.'

I told him what we'd seen earlier, expecting he'd be as shocked as we'd been, but he wasn't.

'Implants, I would guess,' he ventured.

'*Implants?*'

'They're doing a lot of experiments – that's what's been preoccupying her. She wants everyone to have one. At first it was voluntary: people were told it was good for their health, that this thing would sit in their body monitoring them, picking up any early warning signs of disease—'

65

'How the hell does it do that?'

'It can change form: sometimes it's solid, sometimes liquid, sometimes it seamlessly blends with the host tissue. Of course they launched it with a real fanfare, an Infinity campaign to convince us what a great thing it was – and free, too. Then stories started going around about what was *really* happening, that they weren't so much volunteers as guinea pigs, and suddenly no one wanted to know any more ... that's when she *really* went crazy. She started sending out these snatch squads, taking people off the streets, kidnapping them from hospitals ... prisons. They've been working on it day and night, constantly modifying the program, the moment they think they've got something testing it on any number of 'volunteers'. As a result, there are hundreds of screwed-up experiments wandering around.'

'Right. Hence all the crazies?'

'They only let them go because they're so sure they'll find a way of making them respond later.'

'Respond?'

He glanced at me and I sensed that just at that moment he was completely on my side. 'She's working on the removal of all free will.'

'*Jesus!*'

'If she gets her way ... she'll use these things to control us all.'

'What about those guys who spontaneously combusted?'

'At a guess, some kind of variation of punishment implants.'

'Like the satellites?'

'Similar. From what I've heard they sit inside people and monitor what they do; ready to act, not just as judge and jury, but to hand out retribution the moment the host body breaks the law. Do something minor – petty theft, criminal damage – it'll make you feel sick for a while; do something more serious, it might give you months, even years, of chronic pain or unpleasant illness. Unlike the satellites, it doesn't take away your mobility, but something far more precious:

your health. The ultimate deterrent is still the same: when those men were about to kill you, their implants simply executed them from within their own bodies.'

Again I found myself just staring at him. I mean, I'm the original dumb old big guy, it's not exactly an unfamiliar situation for me to find myself out of verbal ammunition – but I couldn't imagine there'd be too many people able to handle what he'd just told me. Like so many before her, Nora Jagger was out to take over the world – only in her case, it sounded like she was well on her way.

'How's Lena?' the Doc asked, as if, amongst all the gathering darkness, he still saw her as a pinpoint of light.

I'd been so caught up in what he was telling me I'd forgotten for a moment why I was there. 'She's fine,' I said, but he continued to stare at me, eagerly waiting for more. 'It's a boy,' I eventually informed him.

'Clancy!' he cried, his excitement irrepressible. 'That's fantastic!'

'Yeah. For *us*,' I said firmly, just in case he was getting any ideas.

'I'm so pleased.' For some time he sat there silently, plainly rolling the news over and over in his head. 'I'd love to see him.'

I was shaking my head even before he'd finished the sentence.

'She'd never know,' he added. 'I give you my word.'

'Last I heard, a thousand of your words couldn't buy bird-shit,' I said, reminding him of how he'd double-crossed us.

Again he went quiet, I guessed appreciating how he was sitting smack-dab on the most delicate of fault lines, and I glanced over to check Gigi was all right.

'People are starting to get that bit healthier. There are certainly fewer zombie-sick around,' he told me, obviously electing to try reason. 'Jimmy did everyone a big favour destroying the satellites and stopping the pollution, but' – again he hesitated, and I had a pretty good idea where he was going with this – 'despite the occasional pregnancy, to my knowledge, no one's actually had a healthy baby.

The terms have got longer, one or two premature ones we had hopes for, but as yet it's just you two.'

I sighed: he might've had his priorities but I had mine, too. 'Lena's gone blind again,' I announced.

'Oh . . . I'm sorry.'

'That day we escaped – probably 'cuz of the Bitch throwing her up against the wall,' I said, feeling a certain pleasure at taking up Gigi's nickname for Nora Jagger.

'I did warn you,' he said. 'It's rare, but it does happen. Mind you, it was a heavy impact.'

For a while we sat in silence, both of us, I think, beginning to appreciate the cards we were laying out on the table. I didn't have to say it, but I did anyway. 'Can you operate on her again?'

He hesitated, the expression on his face slowly changing. 'Well. I don't know,' he said, and for the first time in the conversation he was sounding his smooth old confident self. 'I'd have to take a look, do some tests.'

'I thought you might,' I replied sarcastically.

'It would be better if I came to you,' he said.

'For who?'

'Everyone.'

Again I went quiet, feeling slightly apprehensive that I hadn't thought this through properly; just like when I used to play chess with Jimmy on the Island my attention was so firmly fixed on the main prize, I was always in danger of wandering into a trap.

'I won't harm them, Clancy. I promise you,' the Doc reassured me. 'You can be there all the time.'

'It's up to Lena,' I eventually replied, realising I needed more time to think, that I couldn't make such an important decision for both of us.

I glanced across at Gigi again; she'd powered a window down and was looking distinctly bored. 'Gotta go,' I said.

Despite my fear of doing something unforgivably stupid, and the deeply disturbing things he'd just told me, I gotta say, it was still one helluvan amusing moment. The doc caught sight of Gigi, immediately recognised her, then finally realised what that battered old piece of shit disintegrating away in the corner was.

'Is that my *limo*?' he cried.

'Yep. That's it.'

His mouth dropped open so violently he might've had a small charge of dynamite between his teeth. '*Oh, my God!* . . . What have you done to it?' he cried, tumbling out of the Bentley.

'Just a little wear and tear.'

'Wear and tear!'

I gotta say, I hadn't really given it that much thought, but I could see it was a bit of a mess, what with all kinds of fungus growing all over it from the cave, several panels that'd been ripped off by growlers the night we escaped from Infinity, the paintwork down one side melted and pockmarked from the fire in the barn – yeah, 'a bit of a mess' is what I'd call it.

'I don't believe this!' he cried, walking around the limo, each angle apparently worse than the last.

'We'll fix it up,' I told him.

'Where's the lid to the trunk?' he wailed, his eyes now gaping almost as wide as his mouth.

Gigi gave a pointed sigh, obviously getting a little bored with the whole thing. 'Can we go?' she asked.

'When are you next here?' I asked the Doc.

'What?' he asked, too preoccupied to really pay me any mind.

'When are you next here?'

'Thursday,' he eventually managed to reply, still staring at the limo as if someone had spat on the Mona Lisa or held a dirty protest in the Sistine Chapel.

'I'll think on about Thomas,' I said, climbing in beside Gigi.

I hated myself for doing it, I really did; using access to my baby son as a means of bribing someone felt wrong, but I didn't see any other option. Worse still, I didn't even know if Lena *wanted* the operation – we'd not discussed her sight in ages. I was just going on how she'd behaved before the first time, making out it wasn't that important – but maybe this time it was genuine, maybe she really didn't feel it was something she had to do.

I made a point of shaking Doctor Simon's hand through the limo window before I pulled away, I guess trying to cement our new understanding that we were both starting all over again, as if, if I treated him like a gentleman, he'd behave like one, instead of merely *looking* the part. The last view I had of him was in the rear-view mirror, still gaping after what was left of his former pride and joy.

'What did he say?' Gigi asked, as we emerged up onto street level.

I hesitated. 'A lotta stuff.'

'Is everything okay?'

'More or less,' I replied, not wanting to discuss Nora Jagger or her new powers or ambitions, especially bearing in mind that both of us had attempted to kill her.

What the hell she'd do if she knew the pair of us were back in the City, I couldn't imagine. Rip the whole damn place apart to find us, I'd have guessed – her and her new Bodyguards.

'Turn left here,' Gigi indicated, jolting me out of my thoughts, and I hit the brakes and eased my way over.

The fact that there were more vehicles around and still the occasional street closed off meant we got caught in a kinda low-key rush hour, and by the time we arrived in this old residential street down by the river, the light was starting to fade and Gigi struggled for a few moments to pick out the right place. Mind you, with each and every building daubed with some form of graffiti or urban art, they did look kinda similar.

A good few years back you'd have had to have paid a pretty penny to live in a place that backed onto the river, but after the Crash you couldn't give them away. People who never really had the money to purchase in the first place – even having to borrow their deposits – were forced to put their properties up for sale. The only trouble being there weren't any buyers, and one by one they were repossessed, boarded up, taken over by squatters and now, prompted by what looked like a couple of major fires – maybe accidental, maybe not – there'd plainly been something of an exodus. There were still a few people around, but they didn't look that comfortable about it: keeping their heads low, scurrying away rather than risk being approached, as if a direct question might damage them in some way.

The 'safe house' turned out to be a basement apartment; it might've been more intact than most but it didn't look any more lived-in. We parked the limo in an alleyway leading down to the river and walked back, Gigi approaching with understandable caution.

'D'you think they're still there?' I asked, having my doubts.

'I dunno,' Gigi replied, suddenly acting surprisingly nervous.

'Don't look like it to me,' I commented as we stopped in a doorway opposite and a little ways down the street.

For a moment she didn't say anything and I realised she was getting irritated with me. 'You don't have to be here,' she told me, and I nodded and promptly shut up – I really didn't understand what was going on, what this was all about.

We must've waited for a good half-hour, watching out for any movement – for anyone coming or going – not sure what to do. At one point she went over and peered down over the railings, trying to look through the dirty windows, then turned and headed back.

'See anyone?' I asked, though it was obvious she hadn't.

'Nope.'

'So what d'ya wanna do?'

She hesitated for a moment, took in the way the night was starting to gather, then came to a decision. 'It probably doesn't work,' she said, digging deep into her pocket and bringing out a key.

I was a little taken aback – why hadn't she said something before? – though at least it proved she was telling the truth, that she really had lived there. 'Only one way to find out,' she told me.

We slipped over as unobtrusively as we could: just two more people minding their own business on Mind-Your-Own-Business Street. Gigi briefly hesitated, as if gathering her strength, then went down the steps with me following closely on behind.

To both her and my surprise, the key still worked, and after a couple of shouts of 'Hi!' and getting no reply, we entered. Thankfully, I'd remembered to bring a torch with me from the limo, though I hadn't remembered to check the battery, which, going on its light, was pretty close to expiring.

Slowly we advanced down the hallway, our footsteps deadened by a thick layer of dust, Gigi again calling out, 'David! . . . Isla—?' but still there was no reply.

We looked in the first bedroom but there was nothing apart from an old mattress, some dirty clothes on the floor and a rucksack with a broken strap. The next one was a similar story: a few stacked boxes and for some reason, the mattress sprawled out across the room at a forty-five-degree angle.

'Been gone some time, by the looks of it,' I muttered, stating the all-too-damn obvious.

Next we tried the kitchen, Gigi giving this little cry at the disturbing number of giant roaches there were around, torchlight and shadow doubling their size as they scurried across the floor. They must've found something to eat to stay there, which maybe indicated Gigi's former companions had left in a hurry.

Impatient to explore elsewhere, Gigi took the torch and went through to the main room with me reluctantly following on behind. As far as I could see, we'd got the picture – they were long gone – and I didn't really see the point of staying. And anyways, there was something about that place I didn't like, but she obviously needed to check it out to her satisfaction.

She reached the doorway, went to enter the room, then suddenly stopped, giving out with this low moan and backing out so quickly, she collided with me.

'What's the matter?' I asked.

She slapped the torch back in my hand so I could see what she'd seen, then turned away, panting like a nervous dog.

There was a big old imitation leather sofa and several easy chairs, and sitting in them, almost as if it'd been some kind of social gathering, were the long-dead corpses of six people. They weren't much more than skeletons, with little bits of withered, nibbled flesh clinging on here and there to the bones. I don't know – rats maybe, or even those big fat roaches? But that wasn't the worst part of it, nor even the remnants of the foul odour that lingered; it was the fact that all of them had had their heads torn from their bodies.

I shone the dull light of the torch around the room, knowing they had to be somewhere, and sure enough, piled in the corner, like a mound of rotted cabbages, were the skulls of all six victims.

'Jesus.'

'It's *her*,' Gigi moaned.

I didn't reply, just turned her gently towards the front door. She was right, of course she was: it was the Bitch and her trademark way of killing.

I don't know what made me do it exactly – instinct maybe? The knowledge that that woman had been there? – but when I reached the front door, I flicked the torch's beam around it . . .

Shit! It was really small but I still should've spotted it when we came in. There in the corner, low down so it'd catch everyone who entered, someone had planted a security beam.

I paused for a second or two, wondering whether to risk going outside or not, the control-box had as much dust on it as everything else, so maybe it was no longer functioning? No one had reacted so far, and we must've been there a good five minutes . . . however, at that precise moment, I heard something large and powerful rapidly approaching up the street.

'Is there a back way?' I asked Gigi as the vehicle – or what now sounded like several – came screeching to a halt outside.

She just stood there, frantically thinking, but it was way too late: heavy – *terrifyingly* heavy – footsteps were running across the side-walk and noisily descending the steps to the front door. *The Bitch's Bodyguard!*

Gigi snapped out of her paralysis, giving me a tug, running through to the kitchen with me following close behind. As I shut the door she started scrabbling at the floor, lifting up the old plastic covering – I didn't have a clue what she was up to. It was a basement, for chrissake. What was she going to do: tunnel her way out?

'What're you doing?' I asked, but at that precise moment the front door didn't so much fall open as explode, sending shards of wood somersaulting down the hallway.

'Shit!' I whispered, but Gigi had hold of something on the exposed floor and with a strong jerk, up came this trapdoor.

She pushed me inside, into a space no more than three feet deep, and immediately followed, closing the door just in time and leaving the plastic covering to flip back into place. Above us, sounding like thunder in the darkness, came the crashing of heavy feet running from room to room, more and more of them, shouting and cursing as they realised we weren't there. Something was thrown and smashed against the kitchen wall above us and I could hear the sound of broken glass raining down.

Gigi was trying to push me forward, but in the darkness I couldn't understand where she wanted me to go and I didn't dare turn on the torch in case someone came into the kitchen and caught a glimmer of its light shining through a crack. Above us it sounded like they were starting a more methodical search, those unnaturally heavy footsteps stomping from room to room, spending more time in each one. I tell ya, that sound, the slurping mechanical stride of those destructive prosthetics – and so many of them! – was enough to frighten the hell out of anyone, whether you'd already encountered the Bitch or not.

I managed to edge a few feet forward, fumbling left and right, eventually locating the top of a ladder that apparently led down to a lower level. Gigi went to nudge me again, directing me to climb down, but accidentally knocked the torch from my grasp – a second or so later there was a splash: there was water down there.

'Go on!' she whispered.

I tried to make my way down as quickly as I could, but the lower I got, the more damp and slippery it became and, shit to admit, I lost my footing and plunged down into the water. It was only the fact that they were making so much noise up there that saved me from being overheard.

I splashed around, unable to right myself in the confusion of darkness and waist-deep water, 'til finally I felt Gigi's hands grab hold of me and I managed to stand up.

'Come on,' she said, tugging me away by the shoulder of my coat, obviously knowing which way to go. Overhead it sounded as if they were starting to take out their frustration on the building itself, smashing the whole damn place apart, the sheer ferocity and force of the impacts like shells slamming into it. Then I heard something else that set my stomach on a bigger free-fall than me falling off that ladder: someone was going around stamping on the floor, moving down the hallway then into the kitchen, obviously searching for anywhere that sounded hollow, and within moments there was the distinct sound of cracking timber.

'Jesus!' I muttered, trying to move quicker but ending up almost knocking Gigi over.

I thought they were about to break through; that a good hard kick from one of those bionic legs would show them where we'd gone, but suddenly all noise ceased, as if something had happened that took precedence over everything else. Gigi and I both paused, wondering what the hell it was; even down there you could sense the tension, as if fear was dripping down through the cracks in the floor. Then a single pair of footsteps, far heavier than anyone else's, began a slow, meaningful march down the hallway.

'Oh no!' Gigi gasped.

It was her and we both knew it, and soon, echoing down from above, came a voice that not only put the fear of God into us, but of the Devil, too.

'They didn't have enough time, you *idiots*!' she yelled.

She spoke with such anger, such pure fury, it occurred to me she must've known who it'd been, that maybe that security beam'd been equipped with a visual? There was a muttered conversation, someone telling her something, sounding like they were trying to excuse themselves or get in her good books, then a brief moment of silence followed by an almighty explosion and the kitchen floor showered down into the water behind us.

Gigi yanked me along what I now realised was a short tunnel. Behind us there was more shouting, then the sound of someone descending the ladder, the clank of something hard against metal – and finally, a loud splash, as if something really heavy had fallen in.

'Go!' I hissed at Gigi, a slight disturbance in the air, a faint glow of light, alerting me to the fact that we were emerging outside, and to the rather obvious realisation that we were in the river.

Behind us it sounded like synchronised depth charges were going off as someone began to run us down, and I made the mistake of looking back. In the palest of murky lights there was this powerful dark figure exploding through the water, those eyes that'd haunted my dreams for the last year or more glaring after me.

'Go on!' I shouted at Gigi, giving her a push, telling her to make her own speed, and soon she was moving away from me.

I tried to increase *my* speed, but every stride Nora Jagger took was more like a leap and within seconds she was only feet behind me. One more and that would be it; those murderous super-limbs would wrap around me and put an end to my life – but as I came into sight of the entrance to the tunnel and the opposite bank of the river, the noise behind me suddenly ceased – as if she'd stopped dead for some reason.

I just kept going, praying she'd lost her footing or something, that I'd been given an extra few seconds' grace, but when I finally did glance back, she was just standing there, glaring after us, her face a picture of absolute furious frustration.

'Fuck you, Clancy—! *Fuck you!*' she screamed. 'I'll make you pay for this. I'll hunt you down. D'you hear me? I'll hunt you down and rip you to pieces!'

At that moment I felt the ground beginning to dip away beneath my feet, the water getting deeper, and knew that, like it or not, I was going to have to swim. I half-dived, half-fell forward, striking out against the incoming tide, still petrified that at any moment I would feel her hand clamp on my shoulder . . . *Why the hell had she stopped?* Was it the water? Would it harm her prosthetics in some way? It didn't seem very likely, but what the hell did?

Way up above me I heard a window being opened; someone thrust out a small spotlight and shone it down onto the river, but they were in a slight alcove and the projecting wall meant they could only cover part of it. Gigi, who was a surprisingly strong swimmer, had slowed so she could lead me through a handful of boats moored nearby, using them as cover as we continued our dogged progress against the tide.

I thought we'd be safe enough there, with the spotlight unable to reach us, but d'you know what? That woman was nothing if not resourceful. Suddenly the wall just along from the window, the one actually facing the river, exploded outwards, bricks tumbling down into the water: she'd actually punched or kicked a hole in it, releasing some of her aggression with a brutal display of strength. She kicked a few more bricks down into the water, pushed her way through the wall and shone the spotlight up and down the river.

Jesus, she was something to behold. Maybe it was the beating she gave me that time, the fact that I knew I'd been lucky to escape with my life, but I couldn't think of her as human, let alone a woman, just some awful result of an uncountable number of sinister collisions that had been allowed to grow unchecked 'cuz no one had known how to stop it.

I hugged the side of the boat where I'd sought refuge, confident she couldn't pick me out of the darkness and grateful for it – but suddenly she turned and appeared to look directly at me, like she'd known I was there all the time. I swear her eyes met mine, that she marked me out like an animal for slaughter.

Gigi ducked underwater, heading off in the direction of the shadow of the riverbank, and I did my best to follow. Like I told you before, I'm not the world's best swimmer, especially not underwater. I kept having to surface, each time finding myself not where I thought I'd be, having to duck under again, yet eventually managing to slip into the shadows and out of the Bitch's sight.

I slowly worked my way along the slimy bank until we reached an old iron ladder, following the silhouette of Gigi up, until the moment we touched solid ground and both of us started to run.

I never imagined I'd be so pleased to see that battered old limo. I started her up and drove carefully away, not wanting to attract any undesired attention, knowing there was probably a Dragonfly hanging around somewhere. For several minutes we travelled in silence, both of us still in shock.

'Why the hell did she stop?' I eventually blurted out, as much to me as to Gigi. 'It wasn't the water—'

Gigi gave a long sigh, as if any kind of thought was way beyond her at that moment.

'She could've had us!' I continued, water dripping down my face from my wet hair and filtering into my beard. 'I just don't get it.'

'Me neither,' Gigi muttered.

'And what about that tunnel?' I asked. 'How come that was there?'

'Service tunnel. In the old days, when they were posh houses, people used to deliver that way. Isla found it by accident – they didn't tell me at first. It was a kinda ultimate emergency exit, when all else failed.'

'Didn't do them a lot of good.'

'No,' she sighed.

I reached across and went to squeeze her hand, but knowing she'd push me away, changed it to a clumsy pat on the shoulder. Even that she didn't look that happy about. I wanted to say something, to reassure her it was going to be all right, but I just couldn't bring myself to do it.

If there's one thing in life I'm not good at, it's telling lies.

CHAPTER SIX

As much as a disappointment as it was, I knew my decision had been made for me, that there was no way I could keep my appointment with Doctor Simon – we had to get out of the City as fast as was humanly possible. It was the same for Gigi: whatever she'd wanted to get off her chest, whatever she'd come to say to those people, it was too late, and everything she'd seen since we'd returned to the City had convinced her that, whether she wanted to be there or not, she was better off going back to the farm with me.

It was a real blow, believe me. I'd been so hopeful I could get Lena's sight fixed again. Still, I gotta admit, it'd troubled me that I hadn't told her that was what I was planning. I'd wanted it to be a surprise, but the truth was, I didn't always get it right with Lena – I tried to protect her too much and it caused more than the occasional argument. I'd come to realise it wasn't right to make assumptions on someone else's behalf, no matter how close they might be to you. Not to mention the fact that to put any faith in the Doc would've been a bit like leaving the cat to babysit the canary. Maybe he *was* just a victim of circumstance, but I never got the impression he kicked too hard against it. As long as he could buy a new limo every year and build yet another wardrobe for all his latest hand-tailored suits and silk ties, he always seemed more than happy to cross the street whenever he caught sight of ethics or integrity approaching. Even if I *had* managed to get him back to the farm, even if it had been possible for him to operate on Lena, I could never have let him go afterwards, not without us having to move on in case he returned with others..

I didn't take the main road back to the hills, instead dodging in and out of side streets, keeping my driving steady and mannered rather than risk setting alarm bells off somewhere. I'd meant to ask the Doc why the limo wouldn't hook up to the power strip, but with all the other stuff we'd ended up talking about, I'd forgotten. In any case, we had a quarter of a tank of gas and far more pressing things to worry about, like getting as far away from that Theatre of Hell as we could.

The most disturbing thing by far was those damn holographic statues. It'd been bad enough when we'd *entered* the City in daylight, but now, at night – and after having had the Bitch literally breathing down our necks – it was a real test of the tightness of the bowels, believe me.

'Speed up, will ya?' Gigi complained, turning away from a statue we were passing.

'It's just a hologram,' I told her, though I couldn't resist checking the mirrors just to check it wasn't chasing after us.

'Feels like she's watching.'

I never said anything, but I knew what she meant, though I reckon it was just coincidence that as we rounded the next bend we came face to face with a Dragonfly hovering at the far end of the street, shining a spotlight down on everything that passed beneath it.

'Shit,' I muttered.

'I knew it!' Gigi wailed.

'It's okay,' I reassured her, 'just as long as they're not scanning.'

As we joined on the back of a growing line it just hung there, as still as the moon: a hi-tech roadblock. I advanced slowly forward, knowing that no matter what I'd said to Gigi, they *had* to be scanning – no way would they just sit there shining a light down. For chrissake, we didn't stand a chance, what with the state of the limo, its identification software removed, the fact that it was still registered with Doctor Simon while being driven by this anonymous old guy and a young girl.

I should've seen it before, but it was only then it hit me why they were there. This was no random roadblock; they hadn't positioned themselves by chance: they were guarding the entrance to the Catacombs.

'The Catacombs' was the nickname of the more properly titled Downtown Traffic Relief system, or the DTR. It'd been built supposedly to alleviate the City's chronic congestion, but it turned out so confusing in there, it'd only made things worse. People frequently got lost and couldn't find their way out. Crawling round and round, eventually having to stop to call for help, emergency vehicles having to be sent in to guide them out – you can guess how much that did to alleviate congestion. It was a rabbit warren – or it used to be – and if I could only get us in there, it was probably the next best thing to going free.

I waited 'til the last moment, 'til we were next to be scanned, then floored the gas pedal. The limo kicked forward, still with plenty of grunt, and the Dragonfly immediately reacted, swivelling around, though not with any great sense of urgency. I guessed 'cuz they thought they had the situation under control, 'cuz they assumed we had a security cut-out and they could stop us whenever they wanted. But Jimmy'd removed it, not for situations like that, need I add, but just 'cuz he wanted it for something else.

It was only when we continued our flight towards the tunnel entrance, showing no sign of slowing, that their attitude changed. They opened up with some kind of heavy-duty automatic, and even though the limo's bodywork was reinforced, it was missing a little in places and bullets were getting through. I swerved to the side, tried to get directly underneath them so they couldn't get a shot in, and then swung back and dived into the tunnel. They dropped as low as they dared, spraying a few more bullets down the hole, but we were gone.

Thank God, I still remembered that place in every detail, mainly 'cuz of the number of people who'd tried to lose me in there – usually a customer of Mr Meltoni's who'd got a bit forgetful about who had first calls on his cash. I squeezed through a gap in the barriers, doubled back, took this service-way I'd discovered one night and finally emerged not that far from where I first entered, heading out through a giant underground parking lot and exiting the other side. It would take a while, but I'd go back into the side streets and thread my way through what was left of the Projects.

As it turned out, leaving the City that way was surprisingly easy, maybe 'cuz that was the route Infinity was hoping the unwanted would take; it was a kinda organised rat-run for all the flotsam and jetsam they wanted flushed out into the wasteland of the Interior.

Once we were completely clear of the suburbs and out into the country proper, the road became pretty well deserted and Gigi fell asleep, leaving me with just my thoughts for company. The City had been far worse than I'd imagined. Fear and intimidation had given way to what seemed more like absolute submission. And you didn't have to be a genius to work out that after the City would come the country, and that maybe the process had already started. Nora Jagger was hell-bent on ruling us all, and as crazy as that once would've sounded, I wasn't entirely sure what could stop her.

I didn't get the implants at all. How many failed guinea pigs were there roaming around, for chrissake – hundreds? *Thousands?* How many different implants had there been? And once the perfect implant was developed, the one that'd make everyone do exactly what she wanted, how were they gonna convince people to get it inserted? Sure as hell

I wouldn't, and I'd fight to the death to stop anyone putting one in Lena or Thomas. I just didn't get it.

Then there were the animals – had they been used for experiments? *Wolves*, for chrissake? It didn't seem very likely. On the other hand, they *had* apparently spontaneously combusted.

As always, far, far too many questions.

The sky had just the faintest pink ribbon of dawn edging it as we reached the cave, the moon in graceful bowing retreat. I drove the limo back up the slope, slipping here and there, a drowsy Gigi already out, preferring to walk up, though actually, apart from the odd cosmetic mishap, that vehicle had proved itself time and time again.

It wasn't easy finding that one approach to the cave, getting the angle just right so the limo could slip in. As I squeezed out, it occurred to me that I should be taking the lasers, but I guess I kinda used the state of the power-packs as an excuse not to bother.

Emerging out into the cool freshness of a new day, I expected Gigi to make some smart comment about how long I'd been, but actually she was standing there with a big frown on her face, gazing around as if something had just happened.

'What's up?' I asked.

She just stood there, shaking her head. 'Weird,' she commented.

'What?'

'Something just sorta . . . "passed through",' she said, struggling to put it into words.

'What d'you mean?' I asked, my suspicions immediately aroused.

'I dunno . . . Everything kinda went dark for a moment.'

I didn't need to hear any more. Immediately I started to climb the slope, for a few moments even breaking into a trot. 'Gigi!' I called back, 'Come on! Let's go!'

We went over the mountain as quickly as we could, but actually, both of us were really tired and had to stop to rest several times. It was well into the afternoon before we finally came in sight of the farm.

I didn't know what I expected to see – a gang of crazies besieging the place maybe, Infinity in force, the house burned down – but actually, the closer we got, the more normal everything appeared. The barn door was open, which presumably meant Jimmy was tinkering away in there; smoke was coming from the house chimney, so someone was cooking. Everything looked fine, and in fact, when we got that bit closer, we were in for a really welcome surprise.

We'd only been away a couple of days but the wheat had really made progress. It had to be six or seven inches high – you must've been able to sit back and watch it happen. The two fields we'd so strenuously ploughed were no longer brown but a slowly growing wash of spreading green.

'Wow!' cooed Gigi, surprisingly impressed.

'This place must be Shangri-La,' I commented. 'Anything grows.'

It was a miracle, all right, and I was mighty impressed, but it didn't deflect me from the miracle that I'd been thinking about every minute of the last couple of days. I couldn't help myself, big old bullet-head I may be, but I couldn't wait a moment longer: I dropped my stuff and ran towards the house like an old Romeo seeking out his beloved Juliet.

As I careered past the barn, Jimmy came out and called across to me, 'See the wheat?'

'Yeah!' I shouted, leaping over one of Lena's wires in my haste, and I heard him give this knowing little laugh, like it was pretty obvious what was going on. I bounded onto the porch, almost misjudging it, but righted myself enough to topple cleanly through the front door.

I found Lena in the bedroom, breastfeeding Thomas: my miracle in two parts.

'Can I have some of that?' I joked.

'Clancy!' she cried, wanting to leap up, but she couldn't disturb the little guy.

I went to her, put my arms round them both, and Thomas, immediately sensing a rival for her attention, started a snorting protest.

'How are you, little guy?' I asked, but he was too busy reattaching himself to Lena.

'Is everything okay?' she asked.

'Yeah. Fine,' I replied, though I knew she'd immediately picked up on the fact that there was something wrong. 'I'll tell ya when you've finished.'

No matter how keen she was to know, she still took her time feeding Thomas, observing all the rituals, making sure he was winded and comfortable, finally putting him down in his drawer. The moment she turned to tiptoe away, he summoned her back with a loud burst on the kiddie-klaxon, but at the third attempt he gave up and with a coupla last weary protests, finally fell asleep.

Lena led me out and into the kitchen. Gigi was already there with the others, still understandably upset about what had happened to her 'resistance' friends, but telling them all about what life was like in the City now.

Plainly Jimmy wasn't that happy with me. 'Big Guy!' he protested.

'What?'

'You didn't bring the lasers!'

'The power-packs were really badly corroded—'

'I can fix that,' he said, as if I was insulting him.

I shrugged, like I should've thought of that but had been too engaged with other things.

'Jeez,' Jimmy moaned, 'not cool. Not cool at all.'

'I can go back for them,' I said, though I didn't really mean it.

Thankfully, Lile kinda brushed him aside, wanting to hear more about the City, and I filled them in on anything Gigi had missed.

'I don't get it,' Lena said, when I finished.

'What?'

'Those two guys that attacked you – they had the same implants as the animals?'

'Maybe.'

'How?'

'I dunno . . . Guess it could be just coincidence,' I conceded.

'Two examples of the same weird thing isn't likely to be coincidence,' Hanna pointed out.

'Sounds odd to me,' Delilah agreed.

Jimmy nodded, for once not of a mind to argue with her, but Gordie couldn't come to grips with any of it.

'*People!* Bursting into flames?' he sneered.

'Spontaneous human combustion,' I repeated.

He guffawed, looking around at the others, appearing genuinely surprised that no one else joined in.

I didn't say any more. How could I? I mean, I'd been there, I'd seen those guys catch fire, flames coming out of their mouths and eyes, and I wasn't sure I believed it either.

'course, that wasn't the only disturbing news we'd brought back with us. There was also – and Gigi made a real point of spelling it out, like she wanted to be sure the nickname would stick and everyone would use it – 'the Bitch and her Bodyguard'. The information that now there was a small army of people who could do what she could – or at least fifty per cent of it – stunned everyone to the degree that it felt like all the life had been drained outta the room, even more so when I went on to tell them what the Doc'd said: that Nora Jagger had it in mind to control *everyone* through implants.

'I wouldn't believe anything that guy told me,' Lile croaked, plainly determined to dismiss as much of this as she could.

'Me neither,' Gordie agreed.

Lena turned to me, a frown on her face. 'Why did you go to see Doctor Simon?'

There was a brief but undeniable hesitation. 'Just . . . to know what was going on,' I replied.

She looked decidedly suspicious, like she had plenty of other ideas, and I thought I might be well advised to change the subject. 'Anything happen around here?' I asked. 'Anything at night?'

'Nothing I heard,' Jimmy replied, as if, if *he* hadn't, then for sure nor would anyone else.

'Thomas slept better,' Lena informed me, plainly hinting I was far too keen on picking the little guy up when he cried.

I chuckled. 'He likes our little father-and-son chats.'

Delilah, assisted by Hannah and Gordie, cooked up a meal, everyone plainly delighted to be back together again; this sense of relief that bordered on denial. The moment everything was eaten and cleared away, Lena was up and taking my hand, ready for bed, fortunately unable to see the smirk on Delilah's face and completely ignoring me when I said I really should take a shower first.

We made love with more enthusiasm, more gratitude maybe, than we had at any time since Thomas was born. The little guy provided us with some fairly noisy accompaniment at one point and I could feel Lena noticeably stiffening, almost on the point of stopping, but in the end she decided to just ignore him and keep going.

I was that tired after hiking over the mountain on no sleep there was no chance of me checking outside that night; in fact, for once I actually slept right through. I woke a little after six, going out onto the porch and scanning around as if I'd be able to tell if anything had happened – but no, it all looked pretty well as it should – well, apart from one thing.

I could hardly believe it. That wheat had not only grown another three or four inches, it'd started developing some pretty ripe-looking ears, too. I squatted down and took a closer look, feeling almost intimidated by how fast it was growing. It looked so damn healthy, too; such a vivid green, the stalks so strong and erect.

A few minutes later, Jimmy came out on his way over to the barn. 'Have you seen this?' I called.

He strolled across, the closer he got, the more impressed his expression. 'Cool!' he cried. 'Nick said it was good stuff – MSI GM.'

'Careful where you stand – it'll go straight up the leg of your pants,' I told him.

Jimmy laughed heartily, for once exposing that gap in his bottom teeth he was so self-conscious of. 'We'll be baking before you know it,' he said, still chuckling to himself as he continued his walk to the barn.

For the rest of the day I kept going over to check. It was unbelievable – a real agricultural phenomenon – by late afternoon it had grown a further two inches. In fact, it didn't look so much like it was growing as *rising up*, as if something underneath was pushing it out.

I brought Lena out, walked her amongst it, thinking she'd be as excited as I was, but she didn't really seem to get it, maybe 'cuz she couldn't actually see what was happening, that we were now coming out of the front door to be met by a whole sea of burgeoning green life.

'Remember how you grew that stuff in the tunnels?' I said, feeling compelled to put it into perspective. 'This is like two whole *fields* of it: the richest, greenest crops you could ever imagine. It's beautiful.'

She nodded, standing for a moment holding a stalk of the wheat in her hand, but still not appearing that impressed, and I wondered if it was the thought of something familiar changing that was damping her enthusiasm. She smiled, made some light comment, then headed back to the house, and for the first time in a while I noticed she was checking her wires to make sure she was going in the right direction.

That night we made love again, but Thomas got the better of us this time, interrupting a man when he least wants to be interrupted. I forgave him enough to use him as an excuse to go outside later, to walk him around the farmyard, even going over in the direction of the woods at one point, listening intently, but there was nothing 'cept the occasional echoing call of a distant owl.

Maybe I was wrong about all this? Maybe the Bitch and her Bodyguard didn't have the slightest idea where we were, our little paradise felt peaceful and trouble-free once more. In fact, the way that wheat was bursting up out of the ground, I couldn't help but think that in some way it was a shining omen of an even brighter future.

CHAPTER SEVEN

I thought my sense of wonder couldn't possibly be tickled any further, but the following morning when I went outside, believe it or not, that wheat had not only pushed up a few more inches, it was showing signs of starting to ripen! I wasn't met by a solid sea of green this time, but the occasional ripple of something closer to gold. It was amazing. It truly was. Some of the ears looked almost ready to be harvested: bulging with life, with the seed we hoped to grind into flour.

I was so in awe of what was happening that it went through my mind that maybe it was that little bit too good to be true, that it was growing at such a rate it wouldn't be able to sustain itself. There's this creek that runs down the side of the property. At some point the adjacent spread (twenty times our size, but with all its outbuildings and farmhouse burnt down) must've blocked it off and diverted it across their land, but since everyone had upped and left, Mother Nature had obviously decided to right a wrong and start it flowing our way again. I'd been thinking we should clear some of the old irrigation channels, and with the wheat growing so fast and possibly needing a little extra water, now would be a good time to do it.

After breakfast we formed a working party: Lena, Gordie, Hanna,

Gigi and me. Delilah stayed behind to look after Thomas, as she often did now – Lena being younger and stronger than her, while Jimmy was obviously also playing to his strengths, concentrating on much more important things out in his workshop – stuff that didn't involve manual labour.

By the time that we'd finished, we'd managed to get several channels cleared and running in the direction of the fields. It didn't seem like it was enough; the ground was lapping the water up long before it reached its destination, but it had to be going somewhere – and I wasn't sure it was needed anyway. Like I said, I'm a city boy and this farming was all trial and error – who knew how those new types of seed worked?

Late in the afternoon, Delilah came out with Thomas. The little guy'd just woken up from his afternoon nap, all dazed and dozy, but he was starting to fidget in that way that usually preceded some fairly loud demands for food. She handed him over to Lena like he was a bomb that was about to go off, giving a short sigh of relief, then stepped back to take her first close look at the wheat.

'What's this?' she asked.

'Wheat,' Gordie told her, like she wasn't being too bright. 'For the bread.'

'Wheat?'

'Yeah.'

Delilah grunted, stepping forward to take a closer look. 'Spent some time on a farm when I was a kid. Wheat didn't look like this.'

'They changed it,' I told her.

She gave a long sigh, turning away as if she'd lost all interest. 'Can't anything stay the same?' she grumbled. 'Not even plants? Why we got to alter everything? What good's it done us?'

In a way she was right: changing stuff hadn't done us as much good as we'd hoped; on the other hand, it hadn't done us as much harm as we'd feared either. I mean, let's face it, no matter how much we try to alter things, we're only here for a while – Nature's the constant.

After we'd eaten and played with Thomas for a while, the little guy eventually heading off to snuggle down with the Sleep Fairies, Lena suggested we went out for a ride on the tandem, and despite it getting late, I thought it might be kinda fun.

It's amazing how much I've taken to that thing. I'm an ex-big guy, for chrissake – I drove every kinda of transport there was, and most of it was fast and furious. That tandem looked like it was the free transport to the Mad Hatter's Tea Party. But something about us going out on it, combining my efforts with Lena's, made me feel like we were a real team.

We gently meandered along the road for a while, enjoying its relative smoothness, then turned up this track, heading through the forest and up towards the first real hills of the Interior.

It's funny; I'd always thought people instinctively sought out high ground 'cuz they wanted the view, but Lena enjoys it as much as I do, so I guess there's something else going on. Maybe it's spiritual, trying to get that bit closer to heaven? If it is, then I gotta say, we did a pretty good job that day, what with the view, the sunset, the final whispers of the day, the way we were holding onto each other like it was the first and last time. It was all we could do to give that final sigh and drag ourselves away.

We started off back down that track a damn sight faster than we went up, and with the light fading, where the trees were at their thickest, my old eyes were really starting to struggle and I had to keep hitting the brakes, bringing us almost to a halt so I could work out which way the track was going, then gather up a bit of speed again. Even then there were a couple of occasions when we almost came off, but you know, just when I started to think it might be safest to walk, I felt her hands on either side of my hips.

'Keep going,' she said.

'I can't see,' I told her, feeling that bit embarrassed.

'Keep going!' she urged, starting to twist my body this way and that, and I realised she was intent on doing the steering for me.

'Lena!' I protested, again hitting the brakes.

'Clancy . . . trust me!' she cried impatiently.

It wasn't easy – I mean, she was blind, for chrissake, how could she possibly see better than me? I kept slowing and stretching my fingers out for the brakes, but each time I did she got more and more irritated.

'*No!*' she shouted angrily, and I knew it'd become something of a test: that I *had* to trust her, I *had* to go along with what she was saying – otherwise what sorta relationship did we have? But she was trying to direct me through areas where the forest was so thick I could barely see, and at speeds I wouldn't've been comfortable about in the daylight and out in the open. A couple of times she left it so late, I braced myself for the impact, but at the last moment she swerved me away from the tree looming up before us. The irony was, the deeper, the darker, into the woods we went, the more I became the blind one, the more she became the one who could see.

It was those special skills of hers again, that she'd acquired down in the tunnels those four years she'd spent alone underground – the ones I'd once mistakenly thought the Doc wanted her for. She could hear sounds bouncing off hard surfaces – in this case, I guessed, the trunks of the trees – and maybe she was cross-referencing that with her sense of smell to map out what was around us.

Whatever her method, I gotta say, it made for one of the most hair-raising rides of my life as we slid one way, then another, the two wheels at the back scrabbling to maintain grip, threatening to skid right off the track. Lena was whooping and laughing away, having the time of her life, maybe 'cuz she knew that if we *did* hit a tree, I was gonna be her personal airbag.

At last the forest began to thin and I could feel her insight fading; the fewer trees there were around us, the closer she was to being blind again. Fortunately, with more light, I was able to regain control.

'Want to go again?' she laughed.

'Nah. Not really,' I replied, trying to sound like I just couldn't be bothered; but you know, when we reached the road, I felt so damn pumped up, I started laughing along with her.

'You're a miracle and I love you,' I shouted.

She took me completely by surprise, throwing herself at me, wrapping her arms around mine – no way could I keep control, and we veered off the road and into a nearby tree with such accuracy, you might've thought I'd aimed for it.

We had to walk the last couple of miles, still chuckling away every now and then, knowing we'd be in big trouble with Jimmy for buckling the front wheel of his invention, but in a way, it was the perfect end to a perfect evening, when even what went wrong was right.

I put my arm around her as we went to enter the house, still unable to resist taking a quick glance back: I gotta say, that valley looked about as quiet and peaceful as an angel's graveyard.

I was actually hoping, even expecting, not to see that view again that night, what with clearing the irrigation channels, going for our tandem ride and just the general mood of contentment between Lena and me. Any normal person would've followed that up with a good seven or eight hours of honest slumber – but not me.

Thomas got going a little after two, in full cry, though it was actually Lena nudging me that really brought me round. I stumbled over to the wardrobe, almost tripping over my boots and sprawling headlong. Yeah, I love him, he's my own little guy, my flesh and blood, but there are times . . .

I took him outside, the night dull and dim, the moon covered by a dozen different veils – the world itself sleeping.

I don't know how long it was before I knew something was wrong. I'd just been doing my usual thing, pacing around the farmyard, jigging and shushing Thomas, when suddenly I felt it: this sense that in the deadness of night, the world was actually coming to life. I stopped, holding the little guy that bit closer to me, staring all around us, trying to work out what the hell it was. There was nothing to see, nothing to hear, just this sense of . . . *movement*! It wasn't the wind – there was none to speak of – but there was *something*: a force, a dissipating electricity leaking out into the night, faintly crackling all around me.

The first one I saw, I didn't even put the two things together. I suddenly noticed something was crawling up my leg: small, black, moving quite slowly – maybe some kinda weevil? But no sooner did I realise that was what it was than I saw others making their way up my pants, over my boots, covering the ground around me – there were *thousands* of them! No wonder I'd had the feeling the world was on the march: an army, a crawling black, wriggling army was encircling me and now venturing up my body.

I started to back away, trying to work out what direction they were travelling in so I could hopefully step aside. I thought it must be some kinda migration, but the moment I changed direction, they did the same. I turned to run but they were all around me, more and more of them, their gathering mass slowly turning my pants black, crawling up my back and front. I tried to brush them off, to sweep them away, but it wasn't easy with a baby in my arms. They were everywhere, and the most disturbing part – that at first I couldn't believe – was that they seemed to be targeting Thomas, finding their way into his blanket, navigating the tucks and folds, doing their best to get to the little guy.

I brushed one off his soft, little head, another from his arm, at the same moment aware of several wriggling down my neck and starting to crawl around inside my shirt. Thomas began to wail, no doubt panicked by what he couldn't understand, maybe by my distress, and damned if one of them didn't try to scuttle into his mouth. I swept it away and stamped on it. Jesus, what kinda nightmare was this?

I ran towards the house, squashing them underfoot, stripping the little guy as I went, throwing away his blanket, his clothes, even his diaper. I could feel them sneaking around all over me, finding any way in they could: up the legs of my pants, my sleeves, down the front of my shirt – my whole body seemed to be wriggling and squirming. But it was the way they were converging on Thomas that was really spooking me, as if they somehow knew this tiny, unprotected baby was the vulnerable one, the weakness they should exploit.

I burst through the front door, ran through to the bathroom and turned on the water; Gordie soon following on behind, wondering what the hell was going on.

'Block the front door!' I cried, sweeping weevils off me and Thomas, stamping on them the moment they hit the ground. 'Anywhere they can get in.'

For a moment he just gaped at me, barely believing what he was seeing, then he ran through the house, calling to Hanna and Gigi to come out and help.

I juggled Thomas from one arm to the other while taking off my clothes, the little guy still wailing as loudly as he could, even before I was naked, jumping into the shower and washing those things away, crushing them before nudging them towards the drain.

Suddenly Lena appeared in the doorway. 'What's going on?' she asked, bewildered.

'I dunno. Some kind of weevil,' I told her. 'There are thousands of them out there.'

'Is he okay?' she said, Thomas' crying not having lessened a single decibel.

'Yeah, just a little spooked,' I told her, trying to sound as calm as I could. 'I think a few might've got in the house.'

Without another word, she went to see if she could help. I could hear Jimmy and Delilah joining in, the sound of stamping feet mingled with the shrieks of disgust echoing throughout the house. As I got out of the shower, a weevil fell from my hair onto Thomas' chest and immediately scuttled up his neck, trying to get to his face. I flicked it off and stamped on it. The body had a kind of hard shell that crunched beneath my foot, but there was something soft, almost liquid, inside.

'Shall I take him?' Lena asked, again appearing in the doorway.

I handed him to her; the little guy still giving it all he had, flushed and bulging, as if he was constipated or something, and she took him away, shushing him as she walked through to the bedroom, I guessed to try to calm him with a feed. I dried myself and wrapped a towel around me before grabbing my clothes, opening the window and throwing them out. I'd deal with them later. A couple of weevils fell out and down onto the floor and went scampering away to hide, but I managed to stamp on them, then returned to the shower to wash my feet.

When I finally went out, the others appeared to have the situation under control; still finding the odd insect crawling around, but one by one killing them off, leaving the floor covered in this slippery greenish liquid.

'What the hell was that about?' I said.

'Some kind of natural phenomenon, I guess,' Jimmy said, looking as disturbed as anyone. 'Like a plague of locusts or something.'

'You reckon?' I said, taking a quick look out the window, but it was too dark to see if they were still there.

'Yuk!' Hanna squealed, finding a couple crawling up the back of her leg. She brushed them off and stamped on them, that green liquid squirting out again. 'Disgusting!'

'Did they bite or sting anyone?' I asked, but no one had suffered anything more than a fright. 'Weird,' I commented. 'Just weird.'

'What about the wheat?' Hanna suddenly asked, and everyone paused for a moment. I mean, none of us were that knowledgeable about farming, but I guess we kinda knew that was what weevils did: they ate the stuff you tried to grow.

'I ain't gonna look,' Delilah quickly chipped in.

'I'll go,' Gigi said, as always, out to prove a point.

'No one's opening that door again tonight,' I said, going to check that any gaps were completely sealed.

'I don't mind,' Gigi persisted.

'Well, I do. We're not chancing letting those things in again. We'll worry about what they've done in the morning.'

One by one we returned to our beds, but for once, I wasn't the only one who couldn't sleep. We had this real fear that they might be trying to get in elsewhere, that there were thousands of them climbing all over the house searching for a weakness. Thank God, 'cuz of the cold winter nights, the windows'd all been double-glazed and sealed and the floors were solid. The only possible other entry point – and once I thought about it, it did really concern me – was the chimney. Would they climb up there and find a way down? It worried me so much that, no matter how unlikely it might've been, I went and built the fire up so high, flames were leaping halfway up the chimney. No way was a weevil gonna come down there.

When I finished, I made one last inspection of the house, then re-joined Lena in bed. Not only was she awake, she had Thomas sleeping with her.

'Okay?' she whispered.

'As if we ain't got enough problems,' I grumbled, gently sliding into bed beside her, not wanting to bounce Thomas awake.

For a while we just lay there with the baby fidgeting and

whimpering, the light left on in case we had any more unwanted visitors, then finally Lena said, 'Clancy?'

'Mm?'

'. . . I'm scared.'

'It's okay,' I told her, 'come morning, they'll all be gone.'

'Not just of them.'

'What do you mean?' I asked, turning to face her.

She had that slightly wild intensity about her she sometimes got, when I reckoned she'd've given anything to have her sight restored, if only for a few seconds. 'Don't you see? The animals, the insects, even the plants . . . there's something wrong with them.'

No matter how badly you sleep, it's surprising how you can easily make it worse. Sometimes when people say 'I never closed my eyes all night', what they really mean is, 'not so I noticed, but pardon my snoring every now and then'. When I say, 'I never closed my eyes all night', I mean it: not so much as a blink.

At first I didn't pay too much attention to what Lena'd said; it was pretty far-fetched – she'd just been upset about all those weevils crawling over Thomas – but her words kept coming back to me, worrying me a little more each time. It *was* kinda odd, as if Nature was going against its own nature, and that *couldn't* be right. Those last few days had really been something: seeing Nora Jagger again, the invasion of the weevils, not to mention those two punks spontaneously combusting. What Doctor Simon had said about them probably being implant guinea pigs, that did kinda ring true, but it also added to this growing sense that in some way our existence was being distorted. I just didn't get it. Not that I felt I was lacking in any way – 'cuz I don't reckon anyone else got it either.

I did finally manage half an hour or so of 'death sleep': that narrow crevasse you fall into around about four or five, that when you wake, it feels as if you were mighty lucky, that death played with you for a while and then let you go. I forced myself up, leaving Lena still sleeping, and Thomas, too – probably 'cuz he was exhausted by the previous night.

The first thing I did was to take a good look out the window, but there wasn't a weevil to be seen, not even a dead one. The stuff we'd used to block up the gaps around the front door – wadded paper, torn-down curtains, whatever – had been removed, so I guessed someone'd already gone out. From the porch I could see the barn door was open, which presumably meant Jimmy was already over there and working. I ambled across, needing to talk to the little guy, though I wasn't sure exactly what I wanted to say.

As I walked in, he was struggling with the bent front wheel of the tandem, muttering away to himself.

'Sorry,' I told him.

'Not cool,' he complained. 'Fork's bent, wheel's buckled.'

'I'll help,' I told him.

'Yeah, yeah,' he said, both of us knowing he was never happier than when solving a mechanical or technological problem, no matter how mundane.

For a while I just stood there watching him, how comfortable he looked with a wrench in his hand, like an artist with his brush.

'Those damn things last night – what the hell was that all about?' I eventually commented.

'Frightened the life outa Lile,' he said, as if it hadn't been a problem for him.

'Didn't do a lot for me,' I told him. 'It was almost like they were attacking us.'

'Nah,' Jimmy sneered, spinning the front wheel of the tandem, still not satisfied it was straight, 'just passing through, eating their way around the country.'

'Did you check the wheat?' I asked, realising I should've done that first off.

'Every ripe ear's gone.'

'No!' I groaned.

'Should've brought back the lasers,' he complained, as if we could've shot them all one by one.

Without another word, I left him to go and look at the wheat fields, and sure enough, every golden grain had been stripped and eaten. I cursed repeatedly as I returned to Jimmy, finding him still bent over the tandem.

'Shit,' I commented.

'Thank God it wasn't all ripe.'

'Might come back.'

'Wouldn't think so; they just keep going 'til they get to their breeding colony, or seasonal resting place, or whatever bugs do.'

'Hope so.'

Again I stood and watched as he dismantled the front of the tandem once more, pulling everything apart with such smoothness and precision it was like watching a motor-racing pit stop.

'Lena's got this, er . . . "concern",' I eventually ventured.

'What d'you mean?'

'She thinks there might be a connection.'

He turned to me, awaiting an explanation.

'The way that wheat's grown so quickly, animals and people bursting into flames, armies of invading insects . . .'

He made this kinda bewildered face, as if to say 'what the hell could possibly connect all that?'

'Nora Jagger?' I tentatively suggested.

At that he stopped and stared at me. 'You think she's trained an army of weevils?'

I shrugged, knowing how crazy it sounded. 'I dunno.'

'I wouldn't put anything past that bitch, but enlisting wolves and weevils – I'd like to see how she does it,' he commented, starting to chuckle. 'And I guess the wheat's gonna attack us in the middle of the night, too, huh? The revenge of the killer corn.'

'Yeah, okay, Jimmy,' I said, always ready to defend Lena. 'You gotta admit, there *is* something a little odd about it.'

'Yeah, well . . . not gonna argue with that,' he agreed, spinning the wheel of the tandem again, this time apparently satisfied. 'Okay. A little breakfast, then maybe I'll go over and have a word with Nick. It might be great at growing, but he promised me that wheat was also parasite-proof.'

CHAPTER EIGHT

A huge storm blew up later that morning, first enveloping the mountains and then sweeping down on us like some invading horde, battering the front porch, shaking the house on its foundations, bombarding us with water. The creek immediately swelled up like it was on steroids, getting all boisterous and aggressive, surging at everyone and everything, dashing down the irrigation channels we'd cut out so that soon the wheat fields were partly flooded and I wondered if what hadn't been touched by weevils might well end up being spoiled anyway.

It meant a whole day of doing nothing but staying inside. Jimmy cancelled his plan to visit Nick, agreeing to do a few jobs around the house, but the kids were so fractious, it wasn't long before he slipped out to his workshop. Hanna tried to practise her ballet on the front porch, but Gigi wouldn't have it, complaining – no doubt as a matter of principle – that she'd been about to sit out there. Gordie tried his hand at peacemaker, but that only riled Gigi more, and in the end he retreated to the barn to help Jimmy. Meanwhile, Lena got into this long, low conversation with Delilah, which, though I barely heard a word of it, I had a pretty good idea what it was about.

She never made a big thing of it, but I knew Lile'd been pregnant on several occasions. For some reason, she'd never managed to get it quite right – either she'd wanted it and miscarried, or her situation'd been impossible and she was forced to terminate. Whatever, it'd been a torturous thing to have to go through, and even after all those years she still had days when it skewered deep down into her guts.

What she never told us – what the birth of Thomas eventually prompted her to confess – was that there had been one survivor. When she was approaching forty and getting acutely aware of the fact that hookers don't go on for ever – taking chances, riding bareback to stay competitive – she fell pregnant yet again, and this time it presented her with a real dilemma: time wasn't only running out on her career, but also on her chance to be a mother.

In the end, the maternal tug was that bit stronger and she set out to reinvent herself, to build a new, *normal* life: renting a little apartment, fixing it up, getting it ready for the baby. She knew it wasn't gonna be easy, and no way could she see more than a month, or even a couple of weeks, into the future, but she didn't care about that, only bringing her child into the world: her contribution to humanity, her family, that would be just as good as anyone else's.

As Life and Luck would have it, little Sean was born with severe disabilities. He couldn't walk, was incontinent – he couldn't even feed himself properly – and Lile was utterly beside herself. She did her best, but with all his special needs, she found it really hard. She left him, she went back, she left him, she went back, she left him – *six times!* The problem was, she blamed herself: the life she'd led, her many cus-tomers, the numerous drugs – recreational and otherwise – all those things she'd done to keep herself from simply getting flushed away.

She thought she could cope, live only for Sean, but she wasn't strong enough, and in the end, she put him up for adoption. The only problem there was, no one else was strong enough either, and he ended up in this soulless, decaying and penny-pinched institution. Every time she visited she came away with yet another piece of her heart cauterised. It hurt so much sometimes she just couldn't go through with it: she'd deliberately miss her stop on the subway, or walk past when she got to the gate, or even get to the door to his ward and see all those that society had forgotten (most, of course, who later ended up on the Island) and not have it in her to enter.

Finally, she gave up: she was a useless knob of shit and no good to anyone or anything. She forced herself never to go there again, even at Christmas, even on his birthday, those times when it hurt the most, she'd go to a bar and drink herself into a memory-free stupor.

She never found out who sent the letter, but it made her cry for almost a week. She hadn't seen Sean for thirteen years; she'd always imagined him still in that God-forsaken institution, dying slowly, or maybe even dead – but it turned out, that wasn't the case. The thing was, just like us out on the Island, trapped in our own version of a God-forsaken institution, little Sean had been given the tiniest drop of hope, of belief and encouragement, and he too fought back. Whoever it was wrote to Lile, they wanted her to know that he was about to graduate from high school.

Lile went along to the ceremony, skulking in the shadows at the back of the hall, sobbing so loudly when Sean struggled up the steps to receive his diploma she had to leave. When she finally calmed herself down, she returned to see him with this couple – older than her, but gentle and homely, delighted smiles on their faces, taking it in turns to give him a hug: her son, who she'd given to the world, who she knew she didn't have the right to cause even the slightest of ripples in his life.

She walked away and never ever saw him again, still feeling like a useless knob of shit, but on this occasion at least, one helluva happy and proud one.

I guess that's the sorta tale you save for a special day, when the weather locks in and won't let you out 'til you confess, or a drunken night that'll have no morning, no dawn to soothe away the pain. For sure Delilah only talked about it when she appeared to have no other choice. Where Sean was now, she didn't know, and actually, I didn't think she cared that much. It was enough for her to know he was happy, and far more importantly, that he'd made a damn sight better fist of life than she had.

I could've gone out and seen what Jimmy and Gordie were up to, maybe even acted as a crash-barrier between Hanna and Gigi, but I had it in mind to give myself a bit of a treat. I still got those books I took from the bookstore in the City: Hemingway, Steinbeck, Dickens and Pasternak. I think I told ya, when I first started reading, out on the Island, I realised two things: the first, that I wasn't anywhere near as dumb as I used to think; and the second, that reading's one of the greatest pleasures life has to offer. Books take me to another place, one that I never would've gone otherwise; they've also helped me to express myself a whole lot better. I can articulate stuff now that before I could only grunt about. And I worked at it, too, I really did, not just for myself, but for Lena as well. She inspired me that way: to be the best man I could possibly be.

I'd read all four books – *For Whom the Bell Tolls*, *A Tale of Two Cities*, *The Grapes of Wrath* and *Doctor Zhivago* – any number of times, but I could always stand to read them again. My favourite was *The Grapes of Wrath* – I'm not declaring it the best, just that it was my favourite, maybe 'cuz of all that trekking across the land, looking for salvation; it's something we could really identify with.

I thought back to the old days, when I was with Mr Meltoni and he used to tease me for being illiterate, for never having read a book or knowing anything about what he called 'the finer things of life'. But ya know, those writers he used to talk about with such authority?

– Shakespeare, Oscar Wilde and the like – I don't think he'd read even one of them. The only thing I ever saw him read was the racing page. He just gave off this aura of being knowledgeable and sophisticated, and everyone believed him. I bet I could speak about literature now and he wouldn't have a clue what I was talking about. All he knew was a few quotes, ones that everyone knows and can smile at with recognition so they can congratulate themselves on how clever they are.

We sealed up the outside door again that night, and any other cracks we could find, but the way it'd rained, I couldn't imagine those weevils were still around. They'd either drowned or been washed away, or maybe they'd continued their migration up to higher ground. In fact, when I thought about it, I wondered if that was it? Instinct had told them a big storm was on its way and they'd been hightailing it up into the hills.

Thomas woke up crying at one point, sounding more than averagely distressed, and I was across that room quicker than I would've thought possible, making sure he wasn't being bothered by invading insects, but there was nothing. I picked him up, Lena sleepily enquiring if he was okay, but she was back to breathing heavy even before I could answer. It was too wet to walk him outside so I just sat in a chair, rocking him back and forth 'til he finally fell asleep.

I stayed there with him in my arms all night, I guess feeling a bit more secure that way, that I could keep a close eye on him. At one stage I had to hand him over to Lena for feeding, but as soon as he'd stopped sucking and started trying to blow bubbles, she gave him back and I resumed my seat, thinking there was no way I could sleep, but actually nodding off within a few minutes.

I awoke to find the little guy silently lying there staring up at me, those big blue eyes again expressing astonishment. I mean, what could I say? Get used to it, kid. I'm your old man and nothing's ever gonna change that.

It was hard to believe we'd had so much rain the day before. Even the areas that had been temporarily flooded were now more or less dried out. I went over to check on the wheat fields and was relieved to find that they'd recovered; everything was pointing skywards again, bursting with life, new ears of wheat appearing and rapidly transforming themselves into golden nuggets for us to grind into flour.

I called in on Jimmy in the barn, stopping dead in my tracks as I entered: the tandem had been given a new paint job, in fact, repainted in just about every colour of the rainbow: yellow, blue, pink, red, purple, the original green. Not only that, it was now sporting stripes, spots, a pair of horns on the handlebars – and it'd been christened 'the Typhoon Tandem'.

'What the hell?'

'Gordie decided it needed a little pimping,' he smirked, almost as if he saw it as revenge for Lena's and my buckling the wheel. 'Cool, huh?'

'Yeah, right,' I said, ready to acknowledge that maybe we deserved it, though Lena wasn't gonna have to suffer the way I was.

'Think I might head over to Nick's later,' he told me, 'if you feel like coming along?'

'Yeah. Sure.'

'I wanna talk to him about that weevil smorgasbord we so generously provided.'

Once again Gigi joined us. You either got her or the 'lovebirds' (as she called them), rarely both, and after the big stand-off on the porch the day before, this wasn't likely to be an exception. I did ask Jimmy, as Lena was staying with Thomas, if he thought Lile might like to come along, but getting up over that hill's quite a challenge for her now. I don't know if she'd ever told him how old she was exactly, but since we'd been out in the country and she'd run outta stuff like make-up and hair dye, Lile was looking a lot older. In fact, I think Jimmy'd been under the impression that he'd taken up with a younger woman; now he probably wasn't so sure. It wasn't just her appearance; she seemed permanently weary, like an old battery that couldn't be properly charged. Not that I reckoned there was anything wrong with her – she was just getting old, like we all eventually do.

After the rain everything felt and looked that bit fresher, and when we got to that point at the top of the hill where you could look down into both valleys it was almost uplifting, like we'd been cleansed along with everything else. However, as we descended towards the other smallholdings, the mood began to change. It was Gigi who noticed first, probably 'cuz she was the youngest and got the best eyesight.

'Where is everyone?' she asked.

I never said anything, just kept walking, expecting to see signs of life at any moment – a distant figure, smoke from a chimney – but she was right, there was nothing.

'That's weird,' Jimmy commented.

'They're around somewhere,' I said, a little dismissively.

We walked on, all three of us scanning the valley, trying not to react but slowly becoming more alarmed.

'I don't like this,' Jimmy muttered. 'Definitely not cool.'

'Maybe they all burst into flames,' Gigi joked, but Jimmy and me didn't even acknowledge that she'd spoken.

As we approached the nearest dwelling, I started to call out, softly at first but then turning it into a real bellow: 'Hello! . . . Hello!'

Still there was no sign of anyone and I went to knock on the door. We waited for a while; I tried again, but still there was no answer.

'Let's go to Nick's,' I said. 'He ain't going anywhere, not with Miriam.'

We went over to Nick's place, again calling out, knocking on the door, but still with no reply.

'I don't get this,' I said, scanning the length of the valley, but Gigi decided on a little more direct action, trying Nick's door and finding it open.

'Hey, hey!' I shouted, but she was already inside.

We followed on behind, going from room to room, noting a few things had been taken. There was no sign of life, not even Miriam; no evidence of a struggle, they'd just upped and left by the look of it.

'Where've they gone?' Jimmy asked.

We went back outside, and stood on the porch, still half-expecting to see someone approaching.

'Something must've frightened them off,' Gigi said.

Jimmy and me momentarily exchanged looks, not wanting to say anything or ponder too much on that idea.

We checked several more dwellings, but it was the same story: looked like everyone had grabbed a few essentials and taken off.

'I don't get it,' Jimmy said. 'Nick's cool. He's not just gonna up and leave.'

For a while we wandered around aimlessly, feeling helpless and confused, wondering what to do. Should we search for them? Did they need help? Did this have something to do with crazies? We even tried shouting up to the hills and the surrounding forest, but there was nothing, not even an echo.

'Big Guy,' Jimmy said, indicating the nearby wheat field.

Their fields stretched way out into the distance and had been well in advance of ours, all of it ripe and golden the last time we'd been there – but that wasn't what Jimmy was pointing out. The whole lot had been stripped and from what we could see, there wasn't an intact ear anywhere.

'Those damn weevils,' I muttered.

'Looks like it.'

It was a hard thing to imagine. Thousands, millions, I guessed, of weevils cutting a huge swathe across the country: a big black wave of them sweeping up from our place, over the hill, and then down into the next valley, on to bigger and riper pickings. It was also surprising that from what we could see, they appeared to have a diet of nothing but wheat.

'Maybe that was what scared them away,' Gigi suggested.

It did make a kinda sense, but it didn't altogether sit that easy. We'd fought them off; surely Nick and the others would've done the same?

Eventually we made our way back up the hill, no one talking, still not sure what'd happened and in a strange way feeling like we'd been abandoned. We'd lost our only neighbours, and been left to face an increasing threat on our own.

When we got back to the farm and told the others, they were every bit as dumbfounded as we were, asking all manner of questions we had no way of answering: why hadn't they sent someone over the hill to tell us? Why hadn't they come to us for help? Were we sure it was weevils?

Later I went out and checked our fields again. Just that one day of sunshine (and maybe all that rain) had created yet another bewildering leap skywards. The overwhelming majority of what the weevils had left was now plump and apparently ready for harvesting. It was a miracle, and time for us to start thinking about how we were gonna mill the wheat, though Jimmy had told us not to bother, that we could leave that to him.

I wasn't really sure why, but for some reason I found myself going around checking on Lena's guide wires; reattaching stuff that had been blown off during the storm, digging a couple of new holes for posts that had become unstable in the sodden soil. It wasn't exactly the greatest alarm system ever, especially as only one of us was guaranteed to hear it, but for some reason knowing it was there made me feel that bit more secure.

It didn't happen too often, and I'm not altogether sure what the reason was, but that night Thomas not only fell asleep with no trouble at all, it looked like he was gonna stay that way. In fact, he was so quiet in that snug little nest of his, I checked on him a coupla times to make sure he was okay. It made for an unusually relaxed evening, and after dinner, Lena poured us both some hooch - unless I was reading the signs incorrectly, in the mood for a little love-making.

It wasn't the way it used to be – before Thomas, I mean – and I wouldn't've expected it either. Maybe it never would be like that again. I just figured that if I left it up to her, let her make the decision, then eventually we'd find our balance again – a different one maybe, but it'd be the right one for us. And anyways, let's be absolutely honest about it, at my age I ain't always got the energy myself. When it did happen, and providing we didn't get any interruptions from Master Thomas, it was still one of the best feelings I'd ever known.

Pardon me for being so indiscreet, but when I was younger, I used to have a more than healthy sexual appetite, but sadly, no way of fulfilling it. Problem was, I was never all that comfortable in the company of women (the archetypal 'big guy' – who never ever got the girl). Some guys can chat away with women they've just met as if they've known them all their lives; with me, I talked to women I'd known all my life as if I'd just met them. It was like that for so long, well into my twenties, that eventually I decided that if I wasn't gonna miss out on that side of life altogether, there was only one way for me to receive a little sexual pleasure.

Took me four months to summon up the nerve. I knew where to go – the wrong end of Union; everyone knew that, but I didn't think I'd ever persuade myself down there. That first occasion was one of the most embarrassing episodes of my life. It just didn't feel right: she was a total stranger, we'd exchanged barely a dozen words, and there we were participating in the most intimate act two people can. But gradually, shit to admit, I did become something of a regular, with several ladies; some who cared, some who didn't, some who I left with a smile on my face, some who I left with my heart so heavy I thought it might've stopped. But my pledge to myself as I skulked back to where I'd hidden Mr Meltoni's limo was always exactly the same: *I'll never, ever do that again.*

See, I wasn't really sure what I was looking for. I remember the last time I went, I got into this slightly weird mood: I didn't want sex, I wanted something else. I wanted this short, rather homely little Latina lady to tell me she loved me, that was all. She didn't have to touch me, or me her, just declare that in that moment she had more feeling for me than any other person on this earth. Crazy, huh? I mean, she did oblige, but not all that convincingly. It even went through my head that those people who ran those places were missing a trick: there should be 'emotional whores' – rooms where you could go and be told you're a special person and worthy of love. I think it'd be a real money-spinner. I mean, I might've been lucky enough to have found Lena, but there are plenty of people, men and women, out there who don't have anyone and I reckon they'd be happy to pay handsomely for someone to spend thirty minutes filling in those great aching voids in their wasteland hearts.

Anyways, what I'm trying to say is – and, please, forgive a tired old cliché from a tired old big guy – having sex and making love *are* two very different things. One reduces us to the animals we unquestionably are, while the other raises us up to the spirits we hope to be. You're not devouring flesh, ransacking the sensation of another's body, but feeling something flowing back and forth, taking away the pain, reaffirming who you are to each other.

*

I don't know what time it was, what with that big cracked cup of hooch and making love, but it was a rare night of deep relaxation and for once I was sleeping the Sleep of the Satisfied Gods. There was every chance I'd've stayed that way too, if it hadn't been for Thomas reverting to type and noisily summoning his nurse, comforter and court jester.

I kind of stumbled across to him, bent-kneed and bent-backed, jigging his drawer up and down, shushing him, hoping he'd settle back down where he was, but he wasn't having any of it.

'Clancy!' Lena wearily complained, which didn't leave me with a whole lotta choice. I gave a long sigh, took a real careful hold of the little guy, fearing how groggy I was that I might drop him, and made my way outside.

I commenced on my usual circuit, hoping it would either make him sleepy or wake me up, but it didn't do either. I went clockwise, anti-clockwise, even threw in a little zigzagging for good measure, but nothing seemed to work. The only times he stopped crying were those when he was summoning up strength for the next round. Eventually I was that tired, that brow-beaten, I just had to rest. I slumped down on the porch, leaning against a post, still rocking Thomas back and forth. Every now and then he'd fall asleep for a few moments, and then me, and then, I guess, both of us . . .

It was one of those occasions when you're awake before you realise you've actually been asleep, when you're jolted there through discomfort or alarm, and consciousness comes in a breakneck rush. I awoke coughing repeatedly, with something sharp lodged in my throat, obstructing my airways, making me gasp for air.

Thomas was screaming in such a way I'd never heard before and I looked down to see something in my arms that at first I didn't recognise. It was black and bubbling with movement, thousands of tiny wriggling bodies, and finally I realised the little guy was covered with weevils. They were *everywhere* – I couldn't see even a glimpse of his skin, just this pulsating dark coating, most of them grouped around his nose and mouth, jostling each other in an effort to get inside him, like flies seeking out moisture.

I leapt to my feet, shaking the little guy as hard as I dared, brushing them off him, only in that moment realising I was covered too, that it was weevils in my mouth making me choke.

I coughed and spat, ejecting what I'd almost swallowed, eventually managing to cry out, '*Lena! Jimmy—!*'

I was about to run inside, to head into the shower again, but those things were everywhere, thousands and thousands of them, stacked high against the front of the house, the door and windows, as if they were trying to break them down.

I could hear someone inside approaching, responding to my call, their footsteps echoing across the floor. '*No! Don't open it!*' I shouted. 'Block it up – weevils are everywhere. I'm going down to the creek—'

I ran over there as fast as I could, sweeping weevils off Thomas all the way, feeling those hundreds of tiny feet crawling all over my body. It was as if they were searching me, prying here and there, looking for something. The moon broke through the clouds, giving me a better view of the surrounding area – Jesus, the entire ground, everything I could see, was covered by this black crawling mass making their way towards the house.

When I got to the creek I jumped straight in and dropped to my knees so the water was up to my chest, splashing it over a shrieking Thomas, sluicing those damn things away as best I could. I fumbled with his tiny clothes, stripping him off, thanking God it was a warm night, just letting them float off downstream. But it wasn't only him, I had to get rid of my own clothes, too. Somehow I managed to tug them off me while juggling him from hand to hand, but at one point he slipped from my grasp and fell in. He was gasping with shock as I pulled him clear of the water, and damned if a number of weevils weren't still clinging on to his downy little head.

One by one I swept them away 'til finally I stood there in the middle of that creek with Thomas in my arms, both of us free of weevils, and utterly naked.

The only thing was, what the hell were we gonna do? We couldn't get outta the water, not with all those damn things massed around us. Over in the house the lights were now on, and I guessed everyone was trying to kill the weevils that had got in and blocking out those who hadn't. I just didn't get it – I thought they'd moved on? Or was this a different lot? A second wave? For sure there were a helluva lot more of them.

I don't know how long I stood there hoping they'd go, but the longer it went on, the more I got it in to my head that maybe this wasn't just them overrunning us on their way elsewhere – that maybe it was us they were after?

I know that sounds crazy – insects don't do that kind of thing, right? But no sooner had the thought crossed my mind than I heard the sound of a branch breaking upstream, and don't ask me how, but I knew what it was even before it hit the water. There were some overhanging trees back there, and I reckoned those weevils had been collecting on them, more and more, 'til finally their weight broke a branch. There was a further crack and another splash, and another – Jeez, a whole damn armada was coming our way.

I tried moving to one side to let the first branch float by, but the creek wasn't wide enough and I was forced to just wait 'til it reached me then stamp on it, push it underwater and hope I'd drown them – but the moment I did, they started crawling up my leg, going for my crotch. All the time I was clinging onto Thomas, doing my best to calm him, while he screamed with all the fear a seven-month could muster. It was mayhem: trying to drown them, splashing them off me, missing the odd one, seeing it crawling over Thomas or feeling it tickling its way over me.

Another branch arrived, another skirmish in our river battle, and this time I used the first branch to sink the others, trying to keep the weevils as far away from us as I could, though the creek was now thick with their bobbing little bodies. Over and over they came, branch after branch, 'til I was so exhausted, flailing away while hanging onto Thomas – I wasn't sure I could take it any more. Thankfully, a few moments later, I realised the barrage was slowing, that maybe they'd run out of overhanging branches.

I was left standing helpless and naked in the middle of that creek, my old chest huffing and heaving, my whimpering baby son clutched in my arms, the enemy probably massing on the bank, looking for another way to attack.

Suddenly I heard this weird sound, muffled and metallic, like someone was trying to vomit into a tin can. It took me a while to realise it was Jimmy.

'Big Guy . . . ! Big Guy! *Can you hear me?*'

I didn't know what he'd done – sounded like he was shouting down a long tube. Maybe he'd found something and pushed it outta an upstairs window, or even the chimney.

'Big Guy!' came the muffled cry again.

'I'm okay!' I called back. 'I'm in the creek with Thomas.'

'Can you get back?' came Lena's voice, also all tinny and distant.

'No! We'll have to stay here!'

'All night?'

'We got no choice. Don't worry, we'll be fine,' I added, though I wasn't as confident as I was trying to sound.

'Are you sure?'

'Yeah.'

So that was what I did: I more or less stayed where I was, wading around in the water to try to keep myself as warm as I could, to stop my old legs from going numb, being careful not to trip on the uneven bottom of the creek, and grateful for the occasional shouted conversation with the house.

Some time in the early hours the weevils came again, several more branches heavily laden down with insects floating down the creek – and ya know the really chilling thing? I never heard a crack or splash. Which left me with only one conclusion: they'd found branches elsewhere and carried them into the water. I mean, it was beyond belief, but what other explanation could there be? Again I had to go to war: sinking, soaking, drowning. A whole gang of them got past me at one point and started swarming over Thomas but he was so exhausted, he barely reacted.

With the slow passing of the night, the temperature began to drop noticeably and I had to keep hugging and rubbing the little guy to keep him warm. I was that tired, I could've almost fallen asleep where I was. Thomas might be no weight at all normally, but for that length of time, my limbs were really beginning to ache. I shifted him from shoulder to shoulder, occasionally looking over at the riverbank, thinking how nice it would be to lie down, but I was sure those things were still there, trying to come up with another way of ... *of what?* I didn't know! What the hell did they want from us?

I thought I saw the first light of dawn a dozen times before it finally appeared. The moment I could clearly see the bank, I realised they'd gone, that they'd slipped away with the night. I gave this real heartfelt groan of relief and began to clumsily splash through the water, suddenly appreciating how stiff and achy I was, Thomas so deeply asleep he didn't even wake as I jolted and shook him around.

I was about to climb the outta water when I realised someone had emerged from the house, hastily shutting the door behind them, like they weren't that sure if the weevils had gone or not. I peered over the bank to see Lena and Jimmy making their way across, both of them looking worried sick.

It might sound odd, but as soon as I saw them I lost all thoughts of weevils, of my aches and pains; the only thought going through my head was that I didn't have a stitch on.

'Jimmy! Get me some pants, will ya!' I shouted.

'You okay, Big Guy?' he asked.

'Fine. Get me some pants.'

He returned to the house, Lena calling to me, making her way over, soon standing on the riverbank before me.

'Take him,' I said, carefully placing Thomas in her outstretched hands, but making no attempt to get out myself.

'You sure you're okay?' she said, wrapping herself around Thomas, so relieved to have him back safe and sound.

'Yeah, we're fine. He's been asleep the last couple of hours. Finally we know what it takes.'

Lena just stood there for a moment, looking a little confused, obviously wondering what I was doing. 'You getting out?'

'Yeah, yeah – soon as I get those pants.'

'Clancy! No one's going to care about that.'

Jimmy came out of the house followed by the others, and I cursed to myself, knowing he must've said something. No matter how cold I felt, I immediately squatted down so the water made me decent.

'You okay, Big Guy?' Delilah asked, as she sauntered over.

'Fine. What's everyone want?'

'Just checking you're all right,' she replied, her smirk telling a different story.

'I'm fine. Now could everyone turn their backs?'

'You gonna put your pants on underwater?' Hanna asked.

'Just go, will ya!' I shouted, being of the opinion that the only women in a man's life who should see him naked are his wife and mother.

Despite the circumstances, how tired and cold I was, damned if they didn't all start giggling.

'Clancy!' Lena said, the corners of her mouth turning up, like she wanted to start laughing, too.

'Look, it's been one helluva night; I don't need to be embarrassed on top of it.'

They kinda saw the logic of that and finally took pity on me, leaving Lena and me alone, though they kept looking back as they returned to the house, little peals of laughter erupting every now and then. I didn't know what they were saying, and I didn't want to, either.

I staggered out of the water, my lingering embarrassment helping me get my pants on in double-quick time despite numbed fingers and a wet body. It was an unexpected end to a truly harrowing night, a little light relief maybe, but what'd happened was certainly no laughing matter. What the hell did those things want? Why had they returned? Jimmy went and checked on the wheat fields, coming back with the worst possible news, that every single ear of wheat had been eaten.

I guess that should've been it, the whole episode explained, but for some reason it didn't feel that way. It was disappointing to lose the entire crop, especially after all the work we'd done ploughing and sowing, but I couldn't help but feel we had an even greater problem. I couldn't believe that had merely been the natural instinct of some lowly insect, some weird quirk of nature. Something else had been motivating those things, and the most frightening part was, whatever it'd been, it seemed to have a measure of intelligence.

CHAPTER NINE

I thought it was just me, that I was the only one thinking those weevils were acting way above themselves, but I wasn't. I crashed into bed the moment I got back to the house and slept all morning, but was woken up later by the kids going off down to the fields with Delilah to see if there was any wheat at all they could salvage. The situation so serious that for once they'd temporarily shelved their differences and all gone off together, Gigi and Hanna included.

I had a quick bite with Lena – Thomas's ordeal had apparently had little effect on his appetite; he was sucking away like some baby vampire – then wandered over to see Jimmy in his workshop.

I walked in to find the little guy staring into this glass jar. To my surprise, inside there were several live weevils.

'Set a couple of traps down in the field,' he explained, handing me the glass. 'Just in case they came back.'

I gotta say, up close like that, just a few of them, they weren't that impressive: smaller than I imagined, black, with shiny green streaks, wiggly little antennae, and unnaturally large eyes. Their movement was kinda slow, not like the previous night, as if not wanting to waste their energy while imprisoned.

'Not so big now, are you?' I muttered at them. 'Not without all your friends.'

Jimmy never said anything, just stood there, plainly heavily preoccupied.

'What's the matter?' I asked.

'I don't know what they are.'

'What d'ya mean? They're weevils.'

'You reckon?'

'Yeah . . . Don't you?' I asked, not understanding this conversation at all.

Jimmy took a deep breath and gave an even longer sigh, leading me over to his workbench. Apparently he'd caught more than just those in the jar; he'd already dissected a few and that gooey green liquid was oozing everywhere.

'Their physiology,' he said. 'Weird.'

'In what way?'

'First I thought it was some kinda parasite – maybe even a GM. Makes sense: subvert the culture, teach them new tricks, stop them eating what they shouldn't – specie reduction or termination, but . . . I don't think so.' Again he paused, like he'd really have preferred not to say what he was about to. 'It's not cool, Big Guy,' he warned me. 'It's not cool at all.'

'What isn't?'

For a moment he studied the dissected weevils on a screen, slowly bringing up the magnification. 'When they were all over you . . .'

'Yeah?' I asked impatiently.

'They didn't—?'

'What?'

'Find a way in?'

'What?'

He enhanced the magnification that bit more. 'See those hooks?'

he said, indicating these barbs on the creature's body. 'Weevils ain't parasites. Those are for attaching themselves to a host.'

I stared at him. '*Me?*'

'They couldn't've . . .' he stopped, making this rather apologetic face, 'got inside ya?'

'No . . .' I said, but the word died in me even before it was properly uttered.

'What?' he asked, seeing the sudden expression on my face.

I sighed, not really wanting to tell him. 'When I woke up, there were some in my mouth. I spat them out, all of them – I'm sure I did.'

Jimmy didn't comment, just stood there thinking it through. 'Maybe I could recreate a host environment, see how they react.'

I shrugged; as ever he was starting to lose me.

'But where the hell they come from, I *do not know*,' he said, unusually for him plainly at a loss.

'GM, I'll bet,' I snorted. 'Two things put together that never should be. How often have we seen that?'

But he'd already lost interest in our conversation, searching high and low for something that might aid him with the thread of a theory, no longer listening to me or even aware of my presence.

In the end, I left him to it and headed across to sit on the porch, more than a little troubled by our conversation. Why did he think those things were trying to get inside us? What the hell for – hatch out a new family? Just the thought made me shudder: thousands of them eating their way outta us? But I'd know if I'd swallowed one, wouldn't I? If I had it inside me?

I sat there turning the problem over and over, trying to get a handle on things. Where do they come from? Where do they go? Do they move on? Is each attack a different swarm or are they hiding somewhere and come out at night?

Without actually making a conscious decision, I got up and ambled over to what was left of the wheat fields, where the kids and Delilah were still searching for any surviving grain.

'You okay, Clancy?' Lile asked, sauntering over, the kids following on.

'I'm fine.'

'Only we were saying, we haven't seen much of you this afternoon,' she said, smirking away, and I realised she was teasing me again.

'Yeah – thanks, Delilah.'

'Not like we did this morning . . . Now I know why they call you "Big Guy".'

'You can stop that,' I said forcefully. 'There was nothing to see.'

'Oh, I wouldn't say that,' Delilah commented, the kids giggling, though more, I suspected, out of embarrassment than any other reason.

'Any wheat left?' I asked, making it pretty plain I had no time for her notions of humour.

'Not really,' Hanna answered, taking pity on me, opening her sack to show me what she'd collected, which sure as hell wasn't a lot.

'Not gonna make much flour outta that,' I commented.

'No,' she said, holding out a handful of chaff and a few seeds in her open hand. She was just about to let it fall back into her sack when suddenly she gave this startled little cry.

'What's wrong?' Gordie asked.

'It moved.'

'What?'

'One of those seeds moved . . . ! Ohhh!' she cried, dropping the sack and backing away. 'That was creepy.'

'Jesus Christ!' sneered Gigi, swooping on the opportunity to project some bile Hanna's way.

'It moved, I tell you!'

Gigi turned away in disgust, but Gordie, as loyal as ever, rushed to defend Hanna, which only ramped things up further as Gigi immediately took the opportunity to turn on him, as if he was the real source of her bitterness.

Tell the truth, I couldn't be bothered; it was just the kids squabbling over stupid stuff as usual. I walked away, leaving them to it – in fact, I must've covered almost fifty yards or more before it finally hit me . . . *Jesus! Of course!*

I ran back, grabbed the sack off the ground and took it over to the barn, bursting in on Jimmy, not allowing the little guy a moment to ignore me.

'I know where they come from!' I announced.

He paused for a moment and looked at me, but his thoughts were plainly miles away. 'Big Guy, I'm a little busy—'

'*I know where they come from!*' I repeated. 'They don't *eat* the wheat,' I announced, 'they come *out* of it.'

I put my hand in Hanna's sack, pulled out the largest and liveliest-looking seed I could find and gave it to him. 'Cut it open . . . *Do it!*' I said, when he looked like he was about to dismiss me.

Jimmy shrugged as if indulging an oversized madman, then dissected it – sure enough, the moment he sliced through the husk the seed started moving and there was a weevil inside.

'Whoa . . . *Whoa!*' he cried. I reckoned as much shocked by the fact that *I'd* come up with the answer as anything else.

'Maybe that *was* what happened with Nick?' I suggested. 'Their fields were five or six times the size of ours. They would've been knee-deep in them.'

Jimmy sifted through the sack, found a few more likely seeds, plump and almost pulsating, and cut them open, and again there were weevils inside, one of them almost managing to scramble away before he squashed it, those familiar oily green insides squirting out everywhere.

He poked and prodded the corpse, putting it under his screen, bringing up the image again. 'You *sure* you never swallowed one?'

'As sure as I can be,' I said, levelling with him.

He returned to the insect, turning up the magnification as far as it would go, going disturbingly quiet.

After a while it hit me that I was being dismissed again and I left him to it, walking slowly back to the house, looking all around me as I went, taking in the view – the mountains, the hills, the endless forest: my family and friends' home, our little piece of paradise. And yet, under that most peaceful of open skies, I swear I could hear the sound of sirens starting their shrill warning.

We didn't see Jimmy again that day. Lile took him down some food, but he never touched it, which was a really bad sign. He finally returned just as the light was starting to fade – I guessed concerned the weevils might come again, but he didn't have a lot to say, which we concluded meant he hadn't discovered anything.

We sealed the house up really carefully. Nothing was gonna get in there, no matter how small or determined. We also imposed a watch rota: two people to patrol from room to room and make sure there were no breaches while the others slept.

Gigi sneered when Hanna volunteered her and Gordie for first watch; saying she wouldn't feel safe with the lovebirds looking out for her, that they might get *distracted*. Jesus, I tell ya, I could've done without it – teenage love triangles threatening to erupt at any moment. I made a point of agreeing, trying to settle things down, saying how I was looking forward to a good night's sleep.

It's funny, when you first sleep with someone you wrap your arms around them all night as if it's everything that you wake up in exactly the same positions – as if to signal a commitment that nothing changed while you were sleeping. Then after a while you start sneaking off on your own a little, to what becomes known as 'your side of the bed'. It don't mean nothing bad – you're not cooling off, maybe just getting more comfortable with each other. Lena and me are far more territorial these days, though I guess that space in between us is a reminder of where Thomas used to lie. But if it's a special night, if we gotta problem, maybe feeling threatened in some way, we still tend to lock our arms about each other. That night it was no surprise that we clung on until one of my arms had lost all feeling, and probably the same for her.

Not that we said a lot – well, no, that's not strictly true; we said everything, the Big Three, that harmonious trio we all believe will change the world and cure all its ills.

'I love you.'

'I love you too.'

I tried to give Jimmy plenty of space the following day, to maybe pretend that what he was engaged on wasn't that much of a concern, but when he didn't come back for lunch, well, that was it. I had to find out exactly what was going on.

The moment I walked in to the barn and he glanced up, I knew it wasn't good news.

'Tell me,' I said.

He gave a long sigh. 'I accelerated the action of one of the weevils when introduced to a host environment, ten times real-life speed.'

'And?'

'It died.'

I stared at him; that wasn't the answer I'd been expecting. 'Yeah?' I said, allowing a little hope to stray into my voice. 'That's it?'

'I thought so. Last night. This morning . . .'

He gestured for me to look at his screen. There were a few scraps of what was obviously a weevil in some liquid – I didn't know what it was, some kind of human synthesis, I guessed, but like I've said many times before, this wasn't my area of expertise and my brain never did travel that well.

'It's gone,' he told me.

'I don't understand.'

Again he sighed, this time even heavier, and I felt my apprehension writhing away like a pinned worm. Normally this would be the moment when he'd start to gloat, to tell me that only someone of his intelligence *would* understand, but on this occasion he was far too preoccupied.

'When I first got out here, saw it had gone, I thought it must've dissolved somehow – that it was one of those quirks of nature where a species seeks out its own demise.' He stopped almost as if he'd unexpectedly run out of breath, and I knew we'd reached detonation point. 'But it hasn't dissolved . . . it's metamorphosed.'

I stared at him, waiting for more, knowing it had to come.

'It's still doing it. Sometimes you can actually see it with the naked eye.'

I turned to the screen, watching as he brought up the magnification, but I couldn't see a thing.

'You remember what the Doc told you?' he asked. 'About Nora Jagger trying to find a way of getting implants into everyone?'

'Yeah.'

He paused, like he was hoping I'd say it for him, but I couldn't bear to put into words what was going through my head.

'I think this is it: the *Big Idea*. These things get inside you, find their way to where they can do most damage, then die. What's left then metamorphoses into an implant that continues to metamorphose so it can travel about every part of your body.'

'*Jesus!*' I gasped.

'I don't know what its purpose is exactly, but you don't have to think too hard to come up with possibilities. They could be used to locate someone, keep an eye on them, maybe even exert control over them.'

For a few moments we both fell to an aching silence. All our fears, our instincts, had been right: the Bitch was closing in – but never in our most paranoid of moments, our worst nightmares, had we imagined an invasion like this.

'I've made this scanner,' Jimmy told me, pointing to the makeshift device he'd been working on when I entered. 'It's real basic, but I think it'll do the job. I'm gonna have to scan everyone.'

'Why?' I asked, though of course I knew.

'Just in case,' he said, plainly trying hard not to sound too worried.

'But . . . we'd *know*, surely?'

Jimmy paused for a moment, looking that bit squeamish. 'You know that stuff that oozes outta them?'

'The green slime?'

'I think it's a kinda lubricant.'

Yet again I was reduced to staring at him, wondering what the hell he was gonna say next.

'It's also got anaesthetising properties,' he continued. 'They could slide in anywhere in your body and you wouldn't know a thing about it.'

'*Oh Jeez!*' I groaned.

He went quiet for a few moments, maybe giving me time to absorb what he'd said, and to tell the truth, I *was* kinda overwhelmed by the immensity – and yeah, I'll admit it – even the damn ingenuity of it. What chance did we have up against something like that?

We had to go and tell the others, gather them around the kitchen table and put them in the picture and, let's be honest, break their damn hearts for them. It was all over. Our utopia was hopelessly compromised. Nora Jagger was probably on her way at that very moment.

Delilah was more horrified by *how* a weevil might've got inside her than if she had one or not. 'You mean that thing might've crawled up—'

'Lile!' Jimmy interrupted. 'That ain't helping.'

'While I was sleeping!' she continued, refusing to be silenced.

'Stop it, will you?'

'Yeah, right!' she sneered, 'typical man. Don't give a damn we girls've got more openings to worry about.'

This time general howls of protest, sheer weight of numbers, made her reluctantly give way.

Lena was quietly sitting at the table with Thomas in her arms. 'Clancy?' she called, like she was cutting through a storm or bobbing over waves.

'He's fine,' I reassured her, immediately knowing what was on her mind.

'You sure?'

'Absolutely.'

'What happens if one of us *has* got a weevil inside them?' Hanna asked.

'It turns into an implant, stupid,' Gigi sneered. 'Weren't you listening?'

'No, I mean, what happens to the person who's got it?'

Yep, damned if she hadn't done it again: that girl always came up with the sixty-four-thousand-dollar question that no one wanted to try to answer. I turned to Jimmy and the little guy made this helpless face, like that was a whole other subject.

'No one has,' I declared confidently.

'But if they do,' Hanna persisted. 'If it can do what Jimmy says – track people, influence them, make them do stuff – are they going to stay here?'

'Maybe we shouldn't do this,' I muttered to Jimmy.

'Clancy,' Lena interrupted, 'we've got no choice.'

I turned and, as always, she felt my eyes on her and gave this slight shake of the head. She was a mother now, and protection of her child was her prime concern. It also went through my mind again about when I woke up with those things in my mouth – did I really manage to spit them all out?

We all traipsed over to the barn, Gigi and Gordie bickering about which one of them was going to go first, both trying to prove they were the toughest and meanest of us, that nothing worried them, 'til finally Jimmy decided we'd do it in alphabetical order, which of course meant me going first.

I had to take my shirt off, and despite the situation that was an invitation Lile simply couldn't resist, asking me if I was 'just gonna leave it at that?' Thankfully there was little other appetite for humour, and Jimmy told the others to go and wait at the far end of the barn.

He ran this thing over me, a kind of a metal pad, studying his screen while I just silently looked away and treated it as if I was having a jab or something.

'Okay, Big Guy,' he eventually said, indicating I could put my shirt back on.

I waited but he didn't say any more.

'Well?' I asked.

'I'm just gonna scan first,' he replied. 'The computer'll interpret it afterwards.'

'Right,' I grunted, discreetly withdrawing when I saw it was Delilah's turn next.

Gigi followed, complaining she wasn't stripping off in front of no old man, not for any reason, so Jimmy had to erect a curtain and instruct Delilah what to do while he checked the images on his screen.

One by one we went through the process 'til eventually we were left with the final person: our son, our little miracle, Thomas.

I could barely stand to watch it felt so wrong, so damned invasive, but I had to explain to Lena what was going on. Our baby son was lying there looking so small and vulnerable, threatening to cry at the coldness of the pad, the sternest of frowns on his bewildered little face. Jimmy went over him really carefully, I guessed for that reason – 'cuz he was so defenceless. Or maybe it was 'cuz it was that much more difficult to scan such a tiny body.

When he finally finished, Delilah complained that he hadn't done himself, but Jimmy told her he had earlier; that that was how he'd tested the equipment.

He immediately started switching things around, unplugging this, sliding in that, 'til finally he had his computer set up to read the scans. No one said a word, just stood there watching as he tapped and swiped, working his favourite arena like a pro, bringing up file after file.

'Come on, Jimmy!' Delilah complained.

'Okay, okay,' he replied, obviously having seen all he needed. 'I'm not enjoying this, Lile.'

'Has anyone got an implant?' she persisted.

''course they haven't!' I growled. 'Come on, Jimmy, stop milking it, man.'

But instead of giving us the all-clear, of assuring us that it'd just been a false alarm, he'd got that look about him, embarrassed and shifty, and I knew he had some bad news for someone, and I had a fair idea who it might be.

'Sorry, Big Guy,' he muttered.

There was a momentary silence, Lena gave this little moan and came and put an arm around me, holding Thomas with the other.

'I got one?' I asked Jimmy. 'You sure?'

'It's pretty clear once you know what you're looking for.'

'One of those things is inside me?'

This time he didn't say anything – and nor did anyone else.

'It won't change anything,' Lena said in little more than a whisper. 'It's always going to be you and me.'

I turned and looked into her face, those sightless eyes imploring me the way they sometimes do. The only thing was, she was wrong and had to know it. It *did* change things – it changed everything. If what Jimmy had said was true, that it could be used to track me down or dictate my behaviour, I was gonna be one helluva liability around here.

'Thing is,' Jimmy said, trying to dispense a few odd crumbs of comfort, 'they can't track you, can't do anything, without some kind of monitoring source. It's too far out for a Dragonfly, a fixed-wing ain't sufficiently manoeuvrable in the mountains – we haven't seen anything else.'

I paused for a moment, not wanting to say anything but feeling I had no choice. 'You sure?'

He knew immediately what I was talking about. 'Come on!' he scoffed. 'What did ya see?'

'Something was there,' I insisted.

He shook his head, like he wasn't prepared to even consider it, that it had no part in this discussion, and turned his attention back to the screen. 'Tell you what, as much as it hurts to say it . . . it's damn smart.'

'What is?' I asked.

'This,' he said, with reluctant admiration.

'Whose side are you on?'

'Think about it,' he said. 'A lotta people have gone missing in the country. She could spend for ever hunting them down – a few here, a few there – why would she bother? But once people get established, once there's a decent-sized group – enough to be a threat – they're gonna get organised, and what's the first thing they're gonna need? . . . Food! So they develop this seed with its own built-in parasite: an implant weevil. People think they're building a new future, becoming self-sufficient, when in fact, they're implanting themselves and dedicating their future to her . . . Not cool, I know, but shit, it's damn smart.'

'What about the animals that got burned?' Delilah asked, not fully following. 'George's dog, the wolves – where do they fit in?'

'And those two guys,' Gigi added.

'I guess the weevils were implanting *all* living creatures. Maybe it was a prototype that went wrong,' Jimmy suggested, but Hanna had other ideas.

'They were all killers,' she said, her voice so soft we almost missed it.

I turned to her, at first thinking it was a little out there even for her, but then began to see what she was saying, *and* that she was right. 'Jesus, yeah!' I gasped. 'That dog of George's was for ever killing rats, the wolves were about to kill the deer, and those guys had been about to kill me. Even the bird was some kinda hunter – *that* was the connection. All of them must've had punishment implants.'

'What about Clancy?' Lena asked Jimmy. 'Is his implant functioning?'

'Not properly. Not yet,' he replied. 'It seems to be configuring itself in some way, but I reckon it has to be turned on, keyed in some way, before it's fully operational.'

Again there was silence, the immensity of it, how quickly things had changed, almost too much to cope with, and finally I asked the question I'd wanted to ask from the moment he first told me.

'Can it be removed?'

'I dunno . . . Maybe. I'm no doctor.'

I don't think it was exactly his intention, but his words gave me the faintest cause for hope, the thought that there was something I could do.

I put my arms around both Lena and Thomas and joined her as she went to leave, the others tagging on behind, feeling it was time to go away and digest everything that'd been said.

But Jimmy hadn't quite finished. 'Sorry, guys . . . Sorry—' he called, before we reached the door. 'There's one other thing.'

We paused, waiting for his postscript, a summing-up, but he had that squirming uncomfortable look about him again, and this time I knew it was gonna be a whole lot worse.

'Someone else's got one, too.'

For the first time since Thomas was born, Lena cried openly, in fear and concern. Out here, in the middle of nowhere, and without any sign of trespass, our lives had been stolen from us. Bad enough *I* had an implant in me; but little Thomas as well . . . ?

I was so sure I'd protected him, that none of those damn things had got through, but sometimes blind faith isn't enough. Lena and me spent that night tossing and turning on a bed of nails, echoing each other's words of futile remorse. Meanwhile, the little guy was sleeping unusually peacefully, unaware that he'd been invaded, that he had this parasite going about his tiny body. He wasn't exactly sick, but I guess we felt that terrible dragging helplessness that every parent does when their child's in danger and there's nothing they can do about it. Over and over I kept telling Lena it would be all right, that we'd come up with something, but it was just noise and she knew it as well as I did.

Jimmy would do everything he could; we knew that, but we also knew that for once maybe even he was out of his depth. If those things kept changing all the time, one moment a tiny capsule lodged in a minor crevice of your brain, the next a liquid oozing its way around the streams and canals of your body, what chance did anyone have?

'What are we going to do?' Lena asked for the umpteenth time.

'I dunno,' I told her. 'Jimmy wants to scan me and Thomas again tomorrow, maybe get some ideas. You know what he's like,' I said, trying to sound encouraging.

'Yeah, and I know what *she's* like,' Lena replied.

I never said anything; after spending some time as Infinity's prisoner, she was better placed to talk about them – and, in particular, Nora Jagger – than I was.

'What if you and Thomas *can* be tracked?'

'I dunno,' I said, after yet another helpless pause.

'Are you willing to take the risk?'

I knew what she was getting at: was I prepared to chance leading the Bitch there, to maybe getting everyone killed – or at the very least, implanted?

'Let's see what Jimmy comes up with,' I told her.

For some time we both lay in stillness and silence, all talked and worried out, 'til finally her breathing became heavier and I realised she'd fallen asleep. It didn't take me long to appreciate that there was no chance of me following her, not with all the stuff I had pinballing around in my head, and I gently prised myself out of her arms and slid out of the bed.

I emerged out onto the porch that bit warily, making sure there were no weevils around, but I guessed they'd done their work already. Mind you, only Thomas and me had implants – would they keep coming back 'til they finally got one in everyone? How would it work otherwise, some with, some not? Was there some provision for that?

I couldn't stop thinking about what Lena'd said: was I prepared to take the risk of bringing Nora Jagger here? If only Thomas hadn't got an implant. If it'd been just me, yeah, it would've broken my heart, but I could've taken off on my own. As it was, knowing Lena as I did, I suspected it would be all three of us or no one at all.

It's truly amazing how light Hanna is on her feet. Admittedly I was lost in thought, staring blankly out at the mountains, but the first I knew that she was up and about was when she appeared at my side.

'Jesus! You frightened the hell outta me,' I complained.

'Sorry,' she said.

'Can't you sleep?'

'Not really.'

I paused for a moment, returning my gaze to the mountains. There was no point, nor need, for any pretence. We both knew how serious the situation was.

'Clancy?' she whispered.

'Yeah?'

'Don't leave us, will you?'

CHAPTER TEN

Lena was up before me in the morning and already out on the porch feeding Thomas. To see them there, bathed in fresh sunshine, against a canvas of the forest and the mountains, I tell ya, it was as perfect a scene as you could hope for. The only spoiler was that our baby boy had an implant burrowing away somewhere inside him, and for that matter, so did I.

I just prayed Jimmy would come up with something, though when I got over there, he didn't look that confident. He spent forever going over my body with that scan of his, barely saying a word apart from the occasional muttered expletive. Several times he lost the implant altogether, only to find it somewhere else entirely, morphed into a totally different form. He got me to hold onto Thomas while he did the same thing to him. The little guy had one of his wriggly days on, trying to rock himself over and maybe attempt a little crawling or scooting along on his stomach. Whatever, I wouldn't let him, and copped some pretty heavy-duty protesting while I held him down.

Eventually Jimmy let him go, shaking his head and giving one of his long sighs. I mean, he ain't exactly what you'd call a closed book, you always know pretty well what Jimmy's thinking, and it was obvious he was no further forward.

We never saw him again that day, not until night began to fall; it wasn't until the third time of asking that Lile finally persuaded him to come in.

Over dinner everyone did their best to pretend nothing was wrong, talking away about all manner of unrelated stuff, as if life was going on as normal, though we knew it couldn't.

'I been thinking,' I eventually said, knowing I couldn't put it off any longer, 'maybe it'd be best if I wasn't here.'

'What—! Why?' Lile cried.

'Big Guy!' Jimmy chimed in. 'Give me time, will ya?'

I paused for a moment, waiting for Lena to say something, knowing the next move was hers.

'We'd never forgive ourselves if we led Nora Jagger here,' she said.

I couldn't help but momentarily smile to myself: we 'd actually skirted around that discussion, and I hadn't wanted to assume, but like she often said: it's always gonna be me and her.

'Don't *you* take any responsibility,' I told her. 'It's *my* fault.'

'It's no one's fault,' Jimmy countered.

'Clancy, you *promised*!' Hanna protested.

The whole table fell to silence, no one knowing what else to say, and I couldn't help but feel that part of that was down to the fact that they knew we had a point.

'We could head off, see what happens, come back later,' I suggested.

Gigi gave this slight shrug, like that made a kinda sense to her but she wasn't sure how the others would take it.

'We're a family,' Delilah reminded us, in case anyone had forgotten. 'You're not going anywhere. Whatever's coming our way, we face it together . . . Agreed?' she said, asking the others.

They all nodded, though again Gigi had this look about her, as if she felt the discussion could be that bit more wide-ranging.

'What if they *can* track the implants?' Lena persisted.

'Give me a coupla days,' Jimmy said. 'It can't be that difficult.'

'Maybe we don't have a coupla days?' I told him.

But it didn't matter what we said, how valid our arguments, they wouldn't entertain the possibility of us leaving, and Hanna repeatedly reminded me that I'd made a promise.

'We'll sort it out,' were the last words Lile said as we went to retire. 'My little genius,' she added, putting her long, sinewy arms around Jimmy and kissing him on his bald head, 'he can do anything.'

Lena and me filed through to our bedroom but neither of us made any attempt to undress. We lay on the bed, our arms around each other, both silently going over the situation in our heads.

'What d'you think?' I eventually asked.

She paused as if she didn't want to say, but knew there was no other choice. 'We have to go.'

'Yeah,' I sighed. 'Me, too.'

We waited 'til we were sure everyone was asleep before quietly packing what we thought was essential. Lena extracted Thomas from his drawer and tied his blue and white blanket into a papoose. She hadn't been at all happy about it, but earlier had drunk a bit of hooch, not a lot, just enough that when she fed him she'd hopefully buy a little extra silence. The little guy did stir, but he almost immediately nodded off again. I got everything I could into my backpack, then snuck out into the kitchen and took a little food – just the absolute minimum; I didn't think it was right to take any more. When I saw I had the tiniest space left in my backpack, I grabbed my copy of *The Grapes of Wrath* and jammed that in there, too. Like I said, in some ways it reminded me of our situation, and now, with us heading out across country, it felt like there was even more of an affinity.

We didn't dare risk going out the front door, not with Gordie sleeping on the sofa, instead, softly, and agonisingly slowly, slid up the sash and climbed outta the side window. I felt so damn *guilty* – we both did – sneaking away in the middle of the night, leaving them to fend for themselves. What sorta friends were we? Then again, what choice did we have? For all we knew, Nora Jagger could've been on her way that very moment, and if she *was* tracking us, what we were doing might well lead her away from them.

'Where are we going?' Lena asked as we crossed the farmyard, at the last moment remembering the booby-trapped wire to the barn in front of her and veering around it.

'I dunno. The Interior, I guess,' I replied. I thought it'd be the safer option.

'Long way to anything,' she commented.

I paused for a moment, thinking it through. 'On foot,' I agreed.

'What d'you mean?'

I urged her to wait where she was and headed over to the barn.

'Clancy!' she hissed after me, but by the time that I'd returned she'd obviously worked it out, 'cuz she showed not the slightest surprise when I wheeled the tandem towards her. 'We can't go on that,' she told me.

'Put a lot more distance between us and them, and a damn sight quicker.'

She didn't take a great deal of convincing, especially as Thomas was starting to stir again, and within seconds the two of us had mounted up and were peddling away down the track, fearing a cry of discovery like a pair of common thieves.

'This feels so wrong,' Lena muttered.

'I know,' I told her, 'but it's not.'

Thank God it was a moonlit night and I could see where I was going. I glanced behind me, checking Lena and the baby were okay, despite the situation, smirking to myself. I mean, what kinda getaway was this, for chrissake? Our superheroes, laden down with baby and diaper-filled backpack, peddling off into the night on the weird and wonderful Typhoon Tandem.

I don't know how far we went exactly – a good ten miles, I'd guess – but eventually we had to get off the road, head up into the hills and over to the Interior, and immediately things became that much more difficult.

Jimmy had always claimed the tandem was an off-road vehicle, but he'd never actually tested it, and though we'd been cross-country a few times, it hadn't been laden down with lotsa stuff, or pedalled up and down some fairly steep hills. The main problem was that the only gears he'd been able to find were very old, making this a basic four-speed, and with all the bits and pieces he'd used to reinforce the frame, it was such a weight. It really wasn't up to the job. Particularly as we found ourselves having to get off and push more and more, and by sunrise all we'd managed was to get up one hill, freewheel down the other, and then start on the next one.

Thomas woke up with the birds, immediately starting to cry, and we decided the time had come to stop and feed him – and maybe have a little something to keep us going, too.

It was just as we were finishing off and packing our stuff back in the rucksack that I saw him, over to the side, a hundred, maybe a hundred and fifty yards away, wandering outta the trees a bit like he wasn't accustomed to daylight any more. At first I didn't recognise him, partly 'cuz of the way he was dressed, the state he'd got himself into, but more his general bearing, the way he was holding himself. Before, he'd been this relaxed guy, easy-going, full of energy; now everything about his posture looked tortured.

'What is it?' asked Lena, immediately sensing my reaction.

'It's Nick's boy . . . George? You know, whose dog got combusted.'

'Is he okay?'

'I don't know. Looks a bit odd . . . George!' I called out. '*George!*'

It was the weirdest thing: he might've been some way away but when he turned, even from that distance I saw an expression on his face that damn near stopped me dead. He was so white, so haunted – not so much the face of a ghost but of a corpse. For several achingly long seconds he just stood there, staring at us, then he appeared to panic and ran back into the trees.

'Jesus!' I muttered.

'What happened?' Lena asked.

'I dunno. Maybe he didn't recognise us.'

'Has he gone?'

I thought about jumping on the tandem and chasing after him, but there didn't seem to be much point; by the time we'd got organised and gone down and up, he could've been anywhere. 'Yeah,' I eventually replied.

'Just him?'

'Didn't see anyone else. No sign of the family.'

It was a mystery all right, but also a reminder that we might've been in the middle of nowhere but weren't necessarily alone. A lot of people were out there for a whole variety of different reasons and I'd've been willing to bet there were plenty who'd probably been used for implant experiments – or as we used to call them, 'crazies'.

For the rest of the morning we had to make our way through forest that became so dense, not only did it slow our progress, we were repeatedly getting lost. Or maybe it'd be truer to say that, as navigator, I kept getting lost. Trouble was, the tandem really needed a path, and I kept taking these ones that'd presumably been made by animals, only to realise time and again that their priorities were rather different to ours. We weren't looking for water, just a way out, and were constantly having to double back on ourselves.

We weren't giving too much thought to where we going, we just had some vague notion of 'inland' and as far away as possible. After all, cruel irony though it might've been, the further we got from those we loved, the safer they would be.

A couple of hours and several more hills later, this wall of daylight began to filter through the trees and we emerged out onto this huge open plain, most of it just scrub with the occasional lone tree, but mercifully flat, and the Typhoon Tandem soon came into its own again.

For some time neither Lena or me had said a word and it was pretty obvious why: try as we might, we couldn't shake off that burden of guilt. The gang would've discovered we'd gone by now. Jimmy'd be coming back from the barn, asking where I was, and Lile'd be saying that she thought I was with him and where the hell was Lena and Thomas come to that? They'd go into our bedroom and find it empty, and it wouldn't take them long to work out what we'd done. The kids'd be coming in, Hanna shedding a tear or two, setting off Delilah ... *Oh shit!*

In a strange way it kinda helped, reminding us of who we were trying to protect, and our progress became even more determined. I was driving my old legs as hard as I could, ignoring my bitterly complaining muscles. Our only stops were determined by Thomas, and when he started up again mid-afternoon, throwing in a few tears for good measure, we headed for one of those solitary trees for a little rest and shelter.

Lena fed and changed him, stowing the dirty diaper for when she had a chance to wash it, and that'd obviously been the problem 'cuz the little guy's mood immediately changed and he began smiling and chuckling, waving his pudgy little hands and feet in the air, instantly cheering up his mother no end. Mind you, after a few moments it kinda rebounded on her; she caught her breath and turned away and I knew she'd been thinking about his implant.

'Can you feel it?' she asked me.

I turned to her, knowing immediately what she was talking about. 'Nope.'

'He's been crying a lot.'

'Hey,' I said, 'that kid is to crying what a vampire is to blood.'

'I hope Jimmy's right,' she said, ignoring my feeble attempt at humour.

'What?'

'That it's got to be keyed.'

I just shrugged. What the hell did I know, other than what Doctor Simon had told me and what I feared to be true: that the Bitch was gonna use them to take over the world.

'It'll be all right,' I told her, damning myself for coming out with the same old weary platitudes, but having no idea what else I could say. 'Promise.'

I put my arm around her, Thomas still cooing and smiling away in her lap, obviously having no idea of the situation, and thank the Lord for that. 'Come on,' I said, 'let's go.'

There was this ribbon of hills in the distance and we decided to make it our target for the night, but the plain, which up to that point had been pretty smooth-going, started to throw up a few obstacles and we rode into areas so wet our tyres began to disappear into the mire. We had to turn back and work our way around, rather than risk being swallowed up by the ground. Other times there were these huge areas of brambles, impenetrable fortifications that once again forced our retreat.

In the end it got to the point where exhaustion simply overwhelmed us and we had to stop for the night under one of those rare trees, as if they were Nature's hitching posts. The night got so dark it was as if we were in the shadows of the walls at the edge of the Universe. I had to use a torch to sort through what we had left to eat, which I wasn't very happy about. No place ever fitted the description 'the middle of nowhere' better than that one, but with everything that'd been going on, I didn't want to advertise our presence to anyone or anything.

I thought about conjuring up some kinda makeshift weevil protection – I didn't expect to see any out there, but what did I know? But what with our lack of sleep the previous night and a whole day of peddling and pushing that heavy tandem, I was so tired I more or less passed out where I was lying, and habitual insomniac or not, slid away to the next world before Lena could even settle Thomas next to her.

I guess it was for that reason – that I was so drained – that whoever it was, was able to sneak up on us so easily. I awoke to the sound of Lena's screams, just about able to make out in the darkness that she was backing away from someone and towards me, holding onto Thomas for grim death, determined to protect him.

It was the old 'big guy' instinct, I guess: I leaped forward, staying low, pivoting on one hand and sweeping out with my feet, sensing more than anything that there was someone in the shadow of the tree. I made heavy contact with a body, kicking them around about the knees with enough force to knock them sideways, and took the opportunity to put myself between Lena and Thomas and our attacker.

'He's got a knife,' Lena warned, guessing I'd been about to dive in, and I realised he must've somehow threatened her before I awoke, that that was what'd set her off. It was so damn dark if I rushed him there was every chance I'd impale myself, so I stayed where I was, not making a sound, crouched in front of Lena and Thomas, protecting her the same way she was protecting him, like those Russian dolls, each one covering the other.

I remembered the torch and started fumbling around until I finally found it near my backpack. It wasn't that heavy, but it'd surely hurt if you hit the right spot. I took a coupla swings, just in case the attacker was making a move our way, but there was nothing but empty air.

Finally he ran at me and I raised the torch, ready to hit him as hard as I could, but d'you know, he went to sidestep me – his only apparent interest was Lena and Thomas. I turned and swung in his direction, and managed to smash down on what I hoped was the hand holding the knife.

'Clancy!' Lena cried, not knowing what'd happened.

'It's okay,' I reassured her.

There are certain things in life a man will do anything to protect, and I guess his family is right at the top of that list. I swung at our attacker again, missing a coupla times, then hitting him unexpectedly hard on the shoulder, the force of the impact jarring the torch outta my hand. He lunged at me, his knife actually pierced my coat, but thankfully not my body. But d'you know, again he didn't bother with me, just headed for Lena and Thomas, and the moment I realised that was what he was doing, I dived at him, trusting in God his knife wasn't directed my way, grabbing him around the neck and shoulders and dragging him away. Lena was up and at him like some wild thing, Thomas still in her arms, repeatedly kicking him, while I just about tore his arm off in my efforts to get rid of that damn knife. Finally he dropped it, making the contest a whole lot fairer, and I promptly hit him as hard as I damn well could. He flew backwards and fell over the tandem on the ground. I scrambled across to hit him again but tripped over that thing myself and by the time I was up, he was away, his footsteps rapidly retreating into the distance.

'Are you okay?' I called to Lena.

'Yeah. Yeah, we're fine,' she said, trying to calm Thomas, making sure he was all right, though the amount of noise he was making, there wasn't a lot wrong with his lungs. 'You sure he's gone?'

'I reckon,' I said, locating the torch, finding it still worked, shining it in the direction our attacker had fled, realising that was probably how he'd spotted us – when I'd used it earlier.

'*Why?*' Lena cried, every bit as shocked and confused as I was.

'Don't ask me.'

'Was he trying to kill me or Thomas?'

'I dunno.'

'What if he comes back?'

'He won't,' I said firmly, 'not without his knife.' Though really, I had no idea. 'Go back to sleep.'

'Are you kidding?' Lena cried.

I paused for a moment, trying to calm the situation, to treat it like a one-off. 'I'll stay on watch. I'm the insomniac, remember?'

It took a lotta persuasion, but eventually, with Thomas in her arms and her in mine, my back set to the tree, she did finally fall back to sleep.

I just sat there, my ears stretching out into the darkness, listening as hard as I could, though I really didn't expect him to come back. His knife had flown over into the scrub somewhere and it went through my head that maybe I should think about trying to find it in the morning.

There was just one thing I didn't understand. Mind you, it was one helluva concern. I hadn't said anything to Lena – she'd found it difficult enough to fall asleep as it was – but despite how dark the night had been, while I was wrestling with our attacker, I'd realised I'd known who it was.

It was one helluva shock, believe me. I couldn't get my head around it at all. *Why the hell had George followed us out here and attempted to kill my lover and child?*

CHAPTER ELEVEN

I did doze off for half an hour or so, slipping over the precipice, barely able to claw my way back up, waking to see Lena feeding Thomas, her eyes still closed, obviously trying to grab an extra few minutes.

Without a word I began to sort out what little food we had left, both of us, I reckoned, not only exhausted, but also that bit depressed by the turn of events. I just couldn't get over who'd attacked us – George was one of the nicest, most upstanding young guys you were ever likely to meet.

'You okay?' Lena asked wearily.

'Not really.'

'What is it?'

I took a deep breath, knowing I didn't have much choice but to tell her. 'I know who it was last night.'

'Who attacked us?' she asked, despite her blindness her eyes suddenly snapping open.

'Yeah.'

'Who?'

'George.'

'Who we saw earlier?'

'Yeah . . . I thought he looked a bit strange.'

'Oh my God,' Lena groaned, like it was the final proof the world had gone crazy – not that we needed it.

For a while we both sat in silence, as if we were determined not to discuss it, not to let it affect us in any way.

'Gotta get up into those hills,' I eventually ventured, tearing off half of our last piece of stale flatbread, pouring a little oil over it and placing it in front of her.

Lena juggled Thomas from one arm to the other, then began to eat.

'We'll find somewhere to settle,' I continued, trying to sound optimistic, 'where we can live off the land.'

For a moment she never said anything and I wondered what was going through her head. 'They're just going find us again,' she eventually sighed. 'You know they are.'

'I don't know anything,' I replied.

'Especially with what you've got inside you.'

I never said any more. I could've argued the point, reminded her that Jimmy didn't think they were functioning yet, but I preferred to ignore the whole subject. I mean, hopefully it'd been my imagination, but a coupla times in the night I'd had this sense that I could feel it inside me, like an ice-cold chrysalis lodged somewhere deep in my brain, its inhabitant occasionally stirring, getting ready to slide out and take me over.

Whether I was getting carried away or not, it was still deeply disturbing. Doctor Simon had told me a little about the implants, but I'd never thought about them from the point of having one – and anyway, was the weevil implant the final solution or just one more experiment that might malfunction? Whatever, it was getting harder and harder to ignore, not to give in to a wave of revulsion that was bidding me to reach down inside my throat and tear that damn thing outta me.

A little later we packed up everything, I helped Lena secure Thomas, she helped me secure the backpack, and we wearily mounted the tandem and rode away.

It took us a couple more hours but finally we reached the hills and soon we had to get off and push again. I'll tell ya, that crazy tandem might've been a blessing some of the time, but the rest it was a damn curse.

It wasn't long before we had to stop, both of us out of breath, and I took the opportunity to look back across the wide expanse of the plain.

'Not a soul,' I commented.

Lena nodded, her mood now slightly more approachable. 'Where are we going exactly?' she asked, which was a good question.

'We'll know when we get there,' I replied, the light tone in my voice begging her not to pursue the subject.

She sighed but didn't say any more and the two of us continued our climb, not so much pushing the tandem as leaning on it and letting it slip out from beneath us.

When we got to the top, we were rewarded by a whole range of hills, hazy blue-green swells and folds repeating as far as I could see, most of them covered by forest. I hesitated for a few moments, beginning to wonder how much longer the tandem would be useful, but Lena had her mind on other things. She started to sniff, like she'd caught the scent of something.

'Wood smoke,' she said, and I looked around, squinting as hard as I could – if she said it was there, it was somewhere. And sure enough, I spotted this slight blue trail wafting out of a valley a couple of hills over.

'Yeah. Over there,' I told her, pointing in its direction and placing her hand on mine.

'What does it look like?'

'I dunno. Could be anything.'

'Let's go and see,' she commented, sounding just that bit hopeful.

'Okay,' I replied. I mean, I knew she was right, we had to check it out, but I was a long way from comfortable about it.

We eased slowly down the first hill, hanging onto the brakes to stop the tandem running away from us, swerving left and right to avoid trees, Thomas making these little cooing noises, though whether out of joy or fear, I really couldn't say. At the bottom it was a climb and a push back up the other side, and from that summit, a slower descent down towards the source of the smoke.

About halfway down we decided to stop and hide the tandem. If we did have to make a run for it, we didn't want to be pushing its weight back up the hill. I did suggest to Lena that I went on alone, that her and Thomas should wait, but she brushed it aside, as if, just at that moment, she really didn't care what happened.

As we got closer, I could see through the trees occasional glimpses of a clearing and a camp: lots of simple shelters made out of branches, even the occasional tent.

'I'm not sure about this,' I muttered, stopping for a moment, but Lena wouldn't hear of it.

'Come on.'

Somewhat against my better judgement we worked our way further down; I was beginning to appreciate that the clearing was bigger than I'd first thought, with a lot more people. I hesitated, lurking behind this large tree, aware that it had to be my decision – I was the one who could see. Was this a village for refugees, or a camp for crazies?

We were just standing there, awaiting my verdict, whether we should go and introduce ourselves or not, when this guy came out of nowhere – older, a bit of a limp, like Jimmy – and walked past carrying some firewood.

'Who was that?' Lena asked.

'Some guy. Barely gave us a glance.'

She shrugged, like surely that confirmed it was okay, and we cautiously followed in his footsteps, still ready to turn and run at a moment's notice.

There must've been thirty or forty dwellings varying in size from those able to house a small family right down to those not much bigger than a grave. Most of them were set in a tight communal circle, but there were a few outcrops elsewhere, plus the occasional solitary dwelling right on the edge of the forest. The thing that impressed me most, that was noticeable straight away, was the atmosphere. That smoke drifting leisurely up into the sky said it all. There was a real sense of peace and relaxation about the place. Why, I didn't know; maybe being so far out gave them a greater sense of security? One or two looked over, a couple waved, but no one actually bothered us . . . leastways, not at first.

I guess I should've seen it coming. We were just idly wandering around, wondering who to approach, or if anyone would approach *us*, when as we're passing this small shelter a woman came out, emerging on her hands and knees, stretching herself once she was able to stand upright.

I guess she was in her forties; small and dark, with the kinda face that made you think she might've had problems with alcohol in the past. Her jowls were so heavy you wouldn't have thought her able to express emotion, yet she let out this cry of excitement and rushed over and I realised she'd caught a glimpse of Thomas' leg, hanging outta the papoose.

'Whaddya got?' she asked, her voice that of a curious child.

Lena instantly untied the blanket and wrapped it around Thomas, trying to not reveal him, but it was too late.

'Is thatta *baby*?' the women asked incredulously.

Lena turned to me for guidance on how she should react, but I wasn't sure myself. 'Yes,' she eventually replied.

'He's sleeping,' I said, as if that might mean something.

'*She's gotta baby!*' the woman shouted, at first completely ignored by the other villagers, as if she was well known for saying odd things, but she just kept on, '*It's a baby!*'

Finally, in ones and twos, people began to wander across, more out of wanting to know what was going on, I reckoned, than believing what was being said. But when the cry started to be taken up by others, a real surge swept around the village. I just stood there wondering what the hell was about to happen, if I was gonna have to fight for my partner and child again, cursing myself for not having anticipated such a reaction. After all, if Doctor Simon had been telling the truth, none of them had seen a baby in *years*, so it was hardly surprising how they were behaving. More and more of them started to make their way over, streaming outta shelters and even outta the forest: it was like the Baby Jesus was back in town.

'It's okay,' I whispered to Lena, praying it would be.

We just stood there, surrounded by the gathering crowd, all jostling in on us. I was ready to start swinging at the first sign of trouble, but I soon appreciated there wasn't gonna be any; that all they wanted was to take a look at the little guy. As one they all began cooing and awing, expressions on their faces of the simplest joy, a couple of older women and a man wiping away their tears.

'He looks like my Ronnie!' one woman cried. 'Ronnie!' she repeated, as if Thomas had somehow reconnected her with her lost family.

It wasn't long before the little guy woke up, his bottom lip immediately tucking down at the corners, soon bursting out into what he does best – and you know what? They absolutely loved it! A choir of angels singing God's latest composition wouldn't have got a more enthusiastic response. When Lena finally persuaded him to stop, I thought they were gonna give him a round of applause. For sure, it seemed to confirm everything the Doc had said – that there hadn't been any babies born, or at least, none that anyone there had seen.

I don't know how long we stood there, Lena clutching the little guy to her like a mother bird enfolding her chick within her wing; just about everybody'd had a peep, but there was no sign of their enthusiasm waning. I was starting to wonder how we'd bring this to an end when this woman emerged from what was probably the most substantial dwelling in the village and started making her way across, looking a little like we'd disturbed her sleep.

She stopped when she saw us, a look of real surprise on her face. 'You know, it amazes me how everyone seems to end up here.'

'Is that right,' I replied, not entirely sure of her attitude.

'My theory is we've chosen a bad place: that if people want to run away into the Interior, once they get over the mountains, the natural contours of the land lead them this way.' She hesitated for a moment, giving me a slightly weary but still welcoming smile. 'Ya don't remember me, d'you?'

I stared at her more closely. I guessed she was around the same age as me, stocky, roughly cropped thick silver hair, a no-nonsense expression – like the teacher who used to terrorise you at school – and the way she moved, the way she handled herself, she looked to be in pretty good shape, too. But no, I didn't remember her. 'Sorry.'

'I was a buddy of Bailey's,' she told me, holding out her hand and giving mine a surprisingly firm squeeze.

Again I studied her . . . And this time – *yeah!* I did remember her! She was one of the ex-soldiers who'd fought against the Wastelords that night – when we'd descended that steep hill in the fog she'd taken a bit of a fall, along with a couple of others; later she'd done everything she could to save Bailey.

'Sheila!' I said, the name popping outta nowhere.

Poor Bailey, he was maybe the bravest and most ornery Villager on the Island. He died at the hands of a group of machete-wielding Wastelords, but the old soldiers he'd recruited were probably the difference that night – well, them and the kids.

Sheila was about to add something more when the first woman who'd spoken to us tugged at her sleeve, like a little girl trying to get her attention. 'She's gotta baby,' she said, pointing at Lena.

Sheila might've been an old soldier, and a pretty tough one at that, I reckoned, but her reaction was no different from anyone else's. She peered over the top of the blanket and immediately broke into that now familiar expression of universal joy. 'Will you look at that,' she purred, and for once Thomas was awake but undemanding, gaping back at all those gaping at him. 'I haven't seen a baby since I was sent out to the Island.'

'He's *beautiful*!' the dark little woman cried, then, 'Handsome,' she corrected herself.

Sheila took in the situation, that we were obviously feeling a little hemmed in by all this simple-natured, slightly overwhelming enthusiasm, and invited us into her lean-to. There were several groans and protests but she just waved them away, and Lena and me stepped into a dwelling that had obviously been laboured over for some time. Some of the timbers had been smoothed off, with proper joints and cross-beams for extra strength. Smoked meat and a couple of pheasants were hanging from one of the beams, and there was even a small portable generator and a coupla cans of what I presumed to be gas, in the corner.

Sheila couldn't keep her eyes off the little guy, acting as if he was a new-born unicorn or something, shaking her head and smiling in disbelief. 'That's the most wonderful sight I've seen in a very long time.'

'You won't say that when he starts crying,' Lena told her.

For some time the little guy remained the centre of attention, with an awful lot of cooing and ahhhing going on, but I had a lotta questions and a growing curiosity.

'So how did you end up out here?' I asked.

'Just happened,' Sheila replied. 'When we finally got outta that hellhole of a city we kept going 'til we couldn't smell it any more – over the mountains, the hills, across the plain, 'til finally we stopped. There were five of us then, three of us Island escapees. Since then – you've probably noticed – we've become something of a haven for those desperately in need of shelter.'

I don't know why, but despite taking an immediate liking to her, I found that a little odd. It was a nice enough spot, and I guess there was plenty of food around – I'd seen deer being smoked on our way in – but I still didn't fully understand. Why *there*? So many *challenged* folk, and for some reason they apparently all felt safe and secure. Did it have anything to do with that atmosphere we'd felt when we arrived? Was that part of the attraction?

'Where're the rest of ya?' Sheila asked. 'The mad little guy—?'

'Jimmy,' I said.

'Yeah.' She grinned. 'God, did he move the world ten yards sideways.'

'They're back a ways,' Lena said, jumping into the conversation, I guessed 'cuz she wanted to ensure I didn't tell Sheila why we'd headed off on our own. 'On a farm.'

'Well, if you're out here looking for somewhere else to settle, you're more than welcome. All of you.'

'Thanks,' I said, though still nagged by the idea that we weren't getting the whole story; that she wasn't letting on about something.

'We gotta few characters – a few oddballs,' she added, 'but all told, it works pretty well.'

I hesitated but decided that if there was something she wasn't telling us, the best way to earn a confidence was to give one. I related just about our entire story, right from when we got off the Island: being trapped in the City, Lena being kidnapped, Arturo being killed, and of course, busting into the Infinity building and confronting the Bitch.

'Thank God you're outta that,' Sheila commented.

'Yeah,' I agreed, deciding I wouldn't say anything about implants for the moment.

She offered us something to eat, and we gratefully accepted, following her back outside and sitting around the fire in front of her hut. The small dark woman – Sheila introduced her as Isobel – came over with several others, wanting to see the baby again, but Sheila shooed them away.

One thing I gotta say about Sheila: I don't know where she learned, but she sure could cook. In fact, she had that air about her, like she'd excel at just about anything she put her mind to. I reckoned she could probably shoot a deer from a thousand paces so it suffered no pain at all, whip you up a gourmet meal and serenade you with a coupla bawdy drinking songs at the same time. Even allowing for how hungry we were, I swear it was the most delicious meat I'd ever tasted, and though I ain't never been much of a salad guy, that wild stuff she'd picked, well, I'd happily eat it anytime.

Lena also made a bit of a pig of herself, accepting Sheila's offer of more meat, the pair of us sitting there chomping away with well-satisfied smiles on our faces. Thomas was propped up in Lena's lap, studying everything going on, even sampling a little of his ma's food, though he immediately made this revolted face and spat it out.

I tell ya, what with the warmth of the fire, the unusually rich food, how little we'd slept those last few days, and yeah, maybe a feeling that we were safe and amongst friends, it was no time at all before we fell asleep.

I don't know how long we were there exactly; an hour or so, I'd guess. All I did know was suddenly being awakened by Lena screaming and yelling at the top of her voice.

'Where's Thomas?' she wailed, groping all around her, blindly fumbling her way across the ground. '*Where's my baby?*'

It was one of those moments when you could believe the whole world had stopped to listen. That everywhere, from pole to pole, people were still and silent, standing with horrified expressions on their faces, waiting to hear what would happen next. The only sound to be heard was Lena screaming, all that you knew, the absolute terror of a mother who'd lost her child.

I scrambled to my feet, instantly realising that I should've been more careful, that I'd been far too quick to let my guard down. I'd *known* there was something odd about that place. And where the hell was Sheila, for chrissake? Had *she* taken Thomas? I looked all around, spinning left and right, being her eyes, hoping for a glimpse of something that might help us, in that moment seeing Isobel hurrying our way, Thomas in her arms.

'It's all right! It's all right—! He's here!' she cried, running over and putting him in Lena's arms.

I thought Lena was gonna deck her – I truly did. 'What the fuck!' she screamed.

'I'm sorry, I'm sorry!' Isobel wailed, promptly bursting into tears.

'How dare you!'

'I'm sorry!' Isobel repeated. 'You were sleeping, he was wriggling around, trying to turn over – I was scared he might get burned by the fire.'

'Don't *ever* take my baby!' Lena yelled. 'Not for *any* reason!'

'Lena . . . He's all right,' I said, trying to calm things down, realising it was her blindness speaking as much as anything, her helplessness in such an immediate situation. 'It was my fault – I should've stayed awake.'

Sheila came hurrying back, alerted by the screams, carrying a couple of cans I guessed she used for fetching water from the nearby stream. 'What's going on?'

'Nothing, just a misunderstanding,' I told her.

'Isobel!' she challenged, turning on her like a mother who always thinks her child's the one who's done something wrong.

'*I'm sorry!*' she wailed, her face all white and wide-open with distress.

'It's okay! Really,' I insisted, a little alarmed at just how upset she was. 'No harm done.'

In the end, everyone calmed down: Lena apologised to Isobel, Isobel kept apologising to her, and I think Sheila and me threw in a couple more just for good measure. I mean, it was nothing if not understandable: any mother would be fiercely protective of her child, let alone under these circumstances.

For the rest of the afternoon, Lena wouldn't let go of Thomas – even I had to fight for my turn with the little guy. Sheila told us we could stay as long as we wanted, that she would make up a shelter for herself and we could use her place, but we were much too mindful of the implants and what we might bring down on them. Finally we agreed to stay for the night, and 'cuz of her kindness, I insisted on spending the last hours of daylight building up her pile of firewood.

The clearing wasn't entirely natural: they'd chopped down a few trees, but only for building materials; firewood had to be gathered the traditional way. Lena and me wandered out into the forest, picking up as much dry and dead wood as we could. Thomas was making it a little difficult for her, but she still brought back the best part of an armful, throwing it on the pile and going back out again. We had to go further out the second time, the natural regeneration of the forest obviously not able to keep up with the demands of the growing Commune.

In the middle of this dense, dark concentration of trees, we came across this small open area – I mean, in its own way it was kinda magical. There was a rather dirty-looking pond, but it was plainly the waterhole of choice, for all around various animals and birds were waiting their turns to drink, all obeying some kinda instinctive hierarchy. You could almost imagine it as a social gathering, that at any moment they were gonna burst into a song-and-dance routine from one of those old cartoons.

There was a fair amount of noisy fleeing and flapping when we appeared, but most didn't go very far. Lena walked Thomas forward, listening to the various screeching and snorting sounds she could hear and giving him a cooing rundown on who she thought was making them.

At first the little guy cottoned onto her enthusiasm, but it wasn't long before he started thinking about other things, giving out with noisy demands to be fed that appeared to take even some of the louder wildlife by surprise.

Lena squatted down next to a tree and taking out a breast, silenced him, and for a few moments I just stood there watching Mother Nature from the front row – then I decided I might be better employed carrying on looking for firewood.

I walked in a semicircle around the clearing, meeting this kinda cliff-face that formed a back wall to the area. Bearing in mind we were in the middle of a forest, there was a surprising shortage of anything to burn. Every now and then I'd glance back through the trees at Lena, just to make sure her and Thomas were all right, that I still had them in my sight, but I guess I got distracted, just for a few moments.

There was this large broken branch hanging onto a tree by a sinew or two, ideal for firewood. I had to jump up and give it a real tug and a twist, dragging it down 'til eventually it broke off. I glanced back towards Lena, wondering what she'd made of the noise – if she'd guessed at my clumsy antics and was having a little chuckle to herself. She was still squatting next to the tree, Thomas in her arms, but it was the way she was locked absolutely still, listening so intently, that alerted me. At first I didn't get it, then I saw this figure slipping through the trees towards her.

I think I hesitated for a moment 'cuz of what happened earlier with Isobel, 'cuz of that misunderstanding and not wanting to have another, but something about the purposeful way that guy was moving made me forget all about that and I started to run, shouting to Lena, warning her. She momentarily turned my way, as if assessing how far I was from being able to help, then turned back in the direction of the advancing figure, sensing there was danger even though she couldn't see the heavy club raised over his head, nor know who it was holding it.

She didn't stand a chance. She had the baby in her arms, his defence her first priority; she was blind, she couldn't have been more vulnerable – and George must've known it. I wasn't gonna get to her in time; I could see that already. I couldn't take those blows for her; I couldn't fight her fight. He drew the club back, ready to smash it down on her defenceless head, and she instinctively crouched over Thomas, putting a hand up to protect herself. I screamed out in protest, even in that moment realising I was dealing with a madman, that it would do no good, then suddenly – *oh my God!* – I heard a frighteningly familiar sound.

I couldn't believe it . . . *What the hell?* George was lying there, damaged to death, his body violently twitching, the excess power in him finding its way out of every pore. It couldn't be—! It just couldn't—! Surely they'd all been destroyed . . .

I grabbed Lena and helped her up while she clutched Thomas to her body like some over-protective marsupial.

'What happened?' she asked.

'It was George – he must've followed us,' I told her, staring down at that frozen face of horror, his eyes so wide they were leaking blood.

'But what *happened* to him?'

I paused for a moment, still not believing it even as I spoke the word. '. . . satellite.'

'*What?*' she gasped, every bit as shocked as I was.

'Looks like it.'

I could see people running through the trees towards us, Sheila in the lead, wearing a kinda vest, like she'd been working out. It was only when they reached us, when they were all gathered around, that I realised something: they were concerned all right – but they weren't that surprised.

So that was it: that was what was so unusual about that place; that was what Sheila had been offering us: an old form of policing and protection.

'What the hell happened?' she asked.

'He must've been following us,' I told her. 'George.'

'You know him?'

'Yeah. Friend of mine's boy – great kid – or at least, he used to be.'

'Jesus—'

'Why didn't you tell us?' I interrupted.

She looked a little embarrassed, for a moment not knowing how to reply. 'We decided – when we first found out – we wouldn't tell anyone. People would make their own fates.'

I saw immediately what she meant. 'So if they behave themselves, they don't need to know; if they don't, they find out soon enough?'

'Something like that.'

'How d'you find out?' Lena asked.

'Originally we'd just camped here for a few days, then there was a fight and someone pulled a knife – out of the blue he got zapped. It came as big a shock to us as it did you. I reckon it got hit, like all the rest, but it didn't come down, just got knocked off its orbit. For sure it's damaged – it doesn't always work – but it's up there, limping around, watching over us . . . Anyway, we talked it over and decided to stay.'

'I thought I'd seen the last of them,' I muttered.

'Thing is,' Sheila continued, 'word's starting to get out. That's why a lot of those who feel especially vulnerable have ended up here.'

I could've almost burst out laughing: all those years of trying to get away from those things and now people were gathering to shelter under one. And yet, bearing in mind what was going on – the Bitch and her Bodyguard, all the implant crazies – it did make a kinda sense.

Some of the villagers were getting a little upset at the sight of George's body, whining and pointing, and Sheila asked a couple of guys – I didn't recognise them, but I bet they were the old soldiers from the Island – if they'd mind burying it in the forest. We walked back with her to the Commune and her hut, my arm still firmly around Lena. I mean, can you imagine how that must've felt? For someone to have attacked you and your baby, hell-bent on battering you both to death, then being zapped by a satellite right next to you – and you didn't see any of it? Not to mention *who* it was. And that was another question that needed answering: *What the hell had happened to George?*

'Now that you know,' Sheila said, squatting down to chivvy up her fire, 'you can see how useful Jimmy'd be around here. He could maybe sort that satellite out, make it do more what we want. I mean, maybe things are just fine where you are, but you gotta be out here for a reason.'

She put some water in her coffee pot and put it back on the fire. I turned to Lena and as usual she was way ahead of me, giving a slight nod.

'Thing is,' I said, 'as we're being honest, you wouldn't really want us. Or not me, anyway.'

'Whaddya mean?'

'You're right, we are out here for a reason ... Me and the little one've got something inside us.'

'Implants?'

I nodded.

'What sort?'

'Not sure.'

'Weevils?'

'Yeah.'

I was half expecting her to tell us to leave then and there, that we were a liability, that Infinity could be on their way at any moment, but she looked more concerned on our behalf.

'How long?'

'Three days.'

She thought for a moment, then sighed. 'Five to go.'

I stared at her, not understanding. 'Sorry?'

'More if you're lucky.'

'Five days?' Lena asked.

Sheila paused, realising we hadn't kept up. 'That's what I've been told, at any rate: it starts to work immediately, analysing you and configuring itself, working on your thoughts and behaviour, but it doesn't actually take over 'til it's been keyed.'

'Jimmy said something about being "keyed" – so what does it?'

'Don't ask me,' she said, holding her hands up. 'I just hear stuff from people passing through. This is a bit of a crossroads.'

'Did you ever hear of anyone getting one removed?' I asked.

'Nope,' she replied. 'In the City maybe.'

I turned her words over in my head a minimum number of times. As far as I could see, we were left with only one course of action. 'We gotta go,' I told Lena, immediately getting up.

'Where?' she asked, a little taken aback.

'Back to the farm. Then I'll take Thomas with me into the City.'

'I'm coming with you.'

'Lena, no – I'm sorry. Not for this,' I told her.

'I can't lose you both,' she said.

'If we've got five days—'

'*Maybe!*' she interrupted.

'At least it gives us a chance. After that,' I paused, really not wanting to complete the sentence, 'maybe we won't even know who you are.'

She turned towards me. She might not be able to see my face but she could read all too clearly what was in my mind, and she didn't like it one little bit.

'If anyone can get rid of these implants it's Doctor Simon,' I told her. 'And he'd do *anything* for Thomas.' I was already collecting our things, aware that we had a deadline, that we didn't have a minute to waste – that each and every second took me and Thomas that bit closer to the rule of the Bitch.

Lena allowed my urgency to sweep her along, though I knew the subject was a long way from fully discussed. Sheila took us back into her shelter and gave us a substantial amount of cooked meat to take, then showed us this flap at the back where we could squeeze out and not have to run the gauntlet of what would undoubtedly have been a protracted farewell. It meant a bit of a detour, but Sheila knew the forest like the back of her hand and soon we were weaving through the trees, climbing the hill.

She burst out with loud laughter when we pulled the tandem out of its hiding place. 'You came on *that*?'

'It's okay on the flat,' I said, a little defensively. 'Not so great on the hills, I grant you – or not going *up*.'

She hugged us and wished us both farewell, and reminded us to ask the others how they felt about moving to the Commune, then stood there waving as we pushed the Typhoon Tandem up the slope, her steadfast face slowly disappearing into the dusk of evening and the dark of the forest.

When we reached the top, I paused for a moment and took a look back. I couldn't get over that place: all of those people down there sheltering under the protection of a rogue punishment satellite – and yeah, I guessed they were safer, and it was a nice enough spot, but in some ways they had no more freedom than we'd had back on the Island.

'Let's go,' I said, helping a rather subdued Lena and Thomas onto the tandem, managing to balance myself on the front despite the extra weight of the meat Sheila'd given us.

No matter how anxious I was to make every second of our time count, once we were out on the plain, I knew my plan to ride throughout the night wasn't gonna work. This great oil slick of a cloud slid out across the sky, prematurely bringing down the night, emptying its contents over us as if outta buckets.

I did my best to keep going, Lena's silence not only damning my obstinacy but probably adding to it; however, it almost cost us dearly. I'd noticed how much harder it was getting to peddle, that the wheels didn't seem to want to turn so easily, and belatedly realised I'd steered us straight into a swamp; that the ground wasn't just soft beneath us, it was swallowing us up.

Almost immediately we lost balance and went over, Lena's cry behind me as much of anger and impatience as of distress. I tried to push my way back, to return us to firmer ground, but there was nothing to brace myself against and it felt a bit like I'd steered us in to this big muddy mouth that was now sucking us down as hard as it could.

I soon realised I had to stop struggling, try to lie flat and prevent myself sinking any further, but the rain was beating down on me like fists, pummelling me as if it was the bog's accomplice, and I continued to sink ever lower.

I couldn't move, couldn't even risk turning to see where Thomas and Lena were; even the action of calling to them seemed to drive me down that bit quicker. It was an utterly unexpected horror, and

I gotta admit, as the rain pounded down on me and I slipped ever deeper, I was in something of a state of shock: out of all the ways we could've perished over those last eighteen months, were we gonna die like that, swallowed up by the ground and no one would ever know? I could feel the mud working on my big-guy body, using my own weight against me, and it went through my head that it was entirely appropriate that my bulk that had been so much a part of my life should ensure my eventual demise. But suddenly I felt the tandem jolt as if it'd come into contact with something; I stopped sinking, just hung there for a moment, then slowly began to slide backwards . . . *Jesus!* Lena had managed to get Thomas to a place where he was safe, grabbed hold of the tandem and was now doing her best to drag it – and me – out.

Thank God, she was so strong: she had hold of those two back wheels and was heaving with all her might, grunting with exertion as inch by inch she dragged me back to a position where I could finally struggle out on my own.

'Lena!' I cried, going to take her in my arms, so aware it wasn't the first time she'd saved my life. But d'you know what? She was as mad at me as I'd ever seen her – I was damn lucky she didn't take a pop. Over and over she told me I'd been reckless and stupid, that even the slightest of chances would be no use if I was gonna get us all killed.

'I know, I know. I'm sorry,' I told her. 'Let's rest here 'til daybreak.'

She made a point of finding herself a spot a little bit away from me, sitting there hunched over Thomas, shielding him from the rain, and to my surprise the two of them fell asleep within minutes.

I just stayed where I was, unable to bridge that eight- or nine-foot gap for any reason, knowing I wouldn't close my eyes all night.

Thankfully the rain stopped a little later, though the passage of the early hours was as slow as ever, and I found myself fretting over that thing inside me. Where the hell was it now? I could've sworn I could feel it in there, clinging to the apex of an archway, monitoring my thoughts as they passed through, memorising the ones it didn't like, those it'd punish me for when it took over. Other times it seemed to be oozing its way around me like some thin, eerily transparent octopus, slithering around my head, tucking itself between my brain and skull, sliding off down through my veins to the distant pulsating rhythm of my heart.

It was enough to drive anyone crazy. For sure I was never more grateful to see the glow of dawn stretching out along the horizon, to catch the first sight of a much friendlier sky. Mind you, what a new day would bring was anyone's guess.

CHAPTER TWELVE

Before Lena awoke I had a good look at the lie of the land around us – trying to get back into her good books, I guess, to reassure her I was gonna take a more measured approach to the day. It wasn't immediately obvious, but I began to see that the nature of the grass changed wherever it was boggy: it grew in these heavy island clumps. I spent a while testing my theory, prodding with sticks, risking a few footsteps here and there – the last thing I wanted was to be wrong – but eventually felt confident enough to go back and tell Lena what I'd discovered, though I gotta say, she could've been more interested.

A little later, after we'd wordlessly breakfasted on some more of Sheila's venison (though Thomas stuck to his dairy diet, of course), we picked the mud-covered tandem up off the ground and with me making great play of taking 'the safe route' that I'd charted, we headed off, conversation between us still decidedly sparse.

Having said that, it wasn't long before the rising sun warmed us with a little of its optimism and things began to improve. Eventually we stopped to give each other a hug, from then on feeling that bit stronger, more up to the task at hand, and we returned across that plain a damn sight quicker than we'd first crossed it. By the afternoon we were back up in the hills and amongst the trees, keeping up our pace the best we could, only stopping when we had to, the rest of the time, even when we needed to eat, keeping moving. My only thought was that we had to get back to the farm before nightfall, that we couldn't afford to lose another day.

We just about made it. Those last ten miles or so we were pedalling through the dark, but as it was mostly on the road, it wasn't a problem. Finally we turned up the track to the farm, our mood a mixture of excitement and apprehension; neither of us had actually said it, but we were both aware that anything could've happened in our absence, that like it or not, we'd do best to steel ourselves for what might be bad news.

It was one helluva relief to enter the farmyard and see them through the window, sitting around the table, the remains of a meal in front of them, Jimmy on a bit of a lecture, the others exhibiting fading degrees of interest.

'Clancy?' Lena asked.

'It's okay,' I reassured her, 'they're all fine.'

If everyone hates goodbyes, then I reckon that must mean they love hellos, 'cuz that was one helluva noisy and touching reunion. We had people hanging off us all over, screaming and laughing, Lile planting far more kisses on me than I was comfortable with. 'course, they had to have their say about us leaving the way we did, not prepared to listen to any excuses, battering us with it until eventually they squeezed out our most embarrassed and repeated of apologies.

We told them the whole story, everything that'd happened since we'd left, top billing, of course, going to what Sheila had said about the implants not kicking in for a few days, that for the moment, Thomas and me weren't putting them in any danger. But they just brushed that aside, far more interested to hear that a punishment satellite was still functioning.

'Still one up there!' Jimmy exclaimed.

'Yep.'

'Cool! I wouldn't have thought it possible.'

However, Gordie, who'd been on good terms with Nick's boys, was more concerned by what the satellite had done. 'George!' he moaned, as if he couldn't believe it.

'Yeah,' I sighed, 'but it wasn't George, not as we knew him.'

'Nice kid,' Jimmy commented, 'but a bit too sensitive.'

Delilah grunted. 'What's happening around here is enough to drive anyone insane.'

I went on to tell Jimmy about Sheila suggesting we moved over there, that it was safer, and that they were wondering if he could fix the satellite.

'And get it to do what?' he asked.

'I dunno. I think they got some ideas.'

Jimmy made this face, like if he was gonna reprogramme a satellite he'd want some part in deciding what it'd do.

When we finally finished telling them about our adventures, right down to the obligatory account of how Thomas had handled the whole thing, Lena asked what had been happening around the farm, but as no one had much to say I took that to be to be a good sign that everything was pretty well back to normal.

'No more weevils?' Lena asked.

'Nope,' Jimmy replied, and I gave a bit of a sigh, feeling a sense of relief, but he hadn't quite finished. 'I just don't get it.'

I was tempted to ignore him, to change the subject, but, of course, I couldn't. 'What?'

'Well, you know? Was that it? The Big Idea? A full-on implant assault? Or just another experiment?'

'Pretty effective one,' I told him.

'Not really,' he shot back. 'Out of seven people, only two – and one

173

of them a baby – ended up being implanted. With all those thousands of weevils?'

'It was enough,' I told him.

Jimmy shrugged, aware I was getting a little irritated but as usual ploughing on, 'Doesn't sound right to me.'

'Don't tell me there's gonna be more?' Delilah complained.

'Maybe,' Jimmy replied, making this face as if marking the moment in case sometime he needed to say 'I told you so'.

'Can you feel anything, Clancy?' Hanna asked.

'Nope,' I answered, knowing immediately what she was talking about. I mean, it wasn't strictly true, but I was still putting it down to my imagination.

She came and put her arm around me, the way she did now, as if she might only be a kid but she was auditioning for the role of big sister. Gigi pointedly raised her eyes to the ceiling, as if she'd never seen anything so pathetic in her life, her resentment still as acute as ever.

'What are you gonna do?' Gordie asked.

I took a deep breath, glancing at Lena, knowing she wasn't exactly with me on this and possibly about to resume saying so. 'Take Thomas into the City. See if I can get these things removed.'

But if it was Lena I was worried about running me over, I soon realised there were a whole lotta other trucks forming a line behind her.

'What!' Delilah croaked.

'What's the matter?'

'You gotta be kidding!'

'What's *your* idea, then?' I asked, getting a little defensive.

'Big Guy!' Jimmy said, as if I was a little kid who'd just announced he was walking to Africa. 'No way.'

'You can't take him there,' Gordie told me.

'You saw how those people reacted in the Commune,' Lena said, for the first time acknowledging the fact that Thomas might actually be the miracle Doctor Simon always said he was.

'I'll keep him hidden,' I replied stubbornly, immediately realising that was a real dumb-ass thing to say – I might be able to keep him hidden, but sure as hell I wouldn't be able to keep him unheard, not with those prize-winning lungs.

'Get the Doc to come here,' Gordie suggested. 'Make a house call.'

'Yeah, right,' I muttered irritably, but then stopped, realising he might have something. I could do just that: go into the City, get the Doc and bring him back – the way he'd wanted. It'd be a helluva risk – he wasn't only Nora Jagger's personal physician, he was the guy who'd double-crossed us and imprisoned Lena. Did we really want to chance bringing him to our secret paradise? Then again, what alternative did we have?

It was a long way from perfect, and Lena wasn't that much happier about it, but at least it meant Thomas stayed with her, and in the end, it was what we decided to do.

I debated long and hard about whether I should take someone with me, and who that should be. What I had no way of knowing was if there'd be a situation where I might need someone who *didn't* have an implant, who *couldn't* be scanned and classified. In the end, I decided to take Gordie; we'd just get in and out as quickly as we could. Jimmy also insisted that Hanna went with us as far as the limo so she could bring back the lasers and corroded power-packs for him to try to fix.

I tell ya, it was one helluva pleasure for Lena and me to be back in our own bed that night. We were too exhausted to make love, but still held onto each other like we might somehow fuse together, that when we came to untangle ourselves in the morning we'd find we'd swapped a part or two.

Thomas did us a favour by not waking 'til six, which was a small miracle in itself – though he made up for it by immediately demanding to be changed and fed like some half-pint-sized dictator. Not that I minded; I had to be up and on the road as soon as possible, and for sure there was no chance of grabbing a few extra minutes with that racket going on.

I took my coffee out on the front porch, hoping for a few moments' peace before setting out on what was plainly gonna be one helluva dangerous journey. I hadn't been out there more than a couple of minutes before I glanced down the track and saw someone approaching.

It took me for ever to work out who it was: there was a guy pulling some kind of cart, really having to work at it, his exhausted body bent forward almost horizontal, straining at this taut rope. My first thought was that it was one of the crazies dragging his possessions, that it could be trouble – then finally I realised what I was looking at.

It wasn't a cart, it was a bed: a single bed on wheels with a couple of boxes heaped on it and, most surprising of all, someone lying under a blanket. I don't know how much all that weighed, but whoever was dragging it looked just about all in. It was only as I stood there staring at such a bizarre sight and he got that bit closer that it finally hit me – maybe 'cuz he'd lost so much weight, 'cuz he was so bent and ragged – it was Nick.

I ran down there as fast as I could, still barely able to believe what I was seeing. He had Miriam with him, his wife, towing her in that bed she'd been in for the last God-knew how many years.

Nick fell to his knees as I approached, tears in his eyes, and I gotta say, I'd never been a great hugger, but I pulled the guy up and embraced him. If ever a man looked like he needed it, he did.

'Nick, what the hell happened?' I asked, staring into his haunted face, seeing echoes of something ugly etched deep on there.

'Help me get her into the house?' he replied, like he couldn't say or do anything until Miriam was safe and taken care of.

I went to the back of the bed to push it, just the top of Miriam's grey head appearing outta the covers. As we approached the house, the others came out, standing open-mouthed on the porch, looking every bit as shocked as I'd been. Going on Nick's appearance, the state of the bed – a little rusted, covered in mud, even a bit mildewy – he'd been dragging her around for some time, and no matter what route he'd taken, it would've included any number of steep hills. I tell ya, it just didn't bear thinking about.

We lifted the bed up onto the porch as carefully as we could, within minutes Delilah returning with some breakfast for the pair of them. Nick ignored his, instead concentrating on propping Miriam up and spoon-feeding her, though he gained no response other than some endlessly deliberate chewing and what looked like the occasional glare in his direction.

'See that?' he said. 'Never used to do it. God knows what she's thinking.'

After a while, and having to stop every now and then to wipe food off Miriam's chin, he started to tell us what'd happened over in his valley. Several times I caught someone's eye – Hanna, Jimmy – all of them, like me, wondering if he knew about George – if it'd come up or if we were gonna have to tell him.

Turned out, it *was* the weevils that drove them away: they came night after night, in far greater numbers than we'd suffered; crawling all over the houses, doing everything they could to find a way in, sometimes succeeding through sheer weight of numbers. They'd come massing against windowpanes, layer upon layer, 'til finally the glass gave way and they poured in, streaming out to every corner of the house, looking for any bodily orifice they could enter.

'It went on for ever,' Nick said, looking as if he was hypnotised by the memory. 'No one slept, just waited to see if what we'd used to seal up our homes would hold; ready to kill those who made it through . . .

It was war. We got so tired, we had to sleep in the day and fight at night. We were just about holding out, wondering for how much longer we could, when suddenly it stopped. We thought we'd beaten them, that they'd moved on. One night went by, then another, and we started to relax, to go back to our normal routines, working during the day, sleeping at night . . .

'The moment we did, they came again, like the whole thing had been planned. They were in our homes before we knew it: every-where, over the walls, the ceiling. I woke up to find Miriam covered from head to toe, as if they knew she was defenceless, that she was an easy target.' He paused for a moment, as if, no matter how many times he told that tale, it didn't reduce the impact. 'They were in her mouth, up her nose – anywhere they could get in . . . I'd heard her making these little noises, but I'd been so exhausted, I couldn't wake up. I guess she'd seen them coming, crawling up the bed towards her, but hadn't been able to do anything about it.'

There was a long pause. He looked so destroyed I leaned over and patted him on the back.

'You know what they are, don't you?' Jimmy asked.

'Do now,' Nick replied. 'She's got one inside her, for sure. I been told there are different kinds, but they've all got one thing in common: in the end, Nora Jagger's gonna control us all.'

There was a pause, and I knew I had to find out if he was aware what'd happened to George or not.

'What about your boys?' I asked.

He gave a long, haunted sigh. 'We went into the forest, all of us taking it in turns to drag and push their Ma until we finally found a place to lay up. One day the boys went out hunting . . .' He stopped, and again I could see the slight oozing of a tear. 'Never came back, not one of them. Some days later someone found Edward and Daniel shot dead. I don't know what happened to George.'

I paused for a moment, everyone plainly waiting on me to speak. 'I do,' I told him.

He looked at me, realised I had something to say and walked out into the yard, plainly expecting me to follow. I wasn't sure whether it was 'cuz he wanted to be on his own to hear the news or 'cuz he didn't want Miriam to hear in case she understood.

'I'm sorry,' I said, just in case he had any illusions about which way the conversation was gonna go, but he just beckoned for me to tell him.

I gave him the whole story – that George was killed by a rogue satellite, and why, expecting him to be devastated by the loss of his youngest and last-remaining son, but I think he'd already guessed; he just didn't know the details.

'He was never gonna get through this,' he admitted. 'The least chance of any of them.'

Without another word he returned to the porch and this time commenced on his own breakfast; his sunken cheeks, how quickly he ate, giving a fair indication of how long it was since he'd last had a good meal. Within minutes he'd cleared the plate and we were back to discussing the implants, Jimmy wondering if, as Miriam was lying stationary, he might be able to come up with some kinda shield to stop her being read or reporting. I also had to explain to Nick that Gordie and me were going into the City, and why.

'You got one, too!' he gasped, showing real concern.

'Yeah. And Thomas.'

'Jesus, no—'

'If I can get this doctor to come back with me, if he can extract them, he can fix up Miriam too.'

For the first time since I saw him struggling up the track, Nick smiled, though it looked a little awkward, like he hadn't done it in a while. 'Thanks, Clancy. That'd be great.'

We didn't stay much longer. Gordie and me gathered up everything we needed, no one making an occasion of it, though I did take Lena into the bedroom so we could be alone for a few minutes, promising I'd return, that I'd find a way of getting that thing out of Thomas no matter what.

The irony was, the little guy'd got one of his real smiley moods on, repeatedly exploding with light and laughter as I solemnly tried to say goodbye, staring at my face as if he expected me to make him laugh at any moment. I'll tell ya, kids got no sense of occasion.

I don't know why exactly, but as we set out – me, Gordie and Hanna – I found myself thinking about this book I read out on the Island: *Don Quixote*, all about this old guy who goes a little crazy and thinks he's one of those old-fashioned knights, setting off with his foolishly loyal sidekick – Sancho someone – to battle giants and demons and put the world to rights, but the thing is, he's got no chance; the world's gonna win and he'd know it if he wasn't so soft in the head . . . D'you see where I'm going with this? I was beginning to feel a definite affinity.

If it hadn't been for Nick's arrival and not being able to leave as early as we'd hoped, we probably would've made it over the mountain that day, but as it was, and despite going as fast as we could, we were again left with that decision of whether to descend the far side in darkness or not. We talked it over and decided to give it a try, but almost immediately Gordie slipped, grabbed at Hanna, and though he saved himself, sent her tumbling down a slope. She bumped and slid her way yelping down into the blackness. Me and Gordie came scrabbling after her, repeatedly threatening to also lose our balance, eventually finding her at the base of an outcrop of rock. I was worried to hell 'cuz she wasn't moving. She had this large bruise on her forehead, and obviously a few more on her body, but she slowly got to her feet, all the way testing that everything was still working okay.

Gordie apologised, over and over, and just for a moment I thought she might lose her temper and weigh into him, but that girl's serenity itself. We took it for a warning though, and stopped then and there so we could try to get a few hours' sleep, knowing we were going to need them in the morning.

The last thought I had before I fell asleep was that now it was just four days before Nora Jagger would take control of me, and that when I awoke, it would only be three.

The following morning we were up and on our way probably earlier than was good for us. The only method by which we could've descended that mountain quicker was by falling down it, and what with the lack of light and a heavy dew on the ground, we got pretty close a couple of times. Finally we found our way down to the cave, where the limo was looking just a tad older and mouldier, but as usual, started first time.

I dug the lasers out of the trunk, debating for a moment and eventually pocketed one, keeping it for show. You start waving a laser around, people are seldom of a mind to ask you about the state of the power-pack, and it just might come in useful at some time.

I made a bit of an epic outta backing the limo out and down to the forest floor, leaving those two alone for a few minutes, letting them say their goodbyes any way they wished. Like I said before, it wasn't none of my business and I didn't want it to be either.

However deep Gordie's feelings, his farewell was about as warm as to an ill-favoured aunt with halitosis – I made more of a thing of it than he did. We stood and watched for a few moments as Hanna headed back up the mountain, all slim grace and swaying long hair, then I turned and gave him a bit of a look.

'What?' he asked, but I never replied, just shook my head and went to get in the limo, waiting for him to join me.

When we got to the main highway, just like before, the power track wouldn't hitch up. Again I was gonna have to find gas, and this time I'd have to be a whole lot more careful about it. I tried to keep my right foot as light as a feather, to conserve what fuel we did have, but we were even shorter of time than we were of gas. I couldn't keep my speed down, no matter how many times I reminded myself, it'd creep back up again.

I tried stopping a couple of times, approaching this old-timer on his front porch and getting a rifle pointed at me for my efforts. It didn't leave us with too much choice other than to keep heading for the City and to pray that gas gauge was being far too pessimistic.

Finally the inevitable happened: there was no reserve, the gauge was spot-on and we coughed and spluttered to a halt. I cursed in frustration, repeatedly punching the steering wheel – we still had fifty miles to go. If we had to walk, it would take just about every minute I had before the implant was due to kick in.

The only other possibility was hitching, but neither Gordie nor me held out much hope; it wasn't exactly a popular activity any more, and who the hell was gonna pick up what must've looked like a pair of stand-out crazies?

I felt a real strong compulsion to keep on going, to keep whittling that distance down, even if only by a mile or two, but decided it was best to stay with the limo; as if it gave us some kind of status, that people could see we were out of fuel rather than luck – though with the bullet holes, the dents, the missing bodywork, the dirt and mould, I'm not sure how impressive it was.

I'd just about given up hope and started to think that we might as well start walking when this guy in an old pickup pulled to a gentle halt a few yards in front of us. He was thirty, maybe, bespectacled and balding, not that friendly, but hey, he was offering us a lift, so who was complaining?

'You think the limo's all right there?' Gordie asked, glancing back as we pulled away.

'It's a wreck with no gas – what d'you think?' I replied, and the driver nodded repeatedly, like that was his way of laughing.

He'd introduced himself as Dan – just that, nothing else, as if it was all the information anyone could ever possibly need. In turn, we gave him our names, attempting to keep the conversation going, mentioning all sorts of stuff, but it was like trying to get into an advent calendar after your baby brother'd been playing with the glue – no matter what the subject, the door was tightly closed. In the end, we also lapsed into silence. I mean, he was taking us to the City, his driving seemed okay, who needed conversation?

When we finally peaked the last of the hills and the City loomed into view, it was like something huge and dark squatting on its haunches, getting ready to leap at us, and I wouldn't have been in the least bit surprised if it'd been Nora Jagger either. Dan slowed for a moment, I thought to take in the view, but it was more like he was being energised in some way: he sat up straighter, took more note of what was happening, actually sped up a little as he began the many twists and curves of the descent.

Signs of Infinity began to appear almost immediately – a distant Dragonfly, a glimpse of a laser statue – and Gordie, who hadn't been there since we escaped, immediately looked that bit on edge. However, that was as nothing compared to what was about to follow, which, I'll tell ya, was one of the most bizarre things I've ever witnessed. It was such a shock it took me a while to appreciate what the hell was going on. Dan suddenly opened his mouth really wide, almost as if he didn't have a choice about it, and started making these gurgling, guttural noises, *guck-guck-guck*, then ran through a whole lotta random other sounds, spilling them out as if his voice-box had been kick-started and revved as fast as it would go.

'Let me outta here,' Gordie muttered, backing away as far as he could. But just as abruptly as he'd started, Dan stopped, almost as if he'd been through some kinda checklist. There was a bit of a pause, then finally Mr Single-Syllable spoke properly – I mean, *real* sentences, that made sense, not one-grunt replies. Suddenly Dan had lots to say; the only thing was, it wasn't his voice.

'Due to the fact that there is a non-implanted person in this vehicle, I am changing my route and heading for the nearest Infinity fort.'

I turned and stared at him, spellbound by the mechanical opening and shutting of his mouth. *What the hell?*

It was her voice, of course: the Bitch, somehow talking to us through Dan, or more accurately, I guessed, his implant.

'The doors have been locked for your safety and security. An Infinity Dragonfly will be with you in' – he paused for a moment, as if calculating – 'one minute and forty-four seconds.'

'Clancy!' Gordie cried, though he couldn't have been any more alarmed than I was.

'Pull over,' I said to Dan, seeing a distant Dragonfly change course and start heading back in our direction. '*Pull over!*' I repeated, taking the lifeless laser from my pocket and holding it to his forehead.

'The harming of a fully-registered imp by a non-imp is a serious offence and punishable by death,' said the Bitch's voice out of Dan's flapping mouth, which, even in that moment, at least gave me the comfort of knowing I still hadn't been keyed.

'Pull over!' I shouted, jamming the laser harder to Dan's temple.

To be honest, it was a bit of an empty threat and he probably knew it. Not only did my laser have no power-pack, I was hardly gonna shoot him while he was negotiating the twists and turns of a hilly road. Instead, I started to wrestle with the guy, trying to get him to pull in, yanking his feet off the pedals and hitting the brake. Out of the corner of my eye I could see the Dragonfly getting nearer and Dan announced that it was *one minute and three seconds away*. That didn't leave me with a great deal of choice. As he slowed to take the next hairpin bend, I yanked the wheel so that we hit the barrier side-on – trying to scrub off some speed and hopefully stop, but somewhere amongst the struggle, I lost control and the pickup flipped up and over the crash-barrier.

Don't ask me how it happened; I'm only grateful it did. There was a bit of a shelf and then a fifty- or sixty-foot-drop beyond that crash barrier, but somehow as we sailed over it, the pickup's cabin got caught on the rail and we ended up just hanging there upside down, still secured by our seatbelts. The windshield was partly broken, so I kicked out the rest and Gordie and me freed ourselves and scrambled out. The Bitch's ventriloquist's dummy was no longer spouting her words but pinned in his seat by the steering wheel, blood running from his cheek where his glasses had broken, sliding down his forehead and collecting at the top of his bald head.

As I briefly balanced on the crash-barrier, I noticed this storm drain opening below us on the shelf. We had just enough time to scramble down and get ourselves inside before the Dragonfly loomed up over the rise in front of us. We could hear the pilot hovering, I guessed trying to work out what the hell had gone on, then he started to circle, not realising that Gordie and me had already emerged on the other side of the road and were weaving our way down through the undergrowth. By the time he started doing wider sweeps, we were well away, sticking to cover and not rejoining the highway until much further on.

The whole of the way through that scrub, all I could hear was Gordie behind me repeating, over and over, expletives of the most amazed variety. He couldn't believe it – and, frankly, neither could I. Nora Jagger could speak through the implants! It must be some kinda automatic response, I guessed, and presumably not available with all versions – but it was still one helluva shock.

'I thought she was there!' Gordie moaned. 'Then I thought it was the radio.'

I never commented, no more recovered from the experience than he was.

'Jesus, Clancy!' he suddenly exclaimed, pausing and staring after me. 'Does this mean she's gonna be able to speak through *you*?'

I kept moving, refusing to answer or even consider the prospect. 'Let's find the Doc, shall we?' I said.

CHAPTER THIRTEEN

I knew it wasn't one of the days Doctor Simon had a surgery at St Joseph's; he was either at Infinity or his private clinic at his home in the foothills. Bearing in mind we were on foot and that swanky enclave wasn't that far away – not to mention that I wouldn't have gone anywhere near Infinity if you'd paid me, the decision had more or less made itself.

It took us most of a couple hours to get there, the size and forbidding nature of the properties growing by the suburb, security guards for ever coming out to make sure we kept moving, that we didn't end up on their patch. There was some common ground a few hundred yards down the street from the Doc's estate and Gordie and me waited there in the bushes for that big shiny Bentley of his to come purring along.

The only problem was, it didn't. We waited there for hour after hour, and the longer we did, the more I became aware of the seconds ticking away, that each one was progressively growing in importance. By late afternoon I was beginning to think I'd made a really bad decision, that the Doc was staying down in Infinity, or maybe even away somewhere.

Gordie was just getting going with his complaints that he was bored and hungry, starting to irritate the hell outta me, when the Bentley almost sneaked past us.

I jumped out into the road, praying the Doc was inside, ready to lay myself down in front of him if I had to. However, not only did the car come to an instant automatic stop, but it was the man himself at the steering-wheel.

He slid the passenger window down a few inches, a waft of expensive after-shave almost knocking me over, as usual dressed like he was about to do a cover shot for middle-aged self-satisfaction.

'Clancy. What the hell are you doing?' he asked, furtively looking all around.

'I had to see ya.'

There was a long pause while he continued to check about him, then the back door shushed open almost noiselessly and I quickly slipped inside, followed by Gordie.

I didn't bother with fluffing up the conversation – there wasn't time. 'I gotta implant inside me,' I told him.

'Oh,' was all he said, not sounding anywhere near as concerned as you'd want your doctor to be under such circumstances.

'A weevil,' I added.

He shrugged a little helplessly. 'It's a common story, I'm afraid.'

'You got one?' Gordie challenged.

'Er . . . no,' he stuttered, sounding a little taken aback.

'So?' Gordie persisted.

'I've got an original – a *private* one.'

I didn't know what that meant, and just at that moment, didn't care, either. 'How much d'you know about them?'

'A fair bit.'

'Can they be removed?'

He paused for a moment, plainly not sure what to say. 'Erm . . . Officially, no.'

'Unofficially?'

'Still no,' he replied, though in such a way you knew there was a story.

I turned to him, ready to hit him with my best shot. 'Thomas has got one, too.'

I never seen anyone's attitude change so abruptly. '*What?*'

'Yeah.'

'Oh no! Oh, shit!' he said – Jeez, he even swore like a gentleman.

'Can you remove it?' I asked, feeling he might take it a bit more seriously now.

'How long have you had them?'

'I've got two more days before it can be keyed, or so I'm told. Thomas too, I guess,' I replied, feeling that deadline creeping up over the horizon like some black dawn. 'What does it mean exactly? To be keyed?' I asked.

'I told you, you'll no longer be the master of your own mind . . . "Chained" would be a much better word than "keyed".'

'Shit!' Gordie exclaimed, swearing like he was much more used to it.

'But how does someone actually get *keyed*?' I persisted.

'I don't know. It needs some kind of conductor to "talk" to you, to switch you on. Over the mountains you might get a few days' grace – or you might not. A lot of people know a little about it; only one knows everything.'

I didn't need to ask: that was so typical. Everyone involved was allowed their piece of the puzzle, but only she was allowed to put them all together.

Doctor Simon sat there for a while, staring at the road ahead, obviously thinking it through.

'I have to go to the hospital,' he eventually announced. 'I need to pick up some equipment, speak to my assistant.'

With that he started the engine and was about to pull away when he obviously thought of something else.

'You've got one, too, I hope?' he asked, turning to Gordie.

'What?'

'An implant.'

'No.'

'Jesus!' he groaned, fumbling in his inside pocket, taking out this plastic container and extracting from it a tiny grey disk that he handed to Gordie. It looked a bit like a tinted contact lens. 'Put it somewhere safe and always have it about you, no matter what,' he said. 'Do you hear me?'

'Sure,' Gordie smirked, like he was humouring the Doc.

'It'll save your life a hundred times over.'

At that, Gordie exhibited a little more interest, examining it closely before showing it to me.

'Is this what I think it is?' I asked.

'Early version, but still readable,' the Doc replied.

I gave it back to Gordie and he carefully placed it in his jeans pocket.

'You have no idea,' Doctor Simon warned us before flooring the Bentley and sweeping away.

Despite how recently I'd been there, it didn't take long to get some idea of what he meant. There was a sense of madness gaining an almost irresistible momentum, rolling towards an unforgiveable conclusion. Nora Jagger was even more widespread – more statues, more screens – but it wasn't just that; I had this suspicion that her clean-up of the City was gathering pace, that in some areas everything and everyone had been swept away and sterilised. Yeah, there were people there, but they weren't like any I'd seen before. Something was missing from them, something had been taken away, and I got the feeling it was pretty fundamental.

'Does everyone in the City have an implant?' I asked.

'Not everyone, no,' the Doc replied.

'These people?'

He turned and looked outta his window. 'I'd guess so.'

I stared out for a while. They weren't robots or anything, but there was this sense that something wasn't quite natural.

'What's a "private" implant?' Gordie suddenly asked.

'An old credit or identity implant that's open to be adapted at any time,' the Doc replied, sounding matter-of-fact but also that bit concerned.

'So you're screwed, too,' Gordie commented.

The Doc sighed to himself, but never actually bothered to reply.

Slowly, as we got into the more congested and poorer areas, you could feel yourself crossing boundaries, entering unmarked ghettoes, and the people changed, too: more diversity, less order, rawer emotions.

'I shouldn't have come this way,' the Doc muttered to himself, as if a shortcut had gone wrong and he was regretting overriding the Bentley's program. We turned a corner and found ourselves in a large open square. In the gathering gloom, I couldn't exactly see what, but something was going on over on the far side. There was an agitated mob running around without rhyme or reason, like those huge flocks of birds you see sweeping wildly across the evening sky.

The Doc ignored it, like he'd seen it all before, but we continued to stare.

'What's going on?' Gordie whispered to me.

At first I didn't understand what he was talking about – it was just confusion, a crowd, a fight maybe – but then I did catch a glimpse of something. There was a squat dark shape running through the crowd, causing any amount of panic; what's more, the way people were scattering, there was more than one of them.

'What is it?' I asked Doctor Simon.

'Shadows,' he replied, like he really didn't want to talk about it.

I didn't know if he was joking, saying we were seeing things or what. I looked back outta the rear window, but as I did, we turned a corner and whatever it was, was lost from sight. I could still see people leaving the square though, running as fast as they were able, as if their very lives depended on it. Obviously what the Doc had said earlier was right: we didn't have a clue what was going on, and maybe it was best left that way.

The further we travelled, the more I began to notice a developing pattern: areas where Infinity were in control; areas where they weren't. Whatever was back there in the square, we never saw it again, but there was this frequent shift from order to chaos. As we approached St Joseph's, there was even a little looting, this arcade being plundered, just like when we were living in the City, the only difference being that there felt like much more urgency about it, as though, unlike before, they feared the authorities might appear at any moment.

The Doc left us in the basement at St Joseph's, parked in the darkest corner he could find, while he went to collect a few things and have a word with his assistant, assuring us he'd be back in thirty minutes.

From the moment that those elevator doors slid across his polished face and we were left alone, I was at the mercy of my fears. Why the hell was I trusting this guy, after everything he'd done? He could come back here with a whole pack of Infinity Specials and force us to take them to Lena and Thomas – not that we would, and I guess he knew that.

'If we drive through the night,' I said to Gordie, trying to engage myself with other things, 'we could be there by midday or so.'

'We're gonna drive the whole way?' he asked.

'The Doc ain't gonna leave this in the middle of nowhere,' I said, referring to the Bentley.

'We gotta lock-up,' Gordie joked.

'Yeah, I can just see this in the cave,' I said, stroking the hand-stitched and monogrammed leather.

'What about our limo?'

'We'll have to leave it, for the moment.'

Gordie paused for a moment, looking that bit thoughtful, 'I just hope he can get those implants out.'

'As long as he can remove the one in Thomas.'

'Both of yous. What you and Lena got . . . it's special,' he said, with an awkward honesty. 'One day, you know, I'd like to have something like you two. Maybe,' he added, and I realised where this was coming from.

'You gotta treat her right,' I told him. 'Let her know how you feel.'

'Oh yeah, yeah. I know all that,' he said dismissively, and I was tempted to remind him of how offhand he'd been with Hanna when they parted company on the mountain, but I wasn't sure if my credibility was up to it.

Again he went quiet, but I could see I'd set him thinking. 'How long d'ya think the Doc's gonna be?'

I checked my watch. 'Another fifteen,' I said, knowing that, if nothing else, Doctor Simon was usually punctual.

'Can I have the laser?' he asked, as if he just wanted to take a look, to play with it until the Doc reappeared.

I handed it to him – I mean, without a power-pack, it didn't represent any kinda threat to anyone.

'That arcade around the corner,' he said, referring to the looting. 'People always drop stuff when they're running away. I might go and see if I can find something. Sort of a present,' he announced, stuffing the laser into his pocket and opening his door.

'Hey, hey!' I told him. 'Forget it.'

'I won't go in – just check the sidewalk. I wanna take back something for Hanna,' he said, knowing how fond I was of her and hoping it might sway me. 'Please!'

I hesitated for a moment. It wasn't like him to beg, and it *was* only a coupla hundred yards away. On the other hand, I didn't feel comfortable about it.

'The Doc'll be back soon,' I said, trying to put him off.

'So will I.'

He was so keen, in a way I didn't associate with him, that in the end I gave in. 'Just the *street*. Don't go inside,' I said, pointing my finger at him.

'Promise.'

'And leave that, too,' I said, wrenching the laser out of his pocket, not prepared to risk him waving it around and someone getting the wrong idea.

He gave me a bit of a look, like I was undermining his masculinity in some way, and I was reminded again that he wasn't a kid any more, that it wouldn't be long before that look sent people back-peddling for the door.

'Just think of me as the mother you never had,' I told him, as he got outta the Bentley. 'Ten minutes, no more.'

'Yeah, yeah,' was the last thing I heard him mutter before he made his way to the ramp and disappeared up to street level.

It wasn't 'til he'd gone that I fully appreciated how I'd just doubled my problems: now I had two people to wait and worry about. I sat there idly playing with the laser, checking its settings, so mindful of the time I forgot, how things would've been so different now. If Doctor Simon was up there talking to her on the screen, double-crossing me again, there'd be no reprieve this time.

But he wasn't; in fact, the doors to the lift slid open precisely forty-five seconds short of the thirty minutes he said he'd be. He made his way to the Bentley carrying one large and obviously heavy case, and one small, shiny black one that had an air of importance about it. He put the large one in the trunk, then opened the passenger door and placed the small one on the seat, carefully folding his jacket and placing it on top as if to make sure no one saw it. He then made his way to the driver's side and got in, only then realising Gordie wasn't in the back.

'Where's he gone?'

I half-smiled, a little embarrassed that my ten-minute curfew was about to lapse. 'Get something for Hanna. He won't be long.'

Doctor Simon turned and stared at me. 'Not in the arcade?'

'Just the street – I told him.'

'Jesus!' he gasped.

'What?'

'Please, tell me he's got the implant?' he said, starting the engine.

'Sure,' I said, and then, I don't know why, maybe instinct, but I looked down at where he'd been sitting, and despite how small it was, it caught the light and I spotted it instantly. I also knew how it'd got there: when I'd jerked the laser out of his pocket, I must've pulled the implant with it. 'No. No, he hasn't.'

'Oh no,' Doctor Simon moaned, accelerating towards the ramp.

'What's the matter?' I asked, thinking he was overreacting.

'I told you, you don't know what goes on any more!'

He hit the speed-bump at the top of the ramp so hard I banged my head on the roof. 'For chrissake!' I shouted. 'What's the problem?'

But as we sped up towards the arcade, I began to get some idea: a whole crowd of looters had been flushed out of the building and were now scattering in every direction; it was the same sorta chaos, the same sorta panic we'd witnessed earlier back in that square.

'What's going on?' I asked, sliding my window down to get a better view.

The Doc pulled in a little down the road from the arcade, and on the opposite side. 'I told you,' he said, fear now slicing at his voice. 'Shadows.'

Before I could ask him to explain, this group of people, homeless by the look of them, came running past as fast as they could, their mouths wide open, their eyes bulging with fear. The last one, a woman, was screaming this constant, shrill note at the top of her voice. This was obviously why everyone had wanted to get in and out as quickly as they could, what they'd been running from earlier – but what the hell was it?

Then I saw them, coming out of the arcade, one by one: squat black things, moving like launched missiles, the first one gaining on the homeless group with every stride. And suddenly I realised there was something chillingly familiar about that pursuit.

'Is that what I think it is?'

The Doc nodded, visibly shaking. 'I hate those things.'

'Growlers?'

'Yes.'

Infinity kept growlers in underground bunkers around their headquarters: anyone who tried to break in, who got through the fence and attempted to cross an expanse of grass, was chased and simply torn to pieces – as we so nearly found out to our cost one night.

'I thought they only functioned in the Infinity compound?'

'They're shadow-growlers,' he told me. 'They've got another remit altogether.'

At that exact moment, the pursuing growler caught up with the fleeing group, leaping through the air and knocking the woman flat on her face, clamping its huge jaws around her waist while she screamed and writhed with the raw terror of impending death.

I'd never seen anything like it and I never wanna again either, not as long as I live. With her body just hanging from its mouth, it shook her from side to side so violently and with such force that she fell apart, the bottom half of her flying off into the street.

'Jesus!' I groaned.

Her companions must've heard her screams but they didn't even look back, just continued their hysterical flight, and within moments the shadow-growler was joined by another and they both turned and went chasing after them.

'They won't get far,' the Doc said quietly.

It was only then, as I leaned outta the window to watch the pursuit, that I realised there was another shadow-growler standing right beside the Bentley, so close I could've reached out and touched it. It fixed me with these cold slashes of eyes, obviously checking me out, sifting through its software, and I gotta say, it damn near frightened the life outta me.

They weren't the same as the ones that guarded Infinity: dull black rather than shiny silver, stockier, with feet wider apart, I guessed to make them more stable. But it was the head that was most different: much broader – to accommodate even larger jaws – and across the expanse of its forehead a row of vicious spikes. At the centre of the 'face' where the nose might be was a gaping hole that looked like it might just latch onto you and suck out everything in your body. Jeez, it was an evil-looking thing, and I guess that was the whole point; someone had laboured long and hard to design the most frightening deterrent a human being could ever have to face.

God knows why, but I pressed the window button, wanting something between that thing and me, though I suspected it could probably jump straight through the glass, bullet-proof or not.

'It won't touch us,' the Doc said.

'How d'ya know?'

'It's already scanned us for implants; it's only non-imps it's after.'

So that was how it worked: if you didn't have an implant, one of those things would eliminate you. And the moment I appreciated that, it hit me that Gordie was out there without one.

'I gotta find Gordie,' I said, fumbling at the door.

'Clancy!' Doctor Simon cried. 'It's too late – he's gone.'

'How d'ya know?'

'No one escapes the shadows. Believe me.'

He might've been right but I didn't take any notice, just carefully put Gordie's implant into my pocket, then opened the door, the Doc again begging me not to do it.

The shadow-growler stood there as I eased my way out, studying my every move – Jeez, all it would take would be one spring and a snap of those huge jaws and you could toss me on the barbecue ready jointed.

'Clancy—' Doctor Simon pleaded.

'I'll be back soon,' I told him, sliding along the side of the limo, keeping my eyes on the growler.

'I warn you, even with imps there's often collateral damage.'

With those words still ringing in my ears, and the memory of how the Infinity growlers had attacked almost everyone that night we got in there, I ran towards the arcade, deciding to go with the worst-case scenario: that Gordie hadn't been able to find anything for Hanna in the street, and not wanting to go home empty-handed, had gone inside.

It was one of the older-style shopping centres: four floors with balconies and the familiar laser-waterfall cascading down in the middle. All kinds of stores – furniture, clothes, techno – though food had obviously been the main reason for most of those people to risk their lives. For sure, a lot of them hadn't lived long enough to regret it: the place looked more like a slaughterhouse than a shopping centre – dismembered bodies were strewn everywhere, lying in pools of blood that in places had merged into congealing crimson lakes. One or two folk were still looking for food amongst the carnage, trying to keep a low profile; I presumed they were imps.

'*Gordie!*' I hollered, my concern ousting all caution. '*G-o-r-d-i-e!*'

I started to check through the corpses, saying a silent prayer he wasn't one of them, still calling out his name from time to time.

There was no sign on the first floor so I went up to the second, again working my way through the corpses, though there were far fewer up there away from the food halls. I turned a corner, calling out to Gordie once more, the name dying on my lips when I was suddenly confronted by this shadow-growler standing directly in front of me.

It seemed to be staring, but I guess that I was being scanned again; that weird hole in the middle of its face was expanding and contracting like it was breathing. It was one helluvan irony, but for the first time since I'd discovered I'd got it, I was glad I had that implant inside me.

In the end I just plucked up courage and walked around it, again giving one of those things as wide a berth as I could manage. I told myself not to, but after a few moments I took a quick glance back: it was still standing in the exact same place, watching me as if it was calculating, maybe even thinking. I walked on, trying to act as casual as possible, what the Doc had said about collateral damage going through my head. I was so grateful to turn another corner and be outta sight.

I came to this menswear store. God knows why, but it was a real mess. Someone – or *something*, maybe even the shadow-growler I'd just bumped into – had more or less totalled the place. The display window had been smashed, the counters flattened, the old-fashioned mannequins reduced to little more than piles of dismembered bodies and smashed limbs, as if they'd been massacred.

I entered for a moment, slightly bemused by the completeness of the destruction, then returned outside. *Jesus, Gordie, where the hell are you?*

I was just about to move on, when I heard a voice, 'Clancy!'

It wasn't much more than a loud whisper, but I still recognised it, and that it was coming from the menswear store.

'Gordie?' I called, going back inside.

There was no reply and I started searching, thinking he was hiding somewhere, but I couldn't find him. '*Gordie?*'

'Here,' came the reply, a lot closer, but weaker, too.

It was crazy: he was obviously only yards from me, but damned if I could see him. 'Where are you?'

It wasn't until he finally managed to move that I saw him, hidden amongst the pile of destroyed mannequins, camouflaged by dismembered arms and legs and battered torsos, and looking almost as smashed-up as they were.

I crouched down, tossing the broken limbs aside so I could disentangle him. 'Are you okay?'

'I think so . . .' he croaked, taking my hand, obviously in some pain as I pulled him up.

'What happened?'

'I hid amongst these guys, hoping it wouldn't be able to tell the difference, but it just went crazy.'

Jeez, was that why that one'd behaved so oddly? They were programmed to recognise the human form, but when it'd scanned the mannequins, it couldn't understand: all those 'people' but only one life-form. Eventually it'd got so frustrated it'd reacted in a worryingly human manner, by smashing the whole place up.

I quickly checked Gordie over. There were a few cuts and bruises, a helluva graze on his back, but nothing appeared to be broken. I searched my pocket for that tiny sliver of an implant, wanting to get out of there as rapidly as I could, but before I could find it, there was a long, low growl behind me.

Jesus! . . . I didn't get it. How much free thought were those things capable of exactly? It must've been suspicious of me, thought it over and decided to return. I also realised that there'd been another modification on the standard growler: it no longer made that same slurping mechanical sound when it walked, so it could sneak up on people like us.

It was standing no more than a leap away, giving out with this synthesised snarling – a sound every bit as terrifying as its appearance, as if they'd somehow managed to mix the growls of the hunter with the screams of the hunted.

Again I rummaged in my pocket for the implant, but it was such a fiddly little thing and that damn growler was gnashing and snapping away as if it was about to spring at any moment. The only thing I could think of to do was to get my implanted body between it and Gordie, to place myself face to face with that evil-looking son-of-the-Bitch.

I don't what they've done to them, but they've definitely got some human – or at the very least *animal* – qualities; it got really angry with me, repeatedly growling, obviously wanting me to get out of the way. I swear it was about to rip me out of there, to maybe consign me to collateral damage, but my fingertips finally located the implant, and snatching it out I thrust it into Gordie's breast pocket.

'What're you doing?' he asked.

But I didn't answer, just stepped aside and let the shadow-growler scan him, in absolute mental agony for those next few seconds. However, to our immense relief, it turned and stalked slowly outta the store.

CHAPTER FOURTEEN

We had a bad couple of moments outside the arcade when we couldn't see the Doc's limo, but he'd just moved it a little ways down the street. Gordie and me tumbled in the back, the Doc urging us to hurry, but once we'd got away we had remarkably little trouble getting outta the City. We saw plenty more shadow-growlers chasing people, creating life-and-death panic, but thankfully, none of them were interested in us.

Gordie was fine. The Doc quickly checked him for any signs of concussion, and even though he'd taken a blow or two he could've well done without, after a bottle of the finest chilled mineral water from the mini-bar, he soon became his old self. Which wasn't something you could say about Doc Simon.

The whole way the guy was nothing but a pile of squirming exposed nerves: doing a three-sixty every time we stopped at a light or junction, scanning the sky for Dragonflies, I guessed, taking the biggest risk of his calculating life. Though to be fair, there weren't many who wouldn't have been packing death in his position: going behind Nora Jagger's back and helping people who'd once attempted to kill her; who'd wanna wear those shoes, no matter how soft the leather?

Then again, I was still far from sure I could trust him. Maybe it was all part of a plan?

Once we hit the long sweep around the mountain and through the pass, the Doc started to get that bit sleepy and I suggested I took over the driving. You would've thought I'd asked him if I could step in for him on his wedding night! I thought he was gonna jam the steering wheel down the front of his pants. But no more than ten minutes later he almost ran us off the road and I had to insist.

He made me swear all kinds of oaths about being careful, keeping my speed down, not doing *anything* without asking him. First five or ten miles, no matter how tired he was, I don't think he drew breath. I reminded him I used to be a professional, that driving for Mr Meltoni was part of my duties, but I don't think he heard a word I said.

I guess you've been wondering – and it went through my head now and then – why I so rarely mentioned Mr Meltoni any more? In fact, why I so rarely talked about the past? When I was out on the Island, especially when I teamed up with Jimmy and a bottle of hooch, there were days when it felt like we were the best time-travellers this damn planet'd ever known. We could practically touch the brickwork of the City (or the way it was years ago), feel the heat of the sidewalk beneath our feet; the sound of the horns, the calls of the traders. We lived the past so well we were positively homesick for it. And I guess when you think about the Island, what a hellhole it was, what future apparently lay in wait for us all, that wasn't exactly surprising. Mind you, like a lot of senior citizens, I guess we were inclined to OD that bit on nostalgia, for ever splashing our memories with a solution of fool's gold.

I mean, yeah, Mr Meltoni *was* quite a guy: someone who set about the amount of time he'd been allotted on this Earth and hacked and chiselled and moulded for all he was worth. And he did a lotta good things. But you know something . . . ? He did far more bad. Some, like I told you before, I did for him, and these days it's *that* I'm more inclined to remember. I'd give anything to be able to change that part of my life, to have spent my time working as a baker or a chauffeur or screen repairman. But you know, that wasn't the reason I so seldom dwelled on the past any more.

Took me a while to figure it out, but actually, the answer was kinda obvious: the way my life'd become, the way everything'd changed, well, the best hadn't gone any more . . . the best was still to come.

I might be nothing more than an old big guy, but I had this woman who I loved and who loved me, a child – *my son* – who also loved me, and maybe more importantly, who I was responsible for. And you know what? All those years of being a big guy, throwing my weight around and putting the frighteners on people, it was only then that I finally saw myself as a man. She'd done that for me – Lena. Fear ain't respect – how could I have ever thought it was? I was feeling so much better about myself, more confident, more sure of who I was, and it was Lena who'd done that. That's why I didn't think about the past any more, 'cuz I'd got my eyes and heart firmly set on the future. Though the irony was, the way things were, I wasn't that sure I'd got one.

We arrived back at the farm late in the morning, everyone coming out when they saw the Bentley approaching. Despite the situation, Lile started teasing me, going on about 'Hadn't I done well for myself in the big city'.

The Doc waited a few moments before getting out. I guessed he wasn't sure what sorta reception he'd get – apart from Gigi, no one had seen him since we'd dropped him off beside the road the night we broke into the Infinity Building. However, when I finally untangled myself from Lena's embrace, when I stepped back and he saw what we'd almost been crushing between us, he was out of that vehicle like a dog out of a trap.

I guess it was his aftershave – she must've smelled him as soon as he emerged from the Bentley, 'cuz Lena instinctively held Thomas that bit closer to her, though the Doc was so busy gaping at the little guy I don't think he even noticed.

'Oh my God,' he cried, erupting with helpless laughter, '*Oh my God! He's beautiful!*'

That was the thing about Doc Simon: he might've been capable of sliding under a snake's belly with a top hat on, but sometimes he could really surprise you. The look on his face as he stared at Thomas was as joyful as any I'd seen. In fact, damned if he didn't have tears welling up in his eyes.

'Wow, little guy,' he cooed, 'you really are something.'

I briefly considered handing him the baby, letting him hold him for a few moments, but Lena must've guessed what I had in mind and immediately shrank away – and bearing in mind what he'd done to her, I guess that wasn't that much of a surprise.

'So, what d'you need?' I asked the Doc, wanting him to get busy as soon as possible.

'Somewhere isolated where I can set up my equipment,' he replied, not averting his eyes from Thomas for a second. 'Power, of course. And just those who've got implants,' he added, making it perfectly plain that no one else would be welcome.

'Jimmy's workshop,' I suggested.

'Whoa! Whoa!' Jimmy chimed in before the Doc could reply. 'You can't use my workshop.'

'Jimmy!' I protested, most of the others joining in with me.

'All my stuff's there,' he told us. 'What about the kitchen? It's perfect.'

'Listen,' the Doc said, sounding mildly irritated, 'I faithfully promise not to touch any of your hammers and nails.'

Of all the comments he could've made, that was not the most

helpful. The look on Jimmy's face, how red he went, I thought we were gonna start our new situation with a fight. He advanced a couple of paces, and the Doc, suddenly concerned he might've badly miscalculated, started backing away.

I had to step in. 'Jimmy, come on, man. It's the logical place.'

'The kitchen!' he persisted.

'Please!' Nick begged, his few infrequent words now always coming across like cries from the heart.

'*Jimmy!*' Lile shouted, about to bring her wrath down on him, and at that he finally buckled – though not before he'd made a big thing of announcing that he'd fixed the corroded power-packs on the lasers, that thanks to him and his workshop we were no longer unarmed.

'It won't be for long,' I reassured him.

But he never answered, just turned and busily pegged it over to the barn, obviously determined to get there before anyone else and put his stuff well out of reach.

Doctor Simon peered into Thomas' blue and white checked blanket one last time. He actually started reaching for the little guy's hand, but sensing Lena's unspoken objection, pulled away.

'Okay, let's get to work,' he said, returning to the Bentley and retrieving his shiny black case, carrying it with more care than Lena bore Thomas.

I grabbed his heavy case from the trunk and followed him over, managing a hushed conversation with Lena on the way, reassuring her we'd done the right thing – although when we entered the barn, I wasn't so sure.

Jimmy and the Doc were already squaring up to each other. The little guy was acting like some ponytailed prima donna, watching everything the Doc was doing, plainly ready to butt in for the slightest reason, snatching his home-made scanner away when the Doc started looking at it.

I was about to intervene when through the open barn door I saw Nick trying to squeeze Miriam's bed out onto the porch. I trotted back over to help, noticing how haunted he looked, those dark Mediterranean eyes that Delilah used to describe as sexy now more like shadows on a skull.

'How is she?' I asked.

He hesitated for a moment, as if he had a story to tell, but obviously thought better of it. 'Not good.'

I turned to Miriam, peering down into the covers. There was never much to see, though I gotta say, I did do a bit of a double-take. Normally she had this kind of quiet absence about her, but this time there was a real sense of tethered agitation.

'Let's hope the Doc can get rid of these things,' I said, wondering if it'd make any difference that she'd been implanted that bit longer.

Nick said nothing more and I helped him lift the bed off the porch and wheel it over to the barn – whatever was troubling him, getting rid of those implants came first.

Jimmy might be a genius, but he's not a tidy one, and when I got back the two of them had moved onto arguing about clearing his workbench. Everything Doctor Simon picked up, he either slammed back down where it'd been, or bore it away as if it was made of finest crystal. Tell the truth, I didn't have the patience for it – I just scooped everything up in my arms and dumped it into a corner.

'Big Guy!' he screeched, ignoring Gordie giggling at how high his voice had gone.

I ignored him, doing as the Doc told me: wiping down the bench, helping him unroll and lay out this thick wired sheet of plastic. At last the contents of that shiny case were revealed as he took out what I guessed was the last word in medical computers.

Gordie, knowing he wasn't wanted, left us to it and headed back over to see Hanna. The only other person who shouldn't have been there was Jimmy, but there was no way he was going anywhere, and actually, as annoyed as he was to see someone threatening his position as the brains of the organisation, I could see he was that bit interested. I reckoned he would've given the growth in his burgeoning ponytail for a session on the Doc's fancy computer – not that he would've ever admitted it. I caught him looking longingly at it, but the moment he realised I was watching, his face turned to a sneer, like he'd just seen a dyed blonde speeding in a pink Cadillac.

'Can I have Thomas?' the Doc said, ready to start.

For a moment I thought he wasn't gonna get him – that Lena might just wheel around and take him out, and I couldn't help but think the Doc would've done better to have started with someone else, but maybe he had a good reason.

'Clancy?' she said, as if to check I was monitoring the situation.

'It's okay.'

She reluctantly handed Thomas over, the Doc unable to resist a moment of just holding him up in front of him, staring at the little guy like he was the eighth, ninth and tenth wonders of the world.

Thomas was so sleepy he didn't, as I'd anticipated, start to cry, but instead just nodded off the moment he was placed on the bench. The Doc eased on these big pulsing goggles and started scanning him up and down, searching for the implant. A couple of times he paused to scrutinise different areas, frowning, then finally decided he'd seen enough.

'What is it?' Lena asked, sensing an atmosphere.

'Nothing,' the Doc replied, handing Thomas back to her. 'Clancy?' he said, and indicated that I should lie down, also scanning me with those odd-looking goggles.

'Can you see it?' I asked, but Doctor Simon had fallen into medical mode and completely ignored all my questions.

Miriam was wheeled over, still motionless in bed, and Nick and me helped the Doc get her on the bench. As if he'd known it'd be there, he went straight for her head and immediately appeared to find what he was looking for.

'Well,' he said, taking off his goggles, 'I've got bad news . . . and good.' He paused in a rather practised manner, as if he'd delivered that particular diagnosis a million times.

'What?' Lena cried, as if she couldn't wait a moment longer.

'Sorry, Clancy,' he told me. 'It's really made itself at home – won't be long now . . . And sorry to you, too,' he said to Nick, and I realised no one'd remembered to introduce them.

'No hope?' Nick asked.

'I'm afraid she's already been keyed.'

There was a heavy pause, but Nick never said a word, nor even reacted.

'What about Thomas?' I asked.

Doctor Simon paused for a moment, giving out with a kind of half-grunt, half-chuckle. 'That's the good news . . . he doesn't have one.'

'*What?*' Jimmy cried.

'He doesn't have an implant.'

'Come on,' Jimmy protested, 'I saw it – just like Clancy's.'

'I'm sure you did,' Doctor Simon replied, 'the thing is, for obvious reasons, there's been no research on the effects of implants on babies. I think he's too young: the bone and tissue are still forming. I think the implant simply couldn't get a hold. I would guess that Thomas' implant was disposed of along with the contents of one of his diapers.'

I went to Lena and put my arms around her and the little guy, giving them both a big grateful hug. 'You're sure?'

'Absolutely.'

'Thank God,' I said, kissing Lena on the forehead, but her mind had already travelled on elsewhere.

'What about Clancy and Miriam? What's going to happen to them?'

'I'm not sure. I'll have to give them a more detailed scan.'

'Then what?'

The Doc paused, looking that bit lost. 'I don't know . . . I might try freezing.'

'What good's that gonna do?' Nick asked.

'If we can get the implant in a defined state, stop it metamorphosing, it might make it easier to remove.'

There was a long chunk of silence, no one looking sure what to think. Part of the trouble was, like it or not, we had to trust the Doc, to believe what he was telling us; he could've been stalling, playing for time – maybe there *was* no hope? Or maybe the removal was simple and he could do it then and there, but by hanging around he'd get to see more of Lena and Thomas, maybe even conduct a few tests of his own?

It was only later, after catching up on a couple of hours' sleep, Lena gently dozing beside me, that I remembered about my conversation with Nick. I blearily struggled up, again feeling like death, that maybe that damn thing inside me was poisoning my whole metabolism.

'You okay?' Lena whispered, not wanting to disturb Thomas.

'Just gonna have a word with Nick.'

'Clancy?'

'Yeah?' I replied, my hand on the door handle.

'It'll always be us,' she told me. 'You know that, don't you? I'll choose you over everything.'

I went back and kissed her, then made my way outside. I found Nick around the side, occupying himself by splitting a few logs.

'Trouble?' I asked, his expression telling me he'd been waiting for me.

He sighed then shook his head, as if he could acknowledge what he was about to tell me, but sure couldn't believe it. 'Miriam tried to kill me.'

I stared at him. What the hell was he talking about? She barely moved apart from when she was eating.

'I know, I know,' he said, as if he could read my mind, 'but she did.'

'*Miriam?*' I repeated, not getting it at all.

'I usually stay with her 'til she falls asleep, then go to bed myself. Occasionally, if I'm really tired, I nod off on the edge of her bed.' He paused for a moment, like he couldn't bear to go on. 'The night you left . . . I awoke feeling something really tight around my neck – I tell ya, I couldn't believe it! – she was trying to strangle me with the cord of her dressing-gown.' Again he paused, as if still deep in shock. 'She's barely moved in years. I wouldn't've thought she'd have the strength, but it was all I could do to fight her off.'

I didn't know what to say – partly 'cuz I couldn't believe Miriam was physically capable of such a thing, but also 'cuz – well, why would she do that to *Nick*? I couldn't imagine how he must be feeling. Taking care of her all those years, attending to all her needs, never getting a thing in return – damn it, dragging her in a bed halfway across the country – and for that, she tried to kill him?

Nick slumped forward, his face in his hands, and I noticed how his gut had shrunk. 'Something else,' he said eventually, looking up at me with reddened eyes.

'What?'

'I been thinking . . .' Again he paused, looking like someone who'd rather pull out his own teeth than drag out the thoughts he had in his head. 'Maybe George killed his brothers?'

I never commented, immediately knowing he was going somewhere with this and trying to work out where. He met my gaze full-on, urging me to say it, to save him the trouble, but it was no use.

'Maybe that's why it's not important everyone gets an implant,' he ventured at last, ''cuz those who *do,* kill those who *don't.*'

If I hadn't been sitting down, I reckon I might well have fallen.

Immediately I knew there was something in what he was saying, that that was the answer to Jimmy's little mystery, why it wasn't important that the weevils implanted everyone.

Just like with the shadow-growlers, Nora Jagger's plans had reached a point where if you weren't *with* her, you had to be eliminated. George must've had an implant and once it'd been keyed, set about killing anyone who didn't, including his brothers – and Lena. That was the missing piece of the jigsaw – why he'd ignored me and kept trying to get past me to Lena. Same with Miriam: something in that thing gave her not just the impulse, but the strength to try to kill the nearest non-imp – even if he loved her more than anyone on this earth. And then . . . *Oh, Jesus!* . . . and then finally I saw how all that related to me, and gave out with this loud, almost sickened, moan.

Nick immediately patted me on the back; I guess he'd been ready and waiting for me to reach that point.

'Am I gonna try to kill Lena and Thomas?' I cried.

'No,' he replied, 'the Doctor'll get that thing out. Don't you worry.'

'Jesus, *noooo!*' I moaned, barely able to believe the cruelty of it. I loved those two more than I ever imagined I'd be capable of loving anyone. The thought of harming them in any way made me want to strike myself from the face of the Earth. '*No!*'

'Clancy! It'll be all right!' Nick tried to tell me, but I leapt up and set off for the barn as fast as I could, rushing in to find the Doc studying his computer, plainly not welcoming my interruption but stopping when he saw the expression on my face.

'I gotta get this thing outta me,' I told him.

'I know,' he replied, immediately resorting to his professional bed-side manner.

'I'm gonna try to kill them.'

'Who?' he asked, plainly mystified.

'Lena and Thomas.'

Suddenly I had his full attention and his scrubbed and moisturised brow tangled into a frown. 'What are you talking about?'

I told him the whole story, partly 'cuz I wanted to get it out, but more 'cuz I was hoping he'd dismiss it, but one look at his face was enough to realise it wasn't gonna happen; that Nick was right.

'You gotta get it out of me,' I repeated. 'I don't care what damage it does.'

'I'm trying,' he assured me, gesturing at his computer.

For a moment there was silence, both of us obviously working through what it meant.

'What are you going to do?' he eventually asked.

'What d'you mean?'

He gave this kinda helpless shrug. 'If you present a danger – to your partner and child, to *all* of us . . . with the best will in the world, Clancy, you can't stay here. You're a big guy who used to live his life through violence.'

It's funny, I used to be so proud of that. Like I told ya, it got me what I saw as respect. Now I was ashamed: I was an obsolete liability, a weapon from an old war. Others had taken over now, new ways of fighting where you destroyed the enemy by getting them to turn on each other, where this dumb old big guy could be made to kill those he loved more than anyone in his life. The Doc was right: I had to go. I could no longer protect my family from the enemy. I *was* the enemy.

'Are you getting anywhere at all?' I asked him, unable to keep the desperation out of my voice.

'It's finding other people's bits of the jigsaw,' he sighed. 'And I can't stay much longer – she'll get suspicious.'

'Forget about her,' I told him.

'You know what she's capable of,' he reminded me.

'I don't give a rabbit's fuck!'

He went silent, plainly intimidated by my anger, but there was a much greater force at work here than me and we both knew it.

'So at some point in the next few days I might try to kill Lena and Thomas?' I said, as if recapping.

'Not necessarily.'

'What does that mean?'

'It's not as straightforward as that; there're a lot of things that can influence the outcome, affect the timing. It can vary depending on what type of implant it is, the character of the host, how long you can fight it. Once you're keyed though . . . then it *is* over.'

'And no one knows how that works?'

'Except her.'

I paused, wondering whether to tell him, in the end seeing no harm in it. 'There's something – I don't know what it is – flies around here. You never get to see it, but I swear it's there.'

He shrugged, as if I was a patient telling him one symptom too many – that might confuse the diagnosis. 'It's possible; all I do know is that whatever's used, she's personally involved, so maybe she activates the program herself.'

I left him a few minutes later. To his credit, I gotta say, he had looked genuinely upset. Sitting there deep in thought, even distracted from his computer, conscience and guilt maybe churning over, that age-old realisation that by doing nothing he'd allowed Evil to flourish. Or who knows? Maybe that was giving him far too much credit?

How I could possibly tell Lena, I didn't know, but what the Doc'd said had been right: I couldn't stay; it was far too dangerous. With the exception of Miriam, I was the only one with an implant – I might try to wipe out the whole lotta them.

I paced around the yard for a while, kicking and cursing, trying to come up with another way, but eventually accepted there wasn't one. Like it or not, I had to go and tell Lena.

I found her in the bedroom, sitting in the chair feeding Thomas. She knew something was wrong the moment I walked in. Not that it made it any easier to come out with it

I sat on the arm of the chair and stroked the little guy's soft downy head, that defencelessness that usually made me feel so protective towards him sending a real chill through me.

As much as Lena'd changed *me*, I had the feeling that Thomas'd changed her more. She had another responsibility now, a really big one, and occasionally seemed that much more serious 'cuz of it. I was no longer always number one, not the way I used to be. I guess we guys don't understand that sometimes. We think things should more or less stay the same. Some even get jealous (of a little baby, for chrissake!), especially if there isn't the same amount of fooling around going on – which most times there isn't. But it wasn't simply a case of us two becoming three; there'd been three things in that relationship for a long time: Lena, me, and the love we felt for each other. Now that love had an expression and needed to be shared around a little more, but that didn't mean it was no longer there, that in a time of crisis it wouldn't rear up ready to fight whatever was coming our way.

At first she simply couldn't take it in. She might've believed it of others, of George – she'd suffered that first-hand – but the thought that *I* might try to kill her and Thomas? *Everyone* on the farm? That was too much. I had to keep explaining it, even though I knew she'd understood the first time. Why I had to leave, why I had to get as far away from them as I could. Over and over she said it wasn't necessary, that we'd manage somehow, that we'd always seen things through before, but this was different and she knew it. There was no other way. No matter how much she told me she'd be careful, that she wouldn't leave me alone with Thomas – or maybe *because* she said she wouldn't leave me alone with Thomas – I knew I had to go.

Of course, I tried to sugar-coat it, telling her there was every chance the Doc would come up with something, that the implant still had some time before it would be fully functional, but her smile was every bit as hollow as my words.

That evening, over dinner – with the Doc still out in the barn – I informed the others, though of course Nick already knew. Their reactions were pretty well the same as Lena's: they couldn't believe it, wouldn't accept it, said it would never happen – and yet a couple of times I caught a glimpse of something else. As much as they tried to hide it, their expressions were underwritten by a degree of concern, a fear that I might well run amok, slaying them all like some old-time horror movie, and I found myself endlessly repeating that I'd go, that there was no way I'd stay and risk harming them.

The conversation slowly scratched and scraped its way to silence. I mean, what could anyone say? Though Jimmy did finally come up with the one question that did have to be asked. 'Are you sure that guy's telling the truth?' he said, plainly still with a score to settle.

'I don't trust him,' Gordie chipped in.

'Why would you?' I commented. 'But we can't take the chance.'

'It's true,' Nick assured them, making a rare contribution to the conversation. 'Believe me.'

He then gave them the briefest account of what'd happened with Miriam. He had to stop a coupla times to compose himself. The mood was noticeably darkening as everyone suddenly turned back to me.

I kept it as matter-of-fact as I could, telling them I'd head out in the morning, just until I knew how I'd react to the implant, then, all being well, hopefully I'd be able to return.

'Where you gonna go, Clancy?' Hanna asked.

'I dunno,' I answered, sadness already beginning to invade me. 'Just . . . away.'

Later that evening I returned to the barn. Something had occurred to me and I needed to talk to the Doc again. I found him still busily working away on his laptop, though by the look of him, the frustration hardening on his face, he hadn't made a great deal of progress.

'Anything?' I asked.

'These things take time,' he sighed.

I nodded, actually, as pressing as that was, I had other things on my mind. 'Are all your operations on there?' I asked, gesturing at his computer.

'Yes.'

'Even Lena's?'

He stopped for a moment, looking almost as if he'd been waiting for this conversation. 'We don't have time, Clancy.'

'But if something happens to me – would you?'

'If it's possible. If I get the chance.'

'She's gonna need to be able to see. Tell her.'

'Doesn't she want the operation?'

'I'm not sure.'

'I've got to have her consent, Clancy.'

'I know, but . . . try and persuade her, will you?'

I stayed there for a few more minutes, neither of us speaking, and then, slightly embarrassed by the conversation, I left him to it.

The thing was, Jimmy was right, *everyone* was right: I still didn't know if I could trust the guy. I was grateful he couldn't communicate with anyone, that without aerials or satellites he couldn't get a signal over the mountains, but that didn't mean there wasn't something else organised. I guess the truth was, as it always had been, that I *had* to trust him, at least to some degree. I was leaving him with the two most valued treasures of my life, and even though I knew the others would be watching every move he made, I was still a long way from comfortable about it.

That night was torture from the moment Lena and me went to bed 'til the moment we got up, mainly 'cuz we were trying so hard to play the whole thing down, to pretend it was just a precaution, that I'd soon be back with her, when really we didn't have a clue. Was I gonna turn into a monster, like in another of those books I read out on the Island: *The Strange Case of Dr Jekyll and Mr Hyde*. Did the implant change your whole character so that you became nothing but a killing machine searching out non-imps, or was it more of a programmed response to some kind of stimulus? Not that it mattered much; whether of its own accord or after being keyed, sometime in the next few days that thing inside me was gonna turn me into a killer again, just like in the bad old days with Mr Meltoni, only this time I'd be taking my orders from the Bitch, and my victim wouldn't be someone who'd got a bit too big for their boots, but maybe my lover, our child, all our friends.

We tried to make love, more, I reckon, 'cuz we thought we should, that it would help, but we were both so sick with worry we couldn't manage it. I mean, no matter how positive we were trying to be, how much we reminded ourselves about the insurmountable odds we'd conquered in the past, this was different.

This time, though I'd never have admitted it to her, or anyone else, it felt a bit like the end.

CHAPTER FIFTEEN

I can't tell you how odd the atmosphere was the following morning, what with me packing up what I thought I'd need as if I was going away on a trip. No one quite knew what to say, how to approach it. Hanna put her arms around me, as if she feared it might be the last time, as if she wanted me to know that she'd forgive me no matter what I did, which damn near broke me up. Jimmy and Delilah tried to act as normally as they could but still had that look about them, like they were about to let a wild animal go free that they'd only just tamed.

At one point Nick gestured for me to join him out in the yard so he could have a quiet word, those circles around his eyes now so dark they were like smeared ashes.

'Clancy, if this thing *does* take a hold of you, if it brings you back here and you end up . . .' He paused and took a deep breath. 'Kill her too, won't you?'

'Nick!'

'She won't be able to exist without me.'

'I'm not killing anyone,' I told him. 'I'd rather kill myself. Anyway, she's an imp.'

'That's why you have to kill her.'

'No one's gonna die, not if I can help it.'

'But—'

'*No one's gonna die!*' I repeated.

I gave him a reassuring pat on the shoulder, then led him back inside, feeling a little guilty that I was making promise after promise that I wasn't sure I could keep. I glanced at Miriam as I passed her bed, for some reason imagining that implant inside her gradually subverting what was left of her mind.

Taking Lena and Thomas into the bedroom to say goodbye was one of the hardest things I've done in my life. No matter how much we tried to pretend it was merely a precaution, that everything would soon be back to normal, we knew it wasn't true, that we were drowning in uncertainty. My conversation with Nick had upset me more than I'd let on; the realisation that like it or not, we'd all have to consider extraordinary measures.

I'd collected one of the lasers Jimmy had mended and now placed it in Lena's hand, hoping that would be explanation enough, but she just stood there staring into deepest nothingness.

'If you have to,' I said eventually. I mean, she might be blind, but she'd still have a good idea what to shoot.

'What?'

'If it's a choice between me, or you and Thomas . . .'

She caught this sudden shallow breath. 'I can't believe you'd even say that.'

'I got no choice,' I told her, I swear that thing inside me was suddenly fluttering and triumphant, like it knew it had scored its first major victory.

'I can't kill *you*!' she told me.

'*You're* not the problem,' I told her, pulling her towards me. 'Listen, something you should know: if I harmed either of you in any way, I wouldn't want to live anyway.'

For a moment she went quiet, lost in her head somewhere, and I got the distinct impression she felt betrayed. 'What's the matter?' I asked.

'I've told you a thousand times.'

I waited, still not getting what she was trying to say. 'What?'

'It's me and you, Clancy, no matter what happens. It always will be.'

I stared at her for a moment. It was rare, but occasionally she'd get this hard look that would remind me she'd once been an Island kid: tough, determined, maybe even that little bit crazy.

'I'd choose you over everything,' she told me.

To be honest, I wasn't entirely sure what she meant by that, but I still hugged her as tightly as I dared. The time was soon coming when we had no choice but to release and retreat, and with one last kiss on her lips and Thomas' forehead, I turned to go.

I knew she wasn't gonna follow me out, that the closing of that bedroom door would be the last sound between us, and I didn't look back, not even a glance, just closed the old world off from the new and headed towards the front door.

Out in the parlour, Gordie and Gigi were so determined to act all hard and nonchalant, to prove that the thought of me running amok didn't worry them one little bit, that they didn't notice the tears in the eyes of the assassin. Hanna hugged me almost as long as Lena had, while the older ones – Nick, Jimmy and Lile – were more solemn and respectful; at their age they knew there were no certainties, and for sure not in this situation.

I didn't encourage anyone to follow me out, diffusing the situation by telling them I was going over to see the Doc, everyone agreeing there was no need for extravagant farewells, that I'd be back soon enough.

I found Doctor Simon still crouched over his computer, his

messed-up hair and unshaven face making him look more dishevelled than I ever imagined he could be.

'Nothing?'

'I'm still working on the idea of freezing,' he told me. 'Unfortunately someone appears to have blocked me off.'

For a while I just stood watching his fingers moving around that keyboard almost as quickly as Jimmy's. 'I gotta go,' I told him.

He turned to me, thoughts and feelings darting all over his face, suddenly looking that bit shifty – not that that was what prompted me to say what I did. I'd been rehearsing that since the moment I knew I had to leave.

'I warn you now, you harm Lena or Thomas in any way, it'll be the last thing you ever do . . . I've told the others; they've got lasers. But if they don't get you, I promise you, I'll override this implant – rip it outta my damn body if I have to – and come for you, no matter where you are.'

'It's okay, Clancy,' he reassured me, looking noticeably shaken.

'I mean it.'

'I know you do.'

I stood there for a moment, wanting to reinforce my position by giving him a long hard blast of the look, but he wouldn't meet my gaze, instead returning his eyes to the screen.

'Don't ever forget,' were the last words I said before I stepped back outside.

I glanced over at the porch, I guess hoping Lena would be there, but it was just Hanna and Lile. I retrieved the tandem, gave them a bit of a wave and headed off down the track, already feeling like some kind of outcast: a leper or pariah, so crazy with sickness nobody wanted him around. And d'you know, the moment that thought entered my head, I swear I felt that thing move inside me, melting to jelly, all purple and shiny, wrapping itself around my guts like some life-sucking parasite.

When I got to the road I stopped for a few moments, looking left and right, having no idea which way to go, nor really caring. All I knew was I had to remove myself not only from the gang, but from the chance of trying to kill any non-imp. Finally I turned towards the Interior, feeling safer that way, that I'd find myself a wilderness where I'd be no danger to anyone.

I got no idea how long I pedalled for. A couple of vehicles went by and some kids actually waved outta the window, but I didn't wave back. It felt wrong, that I had no right, bearing in mind what I was probably about to turn into some time in the next twenty-four hours.

It started to rain a little. No weight to it – wasn't much more than a depressed mist, but it added to this growing sense of unease I had that I'd made the wrong decision; I should've gone the other way, over the mountain. Maybe I could've retrieved the limo – that would've given me any number of options, providing it was still there, of course.

I undermined myself so deeply that in the end I turned around, heading back a damn sight quicker than I'd headed out, like some wily old horse hired out by the hour, and soon I was approaching the track back up to the house, a growing frustration inside me making me ride by faster than I'd ridden all day – what the hell was I doing back there?

I kept up that speed until I turned off the road and headed up towards the mountain, but ya know what? I hadn't gone that far at all before I began to wonder if maybe *that* wasn't the right decision either: once I got over the mountain I was bound to come across people and who knew how I'd react. I might be able to make it to the limo and get away before anything happened, but I couldn't be sure. Not to mention the fact that it was outta gas, which would complicate matters no end.

Again I stopped, just standing there straddling the tandem, gazing in every direction, at all my options, but none of them seemed right.

In the end, I had to admit to myself what'd probably been obvious right from the moment I'd set out: I couldn't do it. I couldn't leave. Lena was everything to me, and Thomas and her together that bit more. I couldn't leave them alone and unprotected, no way – but on the other hand, I couldn't endanger them either.

There was only one answer – or only one a lovesick old big guy who really should've known better could come up with: I'd hide in the woods near the farm. That way, if anything happened, I could be across there in moments. And in case I was keyed and my implant became traceable, I'd keep on the move all the time, taking the tandem on random journeys so I'd never be tracked in the same place twice.

And so it was that almost four hours after setting out I found myself no more than a few hundred yards away, feeling a little rash and guilty, concerned I was taking a chance with something I didn't understand, but also that bit happier. I just had to be careful no one saw me; for sure it would do nothing for their peace of mind to know a big old killer bear was lurking in the woods, that at any moment he might come over and pay them a visit.

I found a spot in the thickest part of the woods and set up camp, eating a little of the food I'd brought, keeping it to a minimum, not sure when and where I'd find more. I'd brought a single blanket with me; hopefully that was gonna be enough to keep me warm at night. My main concern was what would happen the following day: was there some kinda automatic trigger? Would I be keyed straightaway? The thought of someone else controlling me frightened me to death, particularly when that someone else was the Bitch, Nora Jagger. If only I could get to her somehow, get rid of her – then again, that's a mistake that's been made right throughout history. It wasn't just her; she wasn't the only one taking the country hostage. For a start, there was the small matter of her Bodyguard. And anyways, I didn't need to get to her . . . She was coming for me.

I was dwelling on it so much, forever thinking I could feel the implant moving around in me, that I decided to take my mind off things by checking the woods. I set off in a circle, exploring areas I'd never been before, deliberately getting lost so I had to find my way back to the camp in the dark and it was well into the night before I finally settled down. To my surprise, I fell asleep almost immediately, though it was no surprise at all who took the opportunity to enter my dreams; Lena came to me just as I knew she would, leaving the house, stealing across the open ground, slipping through the trees and down into my head.

She was in my arms before I knew it, for some reason in the total blackness of the crypt, the derelict old church where we'd lived in the City. There was a slight stirring somewhere, someone moving, and I realised the others were there with us, all five of them: Jimmy and Delilah, Gordie and Hanna, but for some reason not Gigi but little Arturo. Not that I could actually see them – I was as blind as Lena in that darkness – but I knew they were there all right.

It took me a while to realise that Lena and me were making love, the way we used to down there: as quietly as possible, doing everything we could to make sure no one could hear, increasing the pleasure almost to the point of pain.

'I'll never leave you,' I told her. 'No matter what.'

Jeez, that hurt, more than the total accumulation of every fist, foot, club or bullet that'd ever ripped into me. But I said it again and again, becoming concerned that she wasn't listening.

When we finished making love, when I held her to me, I realised she'd stopped breathing. I squeezed so hard I actually heard one of her ribs crack – but it was too late, she was already as cold as ice on a grave.

I awoke with a real jolt, momentarily thinking there was someone or something standing over me, that this was how you were keyed.

I looked this way and that, squinting into the darkness, my heart pounding so hard it felt like it was vibrating down into the earth.

Finally I struggled to my feet, knowing I had to see the farmhouse, that I needed to know Lena was okay. I stumbled awkwardly across the forest floor, the dense trees reinforcing the night's darkness to a point where I kept almost colliding with them.

When I got to the edge of the woods and gazed over, there wasn't a lot to see, not in the middle of the night and with everyone in bed. There wasn't even a light in the barn, which I took to mean the Doc had given up for the day. I hoped to God he'd made some progress, that there was some cause for hope.

Lena was over there – no more than a few hundred yards away, probably sleeping with Thomas for a little comfort. The thought of those two together so warm and welcoming, I'll tell ya, I could almost feel myself crawling in beside them. But I wasn't allowed – not me. I was too much of a threat.

And it was only then, with all that aching loneliness welling up inside me, that I finally saw what I should've seen long ago. I wasn't the first one in those woods to feel that way: banished from those they loved for their own protection, sickened by the thought of what they might do to them – all that howling and screaming into the night? I'd be willing to bet that'd been the reason. Just like me, they hadn't been able to bear the thought of killing their own, their family, those they loved. They hadn't been wounded or caught in traps; their pain had come from inside, and no wonder it had caused such suffering.

I turned and slowly made my way through the darkness back to my camp, aware of suddenly feeling weak, almost sick, like the first signs of a virus. Was that it then? Was that how it happened? Was I primed and ready? Would that plane or whatever it was swoop down and take away everything that was me? Was I about to lose my life and everything in it? God help me – would I never know Lena and Thomas again?

I awoke the following morning grateful for the fact that my mind still seemed to be my own, but still feeling that bit ill. I lay there for a while, telling myself I had to get up, but the next thing I knew I was waking up again, and again, and it kept happening, over and over, 'til finally I forced myself up, getting halfway, balancing on my creaking old joints, then just about managing the rest.

I ate a little food, chewing slowly and thoughtfully, trying to clear my head. I needed to get on the tandem, make my way to the far side of the woods and head off for the day, but before I did, I had to have the reassurance of taking one more look at the farm.

I made my way over as carefully as I could – the last thing I needed was to be spotted. As I approached the tree line, as the daylight began to seep into the woods, I could hear someone singing – not proper singing, not like Lile, but more like they were intent on keeping a rhythm. I wasn't in the least bit surprised to find it was Hanna, though I *was* a little surprised to see what she was doing.

She was up on one of Lena's guide wires, the one that led to the woods, using it as a tightrope, humming and singing, half-walking, half-dancing along it.

I stopped, even backed away a few paces, nervous of how I'd react to her, that something might've changed. Was it really possible that I'd ever want to harm Hanna? That I'd rush over to that non-imp, wrench her off that wire and twist her graceful long neck until it snapped?

I gripped the tree nearest to me, holding it tightly like I was securing myself, and stood watching her. Occasionally she would sway a little but she always kept her balance, humming that bit louder as if it helped, and I heaved a long sigh of relief on appreciating that nothing had changed between us – leastways, not yet.

Having said that, I was still kinda relieved to hear Gordie call to her, for her to jump off the wire and make her way over to the vegetable garden. Gigi came out of the house carrying a tray obviously intended for the Doc, ignoring Hanna as the two of them almost crossed paths. I s'pose I should've been surprised that amongst everything that was going on, they were still continuing their feud, but I wasn't. You might argue with it, especially at their age, but Love goes deeper than a dagger sometimes, and I wouldn't have minded betting that Gigi would carry that grudge as long as she lived.

I was disappointed, but yeah, also that bit relieved not to see Lena and Thomas. There'd been no response from my implant to Hanna, and presumably there'd be none to them, but I didn't want to put it to the test. Not to mention that with Lena's sense of smell, if anyone was gonna pick up on the fact that I was still around, she would.

I returned into the woods, mounted the tandem and headed off, riding alongside the creek for a while and then down to the road. It didn't really matter where I went, only that I got well away from the farm in case I was being tracked.

Irrespective of my situation, the fact that I wasn't feeling so good, I gotta say, it was one helluva perfect day for a bike ride. There wasn't a cloud in the sky, the sun was taking full advantage, and though the wind occasionally whispered, it never spoke louder. My eyes slid along the chain of the mountains into the far hazy distance. Just as they'd once kept the countryside from the worst of the hydrazine-derivative poisoning and the subsequent fires, now they were all that stood between us and total submission.

To tell the truth, I only glimpsed it for a moment, and it was so far away, I couldn't even be sure it was there. I braked the tandem to a halt, hoping for a better look, but whatever it was had disappeared. I know what I *thought* I saw: over on the other side of the valley, slowly moving across the hills, was this big black shadow.

It had to be a plane, there had to be something up there, but when I looked, when I attempted to correlate the sun to where the shadow had been, there was nothing.

I tried to tell myself I was just getting older, that it was one of those spots I sometimes get before my eyes, but I knew it wasn't: a shadow had moved across the land as if it was searching for something, and I had a terrible feeling it might be me.

I didn't see it again that day, and on my journey back to the woods, I began to think that maybe I *had* imagined it, that I was just on edge 'cuz I knew I was ready to be keyed.

All told, I must've covered thirty miles or so. It wasn't my kinda exercise, and I still didn't feel a hundred per cent, but I was getting used to it. More than anything there was this need to exhaust myself, to arrive back at the woods well and truly spent, fit only for sleeping – though whether by accident or design, after having something to eat, there was just enough light left for me to head over to the farm for a short while, and you won't be surprised to know I took full advantage of it.

I approached the edge of the woods, peering around tree after tree like some nervous animal. But ya know, all that caution was forgotten when I looked over towards the house and saw Lena sitting out on the front step with Thomas in her arms. I couldn't see clearly, not from that distance and in the withering day, but I had the feeling she was crying and it damn near broke my heart. I would've given anything to have run over there and told her it was gonna be all right, that we would prevail, the way we always had, but of course I couldn't.

I stayed 'til the light went altogether, finding myself holding a conversation with her the way she apparently used to have conversations with me out on the Island, before we'd actually met, when she'd secretly followed me around the Old City. I told her about where I'd been on the tandem earlier and how it wasn't the same without her on the back. Occasionally I'd put in her side of the conversation, smiling at the things she 'said', 'til finally . . . I dunno, I just lapsed into a kinda helpless silence.

Something about her sitting out on that step on her own, the baby in her arms, night falling, was starting to gnaw at me. There could be anyone around – crazies, whatever. She should be more careful. I'd always thought Lena was the perfect mother, but as soon as I was outta sight, she was acting that bit foolishly.

As if she sensed my worries, she got up and took the baby inside. Despite how dark it was, I waited for a while in case she reappeared, all sorts of thoughts going through my head, but with no further sign, I gave up and headed back into the woods.

I hadn't gone more than a couple of dozen paces before it hit me what'd just happened back there. When Lena and Thomas had disappeared inside, a thought had gone through my head so rapidly, it was only afterwards that I appreciated it'd been there: all about her, and whether she was the mother I'd always assumed her to be, and what I could do about it if she wasn't. That sometimes, to preserve our young, difficult decisions have to be made.

God help me, it *was* a thought, and it *had* been in my head, but I swear it hadn't been mine. I knew immediately what it was, and what'd come next, what that implant would bid me do, and just the thought alone was enough to tip me over the edge.

I'd always known it was there, that at some point I'd be driven to it: I took in as much breath as my old lungs could contain, threw my head back, and just like all those other animals, gave out with the loudest, most tortured howl you could ever imagine. It was pain-stricken and primaeval, half animal, half something unidentifiable, but I had to let it out, to keep going and going 'til there was nothing left inside me, 'til I didn't have the strength left to do what that implant would tell me I must.

In the end, I fell to the ground, stunned and sickened by what had been in my head. I couldn't hurt Lena and Thomas! *Never!* And suddenly I remembered what the Doc had said, about different people reacting in different ways. No way would I let that thing take me over. *No way!* You wanna fight—? I'm your man.

I dragged myself back up and returned to the scene of the crime as if determined to confront the enemy head-on, daring it to try to put another evil thought in my head. There was a light in the house, and one in the barn, which I guessed meant the Doc was still working, and the moment I saw it, I headed off in his direction.

The thing was, I was no danger to him – he *had* an implant. So who better to talk to about whether I'd been keyed or if this was just the final stages of the implant configuring itself. I also needed to check if he was making any progress with how to remove one – and, of course, to make sure he was behaving himself.

I didn't go directly over, instead following the treeline, heading towards the road, so that when I emerged, I could approach the barn from the opposite side to the house.

I'd only made it a few paces out of the woods when the light went off. Damn, he must've had enough for the day. I began to trot over, hoping to catch him before he went to the house, when I heard the Bentley start up in the lean-to at the back. *What the hell?*

Now I was running, desperate to reach him before he pulled away, but the Bentley had already nosed out and was heading towards the track. What the hell was he doing? Running out on us? I risked a bit of a shout, gaining on him a little as he took it easy on the heavily rutted track, but I was still a good fifty or more yards behind.

'Hey—! *Hey—!*' I called.

I didn't know if I imagined it or what, but I sensed a momentary hesitation, like he'd seen me in his mirrors and was checking, but if that was the case, his immediate reaction was to speed up. Or maybe it was just that he was approaching the road and the ground had levelled out.

I watched helplessly as he pulled out, as the Bentley rapidly accelerated away into the night and the silence of the country returned like calm to a disturbed pond. Where the hell was he going? I hadn't seen anyone in the car. Mind you, if he had Thomas, I wouldn't have been able to see anyway. Maybe he'd convinced Lena that it was safe for him to do some research with the little guy on his own? Maybe he'd won her confidence and now was taking unfair advantage?

I couldn't go over there – I couldn't go to the house and find out, so what the hell was I gonna do? In the end, I came up with what I felt was quite a neat solution. I had this old stub of a pencil I always carried with me, and after a little search, I found a scrap of paper blown up against the side of the barn.

I kept it as brief as I could:

Lena,

I thought I should tell you, the Doc's run out on you. You'd better get away as quick as you can. Maybe he's gonna bring Nora Jagger back with him.

I miss you and Thomas more than I ever could've imagined.

I love you so much . . . What else can I say?

I then went to the wire with the cans tied on it, getting as close to the house as I dared, put the note inside the nearest one to the front door and quickly retreated along the wire to the furthest point and gave it a good hard shake, setting the cans all chinking and rattling away. If there was one person in there I was sure would hear it, it would be Lena. It might take her a while, but she'd find the note, of that I was certain.

I ran back to the woods and waited, wanting to see what the reaction would be to my note. If Lena got all upset, for sure it'd mean that the Doc had somehow managed to sneak Thomas away from her – but as it turned out, she came outta the house with him in her arms.

The others soon followed on behind, turning on the porch light, Jimmy waving a laser around – I guessed they thought it was crazies, or even worse, the Bitch and some of the Bodyguard, but when they saw no one they started checking around, maybe looking for animals.

It wasn't long before Lena broke away from them, getting that slightly obsessed look about her – dammit, could she smell me? Almost immediately she started to work her way along the wire, locating the first can and then the note inside, handing it to Delilah to read.

You could see their mood change almost immediately. They turned to look over towards the woods, and even though I couldn't see their expressions, I sensed a certain apprehension about them.

I was still there, no more than a few hundred yards away: the big old ex-Mob heavy who'd gone a little insane.

CHAPTER SIXTEEN

I was up at first light as strings of misty mackerels started to appear in the glowing sky. I knew what Lena was like, how she'd react to my note, that she'd probably reply, and sure enough, when I crept over there I found a sheet of neatly folded paper inside the can.

I grabbed it and got away as fast as I could, not stopping 'til I reached the refuge of the woods. The first thing I saw as I unfolded it was a lot of cartoon characters on the writing paper – she'd obviously found it in the house, left there by the former owner's kids – the second, that it was her big sprawling hand-writing (as long as she keeps it to a minimum, she can write a note) so I guessed she'd written it while the others were sleeping.

> My Love,
> I knew you hadn't gone. The space around me wasn't empty enough. Please, come back. We really miss you. Together we can fight this thing. You won't hurt us – I know you won't.
> Nothing is stronger than my love for you.
>
> PS Dr Simon told us he had to go. He says he'll come back.

How I would've loved to have done just that: to have run across there, through the house and leapt into bed with her – but, of course, I couldn't. I didn't share her conviction that I wouldn't hurt them (or more accurately, that this *thing* inside me wouldn't).

Most of the time I felt okay, as if I was still functioning normally, but I was having to scrutinise each and every one of my thoughts so closely, just in case it turned out there were those smuggled in by someone else. Maybe it would start with Jimmy – how difficult and childish he could be, Delilah, too, and before I knew it, it would be old folk in general: how selfish they were, interested only in their own survival, no longer caring about the needs of society. What did they expect other than to become estranged and discarded? People like them – non-imps, those too old to change – it was only right to eradicate them . . .

And then I'd stop, realising what had crept into my head and forcibly ejecting it, but fearing that I wouldn't have the strength to do it for ever, that maybe that was what my tiredness was all about.

A little later I was out on the tandem, bumping down the slope to the road and turning in the direction of the pass, cycling along there for a while and then taking a detour: up into the hills, through the forest, the mountains always my reference point, making sure I didn't get lost.

It was when I paused at the top of a hill, puffing and blowing from the long climb, that I saw it again: sweeping across the valley floor towards me like a huge bird of prey. I dropped the tandem and ran towards some nearby trees, but how fast that thing was shifting, I knew I wasn't gonna make it. I could feel it surging up the hill, chasing me down, swooping on me – *Jesus, I was about to be keyed!*

Suddenly day seemed to turn into night, like a heavy cloak had been thrown over me. I swear I could feel the weight of that shadow pressing down, darkening every corner of my mind. I turned and looked up, at least expecting to finally discover what it was, but d'you know what? There was *nothing* there. I mean, Jesus – can a shadow exist independently?

I thought I'd feel it happen, like the turning of a switch, some kinda activation, but there was nothing; in fact, that pool of darkness around me suddenly turned and veered away as if it'd changed its mind, leaving me staring dazedly after it as it slid across the ground and over the trees. *What the hell . . . ? What just happened?*

I remained in hiding for some time in case it came back, at one point convinced I glimpsed it again further up the valley. I just didn't get it. What was going on here? Had it changed its mind about me? Had it been looking for someone else? Exactly how many were there of us hiding out in this area, knowing we'd reached our 'key by' date?

I spent the rest of the day riding from one source of cover to another, keeping an eye out for that shadow, anything moving across the land. It was almost dark by the time I got back and I was so tired I was concerned it might make me more vulnerable to having my thoughts perverted, more open to that thing gathering up madness and momentum in my head.

The irony was, after what I said about no longer feeling the need to dwell on the past, I was beginning to understand that one of the ways of fighting the implant was by dragging up memories, the more vivid, the better. It didn't matter what it was of: my folks, Mr Meltoni, my brother Don, my half-brother Ray, and, of course, if I could bear it, even dear little Arturo, the Mickey Mouse Kid. I had no idea why; maybe it was some kinda 'system restore' thing: taking me back to a point when I was confident my thoughts and senses were entirely my own.

I ate a little, then settled down for the night, as if sleep could somehow halt the battle going on inside me, but if anything, it made it worse. With all the barriers lowered, the situations became more bizarre, the characters more evil.

It must've been the implant, but as I flitted from one side of the unconscious to the other, I became aware that I wasn't alone. Talking to Father Donald at the side of my old man's grave, I noticed this shadow lurking behind a gravestone; helping Don to learn to ride a bike, I was aware of someone chasing up behind us, as if they wanted him to fall and hit his unhelmeted head; and when getting my first real view of the Island from the boat the day I was sent over, someone was standing beside me on the rail, as if whoever it was had been one of the first invited to participate in that particular experiment, that without Death, there'd be nothing.

It took me a while to appreciate they were all one and the same person, and when I did, my heart began to race so fast it almost became a single tone.

Down in the Crypt I demanded whoever it was come out of the darkness; listening to their heavy breathing, the scraping of the stone lid of the tomb as they emerged. At the home of the enticer who'd kidnapped Gordie to steal his organs I threw open door after door in my search, and each time was confronted by a pale, naked, freshly scarred and sometimes still bleeding child. But the person orchestrating it all was nowhere to be seen.

As it turned out – and as I guess I always knew – it wasn't the Devil, but it *was* his sister. I immediately knew where she was and set off over to the farmhouse as fast as I could. Even before I got there I could see this looming shadow going from room to room, sucking out all the life, leaving nothing but a vacuum of smudged waste.

I stumbled in to be greeted by the most sickening sight imaginable: she'd beheaded each and every one of them: Jimmy and Lile, Nick and Miriam, the kids. I ran into the bedroom, shrieking out in protest, but no one had been spared. Lena's headless body was lying on the bed . . . even little Thomas had been torn apart and discarded like so many soggy crimson rags. Nora Jagger – 'the Bitch' as Gigi had so rightly christened her – stood in the middle of all that carnage looking so pleased with herself, those prosthetics of hers flexing and unflexing like they were somehow breathing.

'Why?' I screamed. 'Why did you do it?'

She stared deep into my eyes for a moment, her face breaking into the most chilling and vicious of smiles. 'I didn't do it . . . You did.'

I awoke with such a start I damn near levitated three feet into the air, gasping for breath, sweat coursing down the sides of my forehead.

Jesus! Had that been real? It was too vivid for a dream, surely? Nora Jagger had been real, I'd swear it – and, oh dear God, what had I done?

I jumped up and headed through the woods as fast as I could, bludgeoning my way through trees and darkness. I *didn't!* I *couldn't* have! But shit to admit, maybe that thing inside me could and had.

Apart from a slowly charging moon, the house was in deathly darkness, which didn't do a lot for my peace of mind. I ran over, telling myself I was being irrational, that everything was fine, but I needed to prove it to myself. I'd just about made it to the porch when a light went on in the kitchen and for one truly horrific moment I thought it must be Nora Jagger, still revelling in the massacre – *my* massacre – of my innocents, but it was merely a sleepy-eyed Jimmy getting himself a glass of water.

Thank God and Amen! It *had* been just a dream. I was that relieved, I tell ya, I could've screamed out with joy, though if I had, the little guy might've thought a massacre was on the cards anyway.

I turned and crept away as quietly as I could, feeling so relieved, I can't tell ya. Those images had been so *real!* – especially Nora Jagger – I couldn't get them outta my head . . .

The moment that thought occurred to me, I finally realised the obvious significance: of course, I couldn't get her outta my head! That was exactly where she was; that was where that thing was, lodged somewhere deep in my brain sending out horrific images like Lena and Thomas lying in bed with their heads ripped off, blurring my reality and fantasy.

I had to stop for a moment to take in several lungfuls of cool night air. I stood gazing across at the mountains in the growing moonlight, trying to calm myself down. Then suddenly I stopped and stared . . . *What the hell was that?*

There was this really bright light, way over to the right, on the next mountain. In fact, it was more like a *square* of light – like a sports field or baseball diamond, maybe.

I knew I had to investigate, that it was far too important to be left to the morning – but I had to let the others know too.

I wrote another note, not sure if I should ring the cans or not, in the end just leaving it there poking out for them to see, then hurried back to the woods to retrieve the tandem.

It wasn't easy, not in the early hours and on a crazy homemade tandem without any lights, but thankfully, that moon was now well up and casting out as much light as it could. I was so convinced it was the Bitch and the Bodyguard, it went through my head that maybe there'd be a reaction from the implant if I met her face to face? Would it speed up the process, the damn thing finally keyed? Jeez, maybe I'd end up throwing myself at her feet to pay homage?

It took me several hours to get partway across the basin of the foothills, that square of light getting bigger and brighter the closer I got. I came to this long cut that appeared to go almost all the way up and headed off up there, the climb becoming so steep I had to abandon the tandem; finding a hiding place amongst some boulders before resuming my journey, all the while wondering what the hell was going on up there.

It must've been getting on for four by the time I approached the top; the glow of light now so strong it was almost blotting out the night sky. I clambered out of the cut and scrambled up the last bit of the slope, grateful it was a much gentler incline, finally getting to peer over and see what was creating all that illumination.

At first I didn't get it. There was an area maybe eighty or ninety yards square lit up brighter than day. A couple of tents in the middle, large metal posts that looked a bit like aerials at each corner of the lit portion, and a coupla guards patrolling the perimeter. Though the really amazing thing was, that took me a while to register, the source of the light wasn't *above* the ground, it was *below*: the actual ground itself was glowing.

For a while I stayed where I was, having no idea who or what I was confronting. I could hear this kinda faint throbbing noise that seemed to be in some way connected with the corner-posts, as if they were picking up on a pulse maybe generated from one of the two tents – but what was the point? Just to make the ground glow? To give them greater light and security? And how the hell did it work?

I wanted to get a closer look at one of the guards as they patrolled the perimeter, but when they met – at the right-hand side of the square to me – they stopped to discuss something, one of them glancing at his watch. They were wearing a uniform I didn't recognise, a bit like Infinity's but smarter, with a lot of gold braid, and I had a pretty good idea I was getting my first sighting of the Bodyguard, also that – if it even needed saying – we were in a whole lotta trouble.

I started to crawl towards them, hoping to check them out, but hadn't gone more than ten yards when the light went out.

With all that glow around me, I'd missed the clouds covering the moon, and got a bit of a shock to find myself plunged into such darkness. What had happened, why the light had gone off, I had no idea. Maybe it was the hour? It wasn't that long 'til daybreak. What I *did* know was that I'd been presented with a golden opportunity to slip over unseen to the two tents and find out what this was all about.

I made my way over as quietly as I could, taking a bit of a detour to avoid any possibility of bumping into the guards. It was so uniformly black it took me for ever to locate the tents, in fact, I was almost starting to think better of the idea when I heard muffled voices in front of me, obviously from inside a tent. I paused, wondering if I should go any closer, having no idea what I was up against.

'When you're ready?' I heard a voice say.

Jeez, what the hell did that mean? Was something about to happen? I took a step back, then another, and realised someone had left one of the tents. Worse still, I immediately recognised that unmistakeable slurping mechanical stride of Nora Jagger-style prosthetics. It *was* the Bodyguard, and it sounded like they were heading my way.

I don't what I'd been hoping for by going over there ... maybe an opportunity to do something at last, to strike a blow while I still could? But now all I wanted was to get away. Whether the Bitch was there or not, I didn't know, but for sure the Bodyguard were, and I suspected in far greater numbers than I could cope with.

I thought I was heading in the direction of the cut, but I was a long way from sure. My eyes were getting a little more used to the darkness and I could see that bit more, but it wasn't helping much. Again I heard a voice, and this time it sounded like they were right behind me.

I just ran towards what I hoped was the way I'd come, and almost simultaneously several things happened I could've well done without: firstly, the pulsing started radiating out towards the corner posts again and the ground beneath my feet began to glow. Then I saw the guys from the tent had actually passed me and were already over at the perimeter, and finally, and most unwelcome of all, the moment I started to run, to get the hell outta there, this siren started up as if I'd just triggered it.

Amazingly for a dumb old big guy, I immediately had a pretty good idea what it was about: that pulse going through the ground? It wasn't just creating security lighting but also some kinda cushion between the surface and what was underneath – a pressure pad like the one on the lawn of the Infinity building that triggered the growlers. This had to be a portable version that they carried with them and adjusted to whatever size they needed – they'd just switched it off so they could change the guard, and Jeez, what a shame it was I hadn't worked out all that before.

One of the guards immediately took out his laser and started shooting, but now that I knew where I was, I was already over the side and tripping, stumbling and occasionally falling down the slope towards the cut. The only thing was, the guard with prosthetic legs – I guess he must've been the one I'd heard earlier – was after me in an instant.

It was like being pursued by some super-animal, something unknown that was a whole lot faster than you ever imagined an animal could be. Luckily for me, he might've been able to run a lot faster, but he had even less idea of where he was going. I kinda braked when I saw the cut open up before me, but he didn't, flailing his arms around, trying to stop himself falling, and ending up taking us both down into darkness.

It was a real confusion of body and limb, a struggle for dominance and survival. One second we were fighting, the next we were both clinging on to each other for dear life to prevent ourselves from falling faster than we were already. I hit him a couple of times – I mean, unless he managed to right himself, to bring those damn prosthetics into play, I was at no disadvantage. He did try kicking out, but we were still tumbling down the slope and somehow I was doing better than he was. I hit him again, a real hard shot to the face, and whether it stunned him for a moment or he didn't see it in the dark, instead of trying to dodge a boulder looming up in front of us, he slammed straight into it, taking the major share of the impact.

I reached under his body and grabbed his laser from its holster.

'That's enough,' I said, but you know, even with a laser pointed at him, that guy was still determined to fight on. He tried to swivel around, to lash out, but couldn't get any real purchase on the loose and rocky ground and lost his balance again. Still he wouldn't give up: he was up in an instant, taking another swing, and I realised that members of the Bitch's Bodyguard simply weren't programmed to surrender. I slammed him up against the boulder, his head colliding with a real whack, but you wouldn't have known it. He was like a robot, nothing would divert him, and in the end I had no choice. I shot him through the head – but ya know what? He *still* came back at me. I had to shoot him three times at close quarters before he finally lay still.

I struggled up and started to descend that cut as if it was the backstairs from Hell, slipping and tripping, bumping over boulders, threatening to do myself real harm. Even if I did make it to the bottom, I wasn't confident I'd be able to find the tandem's hiding place now that the moon had disappeared. I went on a bit further, actually fell over at one point, damn near breaking my leg, and eventually decided that there was no other choice; that I simply had to lie low for a while, at least until there was a hint of dawn's light.

There was a group of rocks nearby, surrounded by scrub; no one was gonna find me if I squeezed in there. The only thing was, the moment I did, that same heavy tiredness came back and no matter how hard I tried to repel it, sleep just wouldn't be denied.

It wasn't the morning light that burst through the dark walls of my unconscious but a scream: a howl of outrage and anger, and one I immediately recognised. Instinctively I shrank further back into my hiding place, stifling a little moan. *Please, God, no!*

'Find him!' a voice shrieked, and any small granule of hope I might've had immediately dissolved: it was Nora Jagger, all right, and going on how furious she was, someone had given her a description of me that she'd recognised.

'What the hell are you doing?' she shouted at someone, the muttered and unintelligible response sounding painfully contrite.

'Look harder!' she screamed, rocks violently scattering, and I guessed she'd lashed out with one of those killer limbs.

I raised my head as much as I dared and peered out of a slit between two rocks. All my worst fears were realised: there was a small group of them with the Bitch looking down from slightly up the slope, lashing them with her tongue, burning them with her eyes, ready to dish out punishment at the slightest provocation. Not one of them was daring to address her directly, no matter how brave they'd been programmed to be.

'No one kills one of us!' she told them. *'No one!'*

I don't know why – maybe there was another group searching elsewhere she had to check on – but she turned abruptly and stormed back up the hill, pounding the ground so hard it was as if she was trying to crush it. The five members of the Bodyguard – four men and a woman – resumed their search in earnest, though thankfully they were working their way back to the place where the body of their comrade had obviously been discovered.

Now that it was light I could see where I was, and damned if the tandem wasn't no more than a coupla hundred yards away – if only I'd known that the previous night. Still, I reckoned if I could make it there, I had every chance of getting away. I waited 'til I could see they were distracted – one of them had called the others over to the entrance of a small cave – then slipped out and began to tiptoe down the slope, being careful where I put my feet, wanting to run but scared I might disturb a rock or something.

I guess I'd made almost half of that distance before the cry went up, but it wasn't from one of the Bodyguard – Nora Jagger had returned.

'*You damn imbeciles!*' she screamed, '*look!*'

I started to run, doing my best to keep my balance on the steep slope and uneven ground, but immediately she was pounding after me, giving out with this long, wild scream – God, she was angry.

I reached the tandem, dragging it out of its hiding place before glancing back and seeing this wild apparition bearing down on me, her mouth set in a vicious snarl as if she was getting ready to bite my head off.

I rode that crazy contraption as I'd never ridden it before, constantly in danger of falling off, hearing those pounding footsteps getting ever closer, at any moment expecting that bolt-cutter grip to take hold of me and rip me from my saddle. Outta the corner of my eye I could see her shadow on the ground, chasing after mine, the gap between us narrowing with every one of her giant strides. I swerved this way and that to avoid rocks, time and time again almost losing my balance, only God himself knowing why I didn't go hurtling to the ground.

For a few moments I seemed to be holding the distance, then she made her move, leaping at me, those incredible legs propelling her though the air, and I felt her fingers rake down my back, almost get a hold – but it was her last despairing effort and with it she fell to the ground and was forced to give up.

'*Clancy! Clancy—!*' she screamed after me, but I kept going, the cut finally levelling off and allowing me to ride like I might stay in the saddle for more than a few seconds.

'*Clancy!*' she roared one last time, but I was gone.

I couldn't help myself, for a few moments I roared with laughter. After all the sneers and jokes about the Typhoon Tandem, it had turned out to be one of the fastest forms of transport in the valley, certainly when it came to travelling cross-country. Wouldn't Jimmy just love that? For that matter, so did I.

Whether it was all that hard pedalling, the ordeal, or something way more sinister, I didn't know, but not long after the relief of knowing I was safe, that familiar dense tiredness began to ooze its way back through me. I did my best to keep going, to shake it off, singing and shouting, repeatedly slapping my face, doing everything I could – but in the end I had no choice but to give in.

I went into the forest, feeling a bit like I had a fever, that a battle was starting to rage inside me. In the end I just collapsed into some thick undergrowth, letting the tandem fall to the ground, praying to God Nora Jagger didn't come after me.

Within seconds I was asleep, and almost as if she'd triggered that implant to do what she couldn't, she was there. I was driving Mr Meltoni's limo and somehow my tiredness in real life had carried over into my dream. The person in the back was massaging my shoulders. I thought it was Mr Meltoni himself – tell the truth, I was a little uncomfortable about it. Then suddenly these huge arms snaked around and took a firm hold of my throat: the Bitch was panting like a bull on the back of my neck, squeezing and squeezing, out to decapitate me for sure. I hit the brakes, veered over to the side and bounced off a parked truck as I tried to break the grip of those locked hands, but I knew that, like everyone else, I didn't stand a chance.

I lost consciousness and woke up at the same time; feeling so invaded. That woman was everywhere: in my dreams, my head, my body. I forced myself up to my feet, still so dazed I was rocking back and forth, only then appreciating how long I'd been out, that the day was almost over.

I had to clear my head and mount the tandem; get back to the farm and warn the others she was on her way.

I arrived just after dark, still feeling so tired it was almost a sickness. Through the window I could see Gordie and Hanna preparing dinner, just the top of Jimmy's almost bald head appearing over an easy chair. I scribbled another note and left it in the usual can:

> Nora Jagger's nearby. Don't let her know anyone's living here.
> Stay inside – no fires, no lights.

Then I shook the wire and hurried off over to the woods, several of them emerging almost before I'd hidden myself.

I waited to make sure they did what I'd suggested – turning off all the lights, reducing the house to darkness – so distracted that at first I didn't notice it was happening again, that amongst my many thoughts there was the occasional agitator.

Why the hell did I worry about these people all the time? They'd had their chance and hadn't been savvy enough to take it. Now they were doomed to obsolescence – and honestly, I reckon I'd be doing them a favour if I went over there and put an end to their miserable lives. Gordie first, just inside the door – he'd never know what'd hit him. Nick and Miriam were dying of broken hearts anyway; it'd be a kindness. Gigi and Hanna might be a problem, but they both slept so deeply, I reckoned I could take out one without waking the other. Then the old couple, who should've been put out of their misery long ago: one good hard blow to the little guy's bald head, and if that didn't do it, I could finish him off by choking him with that stupid ponytail of his. As for Delilah, well, that'd be no more than snapping an old dead twig.

I don't know when exactly, but somewhere amongst all those terrible thoughts, I slid down the tree trunk I was leaning against and ended up on the ground. No, I hadn't forgotten Lena and Thomas, and that was the whole point: they were the ultimate test. Until I started thinking up ways of killing them, I reckoned there was hope, but I had to keep them right at the forefront of my mind, to hold them up like some burning torch. As long as I did that, I felt I had a chance of keeping up the fight, resisting everything including being keyed.

But ya know, no matter how determined I was, something about that didn't ring quite true. That Shadow-Maker thing, whatever it was, had caught me on open ground; held me down and appeared to go right through me – I'd been completely at its mercy. Not to mention how weak I'd been feeling, tired almost to the point of sickness … was I *really* putting up such a great fight?

I didn't so much fall asleep as tumble over and over 'til I collided with something harder than my head, all the while that thought nagging away inside me: was I really making it impossible for them to take control? Or was there something else going on?

CHAPTER SEVENTEEN

I don't know how long I slept, but going on how I felt when I woke up, ample time for eternity to have trampled over my bones. On the other hand, it was still night and the farmhouse looked pretty well the same – no lights, no smoke – so maybe it'd only been a few hours.

Thank God, they'd heeded my warning. There were so many abandoned buildings in the valley and so spread out, it would take Nora Jagger for ever to check them all out on foot. The last thing we needed was to give her any kinda clue.

And that was another thing I didn't understand: why the hell *was* she on foot? Okay, so maybe it was too far out for a Dragonfly, but they must have plenty of all-terrain vehicles. I was worried it might have something to do with the Doc – maybe he'd tipped her off where we were, that that was the way we travelled back and forth to the City and she'd come over the mountain to make sure that route was closed off? Didn't seem that likely, I know, but on the other hand, the fact that we'd now trust him *not* to do something like that seemed even less likely.

I scanned the mountains from one end to the other, not sure which way the Bitch and her Bodyguards would've gone. If they had that pressure-field up and working every night, they had to be some way off, 'cuz I couldn't see it anywhere.

I was just wondering what I should do, whether I should go out again and try to locate them, when a light came on in the farmhouse. It was only for a second or two, then it was switched off – I thought someone must've forgotten and accidentally put it on – but it was switched on again, then off, then on once more. Jesus, was somebody *signalling*?

I started to trot over to the house, feeling utterly confused – that was Hanna and Gigi's room, so what the hell were they playing at? But ya know, I hadn't even got across there before I began to get this really bad feeling, a suspicion that I should've known this day would come and I'd been a fool not to have done something about it.

I'd always been fond of Gigi – okay, maybe with slight reservations, but the thing is, I learned long ago that the best way of making someone trustworthy is simply by trusting them. By and large that's served me pretty well. That time in the limo, on the way to the City, when she finally told me what'd happened with her and Nora Jagger – about the resistance, and how she'd got caught between the two of them – I hadn't been in the least bit surprised. Gigi was just one of those people: she could turn just like that and no one, least of all her, knew why, what the fault was inside her that made her do it. I believed her that day – that she'd learned from the experience – I guess 'cuz I'd wanted to, but I'd still had my suspicions. Gigi had to be taken at face value at any precise moment in time, 'cuz a couple of minutes later the wind might easily change and there'd be nothing she could do about it.

There was no way Hanna would flick those lights on and off, and no way she'd be there and let Gigi do it, which meant she wasn't in the room. And if she wasn't in the room, where was she?

It was like a time bomb with a very long fuse. I knew it'd been there, I'd known there was every chance it might blow up one day, and I should've made it safe. I'd seen the way Gigi got irrationally angry if Hanna and Gordie so much as hinted at their feelings for each other. The discovery that Hanna had snuck off to be with Gordie in the middle of the night – and what they were probably doing – well, I reckoned that would just about have driven her beyond all logical thinking. Which was probably why she'd decided to bring the wrath of the gods down on everyone by letting Nora Jagger know where we were. No matter that she was in the Bitch's bad books – that she'd once attempted to kill her and was placing herself in terrible danger – in her mood that wasn't even a consideration; all she wanted was instant and bloody revenge on Hanna and Gordie, everything else would merely be collateral damage.

As I neared the farmhouse I grabbed every wire that would make a noise and rang them all, sounding the loudest general alarm I could. The light in the bedroom went off again and this time it didn't come back on. I could hear panic inside, people running around, the odd shout, and I turned and got away from there as quickly as I could, so aware of that *thing* inside me, that that sliver of the Bitch's heart was darkening by the moment.

I almost made it back to the trees when I spotted some lights: maybe half a dozen or so, coming over one of the rises that led up to the mountains, and by the look of them, heading in our direction. *Shit!* They'd been camped there all the time. Maybe they'd decided not to operate the pressure field, that on this occasion it'd be better to remain secret than protected?

I retrieved my backpack, made sure I had the laser with me and leaped onto the tandem, heading off down to the bottom of the woods, now familiar enough with the route to move at surprising speed even at night.

When I burst through the treeline, I gotta bit of a shock: they were already noticeably closer, their lights bobbing up and down: presumably the leg section of the Bodyguard advancing towards us as quickly as those powerful prosthetics would allow.

I had to cut them off somehow – maybe head up the road a ways and find myself a bit of elevation overlooking their approach. For some reason I had it in my head that Nora Jagger wasn't with them, that even if she'd seen the flashing light she wouldn't have imagined I'd be stupid enough to have anything to do with it. Maybe this was just a patrol, and if I could draw them away from the farm, take out a couple of them at the same time, I'd be doing us a favour.

I checked the laser and made sure it was on full blast (never gonna make that mistake again), aware that I didn't really know my enemy, that maybe the Bitch's Bodyguard might have a surprise or two for me. All I wanted was to create a degree of mayhem, then hopefully get away before they could reorganise themselves.

I waited 'til they were almost past me, those lights on their helmets proving a tempting target, then opened up. Several went to the ground, the rest just scattered, looking for cover – leastways, I thought they had. To my surprise, two of them turned and ran at me like they were the patrol's battering ram or something. I tried to cut them down, but they were firing back, and with something a lot heavier duty than the laser I was using.

I jumped on the tandem and pedalled off, really chancing my arm in the dark, doing everything I could to draw them away from the farm. I fired back a couple of times, just to keep them honest, but there was no need; nothing was gonna stop their pursuit. In fact, it occurred to me what they reminded me of: growlers, ready to sacrifice anything, to be shattered and rebuild, and I wouldn't have minded betting that they shared the same software somewhere.

But just like Nora Jagger, they had a weakness, a human core, and it wasn't long before the weight of those heavy limbs and their exertions started to come into play. I kept going, grateful to see them falling back, firing every now and then, making it obvious which way I was going, the direction they should follow – which, of course, was as far away from the farm as I could entice them.

Not that it was altogether random; I knew the time had come for me to leave, that if I was gonna continue my battle with this inner demon that maybe there was only one fair place for me to do it. I'd go back to the Commune, explain the situation to Sheila. If it *was* possible to fight the implant, to control it, or at least live with it for a while, then I would, but if it wasn't and I ended up attacking someone – if I tried to rub out a non-imp or something – then the satellite would take me out. And as much as I had to live for, for that reason alone it would probably be for the best.

I lost the Bodyguards somewhere in the forest in the early hours, at last able to relax, though it was no time at all before those familiar feelings of achiness and exhaustion returned. Once again I did everything I could not to give into them, getting off the tandem and continuing on foot, but it wasn't long before my legs were giving out beneath me – I was literally falling asleep while walking.

I had to stop, to bed down in some long grass, feeling a little like an addict about to take his poison, and sure enough, poison was what came.

How we ended up in that position, I can't even imagine, but for the second time in my life I saw Nora Jagger naked. She had those incredible prosthetic legs wrapped around me and was forcing me to do stuff I'd rather even not talk about, as if she was humiliating me, making me bow down before her.

When I awoke, I couldn't get that outta my head: I was filled with nausea and self-disgust, but something else, too: a growing suspicion that this was all part of it, that by such means she would eventually make me submit. How tired I was getting, the way she came to me every time I slept? That weevil implant knew I was fighting it, that I was putting up the barricades, so it was coming in through the back door, through my unconscious.

I mounted up, freewheeling down the hill and out onto the plain, heading in the direction of the Commune, wondering about the others back at the farm: if they were all right, what they'd done about Gigi? The last thing on my mind was that Shadow-Maker – in any case, there was a high covering of cloud blocking out the sun – but suddenly I knew it was there. I stopped, looking up, scouring the sky, not able to see or hear anything, but I could feel it all the same. Whatever it was, whatever it was doing, it was up there.

I don't know why, maybe it was instinct, maybe it was coincidence, but for some reason my eyes got drawn to one particular spot. I squinted, trying to make out any kind of colour or shape – and that was when it happened.

At first I could barely believe it; all I could do was to stare. I swear, it just appeared in midair, plummeting down probably a half a mile or so away.

Someone was falling outta the sky. Somehow they'd materialised outta nothing and now were tumbling down to their inevitable death. And yet there were no screams that I could hear, and no sign of any other movement, so maybe they were already dead. There was also something about that body – even from a distance it didn't look quite right, like it was misshapen in some way.

When it finally impacted with the ground, I understood it was probably further away than I'd first thought, but you know, I still heard a real thud echoing across the plain, as if life should never end without some kinda acknowledgement.

I rode over there as fast as I could, having to detour when I saw an area of tell-tale grassy clumps, where I knew there'd be a bog. I negotiated my way around it but then stopped, realising I'd lost myself somehow, but wherever that body was, it couldn't be far away.

I let the tandem fall to the ground and started to explore the nearby scrub, but I found no one and for a moment wondered if maybe I'd imagined the whole thing. It was only when I emerged on the far side that I saw a shattered and bloody leg poking outta the long grass.

I slowly made my way over, steeling myself for what was obviously going to be something of an ordeal . . . but ya know, I had no idea.

It's funny how you don't immediately recognise someone when you see them dead, how it takes you a while to appreciate you once knew them; that you talked and laughed and shared moments and feelings. I guess 'cuz it's just the container that's left, the contents, the person that you knew, have moved on elsewhere. I should've identified her clothes though; they were always so distinctive.

Gigi's body was lying smashed and broken on the ground, and I guess it was shock that prevented me from immediately coming to the obvious conclusion that her injuries weren't all down to the fall, that she must've been dead already. After all, you don't live long after you've been decapitated.

It didn't leave much doubt about who'd killed her – it was her usual barbaric method of slaughter. The question I couldn't answer was how on earth the body had been disposed of? I would've sworn it'd just appeared in midair, even though I knew that wasn't possible, that it had to have been dropped from high up – but I didn't get it, not one little bit. In fact, I was so confused it took me a while to appreciate exactly what it meant – *Jesus!* Nora Jagger and the Bodyguard must've been at the farm! Did that mean *everyone* was dead?

I knew immediately I had to go back, that nothing else mattered. I ran back to the tandem as quickly as I could, mounted up and was about to take off when a laser-blast blew my backpack off me.

I threw myself to the ground, rummaging amongst the smoking

remains, thankfully finding my own laser still intact. *What the hell was going on?*

I raised my head a few inches and nearly paid for it with my life, the grass behind me instantly bursting into flames. I held up my laser, pointed it in the general direction the shots had come from, sprayed some fire, then took another look.

Jesus, wouldn't you know it? It was the same two Bodyguards who'd chased me the night before, who'd apparently been following me ever since – in fact, it went through my head that maybe this was the culmination of a plan: that Gigi's body had been dropped to flush me out. If it was, I gotta say, it'd worked perfectly.

Again a burst of laser fire pinned me flat to the ground and I heard some familiar running, that mechanical slurp-slurp, and knew they were coming for me. I rolled over a couple of times, got off a couple of shots and, I thought, managed to hit one; for sure they'd stopped coming and were now crouched down in the undergrowth.

I prayed it was a moment of doubt, something I could take advantage of, and crawling on my knees and elbows, snaked through the bushes 'til I saw the tandem, then made a run for it. But I didn't get there. Heavy laser fire ignited everything around me, the undergrowth popping and crackling with dissipating energy. I fired back as much as I could, but like I'd said, those guys had much heavier-duty weapons.

There was another blast so close it actually took the heel off my boot. I knew I was in big trouble. No way could I win a straight-out fire-fight with those two, and I didn't fancy my chances of hightailing it outta there either.

I let them have everything I had, raking my laser back and forth, hoping it would buy me a few seconds, then made for the tandem again. I was almost there before they came after me, laying down a deluge of fire, igniting everything around me. Tell the truth, I couldn't believe I hadn't been hit. It even went through my head that maybe that wasn't their intention, that their orders were just to capture me; maybe the actual killing was gonna be done by someone else, and you didn't have to be a genius to know who.

I managed to reach the tandem, to leap on and start pedalling, but with all the long grass and thick scrub, it wasn't a place for getting up speed and those powerful prosthetic legs of theirs were making much faster progress. I turned, fired back at them a couple of times, but then lurched to one side, almost came off, and dropped my laser in saving myself.

I gotta be honest, I can take no credit whatsoever for what happened next. It was just a quirk of Fate. I saw the distinctive islands of grass looming up before me and knew I had to ride around, but the two Bodyguards took what to them was the obvious route, thinking they were about to catch me up.

Thing was, those legs were pretty damn heavy. They'd barely gone three or four strides before they began to sink, another couple more and they were in over their knees. They immediately panicked, twisting their bodies from side to side, trying to work their way out, but that only made things worse. They were sinking deeper by the second. They turned towards me, like they were trying to gauge my reaction, maybe even considering asking for my help, but then one of them decided there was an easier way.

'Get us out!' he ordered, pointing at me with his laser.

Thank God, there were some large rocks nearby, on this kinda promontory jutting out into the bog. I dropped the tandem and scrambled over there on my hands and knees, laser-fire again scorching everything around me, tucking myself down behind this boulder. For what felt like for ever, shards of rock spat and flew around me and parts of the undergrowth erupted with flame, 'til finally the shooting began to die down.

I risked a quick look, wondering if their power-packs had run out, and was answered by another laser-burst – but I could see why they'd stopped. Every time they fired, they sank that bit quicker. They were already up to their chests, screaming abuse at me, threatening what they'd do if I didn't help – and certainly not saying anything that might persuade me to leave the safety of my rocky hide-out and help them.

In their final moments, with only their heads showing and mud already starting to rise over the shorter guy's chin, the human side began to win out over the implants. They started pleading with me to help, and I did think about it for a moment, but the knowledge that they belonged to one of the most evil forces that ever existed, that some of their colleagues had been at the farm and done God knows what to those I loved, was enough to convince me I wasn't gonna complicate my life by saving theirs.

Having said that, those last cries were something I never wanna hear again. They changed in note as death and desperation took over, ending with this coughing, choking gurgle that meant it was over.

I went to step out, but d'you know, I was a moment or two too soon. The taller one had been waiting for me to do just that; his nose and eyes and one arm were still sticking out of the muddy mire, like a crab waiting to mug its prey. His laser was directed my way, and the instant I appeared, he let me have it, determined that his last act on this Earth would be to kill me.

Thankfully, the position he was in meant he got it all wrong. The laser blast went way over my head and the slight recoil was enough to push him under once and for all; for a few macabre moments just his hand and the laser remained, and believe it or not, he was still firing the damn thing, hoping to get in one last lucky shot, 'til finally, that disappeared as well.

For a few seconds I just stood there. It was a real weird thing to witness, believe me: Mother Earth consuming her dead that way, swallowing them whole. I also couldn't help but reflect on the natural justice of it; those murderous prosthetic legs had helped confine them to their fate. But I had more urgent things to contend with, and after running back to retrieve the laser I'd dropped, I jumped on the tandem and peddled off as fast as I could.

By the time I got back to the farm and my usual spot at the edge of the woods overlooking the homestead, I'd damn near popped my lungs, written off the tandem and worried myself to death – though I was rewarded by a view I appreciated more than any other: nothing but normality.

I couldn't see *everyone*, but Lena and Thomas were on the porch, Nick and Gordie were chopping wood, and by the look of the open door, Jimmy was working away in the barn.

What had happened exactly, I didn't know, and the way things were, I got the impression they didn't either; that they weren't even aware Gigi was dead.

I can't tell you how relieved I was to see them – especially Lena and Thomas, of course, but you know, as soon as I calmed down, as soon as my fears were tethered elsewhere, that damn tiredness fell upon me again. I'd actually been thinking about going over there – not too close, but calling out to them maybe, finding out what they knew about Gigi – but I couldn't even manage the walk.

I had to sleep, even though I knew I shouldn't, that Nora Jagger would come to me, but there was no other choice. It felt like an illness, physical and mental, and so immediate and debilitating that once again I more or less collapsed where I was, my eyes closed even before I hit the ground.

CHAPTER EIGHTEEN

I don't know how long I slept, nor how long it took me realise I was awake, maybe 'cuz the crossing from unconscious to conscious had been so seamless, and although I awoke in darkness, I had an idea the place I'd just vacated had been even darker.

As I roused myself and gazed down at the darkened farmhouse I was filled with this sudden sense of purpose. The time had finally come. There were no other options – in truth, there never had been.

I began to stride purposefully across, stopping at the log pile on my way and choosing a heavy branch. I was aware they had lasers, and I'd brought mine, but I was hoping to do this with the minimum of fuss. I could take them out one by one without anyone waking – maybe strangle Delilah and Miriam. Shouldn't be too difficult, not for me. After all, I was the Big Guy. I'd lived most of my life through violence.

I felt almost a sense of liberation, of relief, as if I was finally doing what I'd always been *meant* to do: obeying orders, dispensing with the non-imps. I knew we'd meant something to each other in the past, but the truth was, we couldn't any more – not with the fundamental difference inside us. I took a deep breath, gripped my heavy club tighter, feeling that familiar strength in my right arm. I was getting ready to take the first swing, for the impact of club against skull, the way it would kinda bounce off, the sound of cracking bone, the splatter of blood. As for the baby . . . Thomas, well, he wasn't much more than mush anyway.

I had no idea why, but for some reason that thought stopped me in my tracks. Thomas. My son. He'd *had* an implant – if only he'd kept it, I wouldn't've had to include him. For that matter, why had any of us fought the weevils? It would've been so much easier if we'd all given in.

At that moment I felt a kind of jolt inside, almost like I was being monitored, as if I was being pushed forward: there was no room for discussion any more. All of them had to die and that was an end to it.

Maybe it'd be best if I killed Lena and Thomas first, get that part over with? The others would be easy after that. I could try the bedroom window, see if it was open, get in that way.

I snuck around the house as quietly as I could, grateful there was a little wind, that the odd gust, the creaking of timbers, was covering my footsteps. The window was closed but unlocked, and I slid it up an inch or so at a time, soon feeling the warmth of the room brush past me on its way out, the smell of stale air, of oxygen that had sustained the woman and child's bodies.

The baby snuffled a little as I began to climb through, as if he knew it was me, and I froze, petrified he was about to wake. I knew it would have to be her first, that she'd fight to the death to save her child. I eased my other leg inside, feeling a little like something was beginning to rotate inside me, to quietly slash at my insides. I took a coupla faltering steps forward, raising my club, ready to smash it down on the woman's head, but she changed position, made a slight whimper, the bedding around her rustling. Oh shit, don't tell me she was going to wake? Would she know it was me or think it was some anonymous stranger in the dark?

'Clancy?' she suddenly whispered, like she couldn't believe it, that it had to be a dream. 'Is that you?'

I lost all control, panic ripping through my body like exploding DNA. I heard a voice – my voice, someone's voice – I didn't know. I was being tugged and pulled and wrenched and pushed . . . and suddenly I knew I had to get out of there. *I had to get away.*

I turned and just kinda dived outta the window, crashing to the ground, picking myself up, running . . . *running!*

The baby was screaming back there. The woman was calling after me.

'Go back, go back! They're non-imps!' a voice kept telling me.

'Non-imps! Non-imps!' I took up the cry as I ran through the night.

And then, of course, I understood, and the seismic shock of that realisation gave me my first clear thought of the night. That wasn't *me* screaming. That voice didn't originate from me, no more than all those wayward thoughts had.

'Non-imps! Non-imps!' came the cry again, and I knew she was *inside* me, that the Bitch had taken me over. *'Kill them!'*

I kept running, ignoring her screams like she was a passenger on my back demanding to be taken to a different destination, willing myself to go on no matter what was said by the voice in my head or on my lips.

I ran through the woods as fast as I could, colliding with trees as if I wanted to, almost impaling myself on a couple of occasions. What the hell had happened back there? . . . I'd never ever sleep again! *Never!*

I arrived at the other side of the woods, scratched and bruised from head to toe, 'til finally the night opened up and I burst out to confront an eerily large full-blood moon. I stopped before it, not wanting to go another step or to waste a scrap of the energy I still had left inside me. For what I was about to do, I needed every last drop.

I clenched up my body, threw my head back and gave out with the loudest and longest old wolf howl you could ever imagine. It almost killed me to fill the night with such pain. It was if the animals we'd heard before had been building up to this, that *this* was what they'd been trying to say, the agony they'd never been able to express, no matter how hard they'd tried.

'Get o-u-t—! Get out of me . . . !'

I don't know where I went – I just ran. It wasn't so much about getting away as punishing myself, running myself into the ground until there was nothing left, 'til I was helpless and vulnerable, 'til the strike of a moth's downy wing would slice the flesh from me.

Lena! Jesus Christ – *Lena!* How could that thing have induced me to almost do that to her? Had I been keyed at last? Was there a new level of control? I blundered on, at some point running through the creek, clumsy to the point of drunkenness; frequently falling, sometimes just staying on the ground gazing up into the sky, other times immediately leaping up, determined to use any remaining strength I had to punish myself. I was already battered and bleeding, stiff and sore, but I'd run and run until there was no more.

It became kinda vague after that, everything getting compressed and pushed up together. I can remember being on my hands and knees on the road, blood dripping from somewhere onto the tarmac, and then lights . . . bright lights, coming outta nowhere, moving fast towards me as if they were about to run me over. Then they stopped a few yards away, just hanging there, staring at me outta the night like some nocturnal beast about to pounce.

'Clancy?'

I couldn't answer, couldn't even be sure someone had spoken.

'Clancy? What are you doing?'

A car door opened, someone walked towards me, a dark shadow loomed up out of those high beams.

'It's me, Doctor Simon.'

I just stared at him, still not understanding. He hesitated for a moment, maybe not sure if I presented a threat or not, then kneeled down to look at me.

'Jesus, Clancy. Are you okay?'

'I tried to kill them!' I wailed, even in that moment appreciating what a relief it was to talk to someone I knew I wouldn't attempt to harm.

'Jesus,' he gasped.

'All of them . . . The Bitch is inside me – she got in through my dreams . . . *I spoke with her voice!*' I cried.

'But they're all right?'

'Yeah, I think so,' I replied, wondering if I could be sure of anything any more.

The Doc helped me up then led me back to the Bentley, spreading a travel-rug across the passenger seat – God forbid I should get blood on his fine leather seats, no matter what the circumstances – then got me and himself inside.

For a moment he just sat there looking at me. 'Gigi's dead,' he finally announced, as if he thought he should get all the bad news out and over with. 'Lord knows what got into her – she arrived at the camp out of the blue and tried to persuade Nora Jagger she'd always been on her side.' He finished the sentence with a shake of the head, as if there could've been only one result to that approach.

'I know,' I told him. 'They dropped her body on the plain. Well, most of it.'

Again he lapsed into silence and I began to suspect that in some ways he was every bit as beaten-up about things as I was.

'I can't go back again,' he blurted out, rather to my surprise. 'She'll kill anyone, for no reason at all.'

Just for a moment I actually thought he was gonna cry, he was that upset.

'So she knows where we are?' I asked, presuming Gigi would've told them, or maybe, God forbid, they'd tortured it outta her.

'No – she wouldn't tell them anything. That was part of the reason she was executed.'

I don't know why, but that upset me as much as anything: that poor kid, even staring into the face of Death she hadn't really known where her loyalties lay. 'Why are they on foot?' I asked.

The Doc laughed hollowly, as if he thought I'd never believe it. 'Because of you, Clancy: you're *sport*. That's why you haven't been keyed yet – and the same reason she doesn't carry a weapon. You've really got under her skin. Believe it or not, anyone calling you "Big Guy" risks being killed on the spot. She's determined to show them how much stronger she is than you, to hunt you down the old-fashioned way and kill you with her bare hands.'

'Shit,' I grunted, not really appreciating the irony in that remark, the fact that she didn't have 'bare hands'.

'She's mad as hell at you for killing that Bodyguard.'

I grunted, wondering if she had any idea what'd happened to the other two. 'Can you get rid of this thing inside me?' I asked.

'I've done a bit more research,' he replied, the fact that he didn't immediately say no, that he sounded just that little bit hopeful, almost provoking me to hug the guy – although I knew there'd've been hell to pay if I'd crumpled his clothes or left even the tiniest bloodstain.

'Let's go,' I told him.

The moment we turned up the track to the farm he switched off his lights, coming to a whispering halt around the back of the barn, hustling me inside. He got to work immediately, setting up his stuff, moving with surprising speed: not a mortal any more, but a master of medicine.

'This is a long way from proven,' he warned me.

'I don't care.'

He began by scanning me again, checking on the implant, looking at what it'd been up to, finally giving out with this exasperated sigh.

'What?' I asked.

'It's divided up – it's all over you.'

'Shit.'

He paused for a moment, as if unsure whether to go on or not. 'I can still run the program,' he said, not sounding anywhere near as hopeful. 'We can see what happens.'

It was weird: once he'd hitched me up and turned on the power, I had the distinct feeling that the computer wasn't attached to me, that *I* was attached to the computer. Maybe I was imagining it, but I could feel this kinda force sweeping through me like floodwaters through drains, getting into every nook and cranny, sluicing everything away. It really was an odd feeling – not good, not bad, just *odd*.

'Give it ten minutes,' the Doc told me.

I sat there with the current surging through me, feeling it getting ever stronger, soon needing a distraction to take my mind off it. 'Is it her limbs you have to keep an eye on?'

'They need constant monitoring,' he explained, 'checking for irritation or rejection, and of course refreshing the worms.'

'Worms?' I said, a little taken aback.

He smiled. 'That's what keeps them together, binds composite to flesh, makes them almost real – superworms. They simulate blood-and nerve-flow.'

'Jesus.' I grimaced, remembering that time in the Infinity building when I'd caught Nora Jagger without her limbs; the animate cellulose sludge they were stored in, the way that later her arm had seemed to *squirm* back into place. I also remembered something else.

'When she chased me and Gigi outta the safe house and into the river that time she suddenly stopped, like she had a problem.'

266

The Doc studied his screen for a moment, then returned his attention to our conversation. 'Maybe it was high tide? Fresh water wouldn't trouble the worms but salt water certainly would.'

When I thought about it, he was right, it had been high tide. Not that I could see any advantage in the information; not unless we were gonna attack her with salt shakers.

Doctor Simon saw the look on my face, the way I was turning things over, and shook his head. 'She has no weaknesses. Believe me, I'd know if she did.'

'Maybe not with her prosthetics, but what about the human parts? She's the same as us.'

'Not really.'

'What d'you mean?'

'She's had her muscles boosted almost up to the point where they're as hard as the prosthetics. Just about every vital organ has been changed. She scoured the City for the strongest, the biggest, the healthiest organs to enhance her function and increase her life expectancy ... Her heart's a real freak: it came from this young boy they picked up off the street one night.'

I don't know why, really, it didn't make any sense at all, but the moment those words were out of his mouth, I was utterly embraced by ice. 'What boy?'

'Oh, just some street urchin. No one in particular ... Well, I wouldn't have thought so, not until I saw that heart.'

I was aware I was gaping at him, that I couldn't look away no matter how hard I tried, that a thousand heavy silences had somehow been pressed into one. It couldn't be – it was too much of a coincidence ... but the thought had grabbed hold of me as if it'd never let go.

'The Mickey Mouse Kid?' I finally whispered.

He looked up from his screen – now it was his turn to stare. 'Yes ... Mickey Mouse! He had this tattoo ... How did you know that?'

'Picked up in one of the streets off the Square?'

He thought for a minute. 'Yes, I believe he was,' he said, staring at me, waiting for an explanation.

I damn near threw up. I damn near screamed at the top of my voice in protest at a world that would allow such an abomination. *Jesus, no, no, no—!* Arturo's heart was still living, still beating – but in the body of Nora Jagger. What kinda obscenity was that?

'You knew him?' the Doc asked.

'Arturo,' I told him.

'Not Mickey Mouse?' he joked, and for a moment I almost lost it; I could've almost taken my rage out on him.

'He was a friend,' I told him, my voice as chilled as my heart. 'More than a friend. I was with him when he died.'

'Oh,' the Doc said, now looking more than a bit intimidated. 'I'm sorry – they just brought him in . . . His heart was – well, still is – a freak of nature. Especially for a boy of that age. It's hugely enlarged.'

Both of us went quiet. The Doc's cocktail of drugs, micro-lasers and programming, whatever, was still pulsing through me, but I couldn't think of anything but what I'd just been told. Of all the cruel ironies: that warm, funny, loveable little guy's heart ending up in the body of the foulest, most sadistic person I've ever known. And what I then realised, what made it so much more painful, was that if there was any chance at all of us surviving this, it would mean killing Nora Jagger – or to put it another way, by stopping Arturo's heart all over again.

It was almost too much to take in, so many unbearable thoughts, so many torturous ironies, twisting their blades in my head. Who would've ever dreamed that little Arturo still had a hand to play in this? I mean, it was entirely appropriate that such a special little guy should've had a freakishly big heart, and yet entirely *inappropriate* that it would be used for anything but to delight us.

I knew how much it'd upset the others, especially Delilah, so I swore the Doc to secrecy. Nobody needed to know but us, and that was the way I intended to keep it. Arturo was dead and had been for over a year; the only thing that lived now was his memory, and that would live for ever.

When the program had finally finished running, the Doc unhitched the various connections and put organi-plasters on the points of entry. My legs and arms continued to twitch as if some sensations were still in there looking for an emergency escape route.

He ran the scanner again, this time looking that bit pleased with himself.

'Is it okay?' I asked.

'I think we've got it,' he said, breaking into a smile.

I was just about to give out with a cry of relief, to thank the guy from the bottom of my heart, when he suddenly stopped and frowned. 'Damn!'

'What?'

'There's something left,' he said, pointing at the screen. 'There – prefrontal cortex. It's really dug in.'

'What is it?' I asked.

'I don't know,' he replied, 'but if I had to guess . . . I'd say it's the bit that gets keyed.'

'Total submission?'

'Maybe,' he answered.

'That figures.'

He paused for a moment, as if looking for any compensation there might be. 'But the thing is – at least for the moment, Clancy – you're no threat to anyone.'

I could've celebrated, of course; I could've run over there and rampaged through the house, got them all up, hugged and kissed them, held Thomas in my arms, gone to bed with Lena, but after what had happened earlier, what I'd just learnt about Arturo, I thought I'd leave it 'til the morning.

I spent the night in the barn, despite the Doc's reassurances, too scared to sleep in case Nora Jagger could still invade my dreams, waiting till dawn, letting him go over first to tell them the news.

It took less than a minute for Lena to appear on the porch, Thomas in her arms, calling my name – I was running towards them before she hit the second syllable. We hugged and kissed, cried and laughed, and though I tried to apologise for the previous night, she wouldn't listen. Soon the others came out, obviously having given us a few moments on our own – Jimmy and Delilah, Hanna and Gordie, and a rather spent-looking Nick - but we knew the celebrations had to be kept short, that Nora Jagger might appear at any moment.

We didn't have that many options. I told them I'd been on my way to the Commune, and they all agreed it might be the one place we'd be safe (that crazy irony again: a punishment satellite affording us protection). Within minutes we were frantically packing. Lena and me warned them about how far it was, the many hills, the width of the plain, and I gotta say, Lile didn't look that happy about it, but Jimmy was already rushing around deciding what tools and techno to take, the stuff he absolutely couldn't live without, the glimmer in his eyes no doubt down to the prospect of being reunited with a working punishment satellite.

Gordie and Hanna helped Nick bring the bed outta the house, Miriam's prostrate body shaking a little as they jolted it down off the porch and onto the ground. There was a brief but unquestionably awkward silence: I turned to Lena, and Jimmy and Delilah turned to me. Did Nick really intend to push her all the way, even after we'd told him how difficult it was gonna be? Then again, what choice did he have? He could hardly leave her behind.

There was no actual discussion, but it soon became apparent that the Doc was coming with us. I guess preservation of his luxury lifestyle was one thing but the preservation of his buttered hide was another. Life with Nora Jagger was no longer so much dangerous as suicidal; apparently no one was safe, not even her personal physician and programmer.

Thankfully there wasn't the same hostility towards him that there had been, especially after what he'd done for me – and let's face it, he could've brought Nora Jagger and the entire Bodyguard back with him. Not that I was about to put my full trust in him, not for one minute, but I was happy to sit back and watch for any signs of a long game developing. In any case, I was quietly pleased he was coming along and I guess I don't have to tell you why. The Doc took that fancy medical computer of his everywhere and for sure it would be accompanying him to the Commune. I was still hoping that somewhere amongst all this there might be an opportunity for him to give Lena back her sight again.

We hid the Bentley in the woods, covering it with branches like we had our first limo. The Doc was a long way from happy about it, insisting on overseeing the operation himself, making sure nobody scratched the bodywork – though I gotta say, he was that bit more resigned to the situation.

We sure looked like an odd bunch: Lena carrying Thomas in his favourite blue and white blanket, Lile being her 'seeing eye', leading the pair of them – though to be honest, at times it was hard to know who was leading who. Gordie and Hanna were riding the Typhoon Tandem, circling around us, both still a little shaken by what'd happened to Gigi – though oddly, I think it was more her than him. He'd tried to put his arm around her at one point and she'd pushed him away as if he was being somehow disrespectful.

The Doc was dressed like he was going on a country picnic, all cool in a cream linen suit, except he was carrying that very business-like shiny black case of his. As for Jimmy, despite my warnings, he was laden down with more junk than I would've thought possible, like one of those ants carrying a huge leaf. And finally, and yeah, without doubt the oddest sight of all, was Nick pulling Miriam in her bed, with me following along behind to give them a push.

I've never seen a man so devoted to his wife. He kept talking to her all the time – for sure he had longer conversations with her than he did me. All he said in my direction was to be careful not to upset her by going too fast or over bumps. I mean, what I could see of her, the top of her greasy grey head, the fact that she never spoke, I couldn't help but wonder how he'd know if she *was* getting upset. The only time she'd apparently roused herself since coming to the farm had been when she'd attempted to kill him.

Slowly we headed off towards the Interior, once we reached the steeper hills having to occasionally drag Gordie away from Hanna and the tandem to help with the bed, him predictably grumbling to me outta the side of his mouth.

'If he knew he was gonna have to drag her, you'd think he'd've put her on a diet,' he muttered.

What with Miriam, and Lena having to stop every now and then to take care of Thomas, we weren't exactly making rapid progress – at the rate we were going I reckoned it'd take us a couple of days just to reach the plain. The Doc started to complain about his suede shoes, that he hadn't expected the ground to be so wet, and poor old Lile was getting slower and slower; instead of being an asset to Lena she was actually turning into something of a liability. There wasn't much point in hassling them, we were probably going as fast as we could, but the fact that I was bringing up the rear meant I was for ever looking over my shoulder, expecting to see the Bitch and her Bodyguard coming after us at any moment.

We stopped for the night at the top of this low hill, with a pretty good view all around, a bit of a drop on one side so it had only two approaches. The meal was eaten more or less in silence, everyone keen to turn in, to make up for what had been lost that day and to build up for what we'd need for the next.

For Lena and me, of course, it was something of an occasion. We hadn't slept together for several nights and it felt a bit like a free pass to heaven – and that despite the fact that Thomas was in with us and pretty fractious about all the changes he could feel about him. He cried and grizzled a lot more than he slept, meaning that we had to pack in everything we could whenever he gave us the odd moment of opportunity.

'I've missed you so much,' she whispered.

'Me, too ... not sure about him though,' I joked, the little guy already thinking about restarting his motor.

Lena stuck him to her breast like an organi-plaster, doing her best not to allow him to spoil our mood, reattaching her lips to mine in seconds.

Later, when the little guy finally succumbed to sleep and she'd followed along after him, I was left lying there listening to the breeze climbing the hill, rippling the long grass, the occasional distant echoey hoot of an owl. I was so tired, but every time my eyes closed, every time I felt myself falling, I'd panic and wake with a start. I couldn't rid myself of the fear that the Bitch'd be waiting for me in there, that she might order me to do something truly terrible.

No matter our good intentions, it took us a while to get going in the morning. For some reason Miriam was off her food and had to be coaxed into eating anything at all. Eventually, with the sun just a short bounce into the sky, we set off in our usual laborious fashion.

The first hill of the day was a real thigh-breaker, and the Doc had to join Gordie and me in pushing the bed. All the way up we were hoping that was it; that the top would reward us with a view of the plain, but when we got there, there was another hill or two to go.

The downwards slope on the other side might not have been such hard work, but for sure it was more traumatic: at one point we lost it completely. The bed suddenly swerved to one side, knocked Nick and Gordie off-balance, and the Doc and me, completely caught by surprise, couldn't hold on. Everyone except Lena and Lile scrambled after it, Hanna jumping off the tandem, Jimmy dropping his junk, and eventually, thanks partly to it getting held up by some bushes, we managed to get it back under control. Nick was so upset, scrambling down to the bed and fussing over Miriam something terrible.

'Hey! It's okay, darling! I'm sorry, I'm sorry—!'

The Doc and me exchanged looks, Gordie shook his head like the whole thing was madness, and eventually we resumed our slow and strained descent. It really was starting to be something of a problem. As much as I respected Nick's feelings for his wife, it didn't make any sense for all of us to be caught by Nora Jagger 'cuz of them.

We got to the bottom and started up the other side and once again the summit taunted us, pretending it was close, only to slip away as we got nearer. We had to keep stopping to get our breath back, and the Doc upset Nick by sitting on the bed.

'D'you mind?' he said.

'Sorry,' the Doc replied, glancing at Miriam as if to say that he was sure she didn't care one way or the other.

Doc Simon and me resumed our places at the back of the bed, and once again he gave me a look, but this time it was different. When we'd got going, the bed creaking and groaning, he muttered to me outta the corner of his mouth, 'You know she's dead, don't you?'

I looked at him, continuing to push, not quite taking in his words. 'Really?'

'I had an idea she might be earlier.'

'Shit,' I hissed, the pair of us keeping going, neither wanting to be the one to stop and be asked why.

I can't tell ya how difficult that situation became. We were no longer pushing a sick woman, but a corpse – this was a funeral procession now, and it shouldn't be allowed to hold us up. But how the hell could we tell Nick?

We battled slowly on, Miriam now feeling somehow different: dull, absent – lifeless, I guess. And the odd thing was, one by one the others started to pick up on it. Gordie pretended he had to stop for a moment to retie one of his boots. He took the opportunity to look in at her, and somehow managed to pass on the news to Hanna. But still we kept pushing, still we pretended nothing was wrong, cowering before the thought of breaking this man's big heart.

When we reached the top we paused, finally able to gaze out at the wide expanse of the plain, my heart thumping – I couldn't put it off any longer.

'Nick ... I gotta tell you something,' I said, and the others were bowing their heads, partly out of respect, partly out of embarrassment.

Funny how we're all animals at heart, how we so often revert to instinct at times of stress. He took one look at my face, another at those around him, then leaned forward and pulled back the covers, staring at Miriam's lifeless face.

The odd thing was, he didn't react at all, almost as if he'd been through it so many times he couldn't do it again.

'I did wonder when she wouldn't eat,' he said eventually.

I told him how sorry I was, and everyone echoed my words. Jimmy patted him on the shoulder, while Nick just stood there as if he couldn't bear to be the centre of this particular attention.

'That thing killed her,' he said grimly, 'it made her try to do things she wasn't capable of.'

For a while we all stood in silence, looking out from the top of that hill almost as if some kinda ceremony had already begun.

'Thing is, Nick . . .' I started to say.

'I know,' he told me. 'I'll bury her.'

We all helped. Jimmy didn't have any proper digging tools, but we managed to batter and scrape a bit of a dip with hammers and screwdrivers and cover Miriam's body with a shallow layer of soil, then piled on as many rocks we could find. For some reason we press-ganged the Doc into saying a few cultured words: a bit of a poem, something less of a prayer. As for the bed, well, bearing in mind we were being followed and not wanting to risk leaving any kinda clue, we dragged it to the steep side of the hill and pushed it over.

I had to almost pull Nick away. I don't think it was so much grief – there'd be plenty of time for that later; it was more that he felt lost. He'd been at Miriam's side for so long. Not a minute had gone by without him being aware of her presence, her needs, and suddenly all that was gone – he was finally free, but it looked like it was the very last thing he wanted to be.

We descended the hill and made our way out onto the plain, moving a whole lot quicker, though ironically, with so few trees around, Lena had no points of sound reference and started to struggle. Lile offered to take Thomas, but the old girl looked so weary, Doc Simon said he would. There was a bit of a pregnant pause, Lena looking that bit unsure, but I stepped in before it became too obvious. The look of disappointment on the Doc's face was there for everyone to see except the one person it might've influenced.

I had to warn Gordie and Hanna to be careful where they rode the tandem, pointing out the clumps of grass they needed to avoid in case they ended up going into a bog.

There was still a slightly subdued, almost guilty, atmosphere between them, presumably from the continuing hangover from Gigi's disappearance and death, though maybe Miriam's passing had put that into some kinda morbid context. For sure Hanna blamed herself; if she hadn't started a relationship with Gordie, maybe Gigi wouldn't have got so upset and done what she did? I had to talk to her, dismiss that as nonsense – I mean, you start playing that game, you can pretty well trace every single death since the beginning of Time back to yourself one way or another.

For the rest of the day we plodded steadily on, the fact that we could now see for some distance prompting all of us to take the occasional look back, keeping it discreet, no one wanting to alarm the others. She had to be following, she had to be back there somewhere, and maybe that Shadow-Maker was overhead letting her know exactly where we were?

The others made the same mistake we had the first time we made that journey: seeing the hills in the distance and assuming they were a lot closer than they were. Yet finally, as their spirits started to fade with the light, they accepted the fact that we wouldn't reach them 'til morning, and the next of those lone trees we came to, we stopped for the night.

Jimmy's stack of techno junk had shrunk a little during the day. A couple of times he'd had to bite the bullet, decide what *really* wasn't essential and throw it away, though I'd insisted on him burying or hiding it. On both occasions Lile had given him a real hard time, telling him to get rid of the lot, that nothing good had ever come of it, which, though unfair, was pretty well her standard response. Hanna and Gordie had leaned the tandem up against the tree and draped a blanket over it, creating a shelter; the Doc was the first to take advantage. Meanwhile, Nick just sat where he was, apparently oblivious of whether he was under cover or not.

I took one last, long look behind us through the thickening light, and seeing no one following, settled down with Lena, the two of us making a kinda oyster in which Thomas was the pearl. I was real grateful the little guy was in one of his good moods, chuckling away when I tickled him, complaining only the once, which was to be fed.

I noticed the Doc was using his case as a pillow, not, I'm sure, 'cuz it was that comfortable, more 'cuz of how much value he attached to it, that he couldn't bear to lose physical contact even for a moment. Nick was still sitting on his own, staring into nothingness, and I gestured for him to join us, that he'd be more comfortable. He never replied but did shuffle across. I felt for the guy, I really did. No matter how his and Miriam's relationship had worked, you knew that it had, that they'd been happy together. To think that the last real act he'd seen her perform was to try to kill him . . . mind you, hadn't I been on the brink of doing the same to Lena and Thomas?

I've no idea when I finally fell asleep, only that I woke up 'cuz something had disturbed me. I lay there for a while, listening intently, terrified it might be the approach of the Bodyguard. I couldn't hear a thing apart from all the sawing and wheezing going on around me, but something had definitely jolted me awake. There was a sudden slight breeze, stronger than earlier, the leaves on the branches above us starting to shake . . . *Oh shit!*

I nudged Jimmy awake, putting my hand on his mouth, not wanting him to alarm the others, but he came from such a deep place, I damn near frightened him to death. Eventually I helped him up and over to a spot a few yards away where the others couldn't hear us.

'What's the matter?' he asked.

'It's up there,' I whispered.

'What is?' he asked, plainly grumpy at being woken up.

'Shhh! It's coming back!'

We both stood there, the leaves of the tree trembling, almost as if they were also afraid.

'Feel it?' I asked.

'The wind?'

'No!'

'I didn't feel anything.'

Gradually the leaves calmed and stilled and we were left standing in the night. Jimmy sighed and turned to go back to bed, but I hadn't finished. 'The day Gigi's body dropped out of the sky—'

'Yeah?' he said, a little impatiently.

'—it came outta nowhere.'

'Whaddya mean?'

'It just suddenly appeared in midair.'

A waning moon and slight cloud cover was more than enough light to see the deep frown form on his face. 'I don't get you,' he finally admitted.

I took a deep breath, knowing what this was gonna sound like. 'I think she was thrown outta something invisible.'

At that his frown turned to more a look of astonishment. 'Invisible?'

'Yep,' I replied, with real certainty.

'Come on, Big Guy,' he said. 'There's been a lot of new things invented since I was sent over to the Island, but invisible planes? I don't think so.'

'I was looking up when it happened. The body was just suddenly there.'

'It was dropped from high altitude – it took you a while to spot it.'

I stood there, firmly shaking my head. 'That's what keys us.'

For a while he just stood there, like he was being polite, but it was clear from the yawning his tiredness was getting the better of him. 'Sorry, Big Guy,' he said at last, 'not cool, I know, but I really need to sleep. I got all that stuff to carry, and Lile's gonna need my help to get up those hills.'

He left me where I was and returned to his spot next to Delilah.

For a few moments I stayed put, waiting for whatever was up there to return, concerned that, despite what the Doc'd said, it was searching for me to apply that final touch. At last, with no further sense of it, I headed back to Lena and Thomas.

I hadn't been paying much attention to the land – far too busy looking up at the sky – but just before I sat down I took one last along the horizon, the line of distant hills that we'd descended that morning.

Ah, shit . . . *Shit!* Halfway down, I could just make out this square smudge of light. It was her, of course – the Bitch. Obviously she had a fair idea where we were, and now was slowly but surely catching up.

CHAPTER NINETEEN

The following morning I got everyone up and fed real early so we could set out as it was getting light, hoping to steal a march on Nora Jagger, to put a bit of extra distance between us. I took Thomas, leaving Lena to move that bit more freely on her own, though once we started to climb the hills and there were trees for her to bounce sound off, she was fine again. Delilah, on the other hand, was slowing us right down, that long grey stick really starting to puff, withering like a tree that couldn't get enough water to its extremities. I had no choice but to hand Thomas back and reluctantly carry Jimmy's techno so he could give her an arm to hang onto.

The other advantage of being back amongst trees, of course, was cover, so we couldn't be seen – but it worked both ways: the Bitch and her Bodyguard could be closing on us and we wouldn't know 'til the last moment, which was, I guess, why all of us couldn't stop glancing over our shoulders every few seconds.

I was just starting to field a few complaints about how far it was, how hard I was pushing them, when we crested yet another hill and I saw the smoke of the Commune in the next valley.

'Is that it?' Hanna asked, like the others, noticeably hanging on my answer.

'I reckon.'

There was a general sigh of relief and Gordie leapt on the tandem, waiting for Hanna to get on the back.

'Whoa! Whoa!' I cried, remembering how some of the villagers were on the highly-strung side. 'They're not gonna be expecting us. See that thing come hurtling down the hill with you two on it, you'll frighten them to death.'

Gordie grunted and got off, resuming pushing the tandem, not noticing that Hanna was still on the back, quietly giggling to herself.

At the top of the next hill we all paused as we caught our first sight of the Commune. Even from what little I could see, it was obvious it'd grown since we were last there.

'Don't look much,' Delilah grumbled, plainly of a mood to do little else.

'Maybe,' I commented, 'but just at the moment, it's the safest place we can possibly be.'

Delilah took the point, taking yet another glance behind us; the gesture infectious and copied by everyone except Lena.

Believe it or not, it was Lena who led us down – I guess once she commits something to memory, that's it. I followed along behind, feeling a little ridiculous with all that junk I was carrying, every few steps tempted to just toss the lot away.

'How's it looking?' she asked.

'A lot more people than before,' I told her, 'but, yeah, still pretty relaxed.'

We'd only emerged a few yards out of the treeline before the cry went up, the shouts of welcome, calls of 'They're back!' though I didn't think it was so much for us as the little guy Lena was carrying.

Isobel came running across at speed and with an accompanying screech of excitement, like a jet engine, over and over beginning the sentence, '*Could I . . . Could I, please . . .*' 'til Lena gave in and let her hold Thomas for a few moments.

Sheila appeared looking like she'd broken off from yet another workout, all glowing and glistening, saving a special greeting for Jimmy. In fact, I gotta say, between us, what with all the shouting and excitement, we created quite a Mardi Gras.

Gordie was unable to resist showing off the Typhoon Tandem, riding it around in circles, making an obstacle course of the huts and shelters, Isobel running behind him laughing fit to bust. Hanna undoubtedly added a few more to her fan club just by being what she was, while the Doc and Nick kinda kept their distance, receiving the occasional curious look, I guessed 'cuz they weren't joining in with everything that was going on.

Sheila invited us to eat, chivvying Isobel away when she asked to hold the baby again, all of the gang sitting in a circle around her fire. I told her exactly what was going on, that we were on the run and Nora Jagger couldn't be that far behind us. I also offered to keep moving if she wanted us to, if she thought we might bring trouble down on them.

'We're all here for the same reason,' she said, gazing around. 'Clustered under the protection of a rogue satellite. It had to happen one day. I'm just grateful it's taken so long.'

I took a bit more of a studied look around: the Commune had probably doubled in size from when we were last there, and again, it was mostly society's more vulnerable who'd sought out its shelter; there was even a couple in wheelchairs, though God knows how they'd made it.

'It's an SPZ,' Sheila said, chuckling when I looked a little mystified. 'Satellite Protection Zone.'

'Can you communicate with it?' Jimmy asked her.

'Nope. Not yet.'

He thought for a moment. 'Any juice?'

'Small generator. Haven't got a lot of gas, but you're welcome to it.'

Jimmy was obviously thinking through what his options were. 'Depends how long they take to find us,' he said after a bit.

'*If* they find us,' Delilah chipped in, like she thought it needed saying.

'Not sure they haven't already,' Sheila commented, 'what with that damn thing constantly flying around up there.'

'You've seen it?' I asked, immediately knowing what she was talking about.

'Nah. No one's seen it.'

''cuz it's *invisible!*' I said, directing my comment at Jimmy.

'Big Guy! There are no invisible planes, drones, flying saucers, or anything else come to that.'

We ended up in a bit of a free-for-all, even the Doc joining in, saying he'd heard rumours, but Jimmy kept on laughing the whole thing off as if we'd gone crazy.

However, as the argument began to die down, Lena joined in. 'There *is* something,' she said. 'I've seen it.'

There was silence, no one quite sure how to respond. Jimmy vigorously scratched the back of his head, his ponytail wagging from side to side like that of a happy dog. 'Lena—' he started.

'I'm telling you, Jimmy.'

'Maybe something . . . but not invisible,' he insisted.

Gordie started sniggering, like he couldn't believe we were really arguing about invisible planes, and Hanna flicked him with the back of her hand to shut him up.

In the end we just had to agree to differ; in any case, with Nora Jagger and the Bodyguard so near we had far more pressing problems to deal with.

Sheila immediately took control, putting out her own fire and sending out the message for everyone else to do the same; for the next few days we'd be living off smoked meat, cold stuff, drink only water.

I didn't know if it was a legacy from her old army days or because she was one of the first to settle there or what, but people plainly saw her as their leader, and when one guy started whining about us, the threat we'd brought in our wake, she immediately squashed him down, telling him he could leave anytime he wanted.

The other thing she arranged was for everyone to chip in a little from their shelters – branches and leaves mostly – to help us build one big enough for our whole gang so we didn't have to go out into the forest to find stuff and maybe make a lotta noise chopping it down.

Delilah wasn't exactly gracious, making some comment about how she'd be more comfortable down a rabbit's hole, though she was right about one thing: it wouldn't last for five minutes. Mind you, the way things were looking, I wasn't sure we were going to either.

Lena and me, Gordie and Hanna – even Doc Simon rolled up his sleeves – did everything we could to make it as bearable as possible, finding more branches, some with leaves still on, down by the woodpile, collecting grass and moss to lie on.

It was when we returned from one of those trips, laden down with all manner of stuff, that I realised Jimmy had gone somewhere.

'Where is he?' I asked Lile.

'Back up the hill,' she told me, 'the way we came in.'

I thought about following him, seeing what he was up to, but I guessed he'd just appointed himself look-out and was up there keeping an eye out for Nora Jagger, which made a lotta sense.

He didn't return for a coupla hours, and when he did, was plainly deeply preoccupied.

'What's up?' I asked.

'There's no such thing as invisibility,' he told me.

'Jimmy!' I groaned.

'What there might be are ways of making yourself impossible to be seen.'

'Same thing, ain't it?' I said, feeling slightly bemused.

'No, not at all,' he said, and this time I recognised that look he got when something had revved his motor. 'I've put sensors up there; they should give us some indication of whether there's anything flying around or not.'

'And if there is?' I asked.

'Then I guess we'll have to work out how it's making it impossible for us to see it and try to reverse the process.'

It's amazing, that bad leg of his has always been a barometer: if the little guy wasn't happy, he'd be limping and hopping around like a three-legged dog, but if something'd got him that bit inspired, you'd think he was about to leap on the table and do a tap-dance. He'd got seriously pissed off back on the farm at the Doc taking over his workshop, and probably even more that everyone had started to look on the guy as our 'resident expert' – but now, with the hint of a challenge he could rise to, he'd already gotta bit of swagger back about him.

Early the following morning I awoke to see Jimmy sneaking outta the shelter, stretching his leg over one sleeping body after another, kinda losing his balance at the end and toppling outta the entrance. Curiosity got the better of me and I roused myself and followed after him, though it says a lot that he was so pumped up, he was almost up to the top of the hill before I actually caught up with him.

As usual when he'd got one of his obsessive moods on, he wasn't that pleased to see me, nor much into conversation.

'What's going on?' I asked, but he never answered, instead going around checking on what I guessed must be the vibration meters he'd stuck into the ground. He studied one after another, his face giving away very little.

'Well?' I asked.

'Yeah . . . There *is* something,' he eventually admitted.

'I been telling you that for weeks!'

'So why can't we see it?'

'It's invisible!'

'Nothing's invisible, Big Guy,' he said, with pointedly forced patience.

'This is.'

'Just hidden from view,' he reiterated, checking the meter on his last sensor.

'Whatever,' I muttered, not being concerned how he dressed it up.

'Night and day?' he asked me, and I realised he was reviewing what I'd already told him.

'Yep.'

'Any noise?'

'Just what we heard the other night,' I reminded him, realising he hadn't been paying attention. 'A slight vibration.'

'That's it?'

I shrugged. 'A shadow.'

He turned and stared at me. 'There's a *shadow*?'

'Yeah.'

'Why the hell didn't you say so!' he cried, his thoughts plainly veering off in another direction. 'Oh, Jeez. I need to go back down.' And with that he set off downhill at such speed I half-expected him to lose balance and topple forward flat on his face.

'Jimmy!'

'Not now, Big Guy,' he shouted back as he disappeared amongst the trees.

I stayed there for a while, trying to follow his train of thought but eventually giving up. How many times had we been through this? How many times had we seen him get all worked up this way? On the other hand, to be fair, one way or another, it usually worked out to our advantage.

Before going back down, I headed over to the far side of the hill. In the distance I could see a fair bit of the plain; there was the thinnest trail of smoke drifting up from it, as if a spider had descended from the sky and left its web hanging there.

It could've been anyone, of course. There were probably any number of different communities in the Interior – amongst the hills, out on the plain, in the forest – that didn't know about each other. On the other hand, if it *was* Nora Jagger and the Bodyguard, there was no question they were closing in on us.

If it wasn't for that damn Shadow-Maker ghosting around in the sky, I might've still rated our chances; as it was, I knew it could only be a matter of time. And then what? The punishment satellite wasn't on our side any more than it was theirs – it was like looking to the referee to give ya some kinda advantage. And who knew how well it was working – maybe while we'd been away it'd finally expired? Maybe George's execution had been the last act for both of them? In which case we were nothing but sacrificial lambs waiting for the arrival of the slaughter-woman.

CHAPTER TWENTY

It sure was an odd situation. Normally you'd *prepare* for the arrival of an invading force – fortify your position, check your weapons – but with the satellite supposedly ready to punish any acts of violence, there was nothing to do but wait.

I was still feeling guilty that it was me who'd brought this upon everyone, me who was being hunted by Nora Jagger, but Sheila just shrugged it off like it was bound to have happened one day and we might as well get it over with. The one guy who *had* complained had moved into the forest somewhere and set up home with his partner, but in all honesty, that didn't make a lotta sense, not when no one knew how big an area the satellite covered, how much leeway you had before you were no longer afforded its protection.

Just to make life that bit more difficult, it started to rain heavily, and it turned out, branches and broad leaves weren't much better than being out in the open. Everything was dripping, and most of it ended up going down your neck. Thomas started to get distinctly grizzly, crying for something but not knowing what, noisily rejecting everything that was offered. His mood soon infected Lena.

All of us were sitting in a long line with a damp grass bank at our backs, branches propped over us, peering out through the gaps, the leaves getting more and more weighed down by rainwater. Hanna and Gordie were at one end, not cuddling or anything but in a tight huddle, occasionally giggling and whispering, not helping matters at all. Lile was draped across Jimmy, snoring away, though he was so engrossed in his thoughts she could've been a hibernating bear in his lap. At the other end, Doctor Simon was looking about as miserable as a human being can be, again inspecting his soft suede shoes, obviously appalled by their sad condition – though, actually, I had an idea it might've been more down to the turn of events. Bad enough he'd run away from Nora Jagger, but to be found with *us*? I couldn't help but wonder how he was gonna play it when she did arrive, what excuse he'd come up with. The others seemed to think he'd be damned by association, that by throwing in with us he'd lost all hope with her, but I wasn't so sure.

The final one of us, of course, was Nick – really, there are no words, not for a situation like that. We open our mouths and all those familiar old clichés and platitudes spill out like someone emptying the garbage. I'd tried talking with him a couple of times, taking a more – I dunno – *philosophical* approach, but no matter what I said, not one word of it felt right. The only woman he'd ever loved, the only woman he'd ever made love to, who'd been his closest companion even after losing the ability to maintain a conversation was no more. How can you look at *that* philosophically? That's a gut thing, deep down inside, where you know you only exist to fuel a haunted lonely pain and everything else has gone.

In the end I got so fed up sitting there getting that wet it didn't matter if we were inside or out, that I went out for a walk. Everywhere was sodden and running, with not a sound apart from the muffled, continuous drumming of the rain. All the animals had apparently taken shelter in the forest, while the occasional bird was hunched up in a tree, waterlogged and forlorn, as if they'd never ever fly again.

Oddly enough, it was that that started me thinking: how would this weather affect the Shadow-Maker? Could it still fly? 'cuz if it *was* going about its usual business spying on people, then with visibility reduced, surely it would need to fly at a much lower altitude?

I thought it over for a while and then headed back to the shelter. Gordie and Hanna had also gone out somewhere, the Doc was making polite conversation with Lena about Thomas's crying and Delilah was stretched out on her own 'cuz her old man was busy sorting through his junk.

'I was just thinking—' I started to say, but he held his hand up.

'Busy, Big Guy,' he told me.

'Maybe we should go up the hill?' I persisted.

'You wanna catch your death, that's up to you,' he said.

'With this weather, if that thing's flying, wouldn't it have to get lower?' I asked. 'Maybe we could see it.'

He stared at me for a moment as if I was being real irritating and he was a saint for not mentioning it, then a frown suddenly opened up on his face. 'Yeah, well ... guess we could take a look,' he said, the hurried way he got up and put on his old plastic poncho at odds with his casual voice.

As we made our way through the Commune, Sheila called out to us from her shelter, asking where we were going, and when we told her, invited herself along.

Little rivulets of water were dancing down the hill, turning everything muddy and slippery, but we still made it up there surprisingly quickly. Mind you, when we reached the top and got out in the open, the rain bombarding the ground with such force it was bouncing back up again, I wondered if it'd been such a good idea. There was no shelter at all; we had to stand there getting wetter and wetter, our conversation slowly becoming waterlogged and wasted.

'Maybe it's too wet for it,' Sheila eventually suggested, but neither Jimmy or me felt the urge to comment.

We must've stayed there for an hour or more, behaving a bit like animals in a field, knowing there was nothing to do but wait for the rain to stop and the wind to dry us. It was probably the fact that I was feeling so soaked and miserable that at first I didn't notice Shelia go on alert, that she was standing absolutely still, gazing up into the leaden sky. 'What's that?' she muttered.

I kinda inclined my head in the same direction as hers, wishing my old ears worked better, but yeah, now that I was concentrating, I could hear something – I couldn't tell you exactly what, just a kinda slight *disturbance*.

Jimmy lowered the hood of his poncho so he could hear better. 'It's coming this way,' he said, glancing at me.

It approached so slowly, with such a sense of stealth, of creeping up on us, a coupla times I thought it had stopped. It was more like a hum than a hiss, a soft drumming, getting closer and closer until it was almost right overhead.

'Where the hell is it?' Jimmy cried, staring up, his mouth wide open.

'I told ya!' I said. 'It's *invisible!*'

He just stood there shaking his head, his soaked old ponytail looking a bit like a slug crawling up the back of his neck. All three of us were holding our hands to our brows, shielding our eyes from the ceaseless rain. You could *hear* it, you could *feel* it – dammit, it was *right over us* – but there was nothing there.

'It's invisible!' I repeated, but suddenly Sheila pointed at something. '*There!*' she cried.

At first I thought her imagination was just trying to please, that it was no more than a thickening of low cloud, but finally I did see something: a dark outline moving slowly along the line of the hill, a ghost ship piloting the mists of the River Styx. It was the underneath you could make out, the bit that was darkest, as if there was shadow even if there wasn't light.

'Get down!' Sheila called as it seemed on the point of stopping, and all three of us threw ourselves to the ground, sliding on our stomachs over to some long grass, surprised we could get any wetter than we already were.

For some time it just hovered there, a dull, overbearing shadow, as if stretching out its technological tentacles and exploring all its suspicions, probing and prying, then slowly it began to move on and that soft humming noise faded into the general sound of rain.

The three of us tentatively got to our feet. 'What the hell was that?' I asked, still staring after it.

'The thing that's been spying on us,' Sheila said, all too obviously.

'But was it a drone, or what?'

No one answered, all of us still listening intently, mindful that it might return. There was no doubt in my mind now: whatever that thing was, it would eventually take away my identity, my free thought and will, *and* it was what had keyed Miriam and disposed of Gigi.

'We gotta bring it down,' Jimmy said, as if we had no other choice.

I turned to him, wondering if rainwater had seeped into his head somehow. That was the one and only occasion we'd caught the slightest glimpse of it, and even if we did have a weapon that could do it harm, the satellite would punish us for using it.

'It's only a matter of time if we don't,' he said.

We all fell silent, overwhelmed not only by what we'd seen, but also by what he'd just said. I mean, he was right: we had to bring it down, or at least try, but how could *we* – an unarmed band of rag-tag nomads – bring down something like that?

*

The mood hadn't been that great in the shelter when we'd left, but it was a damn sight worse when we returned and told them our news.

'You *saw* it?' Lena cried.

'Kinda,' I replied. 'Just a shadow. You couldn't really make out a shape.'

'But it was there,' Jimmy said thoughtfully. 'In theory it should've been harder to spot on a day like today.'

'Rain bouncing off it maybe?' I suggested.

'That was the drumming sound,' Sheila agreed.

'Jesus,' Jimmy sighed, like he didn't even know where to begin thinking about what he had to come up with. 'Not cool. Not one tiny bit cool.'

Gordie stared at us, then made this face at Hanna. 'We're screwed,' he whispered, but she pushed him away.

'If it has a shadow, it's *not* invisible,' Jimmy stated, as if he was lecturing himself.

'Maybe it's got holes in it?' Delilah suggested. 'Like that Swiss cheese.'

Jimmy didn't so much as acknowledge her existence, let alone what she said. 'Could be something new, I guess – something I don't know about.'

'We can't shoot it down,' Gordie said, for those who'd missed the obvious, 'even if we had something to shoot it down with.'

'Not to mention the fact that we can't see it,' Sheila told him, plainly a little irritated by his attitude.

'Gordie,' Hanna muttered.

'Don't you know anything?' I asked the Doc, turning to find him white-faced with worry, the evidence of Nora Jagger's growing proximity plainly frightening the hell outta him.

'No, I told you: no one knows the full story of *anything* any more.'

I picked up Jimmy's torch and sat there shining it down from my outstretched hand, placing my fist between it and the ground, wondering what the hell could it possibly be made of that we couldn't see it, but it created a shadow?

'Maybe it's glass,' I suggested.

Jimmy gave me an impatient look. 'A plane or drone made of *glass*?'

'A kinda glass. I dunno – mirrors maybe?' I added, trying to save my position.

'Yeah. Thanks, Big Guy. I'll bear that in mind.'

'Told ya,' Gordie whispered to Hanna, this time being ignored.

'I have to go,' the Doc said, suddenly leaping up, still clutching his case to his chest.

'You reckon?' Lile said, grabbing his arm.

There was a momentary stand-off, all his old survival instincts against Lile's insistence that he was going nowhere, then Nick, who up to that point hadn't said a word or participated in any way, plainly decided he'd had enough. He jumped up and grabbed the Doc by the shoulders, forcing him back down, giving him a glare that told him that was where he was gonna stay.

'Maybe . . .' Jimmy said, still lost his thoughts, 'maybe we don't have to shoot it down.'

'Whaddya mean?'

'Maybe I can hack into it, bring it down that way. The satellite's not gonna punish me for that . . .'

'You hope,' Lile commented.

Jimmy thought on for a while, then suddenly stopped. 'Only problem is, I don't have a big enough battery . . . Maybe enough to get me through their security and into the on-board, but I'd have to know exactly where it was in the first place.'

'Must be some way,' I said.

'Not without using power.'

I grunted, trying to think of a solution, and everyone else was too.

'I could do it,' Lena suddenly announced.

I turned to her: Jesus, she was right. If anyone could pinpoint precisely where that thing was, she could.

I looked at Jimmy, wondering what he'd say, but he was already dragging out his stuff and laying it out around him, working out what he was gonna do. 'Okay, everyone leave,' he said.

'It's raining!' Gordie protested.

'Tough. I got work to do,' he told us.

There was a general chorus of disapproval that was only quietened by Sheila offering everyone shelter at her place, though she warned us it'd be a squeeze.

'It's okay, I'll stay here,' I volunteered, thinking I could help.

Jimmy turned to me like I was being presumptuous beyond belief. 'No. Not cool, Big Guy.'

'I won't say anything.'

But ya know what, damned if he didn't grab me by the arm and steer me towards the exit. 'Out,' he ordered, and I knew that it might not be much more than a few branches and a layer of leaves, but it'd been commandeered as Jimmy's latest workshop and there was only one boss there.

CHAPTER TWENTY-ONE

The bad weather continued for the rest of that day and well into the night, and in a way we were all grateful for it. We had no idea if the Bodyguard had any special problems with heavy rain but assumed they were no more inclined to venture out in it than we were, which hopefully meant they'd been unable to make any more progress in our direction. Nevertheless, I was up at dawn to a day as clear as crystal, concerned enough to make my way up the hill and check.

I kinda half-circled the Commune one way, then doubled back and did the same in the other direction. There was no sign of anyone but it still didn't put my mind at rest. I started to look that bit further out, going over a valley or two, half-wishing (leastways when I was on the flat) I'd brought the tandem with me. I wanted to know exactly where they were, how close to us, but I couldn't find them anywhere. Mind you, several armies could've easily gone missing in that forest.

A little after midday I headed back, relieved there was no immediate sign of Nora Jagger but still laden down with any number of concerns. My major one – or certainly well up on the list – was exactly how well that satellite was functioning. I knew it wasn't a hundred per cent, but was it eighty, sixty, twenty per cent efficient, maybe? Did it have a full working program of offences and appropriate punishments, or was it gonna fry someone for picking a flower? Give a mass-murderer a quick laser internal massage?

If only I could've tested it, found some way of provoking it into action and seen how well it responded. It even went through my head to commit a minor indiscretion – give Jimmy a whack or run off with the Doc's case or something – but just as it might prove wanting, it might also prove terminally heavy-handed.

When I got back to the Commune I was amazed to find Jimmy preparing to head up the hill with Lena, that he'd already made up something to use against the Shadow-Maker. Turned out he'd brought some things with him for communicating with the satellite, that he'd used when he brought them all down – well, all bar *one* – which'd given him a bit of a flying start.

I found him talking to Sheila, getting her opinion on the best place to bring that thing down so it was clear of the Commune and wouldn't give away our position.

I could tell by the way he was going over it with her that he was pretty confident about what he'd come up with. He did start to explain it to me, but try as I might, my eyes glazed over and he gave up. In any case, we didn't have the time. If that thing really was the Bitch's eyes and key, the sooner we got rid of it, the better.

Jimmy, Lena, Gordie and Hanna, Sheila and me made our way through the Commune, ignoring the looks of the other villagers, acting all casual, though several of them took more than a passing interest in the signal-booster I was carrying. A couple did ask what was going on, if Nora Jagger was coming, but we just brushed them aside, as if we didn't know any more than they did.

Isobel chased after us, shouting at the top of her voice if she could come along, and when we said no, offered to take care of the baby instead. I told her Lile, Nick and the Doc had it covered, but she wasn't gonna be put off so easily.

'Can't I go and see him?' she begged, her face filled with all its usual earnest emotion.

'Sure,' I said, knowing Lile wouldn't thank me for it, 'but don't stay too long.'

She turned and ran back in the direction of the shelter as fast as she could go, laughing and shrieking, in every way an over-sized child.

Sheila led us up over the hill, along this gully and then started to climb what appeared to be one of the highest points in the area. It took us half an hour or more and most of us older ones were really puffing as we neared the top. Jimmy stopped, staring up at the sky, a few clouds beginning to return with the cooling afternoon.

'Let's hope it's around,' he said, looking from horizon to horizon as if he still thought he should be able to see it.

'Let's hope you know what you're doing,' I heard Gordie mutter. His new habit of trying to impress Hanna with smartass asides was something I was gonna have a quiet word with him about.

Mind you, on this occasion, he did have a point: it wasn't gonna be so much a shot in the dark as a shot in the dark with your eyes closed after being spun around a dozen times. Jimmy was gonna attempt to hack into the computer of something he couldn't see or hear and knew nothing about apart from the briefest glimpse of its shadow. Maybe it had anti-hacking protection and the moment it felt his intrusion it would blast him to kingdom come? Super-resourceful he might be, but like I said, with this thing, he just might've been out of his depth.

The little guy started to lead Lena and me up to some exposed rocks at the very top of the hill, waving the others away. 'Principals only,' he told them.

'You're gonna leave me with these two?' Sheila protested, plainly concerned she was gonna end up playing gooseberry.

Jimmy ignored her; he was in his element, setting up, what was for him, a slightly more professional-looking piece of equipment than usual: no wires hanging off, no insulating tape holding it all together. What I could make of it, mostly it was just a standard computer, signal-booster and battery, and again I had this feeling of being part of a group of Stone Age people about to throw rocks at the Modern World.

He turned it on, spent a few moments fiddling with it – I guessed setting it up and linking in the signal-booster – then put both in sleep mode, obviously still anxious about how much battery he had.

'It's up to you now, Lena,' he told her.

'There's nothing,' she replied immediately.

'Oh . . . okay.'

We crouched down behind some rocks, making ourselves as comfortable as we could, knowing we might be in for a long wait, but it wasn't long before Gordie ventured up from below to complain that he didn't know why he'd bothered to come along if this was all we had in mind for him. Hanna soon followed, grabbing him and leading him away, I suspected 'cuz Sheila had said something.

It's funny how people often adopt roles in relationships that are completely at odds to their normal ones. The longer those two were together, the more he was inclined to show off, the more she was inclined – not to mother him, as such, but to maybe give him a sense of balance. Worse still, at least as far as I was concerned, their relationship had become all-encompassing, the way love, particularly *young* love, often does: they were spending all their free time with each other and no longer attending to other friendships as much as they should've. I know it's the way of the world, 'course it is, but I really missed them both as individuals.

The night started to slowly mass in the far distance, as if someone had dropped a little concentrated colour just over the horizon. Down below I could see the others getting that bit restless, I guessed wondering how long were we going to stay.

'Nothing?' I asked Lena for maybe the seventh or eighth time.

'Thought there was something earlier, but . . .' She shook her head.

'D'you wanna call it a day?'

Jimmy glanced across, maybe hoping she'd say yes, but she didn't. 'Clancy, what if I go back to the camp to sleep now and this thing keys you in the night?'

'It won't, not from what the Doc said.'

'You can't be sure. Not a hundred per cent.'

She was right, of course – she usually was. I just wished we could get it over with, that whatever *was* gonna happen finally would.

'In that case, I might slip behind a bush,' Jimmy told us, working his way around to the other side of the rocks. 'Damned weak bladder . . .'

'This is crazy,' I muttered to Lena the moment he'd gone. 'We don't know anything about this thing – it might be days before it comes this way again.'

'We've got to try,' she told me. 'That's what we've always done.'

She was right about that too: that *was* what we always did – we *tried* – and that was how we'd managed to prevail in spite of impossible odds so many times.

I was about to put my arms around her and steal a kiss, when I saw the expression on her face suddenly change. 'Jimmy!' she cried out. '*Jimmy!*'

He came stumbling back, doing up his pants as he ran, grabbing his gear, getting in a bit of a tangle. 'Where?' he said, powering up.

She pointed back down the valley in the direction we'd come, looking far more scared than I'd expected.

Jimmy directed the booster to where she was indicating, trying to pick something up but plainly without success. 'Nothing,' he told her.

'It's there.'

He started punching keys and swiping the screen, a look of desperation stamped on his face.

'You sure?' I asked Lena.

'Yes!'

'How far?' he asked, now sweeping his booster from side to side.

'I don't know. A quarter of a mile or so – no, less. Moving really slowly, coming up the valley.'

'Shit! *Shit!* Not cool,' Jimmy whined.

'Don't forget we want to bring it down on the plain,' I reminded him.

'Yeah, thanks, Big Guy,' he snapped. 'Just what I need.'

I knew better than to say any more, that it was best to stand back and let him do his job, but he was as flustered as I'd ever seen him. 'Where the hell is it?' he cried.

I couldn't see or hear a thing, but it was obvious from Lena's reaction she could, that she'd conjured up something in her mind.

'Jimmy!' she pleaded, whatever it was obviously now closing in on us.

'Okay . . . okay,' he finally announced. 'I got something.'

My senses still weren't giving me anything, but they didn't need to, not with the expressions on Lena's face – the growing sense of fear, the way her colour was fading to nothing, was as good as any screen. Yet at that moment I did see something moving across the tree-tops below us: a big black shadow sucking up everything before it.

'*Jimmy!*' Lena cried again, but the little guy obviously wasn't finding it as easy to break into as he'd expected.

'I don't get it,' he wailed. 'I just don't get it!'

All I could do was to stay where I was, studying Lena's terrified expression, occasionally looking in the direction she was facing, feeling that huge shadow getting ever closer – but in the sky above us there was still nothing.

'Got it!' Jimmy cried, his program finally locking on and hopefully doing what it was supposed to.

There were several silent seconds that weighed on us like eternity as we all stared up into an empty sky, not knowing what to expect, then I got biggest shock of my life. I just stood there, my mouth falling ever wider, the hairs on the back of my neck vibrating like the strikers on alarm bells. Suddenly I *could* see something: the smallest piece of fuselage floating across the sky towards us like a blown piece of a jigsaw puzzle. Then another piece appeared, a part of a wing maybe, moving in tandem with the bit of fuselage. Then another, and another, as this image slowly took shape as if pixels were coming to life in the sky.

I had no idea what was going on, but could only guess that somehow Jimmy's program was shutting the thing's camouflage system down, and as it did so it was materialising before us bit by bit. A piece of the tail appeared, then this large tube – maybe part of the engine, for diverting the thrust, hence how manoeuvrable it was – or p'raps some kinda silencer? If it was a drone, it wasn't like any I'd ever seen – it was much bigger than I'd expected, the size of a small plane, and looking like a cross between a huge black egg-box and a giant flying insect, all strange angles and bulging eyes.

'Jesus!' I gasped. I mean, that thing was *evil*. Thank the Lord we *hadn't* been able to see it passing over us.

Jimmy was utterly absorbed, not working his computer any more but watching this big black spectre slowly coming to life before us. It was almost overhead, still moving incredibly slowly, yet suddenly it shook like it'd had a convulsion, as if it was trying to keep going but knew it couldn't. Then the nose dipped and it started to head in the general direction of the plain, going down with every second.

'*Die, you fucker!*' Jimmy screamed, jumping up and down, his ponytail bobbing with him, while I explained to Lena what was going on. '*Die!*'

However, at that precise moment the craft suddenly tilted and rolled, veering to the right, and then went into this long sweep heading back towards us.

'Oh, shit!' I groaned.

'What's happening?' Lena asked.

'It's coming this way.'

'*What?*'

It went through my head that it had some kinda failsafe system – its way of destroying those who tried to destroy it – so precise was its course. As it arrowed towards us, Jimmy threw himself behind the rocks and I grabbed Lena and did the same.

It was so low it actually scraped something as it went over – a tree, I think. The others came running up the hill to check we were all right, but even before they'd reached us it'd disappeared over the next ridge.

We all stood there in silence but there was no explosion, no sudden spout of black smoke or fire, just a distant crunch, and then a loud impact.

Jimmy never said a word, just pegged it off down the slope as fast as he could, the rest of us following along behind, me taking Lena's hand.

We went down to the bottom, then up the other side, climbing up to the ridgeline then making our way along, all the time scanning the forest, trying to see where the drone had gone down, though the fading light was making it much more difficult.

'What the hell happened back there?' I asked Jimmy. 'How come it appeared like that?'

'That's what I intend to find out,' he said, his old turtle-neck wrinkling from side to side as he scoured left and right. 'Gotta pretty good idea though.'

'There!' shouted Sheila, pointing to some distant broken tree-tops, and once again we broke into a trot, all of us growing aware that we were heading back in the direction of the Commune. Slowly Jimmy started to fall behind, and by the time we arrived at the crash site, he was the only one missing.

There was a big scar across the forest – broken branches, uprooted small trees where that thing had come down, but eventually its sheer weight had stopped it in its wayward path. Somehow it'd jerked up on its side, maybe in the midst of a somersault, one of its wings crumpled beneath it, and I gotta say, even crashed and disabled, it still gave off an aura of evil, like it'd come from some dark, alien world. Hanna and Gordie'd got there first and were inspecting it from a safe distance. As we emerged from the trees, he picked up a rock and was about to throw it.

'Careful,' I said, thinking that might be asking for trouble.

However when Jimmy arrived, he exercised no such caution, marching up and prodding and pulling at it, taking a real interest in what the outer skin was made of. Eventually he worked his way to a hatch (from where, I guessed, poor Gigi had been jettisoned) and took a hold of its handle.

'You sure that's okay?' I asked.

'Yeah, yeah,' he replied dismissively, and with that wrenched it open and took a good look in. 'That's what I thought,' he said, and promptly wriggled inside.

'Jimmy!' I called after him, explaining to Lena what he'd done, though I think she already had a pretty good idea.

He wasn't in there long, and to no one's surprise reappeared carrying an armful of looted technology.

'I know how it made itself invisible—' he started to say, but didn't quite get to finish the sentence.

The moment he emerged into the fading daylight with his gathered booty in his arms, there was an old familiar sound – a crackle, a burst of energy and light that almost blinded you – and Jimmy fell to the ground.

On the plus side, I guess we did get to see that the satellite was still functioning, still ready to punish; on the minus side, and particularly at his age, Jimmy could've paid for it with his life.

It must've decided he was Looting, or Breaking and Entering maybe – whatever it'd assessed Jimmy's crime to be, that one remaining punishment satellite zapped the little guy so hard he stayed that way for the next ten minutes, his legs and arms shaking, drool sliding out of the corner of his mouth.

It really shook me. I mean, we *knew* that thing wasn't a hundred per cent. What if it'd got it wrong? Anything could've happened.

Yet finally he started to come round, and even though the shock'd affected his bad leg for some reason and we had to carry him, at least the fact that the Shadow-Maker had arced around towards the Commune meant we didn't have far to go.

'What the hell happened?' Delilah asked as we entered the shelter. Sheila and me dumped Jimmy on the ground.

'He got zapped,' Gordie told her.

'*What?*' she cried.

'I'm okay,' Jimmy rather slurred, not sounding anything like it.

Nick jumped up, wanting to help, but to my surprise the Doc got there before him, looking that bit grateful to have something to do.

'I often wondered what it felt like,' the little guy said.

'Jeez,' Lile cried despairingly, 'is he okay?'

'He will be,' the Doc told her, sounding like a medical professional again.

'What did you do?' Lile asked.

Jimmy hesitated for a moment, still taking in deep breaths. 'I brought that thing down.'

'What?'

'Yep,' he said proudly. 'Got inside it, too. Found some cool stuff.'

At that, Lile's sympathy level noticeably slipped a notch or two. 'Junk?' she asked.

'I wanted to know how it made itself invisible,' he said defensively.

'God save us,' she croaked.

'How did it?' I asked, deliberately talking over Lile's continuing groans.

Jimmy propped himself up, determined to share this with us, even if it was the last thing he did, repeatedly slapping his bad leg as if trying to get some feeling back into it. 'So cool, Big Guy. So damn cool . . . The outer skin has millions of tiny micro-cameras embedded in it. Everything it films is then transmitted – via the projector I was hoping to bring back – to the skin directly opposite, where it's shown on the outside. Whatever's on the other side of that thing, you get to see on this side – hence, *invisibility* . . . Ya get it?'

I nodded my head. Actually, yeah, that *was* pretty damn cool.

'I downed the Bitch's pride and joy!' Jimmy cried, looking like he was expecting an ovation.

But as often, Hanna saw things just a little differently. 'So what do you think she'll do?'

There was a sudden silence as everyone started contemplating the possible consequences – how Nora Jagger might take revenge. Doctor Simon looked up from examining Jimmy. 'Where is it?'

I paused for a moment, not really wanting to say.

'Clancy?' Lile asked.

'It kind've took a diversion,' I admitted.

'Other side of the hill,' Gordie chipped in.

The Doc gaped at me as if I'd betrayed him somehow. '*What . . .?* What am I going to do?'

I paused, not quite knowing how to reply, but Lile did. 'Lie to her,' she told him, 'like you do everyone else.'

'Say I kidnapped you,' I added, 'to look at my child and give my partner back her sight.' I didn't mean it to come out like that – it just did.

'Oh, Clancy!' Lena sighed, and I turned away.

Sheila had asked Isobel to get some food out for when we returned and we gathered at the front of the shelter to eat cold venison and flatbread, and pretty special it was, too. Mind you, that wasn't exactly the time for thinking about food. We hadn't meant to, but having set our trap, we'd put a little sauce on the bait, and now all we could do was to wait for the arrival of the beast.

'The satellite'll zap her,' Isobel chuckled, but no one seemed inclined to match her mood and I couldn't help but notice that neither the Doc nor Lile could bring themselves to eat.

Isobel turned from face to face, smiling encouragingly, urging someone to agree with her, but no one did.

'It's not too late for us to leave,' I told Sheila.

'Actually,' she replied, staring out into the darkness of a heavy, unforgiving night, 'I think it probably is.'

'The *satellite*!' Isobel insisted, as if she didn't like this game, the way no one would play with her.

I don't know if he could sense the general mood or what, but Thomas started to cry his little heart out and Lena tugged up her top so she could feed him. Most of the men looked away, but I noticed the Doc getting a real eyeful.

I was about to say something, but he stopped me dead. 'She wants him,' he announced, as if making a confession.

Lena turned to him, her face noticeably paling. 'What?'

'. . . She wants Thomas.'

'Why?'

'I don't know . . . maybe for her own?'

'Jesus!' I groaned.

'Over my dead body,' Lena said, hugging Thomas that bit closer.

The Doc paused for a moment, as if he hadn't quite said all he meant to. 'I don't know – it might be something else.'

'What?' Lena asked.

He gave this long, faltering sigh. 'Maybe it's more what he represents.'

'And what's that?' I asked.

'Hope . . . A future.'

There was another pause; everyone stared at him as if they didn't want to believe what he was telling us.

'Are you saying she wants him *dead*?' Sheila asked. 'The end of the human race?'

This time he couldn't even bring himself to reply, and once again I was reminded that whatever Doctor Simon was, or had done in the past, he had his boundaries too.

'That's *sick*,' Hanna commented.

'She's a sick bitch,' Gordie agreed.

'And all we can do is sit here and wait for her,' Nick said, with one of the very few complete sentences he'd uttered since Miriam's death.

There was a long pause, no one wanting to reply. 'Looks like it,' Delilah finally croaked.

Nick was right, of course; all we could do was wait. We had just one chance, one vague hope of ridding the world of the Bitch and her acolytes: a rogue satellite she knew nothing about in a tiny area of the country where she wasn't the greatest force. On the other hand, if that thing failed us, if it proved every bit as unreliable as we knew it could be – and bearing in mind that the overwhelming majority of the villagers had probably never resorted to violence in their lives –

there was gonna be one helluva massacre, and probably the easiest victory the Bitch and her Bodyguard had ever had.

Hour by hour we waited, second by second we suffered, as the night teased us with every unfamiliar moment. Sheila hadn't given the order, but there wasn't a sound to be heard, the entire Commune held in the grip of a terrified silence. What few words were uttered were only in whispers, just in case they hid the sound of a twig snapping underfoot, the distant approach of marching heavy feet.

A couple of times the alarm went up, the first stirrings of panic, when a group of wandering deer were mistaken for Bodyguards. Sheila calmed everyone down and doubled the lookouts at the edge of the forest, as much to reduce tension as anything, but there wasn't a lot they could do. We knew we were going to be attacked – that was the whole point.

In the end, I couldn't take it any more. After all, there was no safety in numbers, only in the shelter of that watchful eye. Thomas started to cry again and Lena and me used the excuse to take him out into the night, eventually settling over near the wood-chopping area, leaning up against a felled tree-trunk.

For some time I didn't speak and I guess she began to sense that I was wrestling with something.

'What?' she eventually asked.

I almost laughed; so many times she got there ahead of me. 'If we get through this, will you let the Doc operate on you again?'

'Clancy,' she said wearily, 'let it go, will you?'

'I just can't believe that if you had to choose between seeing and not seeing, you'd choose the latter.'

'It's what I've been given,' she said forcefully.

I sighed, knowing she had a point, that it was up to her, but I still couldn't give it up. 'I love you,' I told her.

'Now I'm really worried,' she chuckled.

I smiled, knowing I maybe didn't say it as much as I used to, but also that when I did, I meant it more. I gave her a hug, accidentally squeezing Thomas as well, almost waking him. Truth was, I was looking for a diversion, something to take our minds off the tension stretching ever tighter around us. Again a branch snapped over in the trees, there was movement across the forest floor, and in response, someone gave a stifled scream.

Lena knew as well as I did why we'd wanted to be alone . . . this was it. This was what we'd been leading up to right from the first day that we'd met down in those tunnels. This was why we'd fought the Wastelords and freed the kids; why we'd escaped from the Island; why we'd gone up against Infinity in that hellhole of a City and somehow survived. Nora Jagger was our last great adversary, and inevitably, the ultimate and most lethal.

'I love you, too,' Lena whispered, and together we stayed there in the night, Thomas lodged between us, waiting for whatever it was that was on its way.

CHAPTER TWENTY-TWO

They came at first light. It hadn't been our intention, but Lena and me, with the baby in her arms, had fallen asleep where we were, not knowing another thing until we were awakened by the sound of screaming.

I struggled to my feet, told Lena to look after Thomas and stay hidden behind the tree-trunk, and ran over to the shelters.

It was her, of course: the Bitch and all her brutal attendants. I don't know how many there were – coupla dozen, maybe? – but bearing in mind that each one was equipped with a pair of deadly prosthetics and would do whatever they were ordered even if it meant dying in the process, it seemed like more than enough to deal with a group of the most harmless people you could ever imagine.

The irony was, they might not have known about the satellite, but in the admittedly short time they'd been there, and despite their reputations, not one of them had used sufficient violence to trigger it. They were pushing over shelters, yanking people out (some made a run for it but were easily caught by those with bionic legs and dragged back) but as yet, no one had committed a crime sufficient to get the satellite excited.

312

In the middle of it all, just as I'd known she'd be, directing events like a conductor overseeing her murderous orchestra, was Nora Jagger, screaming at them to round everyone up into one large group. I couldn't see any of the gang yet, but for sure they'd be brought over soon enough.

I didn't have a great deal of choice; I just strode into the middle of it, the Bitch with her back to me not noticing at first, or not until some of the villagers looked expectantly in my direction.

She turned, met my gaze . . . Jeez, I'd forgotten how evil those eyes were; how they reached down and stabbed something you didn't know you had – the heart of the soul. I could almost believe they were bionic too, that the action of narrowing them would result in a spurt of deadly laser-fire. However, that wasn't the first thought that went through my head when I faced her. It was something else, the thing I'd pleaded with myself to forget, to banish from my mind for ever, but I couldn't, and the instant she was in front of me I wanted to puke up everything under my skin.

Inside that monster was the heart of little Arturo, innocently beating away, all that evil, all that malice and murderous intent being sustained by one of the most loveable characters I'd ever met. Jeez, no matter how much of a freak I'd thought she was before, now she truly was an offence to all Creation.

'Clancy!' she purred, giving the cruellest of smiles, wet-lipped relish spreading all across that flinty face. 'It's been fun.'

I guess if I'd needed confirmation that the reason why I hadn't been keyed wasn't so much down to my survival instincts as she'd wanted to personally pursue and kill me, that I'd been kept in my natural state purely for her sport, that was it.

'What d'you want?' I demanded.

'To see you suffer,' she replied, quite simply.

'Every time I see you I suffer,' I said, instantly trying to provoke her.

She stared at me, a little taken aback by my attitude, a coupla nearby Bodyguards exchanged glances.

'Where's the little maid and the baby?' she asked.

'I sent them away.'

'Really?' she said, belief not being entertained for one moment.

'Coupla days ago.'

'Where are they?' she repeated impatiently, her voice cold enough to run a glacier through Hell.

'By now? Could be anywhere,' I replied in careless fashion.

All I wanted was to get her to attack me, to do something that'd result in the satellite zapping her, maybe even taking her out altogether. We'd still have the Bodyguard to deal with, but given how interlinked their mental processes seemed to be, I was hoping they wouldn't be able to function the same way without her. I mean, enraging her, getting those murderous limbs swishing – it was one helluva risk, but I couldn't see any other option.

'I'm not going to ask you again,' she snarled. *'Where is she?'*

'Go fuck yourself,' I said. 'I guess you've had that wired in too?'

There was a brief moment when I thought I'd done it, when I saw that wild venomous fury erupt in her eyes and those closest to her backed away, but she visibly checked herself and I realised I was wasting my time; for some reason she wanted me alive a little longer

'I want you to know,' she said, 'when this is over, I'm going to make your death the slowest, most painful, I've ever inflicted on anyone ... Oh, and that the last thing you'll see on this Earth will be me dismembering your little maid, ripping her apart bit by bit so you experience the pain of her death before suffering your own.'

She was so damn perverted, so evil, you couldn't believe she was another human being, and once again I shuddered when I thought of my little special guy's heart that had once beat with such love and laughter now pumping her poison.

'For the last time,' she barked, *'where is she?'*

'I told ya, she left a coupla days ago.'

I didn't know if I had any chance at all of convincing her, of sowing even the tiniest of doubts in her mind, but for sure it was gone once that voice cried out from the crowd,

'Leave them alone!' Isobel pleaded, and I instantly knew that though she'd had the very best of intentions, she'd unwittingly confirmed that Lena and Thomas were still in the Commune.

Immediately Nora Jagger turned to her Bodyguard. 'Find them,' she ordered.

Admittedly those shelters were on the flimsy side, but they were swept aside like they were no more than old cobwebs, every painstakingly woven branch and leaf ending up scattered to the wind. I saw the gang – Jimmy and Delilah, Hanna and Gordie, Nick, Sheila, and a little ways behind them, doing his best not to be noticed, Doctor Simon – being marched across to join the rest of the villagers.

It didn't take long for Nora Jagger to spot the Doc, though I gotta say, she barely reacted, almost as if she'd never trusted him any more than we had.

'They kidnapped me!' he blurted out before she could say anything. 'I went along with it because I thought you'd want me to keep an eye on the baby – I knew you'd find us in the end.'

I almost laughed. I'd been waiting to see how he'd react, if there was any chance at all of him manning up, and there was my answer. Mind you, it wasn't him at his smoothest, and plainly Nora Jagger didn't believe a word. I wouldn't have chosen the method – not for one moment – but I realised that finally the Bitch was gonna do something that would trigger the satellite. But you know what? Just like with me, she must've had some further use for him 'cuz she ignored him and his pathetic excuses and again I was left wondering how I was gonna uncork all that seething violence. As it turned out, I didn't have to.

It was one of the bravest things I've ever seen anyone do – mainly 'cuz of who did it. Isobel obviously felt so bad about what she'd said earlier, she'd decided to try to make amends. I hadn't noticed her inching her way towards one of the Bodyguards; the first I knew was when she suddenly leapt forward and wrenched his laser from its holster. He whirled around, went to swing at her with his prosthetic arm, but before he could, she got a shot away.

There was this sudden almighty explosion – a detonation of fiery and general chaos – and many of the villagers started howling with fear. At first I didn't get what'd happened – the grass was scorched, a coupla small fires were burning – then I realised. Punishment satellites were supposed to be so fast they could recognise and define the crime in the split-second before it was committed, leaving the intended victim untouched – but not this one. Both the Bodyguard and Isobel had been fried to a crisp and were lying there on the ground like two hunks of burned bacon and a spool of blackened wire. But it wasn't just them: two other Bodyguards must've drawn their lasers too, 'cuz the satellite had zapped them as well.

'What the fuck?' screamed Nora Jagger, looking at the smouldering chaos around her. 'What *happened?*'

I didn't say anything – I didn't need to. I was also distraught about Isobel, that she should've sacrificed herself like that; getting swept away on those emotions that she'd found so hard to control but were always so well-intentioned.

'There's a *satellite?*' the Bitch yelled.

In that moment it obviously occurred to her what I'd been up to: keeping quiet about it, trying to provoke her to violence so it would take her out.

'You . . .' she snarled, her eyes narrowing.

I reckon that was about as close as I've ever been to seeing a human being have a total meltdown. I thought she was gonna spontaneously

316

combust, like some of her implant guinea pigs, but now that she was aware of the situation, she managed to somehow stop and shut everything down.

'I'm gonna hurt you so bad,' she hissed, 'believe me . . . if I were you, I'd start screaming now.'

'Not with a satellite watching over us,' I told her.

She paused for a moment, obviously thinking it through. 'You gonna stay here for ever?' she asked. 'How big an area does it cover? What about food? Water?'

The villagers started muttering amongst themselves, those kinda concerns not having occurred to them, and Sheila did her best to calm them down.

'You wanna take a gamble on how big an area it covers?' I asked Nora Jagger. 'How many more of these freaks of yours are you prepared to lose?'

She marched right up to me, glaring into my face, our noses almost touching, and I realised she'd had those prosthetic legs made longer so she could be that much taller. 'You couldn't run for ever, and you can't stay here for ever either,' she told me.

I met her glare for glare, feeling the pull of those icy blue pools, those blood-stained Arctic wastes, retaliating with the Look but deep down knowing she was right. We were only forestalling the inevitable; like it or not, we had to have this out, and in some ways it was as much of a frustration to me as it was her.

Without another word she spun around and walked away, presumably to join the search for Lena and Thomas, and one by one the gang edged across to me.

'Where are they?' Sheila whispered.

'I dunno. I left her down by the woodpile,' I told her.

'Shit,' Jimmy muttered, knowing they were bound to begin a more general search once they'd been through all the shelters.

'They can't hurt them any more than they can anyone else,' Hanna reasoned.

I knew she was trying to comfort me, to put a brave face on things, but as the day wore on and the search was widened, comfort was simply beyond me. They combed the whole clearing and then headed off into the forest, but still there was nothing. I didn't get it. They couldn't have missed them, not if they were just hiding behind a tree. The only conclusion I could come to was that Lena'd made a bolt for it while everyone was distracted, that by now she really *was* miles away.

The Bodyguard went around the Commune, helping themselves to everyone's food and drink, scoffing what they could and taking or spoiling the rest, relishing every second of fear they were creating, the way villagers cowered and shook before them, yet always making sure they never did anything to rouse the satellite. They also started playing these mind-games, taunting us, telling us what they'd do when their chance came, which, as they kept reminding us, it inevitably would. A coupla guys in particular wouldn't leave Hanna alone. Jimmy and Delilah, Nick and me, we were just gonna be mashed up and stamped on 'til there was nothing left but pulp, but she was gonna be abused in every way they could think of, 'til her young body was ripped to pieces and they couldn't do it any more. Hanna retaliated with a lotta stuff I never would've expected to hear from her, and Gordie was ready to take them all on, satellite or no satellite, but you could see they were both frightened. At their age, and despite everything they'd been through, it wasn't exactly surprising.

A coupla times I tried to slip over to where I'd last seen Lena and Thomas, to check if they'd really gone, but the Bodyguards wouldn't leave me alone for an instant – even if I went for a leak someone came along. As ever, not knowing was happening was driving me crazy. On the other hand, I thanked God and the heavens that they were still free.

With the sun now beginning its long, slow fall, I heard hammering over at the forest edge: they were driving in those aerial-like poles I'd seen when they were camped out on the mountain, presumably setting up a pressure-field. As soon as the light started to fade, they turned it on. I tell ya, it was really something, and of course, Jimmy was fascinated. The ground glowed like molten lava, only bright white, with beams of light filtering out of all the cracks and holes. They set it out over the entire clearing, leaving just a circle in the middle for everyone. Those whose shelters were still intact and inside the safety zone returned to them; the rest of us, the overwhelming majority, had to sleep out in the open. The gang retrieved what we could of our destroyed shelter, rebuilt it, then filed inside. Nora Jagger of all people had commandeered Sheila's place, so she had to squeeze in with us too.

There was never the slightest chance of me sleeping, not with Lena and Thomas out there somewhere. Was it really possible they were miles away, Lena blindly carrying the little guy through the forest, going further into the Interior, inevitably ending up getting lost? She always took extra stuff for the baby, no matter where she went, but it wouldn't last for long.

The moon rose over the hills, shining even more light through the sparse branches of our shelter, projecting dark shadowy lines like ethnic tattoos across everyone's faces.

'This is crazy,' Sheila suddenly groaned.

No one had spoken for so long I'd had no idea who was awake and who wasn't, but as soon as she said something, everyone stirred and sat up.

'I don't know who's jailer or prisoner,' she added.

'The Bitch is the jailer,' Gordie chipped in.

'I just hope that baby's okay,' Delilah croaked.

'Thanks, Lile,' I told her. 'I'm sure they're fine.'

'One blind and the other still in arms,' Lile muttered, making it plain she didn't share my confidence.

Again there was silence, outta respect for my loss, I guessed, but you knew it wasn't gonna last for long, that people needed to talk.

'You actually fought her?' Sheila asked, picking up on something I'd said earlier.

'Wasn't much of a fight,' I admitted.

'That strong, huh?'

'Like a man-made force of nature,' I told her. 'I don't know about the Bodyguards; in theory, they're only fifty per cent of what she is.'

'Maybe we'll find out,' Sheila said, actually sounding like she was relishing the prospect.

'Jimmy, could you switch that thing off?' I asked.

'What?' he asked, having no idea what I was talking about.

'The satellite.'

'Clancy—!' Delilah protested.

'Yeah, just a small point, Big Guy,' Jimmy said, 'but that's all that's standing between us and being massacred.'

'Just thinking.'

'Yeah, well – not cool. If that's the best you can come up with, maybe you should leave it alone.'

'I don't see you coming up with much,' I snapped.

At that point, with emotions getting a little agitated, and as weird as it might sound, Lile burst into song; all bruised and bluesy, and everyone gladly shut up to listen.

Through the branches I could see the Doc lying where he'd exiled himself, outside in the long grass, about as far away from us as he could get, almost on the edge of where the ground was glowing, as if he was lying beside a luminous lake. He was a broken man, dirty and dishevelled, aware he had a death sentence hanging over his head, that the moment she had no more use for him, the Bitch was gonna take full revenge.

He was still using his precious case as a pillow, as if, no matter what, that was the one valuable he was determined to hang onto. Somewhere in there was a program that, as far as I was concerned, was utterly priceless, but ya know something, in that moment, I didn't care. All I wanted was to know that Lena and Thomas were safe; whether she could see or not was irrelevant – and maybe that was the point she'd been trying to make all that time. Maybe I finally understood?

Several times in the night the pressure-field was triggered, the siren went off and the Bodyguard started running around getting all excited. The first couple of occasions I was terrified it might be Lena and Thomas; my old heart started racing as fast as it could go, but in the end we realised it was only animals wandering into the clearing.

Jimmy kept shifting position, plainly no more able to sleep than I was, eventually moving that bit closer to me so no one else could hear him. 'Why d'ya want the satellite turned off?' he muttered.

'I dunno. Just struck me we might need it at some point.'

'Easy enough,' he said.

'What about your tools?' I asked, presuming he'd lost them when the Bodyguard destroyed the shelter.

Jimmy gave that smile I'd become so familiar with – the old magician still capable of the odd new trick – and proceeded to lift the blanket he was lying on, to scratch and scrape at the mossy grass and reveal a square of turf that he rolled back like a kinda trapdoor. Underneath there was all kindsa stuff: tools, various bits of techno, the small generator and gas Sheila had given him. 'Cool, huh?'

'When did you do that?'

'Last night, after you left.'

'I'm glad you're on my side,' I told him, feeling the little guy deserved a compliment.

We fell to silence for a while, gazing out at that silver patch of ground as if both of us were adrift on our respective seas of concern.

'You know something, Big Guy?' he eventually whispered. 'We've got ourselves in another damn prison.'

'Yeah, well ... let's just hope this isn't the condemned cell,' I replied.

I must've finally dozed off, 'cuz the sound of the pressure-field powering down woke me at first light. I took a long look outside, particularly along the forest edge, I guess hoping to see Lena and Thomas, some sign that they were okay, but there was nothing. I just didn't get it. 'course I was glad they hadn't been captured, *but where the hell were they?*

I struggled up, feeling that stiff I tripped over just about everyone on my way out. I was hoping that, at that hour of the day, I could take a leak and maybe sneak over to the log before anyone saw me, but as soon as I emerged, one of the Bodyguard, a woman this time, followed me.

'D'you mind?' I said, how close she was, wondering if I'd just discovered a long-lost Siamese twin.

'No,' she replied, and damned if she wouldn't even turn her back when I was doing my business, just stood there watching, determined not to allow me even a second outta her sight.

On my way back to the shelter I managed to deviate just enough from my route to be able to see the woodpile in the distance – Jesus, there were a coupla Bodyguards sitting on the actual log! She *couldn't* still be there – not unless she'd tunnelled underneath. And how the hell would she keep Thomas quiet? *Dammit, Lena, where are you?*

When I got back to the shelters the villagers were being rounded up again, penned in by the Bodyguard, their fear of their captors more than enough to make them do as they were told. I thought something was about to happen, that after a night's sleep Nora Jagger'd come up with a plan, but all they did was make us stand there for hour after hour with no food or water.

It was midday before she finally appeared, more than enough time for me to work out that, actually, that'd been part of a plan.

Don't ask me why but she'd slicked her hair back so it was all flat and shiny, which only went to accentuate the killing field that was her face. The first thing she did was to take one look at our partly rebuilt shelter and kick it over again. I glanced at Jimmy; the little guy was looking more than a little nervous that she might plant her foot down in his hidey-hole and he'd lose all his stuff, but she turned to address a couple of Bodyguards, ensuring that none of the villagers had been allowed food or drink.

At the sound of her voice only feet away, the Doc, who hadn't moved from where he'd been all night, instantly tried to slide away on his back like some disorientated snake – but it was no use.

She glared at the him, utterly contemptuous of what he'd become, opening her mouth to say something – but then stopped when she saw his case.

'Is that what I think it is?' she asked.

He hesitated for a moment, looking a little like a guilty schoolboy. 'Yes.'

'Everything?'

'Yes.'

Instantly a twisted smile slithered out of its hole and wrapped itself around her face, as if all her frustration had suddenly been lifted. 'Well, well,' she said, turning to me.

I stared at her for a moment, waiting for her to say more, wondering why she suddenly looked so happy. 'What?' I asked.

'Punishment satellites,' she announced, as if she was starting a speech or reminiscing about the past, and all the Bodyguards and villagers turned to listen. 'Brilliant invention . . . Amazing. Just about wiped out crime at a stroke. A bit crude, but—'

'Got that right,' Jimmy agreed.

She scowled at the little guy, furious he should dare interrupt her. 'But . . . there were rumours; some people reckoned there were errors in the postural programming, that if you went about it right, there *was* still a way of getting away with murder . . . *literally*.' She paused, looking around in such a manner some of the villagers started shuffling backwards, and I could sense the balance in this situation violently shifting; that this stalemate was about to be terminated. 'D'you know how?'

Again she addressed the question to me, but I didn't answer, and nor anyone else.

'Just the one way as far as I know,' she added.

'Is that a fact?' I said, trying to sound as if I couldn't be less interested.

'Injection,' she told me, after a slight pause. 'The satellite couldn't differentiate between what was being given to cure and what was being given to kill. Internal cameras, yeah, of course, but from up there . . .'

She glared at the Doc, then at his case, waiting for him to speak.

'I . . . I don't have anything,' he told her.

'You did,' she reminded him, and the Doc plainly wished she hadn't. 'It's gone.'

She reached forward and wrenched the case out of his hand.

'*No!*' he cried.

'You sure you don't have anything?' she asked, raising it over her head, about to smash it down on the ground.

'No, no – wait—! *Wait*! Maybe I have,' he told her.

She obviously knew what she was after, 'cuz the moment he opened his case she went straight for this one container and handed it to the Doc, ordering him to arm his syringe. It was quite a shock to realise he'd done something like that before, that he wasn't the good guy at heart I'd always wanted him to be.

The Bitch ordered everyone to line up in rows, obviously beginning to enjoy herself as she marched up and down, the steady *slurp-slurp* of those legs frightening the hell outta all of us.

'Where are Lena and the baby?' she casually asked, like she was enquiring about the way to the nearest bank or something. She paused for a moment, looking from left to right, but no one answered, nor even met her gaze, though an older woman a coupla rows back did start mithering like a frightened dog.

'Where are Lena and the baby?' the Bitch repeated slowly, but still no one replied.

She knew she couldn't make a sudden movement, that she couldn't appear to do anything that might look like an act of violence, so just slid her arm around the nearest person – a short, wiry man, maybe in his fifties, apparently too frightened to do anything but just go rigid with fear – pulling him outta the line, hugging him around the shoulders as if they were friends, but plainly using that incredible grip of hers.

'Where are Lena and the baby?' she repeated as if she was losing patience, that this would be the last time.

There was a pause and people started to look from one to another. 'We don't know,' Sheila said.

The Bitch waited a few moments longer, and getting no further response, gestured for the Doc to inject the guy.

'*We don't know!*' Sheila repeated.

'Do it,' she ordered, as if she hadn't heard a thing.

'What about the satellite?' the Doc whined.

'It won't register it – now *do* it!'

'No!' Sheila protested, but several of the Bodyguard crowded around her before she could make any kinda move.

The villagers began panicking, too scared to protest but too horrified not to react; again the Doc hesitated, but I guessed he realised it was his last chance to get back into her good books, to save his own miserable hide, and he jabbed the needle into the guy's arm, turning away as he pushed in the plunger, his victim almost immediately starting to convulse.

Nora Jagger released her hold and let him fall and for several moments there was no sound other than the repeated scraping of the guy's feet on the ground, back and forth, back and forth, as he shuddered and jerked his way to oblivion. The Bitch just stood there smiling at the horrified villagers, enjoying their reactions, giving the fear time to percolate right through them.

'So,' she said, 'who's next?'

I guess Nick had already guessed what was about to happen and had decided what his reaction would be. 'Me,' he said, stepping forward.

'*Nooo!*' Hanna wailed.

'Who are *you*, for chrissake?' the Bitch sneered.

'Does it matter?' he asked.

Don't ask me why, but for some reason she appeared to find the way he'd stood up to her, what he was ready to do, utterly pathetic. She laughed at him like he was some miserable form of life that wasn't worth bothering with. 'Nah, too eager. Where's the fun in that? Let's make it . . .' she teased, working her way up and down the line, '*this* one.'

I wasn't altogether surprised to see her point at Jimmy. There was a score to settle there, too, but for sure that didn't make it any easier. Delilah gave out with this long, croaky cry, doing her best to hold onto him, but he was wrenched from her with ease, and before I could react, I felt four prosthetic arms lock around my shoulders, like I had two of the strongest buddies in the world.

Jimmy struggled, if not hard, then certainly busily, his bald head bobbing up and down, his ponytail flapping from side to side, trying his best to wriggle free. The Bitch glanced up a couple of times, obviously concerned about the satellite, but still managed to clamp her arm around him the same way she had her first victim, the little guy's strength fading along with his colour.

'Now,' Nora Jagger challenged, Jimmy's eyes suddenly looking all glazed and distant, like an animal about to be slaughtered, 'has anyone remembered where Lena and the baby are?'

I can't tell you how bad I felt: I was being asked to choose between my best friend and my lover and child – but what could I do? I turned to the Doc, not saying anything but pleading with my eyes, begging him not to do it, appealing to any scrap of decency left in him, but he just stared at the ground.

'Wait!' I cried, trying to buy some time, wondering if I could tell them about the log – but how confident was I that Lena and Thomas had gone? Not that I was the only one wrestling with a dilemma.

'Clancy,' Delilah called, '*no.*' I turned to her, not understanding. 'We've had our time – don't you betray that baby for us.'

Jimmy stared at her, at first, I thought, kinda shocked, but then he got this look about him, like deep down he knew she was right. He took a deep breath, even puffed up his chest a little, like he was ready to take up his responsibility.

'Do it,' Nora Jagger snarled to the Doc, for some reason infuriated by this sense of sacrifice.

I looked at Doc Simon – he couldn't, not to Jimmy, could he? But he just took a bit of a breath, made sure Nora Jagger'd got a firm grip, then went about his duty.

It happened so quickly, so unexpectedly, it took me a while to appreciate what the hell was going on. The Doc leaned forward as if about to jab the syringe into Jimmy's arm, then at the last moment drove upwards and sideways and tried to stick it into the Bitch's neck.

There was a wild tussle – I wasn't sure whether he'd succeeded or not. One of the Bodyguards joined in, the Doc got knocked to the ground and lay there struggling and flapping like a landed fish. I tried to free myself from the two holding me, but they'd been joined by another. The Bitch was lashing out with those awesome limbs of hers, kicking the Doc so hard she almost lifted his body up into the air.

Gordie obviously decided he'd had enough, that he was gonna step in, and Hanna was only a split-second behind him.

'No!' I shouted, and they hesitated, like me not sure whether that damn satellite was gonna join in or not, just how unreliable it'd become.

The Doc was rolled up like a ball, I thought trying to protect himself, but maybe it was the syringe – obviously he hadn't managed to stick it into her. He tried to get up, swishing it from side to side, but she kicked him down again, so furious at his surprise rebellion she momentarily lost all control.

She saw that precious case of his lying on the ground – his private fortune, so beloved and revered – and kicked it as hard as she could; pieces flying everywhere as it tumbled over and over across the clearing, a whole lifetime's work gone – and yeah, even in that moment I couldn't help but think that something that belonged to Lena and me had been lost, too.

I honestly think the Doc might've been beaten at that point, that he never would've got up again, but he was so angry with her for smashing his case he somehow resurrected himself, struggling to his feet, the syringe held tightly in his hand – only then realising it was broken, that its toxic contents had already spilled out.

Nora Jagger clubbed him back down, briefly hesitating, looking up to the sky, like everyone else, wondering what that satellite was gonna do. For sure it should have reacted by now. Was it misinterpreting? In which case, how much could she get away with? It was written all over her face that she wanted the pleasure of finishing him off, but in the end she decided not to risk it, turning to the nearest Bodyguard, directing him to the Doc.

Like all Bodyguards, he never questioned her for a moment: just stamped on the Doc's head with his bionic foot as hard as he could, exploding it like an oversize pumpkin, and you know what? Immediately the day was lit up by a perfect beam of heavenly light and the killer was felled.

'Shit!' the Bitch exclaimed, obviously more concerned by her lucky escape than the death of another of her Bodyguards.

I can't tell ya what a chilling sight that was. Doctor Simon, Mr Immaculate, reduced to nothing but a squashed head and a splatter of blood and bone. And ya know, I was far more upset about it than I would've expected. The guy was a weasel in so many ways, and yet when it came down to it, when he reached that final decision, he was ready to sacrifice himself for others. As if, no matter what was on the surface, somewhere deep inside he regarded life and its continuation as sacred. He'd proved himself worthwhile, though the irony was, by doing so, he'd got himself killed.

I really don't know what would've happened next – they couldn't continue to terrorise the villagers with injections, and it was clear the satellite was working, though it obviously had some issues. Maybe it was prioritising, saving energy, only reacting to capital crimes? Whatever, it was too slow; the victim was perishing along with the attacker. Still, it *was* working, we *were* being protected to some degree – so p'raps we would've resumed the long game, the Bitch trying to starve us out while continuing to search for Lena and Thomas? But suddenly I heard a cry echo across the clearing from the forest edge that I immediately recognised, and that chilled me to my bones and beyond.

A coupla Bodyguards had found her, maybe she'd been sleeping or something, I dunno, but somehow they'd managed to separate her from the baby and were leading her back like a blind dog following a bone. The one in front was carrying Thomas, leading her, the one behind making sure she didn't deviate. Not that they had any need to worry; a dirty and dishevelled Lena was chasing along behind, begging and pleading to be given her baby, and I'll tell ya, I could've wept.

It was too much for some of the villagers; they immediately started wailing too, all of them so fond of mother and child. I struggled with the Bodyguards holding me, and I guess feeling the situation was now resolved, they let me go free.

I ran over and snatched Thomas from the Bodyguard, wanting to kill them for what they'd done to her, to beat them senseless, but I just handed the baby to Lena. 'It's okay, it's okay,' I told her, though clearly it wasn't.

She clutched Thomas to her, rocking him back and forth, tears streaming down her face. '*Bastards!*' she screamed.

For a moment I just held her, trying to give her my strength. 'I thought you were miles away.'

'I was . . . but I couldn't leave you.'

I could've laughed: just as, back at the homestead, I'd been unable to go any further than the woods, now she hadn't got any further than the forest.

'What's happening?' she asked me.

'I don't know,' I told her, petrified of what her capture would mean. I pulled Thomas' blanket aside to check he was okay, surprised to find him awake despite not making the slightest sound, those familiar hazy blue eyes gazing calmly up at me.

The two Bodyguards decided they'd had enough and led us back to the others.

The Bitch was looking particularly pleased with herself. 'If it's not the little maid and her miracle,' she crowed.

It was the weirdest thing: the villagers were so scared of Nora Jagger and the Bodyguard, I would never have expected them to do what they did, but they acted like some kinda herd animals: the moment Thomas was in their midst they crowded around as if determined to protect the little guy. Nora Jagger did her best to get through, but they wouldn't let her.

'This is not advisable,' she told them coldly. 'Not one little bit.'

She didn't do anything, just stood there glaring at them. At first they stayed where they were, not looking her way, determined to hold their ground ... but they weren't strong enough, and one by one, gave way.

'What d'you want?' Lena asked, hearing the Bitch's slurping foot-steps stop in front of her.

'Him,' she said, pulling back the blanket, for the briefest of moments looking coldly fascinated by Thomas' innocent little face.

'You can't have him,' Lena told her, pulling away.

'But my hormones are playing up,' Nora Jagger sneered, chuckling away to herself. 'My maternal instincts.'

Lena just stood there, her eyes unseeing but her face so strong, so resolute, in that moment I would've backed her up against anyone. 'He's *our* baby,' she declared.

'Not any more,' the Bitch told her.

You might've thought Thomas had understood every word of that conversation, 'cuz suddenly his peaceful mood fractured and he began to cry, and the odd thing was, for several moments no one seemed capable of doing anything other than listening to him, as if his tears heralded something in us all.

'He's hungry,' the Bitch said, as if Lena should know that, but Lena ignored her, for once letting the little guy cry.

Nora Jagger turned to the nearest Bodyguards. 'Hold her,' she ordered, and three of them grabbed Lena, I guessed having some idea what was about to happen. Suddenly her face was filled with such panic as she felt those powerful prosthetic hands reaching out, trying to take Thomas, and she let out one of the loudest, most agonised screams I'd ever heard.

'*Nooooo!*' she shrieked. 'Leave him alone!'

I did everything I could to reach her, but they put this kinda choke-chain on me, and when I started to struggle, ripped it as tight as it would go.

In any normal situation I reckon Lena would've fought to the death to defend Thomas, but with those awesomely formidable hands trying to get a hold on his fragile little body, she had to be so careful. There was this almost absurd struggle – probably only for a minute or so, but it felt like for ever – while she kinda crouched over with Thomas buried in the crook of her body, the little guy shrieking loudly while the Bitch did everything she could to get a hold of him. She grabbed his blanket, wrenched at it, and as the struggle continued, finally managed to get hold of one of his arms. Lena must've thought she had no choice, that if she didn't let go, the two of them might tear the little guy apart.

'Don't hurt him! Don't hurt him—!' she cried, as she loosened her grip and felt Thomas being taken from her, and I recalled that thought that had gone through my head so many times: that by having Thomas we'd created our very own Achilles heel, a soft spot where we were hopelessly vulnerable.

No matter how scared they might've been, the villagers expressed their displeasure in the only way they could, booing and jeering the Bitch. 'course, she ignored them, all her attention focused on that fiery, screwed-up little face bawling away in her arms, staring at him as if she couldn't quite believe what it was.

'I told you he was hungry,' she said, as if she knew more about it than Lena. 'He needs feeding.'

It was like being dragged through the doorway into madness and no longer being sure what human behaviour was. I couldn't believe it: she held Thomas in one arm, undid her tunic, and took out one of her breasts.

There were any number of gasps, one or two sickened moans, and Lena asked what was going on. 'Nothing,' I told her – I mean, what the hell could I say?

'Clancy!' she growled impatiently, and I knew I had no choice.

The look of pain on her face, that sense of utter revulsion, was a real challenge to behold. I didn't know if she was gonna start punching or vomiting. I mean, I'm a guy; I couldn't truly appreciate what it meant, but if it felt like an outrage to me – the ultimate in intimate trespass – what the hell must it've felt like to her?

Nora Jagger took Thomas to her breast, the little guy, not knowing any better, starting to suckle, but ya know what? He reacted almost instantly, pulling away and screwing up his little face like he'd sucked on something truly noxious.

'Stop it!' Lena and Lile yelled the moment Thomas started to cry again.

'He's fine,' Nora Jagger replied, getting hold of the little guy and sticking her nipple in his mouth again. 'Just got to get used to it.'

Jeez, it was an obscenity: my son – my own flesh and blood – was suckling on the Bitch and I couldn't divorce myself from the thought that he was imbibing her poison, just in the same way that Arturo's heart was pumping it. He made a face and pulled away again, and this time she more or less rammed her nipple back into his mouth.

'Leave him, will ya?' I shouted. 'Ya got nothing for him.'

I don't know if that was what finally persuaded her to give up, but just like he was a toy that had proved a disappointment, she threw him back at Lena, who, thank God, with a little bit of fumbling, finally managed to keep hold of the little guy.

'Have your brat,' she snapped, 'and make him shut the fuck up.'

Lena hesitated for a moment, I didn't think so much concerned about feeding Thomas in the middle of everything that was going on as wanting to be alone with him, to appreciate having him safe in her arms again. Sheila promptly led her away to her shelter, not bothering to ask permission, just reclaiming her property.

'If I get the chance, I'll kill that bitch,' she muttered as they went past, and Lena grunted, like it wasn't gonna happen; that *she* was gonna be at the head of that particular line.

I tugged at the chain around my neck and this time the Bodyguards let me go. I crossed to Jimmy, the little guy looking like the events of the last few minutes had sucked all the air outta him.

'Not cool, Big Guy,' he gasped, his voice even higher than usual. 'Not cool at all.'

What I didn't understand was what exactly the Bitch had in mind for Thomas – and I was beginning to think she didn't either: one minute she was acting like all she wanted was to be his adopted mother, to start her own dynasty; the next, like motherhood was a huge disappointment and he'd be the last thing thrown on Lena's and my funeral pyre. Thank the Lord for that satellite (there's something I never thought I'd say!): faulty it might be, but at least it'd bought us a little more time.

Sheila left Lena alone with Thomas in the shelter, returning to the group, exchanging the fiercest of glares with the Bitch, letting her know exactly what she thought of her. Tell the truth, it kinda concerned me: it wasn't her fight, and satellite or no satellite, I didn't want her getting herself killed over it. I went over and tried to tug her away before she got into trouble.

'Leave me alone, Clancy,' she muttered.

'You don't know what you're getting into,' I warned, putting a hand on her shoulder.

I tell ya, it was a real shock: she suddenly turned and shoved me so hard I fell back a pace or two. 'Back off, all right?' she snarled.

I was really taken by surprise – I mean, I wasn't exactly happy with the situation either. 'Okay—! Okay, I'm sorry.'

'Who the hell d'you think you are?'

Again I just stared: I thought I knew her – and *liked* her – but I didn't get this at all. Then she gave this little involuntary flick of her eyes in the direction of the shelter, and even before I looked I knew.

Jesus! I stole a quick glance over, what I saw almost making me cry out.

Lena was scurrying across the dip behind the shelter, bent low so I could only see the top part of her body, Thomas in her arms, completely covered by his blanket, presumably in an effort to keep him quiet. She'd obviously gone out the back way, just like we had once before, and was making a run for it, heading over towards the hill.

I didn't know whether Jimmy saw her or was alerted by my reaction, but suddenly he was at my side, Lile tagging on behind.

'Shit,' he gasped.

'Shush!' Sheila hissed.

'What's going on?' Lile asked.

'Nothing!' I told her, wordlessly urging her to silence.

I chanced another quick look and spotted the top of Lena's head as she made her way along this kinda ditch. I tell ya, I've never been so frightened for anyone in my life. How the hell could she do that? Where did she get the courage? She was out in the open, but for her it might as well've been total darkness, a vacuum, with very little to bounce sound off and no way she could make any noise herself.

I tried not to look in her direction, to keep my eyes firmly fixed on Nora Jagger, noting how she was starting to glance over at Sheila's shelter more and more, plainly impatient to resume her torture of the mother and child. Out of the corner of my eye I caught a momentary glimpse of the pair of them and damn near cried out: Lena was entirely out in the open, still crouching low, running hard, clutching that little bundle to herself. *Go, Lena! Go!*

There was a murmur from one of the villagers and I realised some-one else had spotted her. I knew they wouldn't be able to keep it quiet, that it was gonna spread in a matter of moments; already a Bodyguard was looking to see what all the fuss was about. Instantly I turned and shouted at Sheila, gave her a real shove the way she had me, over her shoulder catching a glimpse of Lena approaching the treeline. If she got into the forest, she just might stand a chance.

'Oh, shit!' Lile groaned, and I turned to see the Bitch stomping over to the shelter. Sheila didn't hesitate, she ceased our little play-acting and instead concentrated on Nora Jagger, and at last I realised the all-too-obvious truth: that Lena and her had worked this out while they'd been in the shelter together.

'You know something,' she shouted, 'I'm glad you're made of plastic and composite, 'cuz I'd hate you to be all woman.'

The Bitch stopped in her tracks, glaring at her, barely believing what had been said, but it had the desired effect. '*What* did you say?' she snarled, doubling back, in her fury knocking a couple villagers to the ground.

'You gotta be really *sick* to do that to another woman's baby.'

There was a sudden awed silence, everyone waiting for the reaction, but as Fate would have it, into that heavy silence fell the sound of a branch snapping over at the edge of the forest.

Everyone turned to look and immediately saw what'd happened: Lena had started to climb a steep slope, must've slipped, and while floundering for something to hold onto, had grabbed a branch that had broken.

Sheila didn't hesitate; knowing the Bitch would chase after Lena and the baby, she immediately threw herself at her.

I gotta say, it was an unbelievably gutsy thing to do. Despite being considerably shorter, she gripped the top half of Nora Jagger's body, those muscular arms of hers locked around the Bitch's prosthetics, knowing that was probably all she had, that once that grip was broken, she was gonna be in big trouble. A desperate struggle began, Nora Jagger swaying back and forth, violently trying to shake herself free, while Sheila hung on for dear life.

The Bitch started to kick out, eventually scything Sheila down, but she didn't break the hold and ended up going over, too. They were rolling back and forth, the Bodyguard, knowing they weren't allowed to intervene, at least having the presence of mind to grab hold of me again. But ya know something . . . ? I could barely believe it, but looking around me, I could sense a miracle coming on.

Up to that point, not one of those excitable villagers had dared to question the might of the Bodyguard – they were simply beyond any resistance they could muster. But the sight of Sheila getting set on – the head of their village, the woman who'd taken them in, who they plainly loved and respected – the inevitability of what was about to happen to her was starting to stir them up. They looked to each other, tentatively advancing forward, as if they were just waiting for someone to make the first move.

Nora Jagger managed to twist herself around and catch a glimpse of Lena and Thomas disappearing into the darkness of the forest, her frustration so great she screamed and stretched her neck forward to sink her teeth deep into Sheila's neck, blood immediately starting to flow.

I couldn't take it any longer: damn those prosthetics, damn that delinquent satellite, damn the Bodyguard, too. I bucked and kicked until I managed to get a hand free and slammed it into the face of one of the guys holding me, and obviously it was what the villagers had been waiting for, 'cuz they pitched in too, no one really having a clear idea what to do, but knowing they had to do *something*.

The Bodyguard were outnumbered three or four to one but they still should've had the situation under control – but one of them panicked, pulled out his laser and shot a villager and instantly got zapped by the satellite, left burnt and twisted on the ground, a bit of a fire starting amongst a pile of leaves and branches from destroyed shelters.

I tried to get through to Sheila, knowing she couldn't last much longer, but some of the Bodyguard had retreated around the Bitch, presumably to protect her.

Hanna and Gordie obviously decided they'd seen enough, leaping at a coupla Bodyguards, swarming over them like rats. Jeez, I'd forgotten how those kids fought. It's all about speed, making up for their lack of strength by moving so fast they're gone before you can hit them. Though now that Gordie was starting to bulk up, you could see he was also starting to punch his weight, too. Together they were a real team: her doing her dance of destruction, pirou-etting and kicking with deadly accuracy; him being more direct, dodging the swish of those all-powerful prosthetics and countering as rapidly as he could.

Nick also joined in, throwing punches as if he'd never thrown one before in his life, plainly letting out some of his demons of the last few days. But ya know, it was the villagers who really surprised me. There was barely a person amongst them who I would've previously thought capable of mistreating a fly: they were the marginalised, the mistreated, those with everything to fear, but they were picking up discarded branches and launching themselves at the Bodyguards, not giving a damn about the consequences.

Again the satellite zapped someone – I couldn't see who; hopefully a Bodyguard. Things were so chaotic, I had no idea what was going on, and I was pretty sure the satellite didn't either. Through the warring bodies I caught a glimpse of Sheila, her agonised face smeared with blood, desperately trying to hang on, but her fingers slowly being prised apart, 'til finally the Bitch broke free.

She was up in a second, kicking out when Sheila tried to grab hold of her again, I thought about to do her worst – but she had something far more important to attend to. She turned and ran after Lena and Thomas as fast as she could, those prosthetic legs of hers propelling her across the clearing at unbelievable speed.

I tried to go after her, but one of the Bodyguards grabbed me from behind, holding on with his prosthetic arm so tightly he damn near choked me. I wriggled this way and that, eventually managing to swivel around enough to ram my knee somewhere where – going on how he reacted, the Bodyguards definitely weren't bionic. But the moment I was free, I was grabbed by another one.

I did everything I could to break that hold, again twisting and bucking, out of the corner of my eye catching a glimpse of Nora Jagger sprinting into the forest – *Jesus!* But in that moment I felt a real *thud* reverberate through me and turned to see Nick had hit the guy on the head with a rock. He crumpled to the ground, but almost immediately Nick followed after him, zapped no more than a couple of feet from me. But d'you know something? He wasn't that hurt: that laser-beam had spluttered and died. That was it: the damn thing had lost its power.

I was finally free to run after Lena and the Bitch – but how the hell could I? The Bodyguard knew as well as I did that the satellite was finished and they could now kill whoever they liked, and even though a lot of them were down and the villagers were swarming all over them, performing incredible acts of bravery, I still felt like a massacre was on the cards.

Immediately several villagers got cut down, and just as the urge to fight had rippled through them, now it was the urge to flee. They looked to one another, no one sure what to do, in that moment of indecision a couple more getting blown to pieces. I tried to grab a Bodyguard, to get his laser, but one of the others damn near took me out. What the hell was I gonna do? I couldn't leave everyone but I had to save Lena and Thomas!

Amongst everything else that'd been going on, I hadn't noticed that Jimmy and Delilah had disappeared. I guess if I'd thought about it I would've just assumed they'd taken cover, that they were getting a little old for that sorta thing. Turned out I was wrong – very wrong – but never in my wildest dreams could I have imagined they'd make the entrance they did.

They suddenly appeared outta nowhere, riding the Typhoon Tandem, Delilah at the front, gamely steering and pedalling, while Jimmy sat at the back, clutching in his arms what looked like a bunch of lighted candles. As they got nearer, he hurled one through the air; it landed amongst a group of Bodyguards and there was an almighty explosion. I knew at once what it was: he'd used the gas Sheila had given him to make petrol bombs. I mean, he might be an ageing whiz-kid when it came to hi-tech, but he never minded turning his hand to the more basic stuff now and then.

He shouted something at Delilah and she altered course, heading towards another group of Bodyguards, and he tossed another petrol bomb their way. I tell ya, you've never seen anything like it! Talk about a change of fortunes: the Bodyguards were scattering this way and that, and every one had a pack of villagers running after them, sheer weight of numbers finally beginning to tell. A coupla fires had begun to take hold, and with all the chaos, the knowledge that the Bodyguards were taking a beating, I turned and ran after Lena and the Bitch as fast as I could go.

I made it to the top of the hill, aware I was going way too fast for my old engine: puffing and panting and already feeling a little dizzy. Where the hell did they go? I stopped and listened, thought about calling out to Lena but changed my mind, then heard a branch snap underfoot some way in front of me and headed off in that direction; soon finding myself careering wildly downhill, out of control and almost toppling over.

At the bottom I stopped and listened again. There was an almost cathedral-like silence and I was starting to panic, to appreciate how little chance I had of finding either of them, when I spotted the Bitch's unmistakeable heavy footprints in some soft earth, their depth and definition a fair indication of her weight and power. The woman was a macro-monster, the product of technology ran amok. I wouldn't stand a chance against her, not even with Lena's help – but what choice did I have?

I followed the direction of the footprints up another slope, the sudden screech of a panicked bird right above my head, the explosion of its beating wings, almost frightening the damn life outta me.

By the time that I made it to the top, it felt like two heavy straps had been secured around my chest and now were being slowly tightened. I slumped forward, my hands resting on my knees, puffing and panting, and at that precise moment saw the Bitch.

She was about sixty yards or so away, over on the next slope, in the middle of a small clearing, standing perfectly still, I reckoned listening for Lena. I don't know exactly what she heard but suddenly she ran on – however, even before I could start chasing after her, she was back; looking all around, trying another direction and returning yet again. Obviously she had no idea which way Lena and Thomas had gone, and I thanked God for it.

I thought about it, and decided my best option was to follow her – that way, if she did find Lena and Thomas, I'd be close at hand to help out, and if she didn't, well, all the better. I went down and up, approaching the small clearing with real caution, not sure which way she'd gone; stopping and starting, dodging behind trees, listening so hard it almost made my ears hurt.

It happened so suddenly, so unexpectedly, I didn't even know what it was. Something came at me from outta the air, outta nothing, and hit me so hard, blood welled up in my head and drowned my brain. I blacked out, the victim of an almighty force, of a fearsome swooping falcon – stunned and helpless, unable to do anything but lie there waiting to be torn apart and eaten.

I guess she'd worked it out, and pretty smart it was, too. She knew how hard it'd be to find Lena and Thomas in that forest, but also guessed I wouldn't be far behind, that all she had to do was wait. Or maybe she'd even spotted me chasing after her? Whatever, she'd climbed a tree at the edge of the clearing – pretty easy with those legs and arms of hers – and just waited; swinging down, smashing into me with those warrior prosthetics and knocking me senseless.

It was her shouting that brought me round; her voice calling out a familiar name: 'Lena—! . . . *Lena*—! I've got Clancy! If you want to save him, bring me that baby.'

I didn't regain total consciousness, not immediately, but I did have a kneejerk reawakening of my instincts. I tried to scramble up, to right myself before I knew what was wrong, everything slowly untangling and telling me what there was to know: that I was in a lot of pain, though I couldn't immediately say where.

I did a quick inventory: my head was a jagged mass of smashed crimson stalactites, my nose a pump run dry – but it was only when I tried to get up that I appreciated my right leg was the epicentre of my agony, that that was where I'd sustained the most damage. I could see blood seeping through my pants and out onto the ground, and a lot of it, too.

The Bitch turned, saw I was conscious and trying to struggle up, and came over and stamped on that damaged leg as hard as she could.

J-e-s-u-s! I gave out with a real howl as the pain took me right to the edge of unconsciousness again, falling back down, even in that moment knowing what she'd done: that she'd crushed my leg with her damn prosthetic to make sure I didn't try to escape.

'*Shit!*' I gasped, praying for that pain to subside even by a single degree.

'Just stay there,' she snarled. 'I need you alive, but that doesn't mean in one piece.'

Again I slumped back, not even sure I was capable of breathing, let alone going anywhere. Now I understood why she hadn't killed me back at the Commune: she'd foreseen a situation like this and kept me alive a little longer.

She took a few paces away, to where the clearing slightly dipped from us and again called out to the surrounding forest, 'Lena!' she yelled, her voice every bit as powerful as the rest of her body. 'I've got Clancy!'

God knows where I got the energy; maybe there's a little reserve that sleeps in us all until it's called upon to save others, but suddenly I was also calling out, 'Lena, run! Get away!'

The Bitch whirled around and with one leap stomped on my leg again, this time grinding her heel in for good measure. Jeez, I thought she'd severed it clean off.

'I'll tell you if I want you to speak,' she told me, 'but thanks for letting her know you're really here.'

Goddammit, I was such a fool. I so desperately didn't want Lena to give herself and Thomas up, but I'd handed Nora Jagger the one bit of leverage that might persuade her to do just that.

'Lena!' the Bitch called out again. 'Give me the baby. You two can go.'

She smiled in my direction, as if she was being surprisingly generous, and I immediately knew why: she knew nothing about the Doc operating on me and was under the impression that, no matter what, there was no escape for us: that the implant would ensure I'd end up killing Lena anyway.

'You've got five minutes,' she shouted. 'If you're not here, I'm gonna start pulling him apart.'

'No, Lena!' I shouted, and promptly received a kick in the ribs for my trouble.

I wasn't feeling separate pains any more; they'd all fused into one that throbbed and pounded so hard throughout my body it was making me wanna throw up.

Several minutes ticked by, the Bitch calling them off one by one, letting Lena know what she was planning on doing to me, that she'd start by pulling my arms out of their sockets – and ya knew she wasn't joking.

'Two minutes!' she shouted.

I really didn't know what to expect – I guess I was hoping that Lena was so far away she couldn't even hear us – but not more thirty seconds or so later she appeared on the far side of the clearing, and if I'd imagined she wouldn't bring Thomas with her, well, I was wrong.

'Well, well,' smirked Nora Jagger gleefully, 'the little maid.'

Lena stayed where she was, thirty-odd yards away and down a slight slope, moving her head slightly from left to right as if giving herself the opportunity to map out the immediate area. 'Let him go,' she said.

'I would,' the Bitch taunted, 'but he's having a bit of trouble walking.'

Lena didn't need to see to know what that meant. 'Don't you hurt him!' she shouted.

The Bitch did this little shrug, like it was all a bit late and unnecessary. 'Give me the baby – you can fix him up,' she replied.

Lena never answered, just stood there biting her bottom lip, plainly having no idea what to do, and the Bitch burst into laughter, so enjoying the expression on her face, her total vulnerability. 'You can always have another baby,' she said.

Still Lena didn't speak or move, almost as if the situation was so unbearable, she'd found a way of hiding it from herself. She hugged Thomas that bit tighter, keeping him to her as if it might attach him in some way.

'Lena, *run!*' I begged, but my words were futile and we all knew it: *she* was gonna make this decision, not me.

'Why do you want him?' she asked, looking down at Thomas all safe and secure in his blanket, having no idea what sort of threat he was under.

'To raise him as my own,' the Bitch answered, though I didn't think she sounded that sure about it. 'He'd be quite the status symbol.'

'I'd rather see him dead,' I said.

'Well . . . we'll see how it goes,' she replied, turning and giving me an unnerving smile.

'Lena!' I called again, but she just shook her head.

'I've told you before, Clancy . . . I love you both more than life itself, but I'll choose you over everything.'

I tell ya, that really shocked me. Just at that moment I would've preferred something else – for her to have despised me.

As if she'd finally made her mind up, that there was simply no other way, she pulled back the blanket and buried her face inside, kissing Thomas, hugging him to her, and even from where I was, I could see she was crying.

'*No!*' I cried, barely able to believe what she was doing, but again she ignored me, slowly collapsing down onto her knees, gently placing Thomas on the ground, leaving him on the far side of the clearing as if that was how these things should be done, that she wanted some leeway before she inspected me and affected the exchange. Once more I cried out in protest, but she walked determinedly away from the little guy, and I'll tell ya, knowing how much that had to be hurting – knowing how much it was hurting *me*, seeing that tiny blue and white bundle left all alone on the ground – was pulling me apart a damn sight more effectively than Nora Jagger ever could.

'*Lena, no!*' I called, but there was no point any more.

There was no confrontation between her and Nora Jagger, no angry words, as if it would be too much, that she simply wasn't strong enough. She found her way to me, helped me to my feet, a whole trainload of pain tearing through me from head to toe.

'As good as new,' the Bitch smiled, obviously taking a certain pride in the agony etched on my face. 'Well – as *old*, maybe.'

Lena never said a word, just supported me as I limped away, following my directions, moving us along as quickly as I could manage. I guessed she needed to put as much distance as she could between her and what she'd done – or maybe it was more 'cuz she didn't trust the Bitch and wanted to get away before she tried something.

I didn't look back but I could sense she was still watching us, enjoying seeing what a broken couple we were, smugly believing she could key me anytime she wanted, that I'd end up killing Lena.

Over and over, I told Lena not to worry, that we'd get Thomas back – but all she did was to shake her head, as if we'd finally been beaten; as if we simply had to accept what'd happened: that our little miracle had been stolen from us.

We got halfway up the slope, despite my shattered leg still able to find a kinda harmony of movement, almost at the spot where I'd first seen Nora Jagger in the clearing – as much as I told myself not to, I couldn't help but look back.

My heart just about drained and imploded: at the very moment that I turned, the Bitch was picking Thomas up off the ground, handling him awkwardly to the point of carelessness – to have to give up your child was bad enough, but to have to leave it with a monster? Who knew what would happen to the little guy? No matter how innocent now, one day he might turn out like her, even carry on where she left off . . . And I couldn't help but reflect on the fate of Arturo's heart, how the Bitch was snatching everything from us that we loved and taking it with her to damnation.

Lena tugged me on, not aware why I'd hesitated, that I was going through a thousand agonies. I tried to pick up the pace, to follow her lead, but couldn't resist one final glance back . . . *Jesus!* What I saw froze me colder than the fridges of Hell. At last I knew why that woman had wanted Thomas and it was just as the Doc had feared: not to fulfil her maternal instincts, not to raise him as her own – but to destroy any hope he represented, any possibility of a better world.

She had that familiar blue-and-white bundle raised up over her head like some ceremonial priestess about to commit a sacrifice. I opened my mouth to scream out in protest, but before any sound came out, she smashed the little guy down onto the ground, stamping on him for good measure.

'*Nooo!*' I wailed. '*Jesus, no—!*'

'Keep going!' Lena urged, trying to make me move faster.

'*Lena! . . . Oh my God!*' I cried, not knowing how to tell her what I'd just seen, but she just kept pulling me on, even trying to increase my speed. '*No!*'

'It's not Thomas,' she suddenly announced.

'What?' I gasped, so shocked I almost stopped in my tracks.

'Keep moving! It's not Thomas.'

Again I hesitated and this time I was abruptly yanked on. 'Who is it?'

'No one! A plucked pheasant Sheila had hanging up. Thomas is with her – hopefully hidden away by now.'

I didn't know whether to laugh or cry – I mean, I thought I'd ridden out the 'dumb old big guy' title but I immediately bestowed it upon myself again. I guess I'd been so unsettled by everything that'd happened things had passed me by without being properly questioned. Had I really imagined Lena would give up Thomas like that – for any reason at all? And once I'd reaffirmed that, it was so obvious what'd gone on, I couldn't imagine why I'd assumed anything else.

When she'd gone into the shelter, Lena had done the switch, wrapping Thomas' favourite blanket around the bird and leaving the little guy where he was for Sheila to retrieve later (maybe again giving him a little something with his feed to make sure he kept quiet). Even breaking that branch at the edge of the clearing had been deliberate – dammit, I'd thought it'd been unusually clumsy for her! She needed to make sure the Bitch followed, and once she was drawn away, Sheila could hide Thomas somewhere safe.

It was a simple but brilliant plan – for sure it fooled me – and it would've worked perfectly if it hadn't been for one thing: Lena hadn't known that the Bitch would cripple me, that she was gonna damn near break my leg and make it impossible for me go anywhere in a hurry.

I did all I could to keep going, to respond to Lena's urging, moving faster than I would've thought possible and not doing my leg any good at all. But I couldn't keep it up for long and soon I noticed her repeatedly looking over her shoulder, knowing Nora Jagger would be after us, that she'd chase us down and tear us *both* to pieces.

We made our way into the thicker part of the forest, doing everything we could not to leave any clues, me checking every time I felt more blood oozing down my leg and getting Lena to scuff over the stain, but it wasn't foolproof by any means.

It didn't take us long to realise we were hopelessly lost, and worse still, with an overcast sky there was no sun to give us any idea of even the general direction we should be heading.

My leg was so painful that eventually we had to stop for a while, scrabbling deep into some bushes, both of us grateful for the rest.

'The more lost we are, the harder we are to find,' I told Lena, though I wasn't entirely sure that made any sense – even to me.

'Maybe she gave up and went back to see what happened to the Bodyguard?'

'That's not gonna improve her mood, is it?' I said, trying to make a bit of a joke, but it wasn't exactly humour material.

Lena paused for a moment, as if she thought she'd heard something, eventually deciding it was nothing to worry about. 'She probably *wouldn't* bother going back – they're not going to look for us at night, and we could be miles away by morning.'

Despite her begging me to leave it a little longer, I insisted on dragging myself up and getting moving; along the way looking for anything that might be familiar, that might help us find our way back to the Commune. For sure I wasn't in very good shape; a couple of times missing my step, almost toppling over and bringing her down with me, yet again having to stop, to wait a while for the pain to subside.

'Can you manage?' Lena asked.

'Yeah. I'm fine,' I replied, though she didn't look that reassured.

From there on she insisted I took the 'easiest' route, even if it meant veering off course – smoothing out the hills as much as I could – but actually, the terrain was getting that bit more rugged, with sheer drops in places. I came across this deer track that ran right along the top of a ridge, though it was so narrow that in trying to make sure she had enough room, I almost went over the edge myself.

'Clancy,' she complained, '*I'll* go first; you hold onto my shoulders and direct me.'

'Okay, okay,' I said, reminded of that time on the tandem when she'd 'steered' me. 'We're a team.'

She stopped for a moment and kissed me on the cheek. 'And always will be.'

I don't know how far we went like that – me steering Lena, looking for the easiest route down so we could get over to the other side, still having no idea what direction we were going in – but suddenly I felt her shoulders go as rigid as stone.

'What?' I whispered.

'Shhhh!'

She just stood there, a frown gathering on her face, her sightless eyes flicking left and right as if panicked by what they couldn't see. My hearing might not be as good as hers, but it wasn't long before I caught it too: the familiar *slurp-slurp* of those bionic legs. Nora Jagger was coming.

I pushed Lena on, trying to get up more speed, but we both knew it was hopeless; how fast those footsteps were closing, she'd catch us in moments. It didn't leave us with a great deal of choice. I wrapped my arms around Lena, held onto her as tightly as I could and dived over the side.

Jesus, the pain as we tumbled our way down . . . I did what I could to protect my leg, but also had to keep hold of Lena, to stop her from crashing into something. At one point the ground levelled out a little, our rapid rate of decent slowed, and I managed to grab this small tree and stop us both – but no sooner did I try to struggle up, the amount of blood in my boot meant my foot slipped and I went over again.

Lena did what she could to stop me, wildly flailing through the air, but couldn't locate me and in the end overbalanced herself; the two of us dragging each other down, rolling over and over, bumping from side to side and finally coming to a shuddering and painful halt against an outcrop of rock.

'Stay still,' I hissed, though in truth, neither of us was up to moving.

Way up above we heard the Bitch's pneumatic stride, bounding along the ridge as if setting up tremors. *God help us* – a man who couldn't walk and a woman who couldn't see being pursued by that aberration.

We stayed there long after her footsteps had faded to nothing, just in case she returned. 'Let's go,' Lena eventually urged, struggling up. 'She'll be back.'

She was right, of course, and you didn't have to be a genius to work out why. The Bitch'd been able to track us by the occasional drop of my blood that we'd missed – once she saw there were no more she'd start to work her way back 'til she found where we'd gone over.

Lena took my hands and went to pull me up, but I wouldn't let her. 'Wait,' I said. 'Leave me. Get back to Thomas.' But she just kept pulling, acting as if I hadn't even spoken. 'She's gonna find us. You know she will.'

Lena paused for a moment, sighing as if she knew it was true, that we had to think about this differently. 'Maybe we should stop for the night? She'll give up once it gets dark. If we head out before dawn, maybe we can get some idea where we are and get back to the Commune before she's even awake.'

I didn't pass comment – I mean, it sounded a little optimistic, even half-baked, but one way or another I knew I couldn't keep walking. Having said that, she took me on a little ways, presumably searching for a place where she felt secure. Occasionally she'd pause for a few moments, listening, going onto her other senses. It must've been the best part of a mile before she was finally satisfied.

'Describe it,' she told me.

There wasn't a lot I could say, most of it I was sure she already knew: the forest was probably denser than anywhere we'd been. In some directions the trees were almost a solid wall, with no space at all between. It was relatively flat apart from a dip in the ground over to one side, but that was about it.

'Okay,' she said to my relief, and I more or less collapsed to the ground.

But even then she hadn't finished. She went for a walk on her own, going around in circles, exploring the immediate area, presumably leaving nothing to chance in case we had to make a run for it.

After a while she came back and asked me if I was up to moving a little further. I just did it – without asking why – finding the new spot had a bit of a bluff to our back. Maybe it helped her hear better? I dunno; I had no idea and was too tired to ask. I just lay there, hearing the wind ghosting through the trees, the rattle of the forest's bones, the night slowly cupping its huge hands over us, and somewhere amongst it all I gratefully fell asleep.

It wasn't sound that woke me, it was sensation: I was suddenly aware of feeling cold, that Lena had left me.

I whispered her name into the dark, wondering if she was taking a leak or something, but the forest felt empty, as if she'd gone.

What the hell? I struggled up, my leg so pained and stiff I almost fell straight back down again. Where'd she gone?

'Lena?' I called into the darkness, but there was no reply.

The trees were so dense, she could've rolled over a few feet and I wouldn't have been able to see her – but there was nothing. I didn't have a clue what to do, whether to lie back down and wait or what, but I had this really corrosive gut feeling that something was badly wrong.

I must've stayed there for a minute or two, waiting, listening, straining to see out into that dark, empty world. Then finally I heard it, dug up by the wind and thrown in my direction – just for a moment, then a few moments more. Jesus Christ—

The Bitch was approaching!

My first thought was to turn and hop away as best I could, even crawl if I had to – but where the hell was Lena? Again I whispered her name into the night, and again there was no reply. *Lena, what are you doing?*

Those familiar footsteps were constant now, fast approaching in my direction, that sucking *slurp-slurp* as if she was extracting life with every footprint and leaving nothing in her wake. I could just make out a faint glow, not a torch, much less imprecise, and finally I realised it was some kinda screen, that she was using its light to guide her.

I tell ya, I was utterly at a loss. What the hell was going on? Was the disappearance of Lena linked to the arrival of Nora Jagger?

She stopped around about the place where I'd first flopped down, waving her screen back and forth, by the look of it, crouching down, and I guessed she was looking for bloodstains.

And that was when I finally knew where Lena was – and why. Suddenly something came out of that dip in the ground at great speed, leaping at Nora Jagger and knocking her over, the screen flying through the air. There was a cry, a half-mouthed expletive, and I realised what was going on.

Lena had picked that spot not to be *safe* from Nora Jagger but to have a showdown with her, to try to finish this once and for all. I was in no condition to do it, that was obvious, but if she got Nora Jagger in something close to her environment, in the dark and with plenty of surfaces bouncing sound, she figured she had a chance. But Jesus, no, Lena . . . not against *that*.

I began to hobble over, it occurring to me as I did that I'd unknowingly been part of setting the trap, that where I'd lain before I'd left blood for Nora Jagger to discover, that Lena had been lying in hiding, waiting just for that. I could hear a struggle going on, a lot of swinging and missing maybe, but apart from that first blow, no one appeared to have really landed one yet.

The one other thing Lena had going for her was that just like the kids, she was fast (as I've found out to *my* cost on a couple of occasions). Once she's made up her mind what she's gonna do, it happens in the blink of an eye. Neither the Bitch or the Bodyguards were that quick, presumably 'cuz of the prosthetics, 'cuz they were built for strength rather than speed.

As I got closer I could hear Nora Jagger goading Lena, calling her *little maid*, telling her to 'take her best shot', and almost immediately I heard the first full-blooded blow from what I guessed was a branch. The Bitch started to laugh, probably just to prove she hadn't been hurt, though I wouldn't've minded betting she had been.

I couldn't see exactly what was happening but I had this sense it was pretty well what I'd imagined: power against speed. You could hear the swish of the Bitch's leg through the air, then nothing – as if she'd fired a blank – but immediately after there would be a sudden retaliatory smack where Lena got in her reply.

I got to within a few yards of them, close enough to be able to make out these two dark shapes facing each other, dodging and ducking, Lena with her stick held high, the Bitch repeatedly leaping and slicing through the air with those lethal legs.

I was about join in, see how I could help, when Lena stopped me. 'Go back!' she shouted, and Nora Jagger chuckled as if I'd made a tactical error and I retreated as fast as I could.

As much as I wanted to, the truth was, not only was I injured, not only was this an environment that suited Lena and not me, more than anything, she plainly saw it as *her* fight. Her revenge for what the Bitch had done to us all: threatening Thomas, enslaving me, killing the Doc and Gigi, all those other people she dispensed with, including, of course, little Arturo – though did she but know it, what she was so desperately trying to do was to extinguish that little guy's heart all over again.

There was another flurry of blows and a real hard smack, like God clapping his hands, and I saw the bigger of those two shadows staggering backwards, losing her balance and falling over.

I could've almost let out a cheer. Lena was on her in a moment, ramming her knee into the Bitch's gut, wrapping her fingers around her neck, determined to get this over with. She'd somehow managed to pin one of those powerful arms but not the other, and I winced a couple of times when she took really heavy blows from the free prosthetic. Still she managed to maintain her grip, just the same way Sheila had, pressing down, slowly choking the Bitch.

But she got hit again – and again. And I began to see that no matter how determined she was, she couldn't hold on, that in the end Nora Jagger would just smash her to pulp.

No matter what Lena'd said, I couldn't hold myself back any longer – but I was too late. The Bitch managed to shove her off, for a moment just lying there, getting her breath back, giving her impacted windpipe a chance to recover, while Lena, maybe fearing it was all over, tried to crawl away. Seconds later Nora Jagger was up and striding after her, kicking her so hard it must've felt like she'd got in the way of a discharging cannon.

I shouted out in protest, tried to follow after them, but I was limping so badly, I couldn't keep up. Lena managed to get to her feet, stumbling across the forest floor with the Bitch chasing after her, intent on finishing her off. I could feel the tension, the world cringing every time another blow was struck, the wait to see if it would be the last. Lena made her miss a couple of times and got in a couple of kicks of her own, but there could be only one end to this contest – or so I thought.

I don't know how it happened exactly – I guess Lena had become completely disorientated. The Bitch kinda leaped at her, there was a bit of a struggle, and suddenly they both disappeared.

I couldn't have been more surprised if night had turned into day. For a moment I just stared, then slowly made my way over to where I'd last seen them.

I should've guessed, what with the more varied terrain, the sheer drops: the two of them had gone over a bit of a cliff and were now lying in a clearing some twenty feet below, neither of them moving.

It's amazing what the human body can do when it has to, when it throws off the restraints of common sense and lets blind instinct take over. I was in so much pain there was no way I could make it down there – but I did. I went over to the side where it wasn't quite so steep – it wasn't exactly an easy way down, but it was a damn sight better than the sheer drop Lena and the Bitch had gone over. All the time I was calling out to Lena, hoping for some sign of life, but there was none.

Just over halfway down I came to a point where I had no other choice but to jump. Jesus, I'll tell ya, I landed on my good leg but you wouldn't have known it. It gave way beneath me and I collided with the ground, my left knee smashed, my right leg in pulsing agony.

I struggled up and hobbled over to the pair of them, grateful that in the clearing at least there was some light. I went to push aside the heavy bulk of the Bitch, to get those damn prosthetics as far away from Lena as I could, but suddenly it wasn't her I had to worry about, it was *me*. One of those huge hands shot out and grabbed me around the neck, pulling me towards her so my face was almost touching hers – gazing into the eyes of the wolf, the grin of the crocodile.

'I said I'd make you pay,' she snarled, 'and I *will*. First the little maid, then you.'

She brought her elbow up and slammed it into my face so hard I thought for a moment I was gonna pass out. I think she was trying to subdue me, to reduce me to a state where I'd offer no resistance and she could do what she'd threatened: kill Lena as brutally as she could, then do something even worse to me.

It went through my head that I might've had some slight cause for hope, that after fighting with Lena and taking that fall she might be weakened, but as soon as I started to tussle with her I knew I was wrong. It was like trying to stand up to an avalanche: rocks and boulders pummelling into me, smashing my outer shell, squashing out my innards. I did everything I could to fight back; despite my leg – despite my *age* – I swear I hit her as hard as I've ever hit anyone in my life, but still she kept coming. For sure, since that last time I'd crossed her she'd had further modifications done. There was this sense that she didn't have *any* weakness any more, that the human part of her was almost the equal of the prosthetics.

Just as before, she picked me up, gave a triumphant roar as she lifted me over her head, like she was the Queen of the Jungle, and threw me across the clearing to bounce off the cliff face. Jesus, the last time I weighed myself I was two hundred and twenty-seven pounds, but I felt like a ragdoll being tossed around by a Great Dane. Before I could recover, she was at my side and once again kicking me, grinding her heel deep into my wounded leg, trying to cause as much pain and damage as she possibly could.

I hollered so loud, I damn near frightened myself, but she just ignored me, picking me up and throwing me at the cliff-face again as if trying to stick me to the wall with my own blood.

I tumbled to the hard ground and this time stayed there. The Bitch stomped away into the night, giving me a few moments of precious respite, but within seconds I heard this scuffing noise and turned to see her dragging an unconscious Lena across the ground by her hair.

'I promised you,' she said.

I couldn't believe it, even of *her*: she seriously intended to kill Lena right in front of me, to perform some foul atrocity that would be the last thing I witnessed on this Earth before she killed me too.

'Leave her alone!' I cried, my voice bubbling out through a mouthful of blood.

She slapped Lena across the face a couple of times, I guessed 'cuz she reckoned it was gonna be a whole lot more fun if her victim was conscious and screaming. When there was no reaction, she just carried on as if, with what she had in mind, she was pretty confident Lena'd come round soon enough anyway.

She paused, turning to smile at me as if to indicate our moment had finally come, then grabbed Lena's hand, dug her foot into her armpit, braced herself and started to pull. She really was gonna do what she'd so often threatened: tear Lena apart limb from limb.

Just as she'd hoped, the pain brought Lena round and she gave out with this loud moan as if she'd been yanked back from the torture of another world to the pain of this. I heard her body crack, maybe even her shoulder threatening to dislocate.

But it's like I said, it's amazing what you can force your body to do sometimes. I shouldn't have been able to get up from where I lay, not in the state I was in, but with Lena screaming, I reckon I would've attempted to raise myself from the dead. I staggered over, looking for something harder than my fist to hit that monster with. Somehow Lena had managed to wriggle free, kicking Nora Jagger off, scrambling away on her hands and knees, but the Bitch leapt at her, jumping on her back and grabbing her around the neck, getting her in that full nelson she was so fond of, and I knew the time had come.

I spotted a rock, not really big enough for what I needed, but hearing Lena gasping for air, fearing it was all over, I picked it up and smashed it down on the Bitch's head as hard as I could.

I was right – it wasn't substantial enough. I'd tried to compensate by hitting her harder, but had ended up not striking her cleanly, and though she slumped over, she was back up almost instantly, those crazy eyes a mushroom cloud of fury as she turned on me, screaming every foul threat she could think of, pounding fists and feet into my battered body before grabbing me, lifting me up over her head once again and throwing me through the air as far as she could.

It was where I landed that finally alerted me to where we were: half-in, half-out, of a pond. We were in the clearing where George had attacked Lena, where all the birds and animals gather to drink, and not that far from the Commune. For a moment I thought about just shouting as loudly as I could, summoning my last bit of breath and strength to try to attract someone, but she already had hold of me again and was about to launch me through the air once more. However, she slipped on the mud at the edge of the pond and suddenly both of us were in the water.

It was deeper than I'd anticipated, maybe four feet or so, and at night, not all that welcoming, but it did kinda even things up a little. She wouldn't be able to leap around so much, or kick me with those damn legs of hers – in fact, looking at it that way, she'd lost fifty per cent of her armoury. On the other hand, I wasn't exactly that light on my feet either, on land or in water. But for whatever reason, it'd become a very different contest, with both of us flailing and missing, losing our balance or slipping on the muddy bottom of the pond, disappearing underwater, bursting back up, launching ourselves at each other over and over again.

I'll tell ya, I was that exhausted I could barely defend myself, but she wasn't a lot better. Time and time again she just stood there staring at me, gasping for air, and once more it went through my head what was sustaining all that extra power, that I was up against the engine of Arturo's prize heart.

It reminded me of that occasion out on the Island when I fought De Grew, the leader of the Wastelords, that sickening moment when I knew I was beaten, not by him, but by Time: that I was just too old for that kinda thing. Though to be honest, even at my peak I doubt I could've coped with Nora Jagger. She came at me again and crunched me with a half-open flailed fist to the side of my forehead, blood instantly streaming down my cheek. She was more or less hitting me at will now, trying to bludgeon me to my knees, to drown me, not showboating any more, no longer intent on giving demonstrations of her superior strength, but so exhausted she just wanted it over.

Again she paused, filling her lungs with as much air as she could, examining me for damage; behind her a little moonlight was reflected on the pond, then she exploded towards me one last time.

It felt so damn brutal, so overwhelming, blow after blow raining down on me, I couldn't even be sure she was still alone, that some of the Bodyguards hadn't arrived from somewhere. I could feel my legs beginning to go, that I was on the point of toppling over; I begged myself not to, knowing if I did I was finished, but I didn't seem able to stop it.

I was underwater before I knew it, the sound of splashing, a distant cursing and a fading consciousness the last things I would know. She had her hands on my shoulders, holding me under, and I simply didn't have the strength to fight back.

What happened next, I really couldn't tell ya, only that I felt like a spring that'd been unexpectedly released. I burst through the surface of the water, still alive, still functioning, while Nora Jagger was gaping at me with, I swear, the ugliest expression I've ever seen on a human face.

I didn't get it, not one scrap – what the hell was going on? Why had she let me go? Was this another facet of her torture? Was she playing with me? But that look on her face, that expression – Jeez, whatever it was, she was every bit as shocked as I was.

We stood there staring at each other, her mouth falling ever wider. *What the hell was it?* Then she looked at her shoulders, first left, then right, and I began to understand.

Even in the dark I could make out some kinda movement around the top of her arms: a squirming where the prosthetics met flesh, and I remembered that time she'd reattached her arm at Infinity, how it'd seemed to *wriggle* back into place. It was the worms the Doc had told me about – the superworms. For some reason they were relinquishing their hold, rejecting the prosthetics and leaving the host. Any number of these long, thin, slimy white strands were emerging from her sleeves, slithering over the top of her collar and dropping out of her tunic – I'll tell ya, it was enough to make ya wanna throw up. But I still didn't get it: *Why?* What'd happened? And in that moment I suddenly realised I had a familiar taste in my mouth, from when I was underwater, and that it explained everything.

The birds and animals didn't come to that pond for *water* – they came for *salt!* That was what I could taste. It was a *salt-water* pond that they used to balance their diets – that was what was so special about it. But salt was the one thing the Doc'd told me that superworms couldn't cope with.

The Bitch felt one of her arms beginning to come out of its socket and made a grab for it with the other, but that dislodged, too – both of them slid down her sleeves and into the water and there was nothing she could do about it. She went to turn, I reckoned to make a run for it, but she was too late; her body just pivoted off her legs and she toppled over into the water; desperately trying to right herself, writhing from side to side, doing all she could to survive, and you know what, I'm not exactly proud of it, but I left her there to drown. Well, not so much 'left her there' as remembered about Lena and couldn't think of anything else. I slithered and slipped my way outta that salt pond, glancing back as I reached the bank, seeing that female devil bobbing around face-down. Jeez, rise up, World! Rise up and celebrate! *Ding-dong . . . the Bitch is dead!*

Lena was in such a state, it made me wanna cry out just to look at her. She could hardly move, was covered in blood, and one eye was so badly swollen you could barely see it.

'Lena! Are you okay?' I asked, though clearly she was anything but.

'I'm fine,' she said bravely.

'She's dead,' I told her. 'It's all over.'

'Thank God,' she sighed, her mouth for some reason looking slightly askew.

'We're near the Commune,' I informed her. 'The pond, d'you remember? I can carry you back.'

'In the dark? With your leg?' she said.

'We can help each other,' I told her.

For a few moments we didn't speak, I think allowing ourselves a little time to recover. I gave her the gentlest kiss I could on the forehead.

'Where is she?' Lena asked.

'In the pond,' I told her, glancing over, for a moment puzzled at not being able to make out Nora Jagger in the dark. Then I saw the limbs and torso had blown over to the far side and were bumping up against each other, for all the world like some macabre spare parts sale.

Lena tried to struggle up to see if she could walk, but couldn't even get upright.

'It's okay,' I told her. 'I'll bring someone back.'

For a moment I just stood there, not wanting to leave her, not after what had happened, but what choice did I have? 'You sure you're okay?'

'I am now,' she said, squeezing my hand.

I kissed her once more, promised I'd be back as soon as I could, then, after finding myself a branch to use as a walking stick, headed off.

But it wasn't easy – a long way from it. I had a fair idea where the Commune was, but I'd only been out that way during the day, and there seemed to be a lot more trees at night, more dips and swells in the ground, and every single stride, whether up, down or sideways, was punished by a body already choked with pain. Having said that, the further I went, the less that became the issue – I really hadn't liked leaving Lena back there. I knew I had no choice, that I had to seek help, and of the two of us I was in better shape, but even though the Bitch was dead, the thought of leaving Lena alone near her body really didn't sit well.

It was almost beyond belief that after all the people who must've wanted to kill Nora Jagger, she'd been brought down by worms – well, not even worms, by a grain or two of salt. They say everyone has a weakness, but who would've ever guessed at that one?

I paused for a moment, taking yet another pain break, letting it subside before moving on, but for some reason couldn't bring myself to continue. This was more than just understandable anxiety, something was nagging at me, telling me to go back.

The thing I didn't get was that Nora Jagger *knew* about the risks of salt water – we'd seen it the day she turned back when we were in the river – so why hadn't she done something about it? Even if it was an insurmountable problem that none of her whiz-kids could solve, you would've thought she would've insisted on some provision in case she did ever accidentally find herself in salt water.

And the more I thought about that, the more it didn't make sense, the more I felt this panic starting to build inside me. I told myself not to be so stupid, that bearing in mind what we'd been through, it was no wonder I was still feeling uneasy – everything was fine, it was over, the Bitch was dead – but it was no use. I turned and started to head back, cursing myself for being a fool, but hopping and limping back to the clearing as fast as my bloodied and beaten old body would carry me.

As I approached the pond my first thought was that I fully deserved all the names I'd been calling myself, that I'd really let my imagination give me the run around. I could see the shadowy bulk of the Bitch's trunk still in the same place, like some dead dog laid out there, her prosthetics all around her ... *What the hell was wrong with me?* I was about to limp over to Lena, to explain and apologise if she was awake, or hightail it out of there if she wasn't – when suddenly I stopped.

Had that body been that far outta the water? I thought the wind had just blown it to the edge ... I started to make my way around the pond, knowing that I just *had* to look, I *had* to confirm she was dead, once and for all. But I hadn't gone more than half a dozen paces before I saw a movement, as if the corpse was slightly rocking back and forth. At first I thought it was some kinda natural phenomenon, probably the lapping of the water, but as I got closer, I saw something else that really shook me: those worms were starting to mass around her again, like they were being called home, and as I watched they started squirming back into their sockets.

Oh, Jesus, no!

She began to rock more violently, I guessed 'cuz she'd heard me coming and was doing what she could to get an arm back into place. I started to run towards her, ignoring my pain as I went slithering through the mud, desperate to get to her before she succeeded – but I was too late. She jammed one arm home, leaning on it, squashing it in amongst the worms, and after that it was just a simple matter of inserting the other.

I still thought I might be able to stop her; that if I could reach her before she got those legs on I had every chance – but she had a real shock in store for me. She had these kinda wristbands on her arms, I hadn't noticed them 'til she began to twist them, dialling them back and forth; I heard them click into place. She then turned towards me, put her hands together and pointed the index fingers in my direction, like she was gonna shoot me or something.

Don't ask me why, but I knew at once what it was. I also knew that it was all over ... that the Bitch had won.

I had the briefest of moments when I felt this pain zip through my head, this sense that my brain had been removed or maybe majorly diverted. I knew what it was, but then it was gone, and I knew nothing more.

The Boss was lying beside me, looking up, studying my face intently, and I bowed my head so as not to meet her gaze. She told me to put her legs on, to be careful of the worms, not to harm them, and 'course I did what she asked.

'Come with me,' she said, and led me across the clearing. There was an injured woman lying there who I vaguely recognised – but she seemed to know me really well. Or maybe it was a case of mistaken identity? For sure she knew my name, but she was coming out with all kindsa weird stuff, getting really hysterical. I didn't understand it at all.

'Clancy, no! *No!*' she kept crying, and then, oddly, 'Clancy, it's *me!*'

I thought she might've been blind, but I didn't bother to look too closely on account of the fact that I'd also realised something else that was far more important: she was a *non-imp*.

'Kill her,' the Boss ordered, watching me closely, as if I was being subjected to some kinda test.

'How?' I asked, still ignoring the woman's screams, how upset she was getting, the way she kept pleading with me.

The Boss looked around, her eyes falling on this large rock. 'Can you lift that?'

''course I can,' I replied, though, actually, I wasn't sure I could.

'Crush her with it.'

I wasn't gonna let the Boss down, not at any price. All non-imps had to die, everyone knew that, and if I could impress her at the same time, all the better. The really convenient thing was that the woman couldn't move, she was just lying on the ground already bloodied and beaten; the *less* convenient thing was that for some reason she still wouldn't shut up, over and over screaming to me to save her.

I locked my arms around the boulder, well, as best I could. It was huge and heavy, probably bigger than anything I'd lifted in my life, but I gave this almighty heave and managed to get it a few inches off the ground – however, as soon as I did, I had so much pain in one of my legs I promptly dropped it.

I tried again, giving it my all, determined to obey and impress the Boss, but once again, as soon as I lifted it, this stab of pain shot down my leg and I had to let go.

For sure the non-imp wasn't helping with all her screaming; she kept begging me to remember who she was, calling out this name over and over. 'Thomas!' she kept repeating, like it was s'posed to mean something to me, 'Remember Thomas!'

Having said that, something about the situation was unsettling me – probably that I was failing the Boss and she was obviously starting to get angry with me. 'Do it!' she demanded. 'Do it!'

Again I tried, but it was no use, my leg simply couldn't take the weight, and finally the Boss shoved me aside, glaring at me as if I was nothing – worse than nothing – determined to show me how it should be done.

I'll tell ya, that woman was really something else. She grabbed that boulder and raised it up to chest-level in one clean, smooth movement, standing there looking at me with this expression of triumph, as if we'd just completed a very long contest that she'd finally and overwhelmingly won. I mean, it *was* impressive – God knew how much that thing weighed. The non-imp was wailing even louder, knowing death was only seconds away, still saying all kindsa weird stuff.

'I love you, Clancy! I love you!' she kept crying out, as if it would make a difference to me in some way.

The Boss raised the boulder right over her head, standing there like some magnificent goddess basking in her glory, beginning to shake a little but still looking supremely confident, obviously enjoying showing me just how strong she was, greedily relishing what she was about to do.

'*I love you, Clancy!*' the non-imp shrieked.

And with that, as if it was the motivation she'd been waiting for – as if she utterly despised what the non-imp had just said, the Boss went to smash the boulder down on the weeping blind woman.

EPILOGUE

Like I told ya at the beginning, we never know what life has in store for us, and never more so when it comes to death.

I don't imagine for one moment that it occurred to Nora Jagger how close she was to hers. And what an even bigger shock it would've been for her to know exactly who was responsible – after all, both perpetrators were already dead.

The first one was little Arturo, and I can't begin to tell you how glad I was that the Mickey Mouse Kid finally got his full glass of revenge. It was an obscenity, not just that someone like him had been slain at such a young age, but the way it'd happened, picked off by hunters on the street, his body stolen for spare parts. Then again, as it turned out, he wasn't down to live that long anyway: it was true that Arturo had an unnaturally large heart, but it wasn't a healthy one. He had this condition called cardiomegaly, and I reckon our second perpetrator, Doctor Simon, had known all along. He must've been managing it for Nora Jagger without letting on, aware that if he ever disappeared, if she decided to take him out for any reason, she'd lose her medication and be liable to heart failure. Like when she was putting too much strain on that immensely strong – immensely *heavy* – hybrid body of hers. For example, pounding through the forest, running up hills, fighting everyone she came across, then finally, lifting insane weights just to prove she was the strongest of all.

The amazing thing was, the moment she died – that very second she crumpled to the ground with that huge boulder falling on top of her, crushing her head the way she had so many others – I was free. Jimmy was right when he said we shoulda known. No way was she gonna leave the 'turning of the key' to a third party. The Shadow-Maker was just her instrument, the actual key was the Bitch herself: those four hi-tech prosthetics, the extra implant she had inside her (one of several, apparently), together they created a kinda techno field. It was that she used to key people, and why, in an emergency, she was able to manually key me.

No wonder she only removed those limbs in controlled conditions, like when she could store them in those special vats at Infinity. No wonder she got so furious with me that day I took one. It was her very own personal configuration, that she trusted to no one, and when she died, the field was broken. My implant stopped functioning along with everyone else's, and I thank every god of the Universe and Time that I hadn't gone through with what she'd ordered me to do, that I hadn't killed the woman I love.

It's funny, in most of the books I've read, certainly in the movies I used to watch years ago back in the City, stories always had a definite ending, and usually a happy one. Well, I guess this is a happy ending, though I wouldn't describe it as altogether definite. If this was Hollywood, maybe the beating the Bitch gave Lena would've resulted in her getting her sight back, waking up and seeing my wrinkled old face before her – but that didn't happen. Lena's finally convinced me that she's fine the way she is. Sure, she might go to the City one day and try to change it, but with what we've got – the farm, our friends, that boisterous little one-year-old, and most of all, each other – she's more than happy the way things are. And, of course, I've come to realise she's right – like I told you before, she usually is.

Sheila and the rest of the Commune talked it over with Jimmy and in the end decided not to do anything about the punishment satellite. They didn't want any more Judgements from On High, or even to dictate what it should punish for. As far as they're concerned it can stay up there till the day gravity finally sucks it back down. From now on they'll work things out amongst themselves, let their notions on morality and law and order develop naturally.

They did ask us if we wanted to stay at the Commune, but we were keen to get back to the farm. We might've only lived here for a short while, and for sure it's got its limitations, but as far as we're concerned, this smallholding is our own little plot in paradise. Nick was the only one who decided to stay at the Commune. I'm not sure why. Maybe the valley reminds him too much of Miriam. Anyways, for sure we'll be seeing them all often enough.

I guess it might sound odd, but we haven't been back to the City yet. Maybe for the same reason Nick couldn't return here? There are just too many memories. I'm sure things are better now that the Bitch is dead and her implant program over – but after everything that happened, we simply can't bear to put it to the test. Out here our victory is complete; in the City, with all those different factions, it might end up being only partial. But still, as someone once said, 'You can't have sunshine without a few shadows'.

Oh, there's one other thing I gotta tell ya, that maybe reassured us a little about the City, that life there would get back to normal, something the Doc would've been truly delighted by.

I know I've come a long way in all of this. Mostly thanks to Lena, I feel so much more confident in myself, who I am, but there are still times when I can be the dumb old big guy. Though in this case, maybe the truth was, I really didn't *wanna* know? I mean, those kids, Gordie and Hanna – what the hell did I think they were up to, sloping off all the time, going missing, taking long walks. They're in love! 'course they are, and well, lovers – irrespective of age – get up to all kindsa stuff.

Anyways, we don't have to worry about whether anyone else but Lena can give birth to a child any more. It was one helluva shock, believe me. When they first told me, I gotta admit, I got really angry with them. They're barely seventeen, for chrissake! But Lena never questioned it for a moment, a little like the way she never questioned the difference in *our* ages, as if all that mattered was that amongst all the terrible things that'd been going on, Love had found a way.

How we're gonna take care of another baby, I dunno, but I guess we'll manage. I mean, ya do, don't you? You have to. That's what I mean about endings rarely being definite – there's always that bit more. The only prediction you can confidently make about this life is that as soon as you get it all neat and tidy, someone's gonna come along and mess it all up again.

THE END

ACKNOWLEDGEMENTS

It would be very remiss of me not to take this opportunity to acknowledge the huge debt I owe to Daniaile Jarry and Penny Karlin for all their work in promoting The Detainee Trilogy. My gratitude forever.

Peter Liney was born in Wiltshire but has spent a large part of his life overseas. He has written sitcoms for ABC and Channel 4, and drama for the BBC and South African radio. The full Detainee trilogy is published by Jo Fletcher Books. He lives in Salisbury.

ALSO AVAILABLE

THE
DETAINEE

When the fog comes down and the drums start to beat, the inhabitants of the island tremble: for the punishment satellites – which keep the tyrannical Wastelords at bay – are blind in the darkness, and the islanders become prey.

The inhabitants are the old, the sick, the poor: the detritus of Society, dumped on the island with the rest of Society's waste. There is no point trying to escape, for the satellites – the invisible eyes of the law – mete out instant judgement from the sky.

The island is the end of all hope – until 'Big Guy' Clancy finds a blind woman living in a secret underground warren, and discovers a reason to fight.

Jo Fletcher
BOOKS

ALSO AVAILABLE

INTO
THE
FIRE

Having escaped the Island - a wasteland that housed those no longer able to contribute to society - ageing 'Big Guy' Clancy thought his fight was over. But they have returned to the mainland to find that it is not the haven they anticipated.

With the punishment satellites that kept them on the Island – and the city under control - gone, hell has been unleashed. A mysterious organisation has begun to decimate the population; those it doesn't kill outright are herded into the streets and then set free to run – for the rich and powerful to hunt. Clancy is about to discover that his work is far from over. The fires of hell don't burn much hotter than this.

Jo Fletcher
BOOKS